THE

VATICAN

KNIGHTS

By Rick Jones

Visit Rick Jones on the World Wide Web at: www.rickjonz.com

BY RICK JONES:

Vatican Knights Series
The Vatican Knights
Shepherd One
The Iscariot Agenda
Pandora's Ark
The Bridge of Bones
Crosses to Bear
The Lost Cathedral
Dark Advent
The Golgotha Pursuit Cabal
Targeted Killing

Stand Alone Novels
Familiar Stranger
Jurassic Run
Mausoleum 2069

Hunter Series
Night of the Hunter
The Black Key

The Eden Series
The Crypts of Eden (A John Savage/Alyssa Moore Adventure)
The Menagerie (A John Savage/Alyssa Moore Adventure)
The Thrones of Eden (A John Savage/Alyssa Moore Adventure)
The Atlantis Series
*City Beneath the Sea **(A John Savage/Alyssa Moore Adventure)***
(COMING) *The Sacred Vault (The Quest for the Emerald Tablet) (A John Savage/Alyssa Moore Adventure)*

Contents

PROLOGUE

Washington, D.C.
Fifteen Years Ago

When Shari Cohen's grandmother was confined to Auschwitz, the sky always rained ashes.

At the peak of the camp's existence, 20,000 Jews were summarily executed daily then burned in the ovens, a tragedy that was memorialized by the photos lining the walls, galleries, and glass cases of the Holocaust Memorial Museum in Washington, D.C.

People milled about as they moved from one display case to another, everyone regaled by the Iron Crosses and German Lugers. Beneath recessed lighting hung German and Hebrew banners, as well as framed paintings that the Nazi regime had appropriated from Jewish owners.

At the end of a corridor, Shari walked along the Memorial Wall that was lined with numerous black-and-white photos and studied each one carefully.

And then she found it; a grainy black-and-white print of camp detainees wearing garments that hung loosely from wispy-thin limbs no larger than broomsticks.

With the tips of her fingers, Shari traced the image of a young woman who stood with her chin raised in defiance. The points of her shoulders and cheeks, the paleness of her flesh, and the death rings surrounding her eyes, all bore testament to her will and courage in the face of adversity. It was the photo of her grandmother.

She immediately felt the sting of tears, her grief, and pity mixed with overwhelming pride.

Then she moved along the cases examining every photo while imagining the storied atrocity behind each one. In one picture she noted bodies hanging from the gallows, then recalled her grandmother saying that corpses would swing for days on end, as a reminder to

Jews of their destiny.

To be a Jew, her grandmother told her, was a fate that always assured death and never a pardon.

Even now Shari could hear the slight accent of her grandmother's voice and the sweet clip of her tone. The way she spoke, with the courage and pride of making it through one of the blackest moments of history, was in itself a demonstration of her fortitude.

When Shari was too young to understand the agony of her grandmother's suffering but on the cusp of learning, her grandmother had shown her the stenciled numerals on her left forearm. Viewing the numbers from one side read 100681, but when the forearm was viewed from the opposite side the numbers became inverted, reading 189001. Same tattoo, different numerals, but something her grandmother had always referred to as the *magic numbers.*

Shari smiled as she remembered her grandmother's amused look the moment Shari's young face lit up as these numbers changed before her eyes with a simple flip of her grandmother's arm.

100681 became 189001, then, when she turned her arm over, 189001 became 100681.

The Magic numbers.

Shari's smile faded. The woman who was so brave and cavalier about her struggles in Auschwitz was so committed to survival, recently died of heart failure in a D.C. hospital at seventy-nine. Shari missed her deeply.

Moving along the displays and observing more photographs, which included pictures of three-foot-tall urns containing the charred remains from the ovens, the moments had been caught on camera of the summary executions of Jews who looked into the camera's lens a moment before the pull of a German luger, as well as mass graves filled with bony corpses.

How her grandmother maintained her sanity was beyond Shari's comprehension. *How could anybody live under the mantle of an Auschwitz sky wondering if her ashes would one day rain down and cover the landscape with a horrible grayness?*

She couldn't even begin to fathom the terror of not knowing what one day held to the next.

Through the museum's photos, Shari witnessed a chronology

of events that reminded her that even though she was a Jew, her country was not entirely without its prejudices. She recalled her grandmother's words at the time of Shari's Sweet Sixteen.

"You're a young woman now," she told her. *"Old enough to understand the things a young woman should know. So, what I'm about to give you, my littlest one, is the most wonderful gift of all: The gift of insight and wisdom."* Her grandmother beckoned her to come close so her gift could only be passed on in whispers. *"I'm a Jew,"* she added, *"as you are. But I was proud and refused to give up. To be a Jew in Auschwitz was certain death. But if you fight from here,"* she said, placing an open hand over her heart, *"if you're truly proud of who and what you are, then you will survive. But never forget this* one *thing: there are terrible people out there willing to destroy you simply because evil has its place. If you want evil to take hold, then stand back and do nothing. But if you want to make a difference, then fight, so that all can live in the Light. Does this make any sense, what I'm telling you?"*

Shari could remember giving her a quizzical look, enough so that her grandmother held her forearm out. The ink of the magic numbers had faded to an olive-green color.

"Because I was a Jew, I was given this mark even though I was a good girl who never hurt anyone. My parents, your great-grandparents, were good people who never received a mark because they were told to go to "the left" with a simple flick of Mengele's cane, which, in Auschwitz, always meant death in the gas chambers. I never saw them again." She smiled, the creases of her face many, but the lines warm and beautiful.

She then reached for Shari's hand and embraced it with gentleness. *"There is goodness in you,"* she told her. *"I know this. I see it within you. And it's people like you who can make a difference in the lives of everyone, whether they be Jew or not. These marks on my arm are a constant reminder of good people who turned a blind eye and did nothing to help me or others when life was at its darkest. And because of this many people died unnecessarily; evil was allowed to succeed. But in you, my littlest one, is a fire so bright I can see it in your eyes. You want to do good for those who cannot protect themselves, yes?"*

At that moment Shari realized that this sudden epiphany may

have been motivated as much by a desire to simply please her grandmother. This discovery, however, since she was only sixteen, remained secondary since her greatest concerns still involved boys. Protecting those who couldn't protect themselves would come later.

Then she could see her grandmother's smile widen within her mind's eye. *"Not to worry,"* she went on. *"Just remember that when the time comes there will always be obstacles. But don't give up. Determination and perseverance will get you there all the time. I was determined to survive Auschwitz. And I did. Now it's your turn to make sure what happened to me . . . never happens to anyone else ever again."*

Shari lifted her grandmother's forearm and turned it over, then traced her fingers softly over the washed-out tattoo. *"No one should have suffered like you did, Grandmama. And I'll make sure no one ever will."*

Her grandmother maintained an even smile. *So smart you are.*

But over time, Shari often thought of her grandmother and wondered if her promises were simply offhand remarks of a sixteen-year-old girl who told an old woman what she wanted to hear, or if she honestly believed that Shari had true conviction. But Shari couldn't have been more sincere since her love for her grandmother had trumped everything, even if she was sixteen and still preoccupied with boys. Good people like her grandmother always deserved better.

"This is my gift to you, my dear. Sometimes the best presents don't come in a box but as a lesson. So, take it and use it well."

She never forgot that lesson taught to her by her grandmother on her sixteenth birthday.

Now, two years later and at eighteen years of age, Shari had been accepted into Georgetown University on a full scholarship. Less into boys and more career-minded, she was working toward her pledge to never let the atrocities that happen to "those who couldn't help themselves," by enrolling into Criminal Justice courses with an eye on greater achievements.

To her right, Shari noticed three teenagers about her age, all dressed in black with matching black lipstick and fingernail polish, and hair that had been dyed raven and their ghostly faces powdered. They chattered excitedly as they referred to the photographs with adjectives such as "sweet" and "awesome" and "cool," words that bit her deeply.

Shari had to wonder that if they had been subjected to the same tortures and suffering as those in the photos, would they still think it was sweet and awesome and cool?

She thought not.

Moving along and leaving her unenlightened peers behind, Shari thought about her grandmother and the way she carried herself courageously throughout the remainder of her life. By surviving Auschwitz her lineage continued. Her grandmother gave birth to three children who extended the line further with seven grandchildren, Shari being the youngest. Without her grandmother's will to continue on in one of history's most notorious travesties, none of them would be alive today.

Thank you, Grandmama.

Shari stood over a glass case as her reflection stared back. She was attractive with an errant lock of hair that curled over her brow like an inverted question mark to the left of her widow's peak. And her eyes, a dazzling copper brown that shined like newly minted pennies, gazed back with something inquisitive about them. *Why was there such fanaticism in the world to warrant the murder of over six million Jews?* In Shari's mind, it seemed all too tragic that mankind had not matured enough to see its downfall.

Sighing, she looked beyond her reflection and saw the Nazi flag resting within the case. The red and white colors were crisp and clean as if new. And the swastika stared back at her as one of the extreme symbols of intolerance and hatred.

"Because you're a Jew," her grandmother told her, *"you'll always be persecuted. But never forget who you are and always be proud, because one day you will be reminded of what you are, and you'll need to fight back to survive. Never forget that, my littlest one."*

Out loud but softly, Shari said, "I won't, Grandmama."

Then she smiled delicately, a small curvature of the lips in remembrance of a remarkable woman. Coming to the Holocaust Museum was not only in homage to her grandmother but also a reminder to Shari of what her grandmother instilled in her—to be proud and bold and never forget where you came from. More importantly, always remain strong in the face of adversity, which is inevitable.

5

"Remember, my littlest one. There will come a time where life may seem to be at its worst. But that *is when you need to be at your best."*

In a country where religion was a constitutionally protected freedom, Shari doubted that being Jewish would cause any marginalization of any kind. But she couldn't quite dismiss it either.

If it became an issue, then it would be one more obstacle to conquer in order to champion the cause for many, she considered. She knew she would always persevere since perseverance was a part of her grandmother; therefore, a part of her, genetic or otherwise.

Walking along the cases from one display to another, Shari spent most of the day reflecting on the courageous people who survived the camps, then prayed for those who didn't.

CHAPTER ONE

Six Miles Northwest of Mesquite, Nevada
Present Day

Two Humvees and a canopied cargo truck moved quickly across the desert floor, with the forward Humvee, which was equipped to handle such terrain, escorting the cargo truck deep into the valley. The Humvee riding aft stayed close to the cargo truck to guard its precious load from attempting to escape its bay.

As the Humvees took the rises and falls of the desert floor with ease, the cargo truck, which was not geared for such an environment, was less cooperative. A commando maintaining vigil inside the bay steadied the point of his MP5 on the eight Middle Eastern prisoners sitting along the benches, their wrists bound by flex-cuffs.

The farther they moved off-road, the more barren and inhospitable the landscape became. Enormous rock formations poked through the parched wasteland as windswept dust sped across the plain like sea swells. The clay was brittle and worn, the surface fragmenting over time from the elements of searing wind and unforgiving heat. And the caretakers—the scorpions, snakes, and lizards—adapted to a wasteland that offered little rainfall and blistering sun, thereby inheriting a kingdom that no one cared to rule.

It was a place of no contrition.

Once the vehicles negotiated miles of ruts and rises and the topography had finally leveled off, the forward Humvee slowed to a stop, with the other vehicles following its lead. As the dust slowly settled, nine commandos wearing desert camo, goggles, and helmets the color of desert sand, exited the Humvees with their assault weapons directed forward.

Through the opening of the gun turret in the first Humvee, a commando with a Laser YardagePro, which was a range-finding system that made the binoculars so heavy that he had to use both hands to steady them, made a slow scan of the horizon. After confirming no movement, he lowered the binoculars. "Clear!"

At that moment the team leader, who sat in the cargo's bay, pushed back the canvas flap and pointed his MP5 to the desert floor beyond the tailgate, the man then shouting in Arabic to those bound by flex-cuffs to exit the vehicle.

The prisoners leapt from the hold with their eyes narrowed against an unforgiving sun. As the desert-clad commandos converged knowing full well their captives had little command of the English language, they barked orders, nonetheless, while prodding them along with the tips of their weapons to a clearing of sunbaked clay.

From the rear of the cargo hold, team leader looked on as his unit escorted the captives to a sandstone formation that stood out like a half shell, its surface brushed smooth by the winds over centuries. He then faced the two Arabs sitting along the hardwood benches in the rear of the hold, while the men in the shadows remained shackled to a steel ring welded to the floor. Then he directed his weapon on them.

"Today marks the beginning of the end," he told them. "So, consider them" –He tipped his head in the direction of the faction standing before the half shell— "the lucky ones." With deliberate slowness, Team Leader pointed his weapon ceilingward. "I'm afraid Allah has a far greater destiny for you both . . . So, your Paradise will have to wait." There was nothing cynical in his tone. It was simply a straightforward statement informing them that death always had its place, but this, however, was not their time.

Though subdued, al-Hashrie and al-Bashrah began to recite a mantra in hushed tones. Recognizing the Islamic scripture, Team Leader became incensed.

"If Allah hears you," he stated with severity, "ask Him for divine intervention for the sake of your brothers. And if He truly is your savior, then have Him strike me down before you as a show of His almighty power. I will grant Him one minute to do so," he said. "Just one."

Team Leader jumped off the truck and slammed the tailgate shut as a sign of his resentment. He walked toward the half shell, his eyes fixing on the Middle-Easterners, and gestured to his troops to force the captives to their knees.

The wind was calm, the sun hot as Team Leader gripped his

weapon and took stock of his enemies, the man exhibiting little emotion as they pleaded for clemency. But their words fell upon deaf ears as he looked skyward.

You now have less than a minute.

The captors pleaded in earnest before him, either begging for mercy or send them to Paradise.

After removing his goggles and helmet, he turned his face skyward to bask in a warm streamer of light that lit upon him, spotlighting his pale complexion that was in stark contrast to his raven hair and even darker eyes. On the base of his chin was a wedge-shaped scar, a keepsake from a suicide bomber several years earlier in Ramallah with the scarred tissue a constant reminder of a constant struggle.

After putting his helmet on and tucking the goggles beneath his shoulder strap, Team Leader leveled his weapon for the kill shot, inciting hysterical pleas from two Arabs who cried out for redemption because their will to enter Paradise had escaped them. Whereas the others stoically waited for the inevitable.

When the minute was up and Allah had yet to respond, Team Leader shifted the mouth of his MP5 from one Middle Easterner to the next, deciding who would be the first to enter Paradise.

Then he spoke to them in a manner that was flat and desensitized. "When you see Allah," he told them with the point of his weapon poised, "tell Him that Yahweh sent you." With no hesitation, Team Leader pulled the trigger.

When it was over, the commandos listened as the sound of gunshots continued to echo across the far reaches of the valley, then dissipate until nothing sounded but the soft soughing of the desert wind.

With the smell of gunpowder cloyingly thick in the air, Team Leader closed his eyes and drew in a deep breath through his nostrils, relishing the moment.

The moment, however, was interrupted by the voice of his second lieutenant.

"Shall we bury them?"

Team Leader opened his eyes, the moment now gone. "I want you to spread the bodies and bury them deep," he said. Although he spoke English, he did so with a clipped foreign accent. "The last thing

I need is for the coyotes to bring them back to the surface."

"Yes, sir."

Team Leader took a step toward the bodies and measured the looks on their faces. Not one seemed to have the repose of gentle peace. Instead, they appeared to exhibit what Team Leader interpreted as a measure of surprise regarding their mortality. *Or was it the sudden revelation of standing before the true face of Judgment?* Considering this, he once more turned toward the sky as if seeking answers but got nothing in return. The Biblical beam of light that once embraced him, had now been cut off by a passing cloud.

Turning his attention back to the Arabs, he could only wonder if they genuinely believed that their God-driven causes would be rewarded with a heaven full of virgins.

It was a mindset Team Leader never fully understood, believing that when man stood erect and walked away from the primordial soup, he also took with him the concept of self-preservation. Yet these fanatical groups were driven by suicidal fascination that eclipsed their need to survive. Fighting for a cause was one thing; dying for one was another.

With the tip of his weapon, Team Leader prodded one of the dead with the action causing the man's head to roll to one side.

"Now the battle begins," he whispered to the body in Arabic. "So, tell me, who will be the stronger god? Allah or Yahweh?" Expecting no answer, the man with the scar turned and headed to the rear of the cargo truck where he would take his place in the hold for the long journey back.

With his MP5 trained on his human cargo, and with al-Hashrie and al-Bashrah continuing their mantra, Team Leader contemplated the fate of the two men before him and anticipated the impact they would have in the near future of the civilized world.

Yes, al-Hashrie and al-Bashrah, you have a much greater role in the eyes of Allah.

CHAPTER TWO

Shepherd One is the Vatican's version of Air Force One, but without the luxurious accouterments such as an office, a Comm Center, and a presidential suite. In fact, Shepherd One is a commercial jetliner owned by Alitalia Airlines, which is often set aside for papal excursions.

Sitting in the fore section of the 747 that was exclusively reserved for the pope and his papal team as it made its westbound trajectory to Dulles from Rome, Pope Pius XIII looked over the itinerary for his two-week visit on American soil. Often, he would gaze out the window, the ocean below him a glittering seascape of tinsel and glass, while thinking about the challenges before him.

Religion was a business that provided faith as its commodity. And with politics and banking the business aspect of the Vatican, he served as the State's head who was responsible to lift the faith in the eyes of his constituency to new levels. For years congregates had been abandoning Mass due to growing liberalism and the Church's refusal to concede its stance on conservative values, resulting in empty pews across the world. The pope's undertaking was to close the ever-widening gap between the Church and its citizenry. What Pius wanted to do was to rekindle the spark of religious hope.

And not by the way of commercializing the Word of God, either. He would let it be known that God had never abandoned His children, but that He loved them unconditionally. And he was not given to preaching the fire-and-brimstone style as a priest, he was not inclined to sermonize in terms of *"God loves you. But . . . if you went to church and accepted the ways of old, He would love you more."*

Evangelizing with the force of admonishment had never been his way. Nor would it ever be.

After rubbing his eyes, the pope sighed as if this responsibility was too much for a man of his age. Despite the fatigue and the occasional discouragement that sometimes struck like pangs, he continued to hang onto that deep-rooted determination to win back the citizenry. He was committed to this aim, no matter the demands levied upon him or the struggles that were sure to come. Now, with the world crying for evolution, the challenge would be to show the relevance of the age-old precepts of Christendom. How to promote unity, however, was the contest that needed to be won by the Vatican.

Pope Pius XIII returned to the scripted speeches for further study and concluded that it would come down to convincing verbiage, in order to win over the masses. And to help him were three bishops from the Holy See (the Vatican's administrative arm), as well as the Eminent Cardinals Alberto Bertini and Attilio Paolo, who served as leading administrators on the Vatican's Commission for the Vatican City State behind the Vatican's president, who was second in command behind Pope Pius.

The pope reread the attached speeches proposed by his administration long enough so when he closed his eyes, he could see the print burn as an after-image behind the folds of his lids. It was here that he decided to speak from his heart, rather than to grandstand from the papal pulpit as if it was a political soapbox.

Like he had always done, Pope Pius would speak from his soul. "Your Holiness?"

Pius opened his eyes to see Cardinal Bertini take the seat opposite him. He was a man beginning to show the puffiness of aging as soft, doughy features began to express themselves with expanding jowls and a developing second chin.

"I'm sorry," the cardinal said apologetically. "Were you sleeping?"

The pope shook his head. "Just thinking." After a brief moment of deliberation, he added, "Trying to win back the masses will not be an easy task, Alberto. I know this. But these" –He raised the documents— "sound a bit scripted. Now I know the Holy See means well, but these documents are without substance." The pope suddenly reached over and patted the cardinal on the forearm, with his smile all-encompassing. "I think these efforts need something more of a direct truthfulness. I need to approach the people without feeling as though I'm trying to sell a pitch, rather than instill lost faith."

"They're simple guidelines, Your Holiness. More like points to touch upon during your speeches. You're exceptionally good at what you do, Your Holiness. Address the current concerns of the people and the Church. You'll be fine."

The pope smiled appreciatively with his lips paring back enough to show rows of ruler-straight teeth. "This is going to be a blessing," he said. "To reach out."

"You're absolutely right about that," the cardinal returned. "If you reach out a hand to those who care to glimpse at the Light, then the Light will reach out to embrace them fully."

The pontiff nodded in agreement.

Cardinal Bertini bowed his head in respect and returned to the rows where the bishops of the Holy See sat judiciously debating amongst themselves as to the best way to handle the media. It was a show of politics to the very end.

Turning his eyes to the ocean below, the pope noted the tiny curls and froths of the churning waves.

The time was 10:47 a.m.

CHAPTER THREE

Dulles Airport, Washington, D.C.
September 22, Late Afternoon

The moment Shepherd One landed at Dulles, the plane taxied under the watchful eyes of thousands who waited to gaze upon the pontiff from areas cordoned off within the terminal. Hand-painted signs waved, people cheered, and the air became electric as the pope exited the plane and made his way down the breezeway in full decorative vestments. After reaching the terminal and giving the sign-of-the-cross as a papal blessing, he then offered his hand to the political principals who either kissed the Piscatorial Ring in greeting or simply shook his hand.

In an area set aside for the media, cameras and news networks recorded the moment of the pope's arrival, capturing the pontiff's first celebrated appearance upon American soil as he and his papal team made their way to a procession of limos.

Raising an arm toward the masses, Pope Pius XIII waved and incited a cheer. Then he ducked inside an armor-plated SUV.

A single man in the crowd, however, appeared indifferent. A man of light complexion neither smiled nor showed emotion as he studied the pope. He gave the impression of someone deliberating with this manner further emphasized by the act of rubbing his fingertips thoughtfully over the scar beneath his chin.

Just before the pope's arrival, Team Leader had received intel that Pope Pius XIII was staying at Blair House, the presidential guest house that was made up of connecting townhomes that faced Pennsylvania Avenue and Lafayette Park on Jackson Place. The residence of the pontiff's team, though the complex featured more than 120 rooms in over 60,000 square feet of living space, had its reserved

14

share of rooms that faced Lafayette Park.

There would be battle-tested agents as security, all high-quality people of opposition.

But Team Leader's unit had seasoned soldiers to the level of an elite force. And despite the president's confidence in the capabilities of his detail, Team Leader knew that taking Blair House would be nothing more than a nominal exercise performed at minimal risk. Come morning, Pope Pius XIII would be within his authority, and the president's detail would be nothing more than a list of names on the obituary page of the morning news.

With inwardly turned enthusiasm, Team Leader envisioned his unit moving through the halls of Blair House with stealth and precision. He had trained his team repeatedly until their motions became involuntary acts rather than practiced maneuvers. This, in turn, developed a higher degree of instinct in decision-making, which now took nanoseconds rather than moments. The infinitesimal time difference could mean the difference between success and failure in such an operation.

As the SUV and its supporting motorcade started away from the airport, Team Leader began to move against the crowd and toward the terminal doors.

CHAPTER FOUR

Blair House.
The Lee Dining Hall.
September 22. Early Evening

Though the Lee Dining Room is normally used for formal banquets, it has place settings for 150 people. Tonight, however, there would be twenty-two people dining with the papal staff, including those from the Senate and House of Representatives who wanted to share a lasting memory with this religious icon who reigned over an empire of more than a billion people.

Matters of religion were obviously discussed as well as the movement of ISIS, the crisis of refugees seeking salvation, and the ongoing tragedies in Syria, especially in Aleppo, where children were seen as collateral damage in the ongoing effort to remove rebels from the city stronghold.

But as mealtime wound down and the time difference between Rome and D.C., which was five hours, the pontiff excused himself. The night, though young, was not so to an aged man who had yet to acclimate timewise.

By eight o'clock, Pope Pius XIII retired to one of the many bedrooms overlooking Lafayette Park. Bishop Angelo, the papal valet, aided in preparing the pope for bed by helping him with his sacred undergarment, a cotton pullover that covered the man from neck to ankle.

As the pope labored to the edge of his mattress, Bishop Angelo assisted the elderly man beneath the sheets and pulled the blankets around him.

"Are you comfortable?" he asked Pius.

The pope continuously shifted as if trying to find the sweet spot on the mattress. "It's not home," he answered. "But it's all good."

Bishop Angelo laid a hand upon the pontiff's shoulder and felt the bony protrusion of a body withered by age. "Perhaps you'd like to read before you retire."

The pope shook his head. "Not tonight, Genaro. Tomorrow's going to be a big day for all of us. So, we'll need to be at our best, yes?"

"Then have a good night, Your Holiness."

On most evenings, Pope Pius XIII often read from the Bible or the passages from *Paradise Lost,* by John Milton. Milton's poetic tale of the fall of Adam and Eve, and by extension, all humanity, in which Lucifer is seen as a sympathetic character who challenges the tyranny of Heaven (an allusion to the Catholic Church), which may have been considered questionable material for the ruler of the Church. Pope Pius, however, found the language and meter of the poem masterful and looked upon the work as an indication that the Church would always be seen through the critical eyes of its followers.

But tonight, he was too tired to flip back the covers to either of the leather-bound volumes. As fatigue began to eclipse him, he switched off the table lamp, causing darkness to sweep across the room in a blink of an eye.

In an attitude of prayer, Pope Pius placed his hands together and worshiped his Lord, thanking Him for raising him from the ranks of obscurity to prominence.

He had come from a family of eleven, all poor, some sickly, but none without hope or faith. He had not been drawn to the priesthood through tragedy, nor did he have an epiphany to follow the Lord's path. Amerigo was simply enamored as a boy with God and everything He stood for, such as the Good and the Caring, and His ability to hold influence over others and lead them toward the world of Light and Loving Spirits.

So, Amerigo dreamed of sermonizing and spreading the Word.

But his father would have none of it as he obligated his son to work the fields of their small farm sixty kilometers west of Florence, alongside his brothers. For his father, the true measure of a man was calculated by the crops he yielded rather than the knowledge he attained.

So, having been taught by his mother at home, having read and memorized all the passages of the Bible, having learned the basics in rudimentary math, and tilling the fields with his siblings for nearly a decade, Amerigo Giovanni Anzalone had become a learned man with calloused hands from driving the yoke, and he came to realize that tilling the soil was not his calling in life.

Every Sunday he went to church with his mother and siblings. And every day thereafter, as he worked the soil beneath a relentless sun, he dreamed of wearing the vestments of a priest and providing sermons. What Amerigo wanted, what he needed, was to be empowered by the Church to give direction.

Upon his eighteenth birthday, and against his father's wishes—but with the aid of the village priest whom his father was unwilling to contest—Amerigo gave up the yoke and headed to the Divinity School in Florence, his first step on the path to Rome.

In the years to follow, Amerigo was recognized as a cardinal and became a respected member within the Curia, which ultimately led the College of Cardinals to choose him as the successor to John Paul II. Upon his acceptance, Amerigo took the name of Pope Pius XIII.

And like his predecessor, Amerigo would offer a hand to every race and religion, leaving nobody out, nobody alone. He would embrace the world with love and tolerance, beginning with the United States.

With that thought on his mind, Pope Pius XIII eventually fell asleep with his hands drifting apart and falling to his sides.

CHAPTER FIVE

He was nine years old when he lost his mother and sister to a suicide bomber on a trip to Ramallah. After going to the market where fowl and goat meat hung from hooks, the boy, his mother, and his twelve-year-old sister boarded a bus for home.

Even to this day, he could recall the pain and confusion of the explosion with fresh intensity as if the blast happened the day before.

It was a hot day in Ramallah. His mother had removed her shoe to massage her foot as his sister sat quietly beside her. From the rear of the bus, the boy watched a man board. His coat much too bulky for such a warm day, he considered, as the man took a seat a few rows ahead of them. As the bus moved along its designated route picking up passengers, he could not take his eyes off this man.

The man appeared nervous and uneasy, his brow slick with sweat as he took several glances around him. Then he spied the boy in the back, their eyes locking. And somehow, he knew that the boy was perceptive, whereas those around him had no suspicion as to what he was about to do. Offering what seemed to be an affable nod, the man in the bulky coat then raised his hand. In it was a dead man's switch. "To all occupiers of the nation of Islam," he said in Arabic, "Allah is great!"

Just as he was about to turn to his mother and ask her who Allah was, the man pushed the button.

With the slowness of a bad dream, the boy watched the man break up into countless pieces. Flame and pressure blew out the walls of the bus. People sitting close to him disappeared within the licks of fire and ash. Piercing cries filled the air, hanging as thick as the acrid smoke. And propelled by the force of the blast, a piece of metal caught the boy on the chin, gashing his flesh into a horrible second mouth that seemed to open wide with the awe of confusion.

After that, he could only remember seeing a swatch of blue sky tainted with greasy black smoke and feeling the heat of a nearby fire.

Only when he awoke several days later to the haggard face of his father, his skin as loose as a rubber mask, did he finally feel the agonies of his pain. With second-degree burns over thirty percent of his body and a severe gash beneath his chin, the boy was incredibly lucky. The real pain came when he learned that his mother and sister had died in the blast.

When he asked why the man did what he did on the bus, his father told him.

That was the day he learned what life would be like for a Jew living in a land of open hostilities.

Taking a deep breath, and with the images of his childhood fading, Team Leader opened his eyes to see the members of his team meditating as the van made its way to Blair House. Every soldier, every stolid commando, as dictated by his constant training, was visualizing in detail his every movement to assure that there would be no room for mistakes during actual combat.

Each man was equipped with an Israeli Bullpup assault weapon—a product of Israeli technology with devastating capabilities. With the exception of Team Leader who dressed as a priest, his team was dressed identically wearing a Kevlar helmet with a formation of gadgetry that marched up one side and down the other, with each having an assemblage of an NVG monocular attached, a convexity faceplate of yellow-hued plastic, and body ensembles that were completely 'Robocop,' with specially designed composite shin and forearm guards.

Unwilling to carry a firearm, Team Leader opted for his weapon of choice, a pair of T-handled push daggers made of a plastic, composite-like material, that he had become accustomed to as a Kidon assassin.

On the floor, Hashrie and Bashrah lay cuffed and dressed in military fatigues.

For the third time in the last five minutes, Team Leader looked at his watch and realized that months of preparation would soon bear the fruit of their labors. And then he closed his eyes once more, the images of that day in Ramallah reminding him why he was about to go to war.

The time was 0258 hours.

CHAPTER SIX

Blair House
3:13 A.M.
September 23

Blair House was a series of connecting townhouses with more than 60,000 square feet of living space. The pope's residence was on the backside, towards Lafayette Park.

Two of the president's security detail were manning the front-desk monitors when one by one they began to wink off.

"What the Hell," said the console officer, who tapped a fingertip against a screen as if the act would bring it back online.

"What?" asked a second officer, who was seated on a barstool-like chair by the double entryway that was constructed entirely of bomb-blast-resistant glass.

"We just lost our feed," answered the first, who continued to tap the screens. "To which areas?"

"All of them."

There was a buzz at the outside doorway. Standing before the glass doorway was a priest wearing a cleric's coat. In his hand was a briefcase.

The man helming the console flipped a switch. "Something I can help you with, Father?"

The priest held up the briefcase to showcase through the glass. "Can you hear me?"

"I can hear you, Father. What can I help you with?"

"I'm afraid I have pressing matters that require the signature of the pontiff."

"You do understand that it's almost three-thirty in the morning, right?"

"I do apologize. But it's eight-thirty at Vatican City. The pontiff will understand once he views these documents."

"Are you from the archdiocese?' The priest nodded. "I am."

The console operator looked at the officer standing by the door. "The guy's a priest. What am I supposed to do? Say no." The operator pressed in the entry code and the door unlocked. "Please, Father, when you come in, I'll need you to place the briefcase on the table for inspection."

"Yes. Of course."

The priest entered through the first set of doors and was coded through the second set of doors. As directed by the second officer, the priest lowered the briefcase to the table next to the console, then the security agent held a wand to the priest's body to detect metals. When the wand didn't go off, the officer instructed the priest to lower his arms and to open the case, which the priest did, the cleric undoing the clasps before lifting the top.

The briefcase was empty.

The officer seemed perplexed by this, the man pointing to the carry case. "What the—"

Sliding weapons that were hidden underneath his sleeves and into his palms, the priest came across in an arc with a pair of T-handled push daggers, which were designed to be grasped in the hand so that the blade protruded from the front of one's fist between the index and middle fingers and slashed the officer's throat. The lips of the man's wound pared back, the opening giving a view of the assemblage of the man's throat beneath the skin. As the man brought his hands up to his neck and his eyes flared to mostly whites in astonishment, he began to choke on his wetness.

Then the assassin in priest's clothing hopped over the console just as the second officer got to his feet and went for his gun and came across with a series of sweeps from side to side and back again, the Kidon cutting, slicing, and dicing the man's forearms and flesh.

As the console officer tried to disengage his weapon from his holster, the assassin through a series of straight jabs with the point of the knife stabbing and punching holes into the man's chest and shoulders, debilitated him. The moment the officer went to his knees, the Kidon drove the points of his blades first into one temple, and then the second blade in the other, killing the man quickly.

With the other officer still on his knees, the Kidon let a blade fly, the weapon crossing the divide between them and lodging deep in the man's forehead. The man's eyes rolled upward, showing slivers of white before falling back, his life extinguished.

When the assassin immediately took over operations of the console, he popped the keypad cover with a small screwdriver to expose the circuitry underneath. He then removed a small, windowed device from the inside pocket of his clerical jacket, connected two wired clips that were attached to the decoder to two specific leads in the circuitry, and started the unit. The entire task from beginning to end took eight seconds.

Red LED numbers began to scroll in the decoder's window, the numbers rolling to identify the breach code of Blair House with the first number being 6, and the second number 7. There were two more numerals to go.

The assassin looked at his watch. *Everything remained on schedule.*

The third number was 3. And the final number was 0.

When the entry code flashed 6730, the doors to Blair House buzzed open on their own.

Team Leader's unit moved quickly, quietly, and efficiently with their weapons leveled as one half of the team went left inside the facility and the other went right, the teams fanning out to certain points within the complex.

Team Leader removed the cleric's band from around his throat, packed it deep inside his shirt pocket, then after removing the decoding unit, he joined his team.

#

The lighting in the hallway was subdued as an agent from the president's detail walked into the cardinal's darkened library and stood silhouetted within the door frame. The moment he raised his hand to the light switch, three muted pops no louder than spits sounded off in quick succession, one right after the other as muzzle flashes winked intermittently from the darkest edges of the room. With icy-cold effectiveness, the perfectly placed bullets hit center mass in a tight pattern, which dropped the agent as fast as gravity would allow.

#

On the second-tier landing where the bedrooms were located, two agents stood vigil at opposite ends of the hallway. When one of the agents began to toy with his earpiece, a darkened shape moved along the wall with incredible stealth, drew a garrote around the agent's neck, and pulled him silently into the shadows where he strangled him with such surgical precision that the agent was unable to produce a sound upon the moment of his death.

After the assassin lowered the body to the floor, he melded so easily with the surrounding darkness that he became a part of it.

And then he was gone.

#

Agent Cross stood alone at the opposite end of the corridor, unaware that he was surrounded by a group of hostiles. The moment he raised his hand to adjust his lip mic, he was taken down. The action was so quick and so proficient, he was numbed by surprise.

Now, with the front line of defense taken out, all that remained was the task of securing the designated targets.

#

The noise was distant, but enough to wake Pope Pius XIII from a vague dream he would have no memory of. While he lay there listening for the obscurest of sounds, he heard nothing more than autumn leaves brushing against the windowpanes from cool outside breezes.

As he labored to a sitting position, he thought he saw the shadowy movement of feet along the floor beneath the door to his room.

"Hello?"

Even though the movement stopped, the pontiff knew somebody was standing on the other side of the door.

And then in a more prudent tone, he asked, "Hello?"

The door quietly opened and two men in military dress stood

silhouetted against the backdrop of the hallway. The only light was the faint blue glow of moonlight through the bedroom's window. Then one man reached up to engage a switch on his monocular headset, which activated a phosphorous green light that gave him the advantage of night vision.

"Your Holiness," said the other. But in such darkness, the pope couldn't tell which one was speaking since one shape was as dark as the other. "Please understand that we're not here to hurt you."

The pontiff's voice remained calm. "What is it you want?"

"Your cooperation."

"My cooperation for what?"

The men in uniform looked at each other for a brief moment before turning their attention back to the pontiff.

"Please, Your Holiness, we don't need to make this difficult."

"Difficult? I'm merely posing a question."

Then one of the voices became a little less congenial. "Roll up the sleeve of your shirt."

Both men moved forward in unison, the one with the monocular holding a syringe, the other an assault weapon. To drive his point home, the commando with the Bullpup pressed the mouth of the weapon's barrel against the pope's temple. "Roll up your sleeve . . . now."

"I don't understand—"

"You're not supposed to. Now roll up your sleeve." The commando forced the mouth of the weapon deeper into the soft flesh, dimpling it.

The pope did as he was instructed, felt the prick of the syringe, and gave way to its effects.

The operation was nearly complete.

CHAPTER SEVEN

Team Leader was pleased that the operation took less than ten minutes as planned. Those dispatched on the opposing team were done quickly and dispassionately.

Moving his operation to the Lee Dining Room, Team Leader felt awash in glory as cold, blue light shone through the east wall windows. Behind him, the portrait eyes of past presidents watched the proceedings with mute detachment.

At the end of the dining table with the brim of his hat screening his face in shadow, a man sat with one leg casually crossed over the other. "Your team did well," he said. "Much better than expected."

Team Leader made his way toward the man and took his position before the operative. "Your job is done here, Judas. Your services are no longer needed."

"And miss the final scene of this magnificent production? I don't think so." The man remained still with the tone of his voice as cold as the stone tiles beneath his feet.

Team Leader nodded. "So be it."

"Then let's get this show on the road, shall we?"

Bashrah and Hashrie were ushered into the dining room and forced to their knees. The mouth of a Bullpup was positioned at the base of each man's skull. Neither captive was willing to show fear, each having resolved to meet his fate head-on.

Team Leader circled them in appraisal, wondering what drove such men to give up their lives for an afterlife he considered to be highly implausible. Then, in Arabic, so that the understanding was between Arab and Hebrew only, Team Leader said, "You came to this soil to make history for your people," he told them. "So, history you shall make if this is what you seek. But not the history you dreamed about or imagined." Team Leader turned his back to them and began to walk away. "Today marks the onset of a brave new world; the beginning for some, the end for others."

Even though the man sitting in the shadows didn't understand the exchange, he couldn't help but smile with malicious amusement.

Judas' voice dripped with malice "Did you tell them that they're about to die?"

Team Leader closed his eyes and drew a deep breath. His hatred for Judas was enormous. Judas was a mercenary whose personal cause was to line his pockets with blood money. It was never for the advancement of the cause itself.

Team Leader turned to the man sitting in the shadows. "What we do, Judas, we do without malevolence, which you seem to have forgotten."

"What we do," he returned, "we do for money. Now get on with it."

The muscles in the back of Team Leader's jaw began to work. Judas was a major player who opened the door and made the cause possible. But Team Leader was not accustomed to taking orders from someone whose only motivation in promoting the cause was financially based. To Team Leader, Judas was nothing but a whore.

However, Judas was right when he said that things needed to move along. Time was not a luxury.

The last standing member of the president's detail, Agent Cross, was guided into the room with a suppressed Bullpup pressed to his skull.

"The area's secured," stated the commando holding the weapon. "Their entire defense force has been eliminated."

Judas stood while running a finger along the brim of his fedora in greeting, then he addressed Special Agent Cross with playful sarcasm. His features were recognizable for the first time in the blue light. Then: "Top of the morning to you," he said.

Cross turned away. His face and eyes, everything about his manner professed disbelief that the man he knew and respected, a man he even idolized at one time, could have maneuvered this team.

Team Leader looked at Cross and intuited that the men knew each other.

Cross looked at Team Leader. The strength of his chin and the determination he exhibited was a sign of stoicism, an action Team

Leader admired.

"Judas," Cross said to the hatted man. "The name certainly fits." Judas's face remained partially hidden by the brim of his hat.

"Perhaps," he answered. "But unlike the real Judas who did it for thirty pieces of silver, I'm doing it for ten million dollars. And I'm sure you would, too, David, if given the chance."

"You'd be wrong about that."

Judas clapped a hand on the agent's shoulder, then addressed him with sarcasm dripping and bleeding like a hemorrhage. "Just so you know where I stand in all this," he told Cross, "I'll be at your funeral telling your wife how much of a good man you used to be and how much you'll be missed. And maybe—just maybe—I'll sleep with her just to help fill that sudden and horrible gap in her life. Sound OK to you?" Judas couldn't help the malice. "Have a good death, David. It's a stop we all have to make someday." Still wearing a smile of dark humor, Judas left the room with all the ease of taking a stroll through the park with his hands buried deep inside the pockets of his long coat.

His lack of respect for fellow agents only confirmed the hatred Team Leader felt for Judas, whom he considered to be a man without honor.

Facing Agent Cross with a neutral expression, Team Leader said, "Your team, Special Agent Cross, was so complacent there wasn't much sport to the takeover. Judas or no Judas, your protection of the pope was completely negligent. Your team would have never been so poorly trained under my command."

Team Leader turned to the commando holding the Bullpup to Cross's head and held out a hand. "His weapon, if you would."

The commando removed a Glock from his waistband and gave it to Team Leader.

"Nevertheless," Team Leader said to Cross while turning the weapon over in his hand to check its weight. "Since you *are* the only one left alive in your unit, I'm going to make you an American hero." Team Leader examined the mouth of the barrel before removing a suppressor from his pocket and screwed the device into the Glock. "I'm sure your family will be extremely proud of you," he said in accented English. "And I'm sure you'll be awarded something posthumous for your efforts in taking down two known terrorists. I think Americans love that sort of thing, don't you?" After the suppressor was fitted, Team Leader placed the weapon by his side so the mouth of the barrel faced the floor. "At least your children will grow up in a safe place," he concluded. "That was something I always dreamed about."

At that moment he raised the weapon and shot Bashrah and Hashrie with shots to the chest and throat. They dropped as fast as the bullets that took their lives.

Agent Cross's knees began to buckle, his balance wavering. The commando forced him back to solid footing. Once the agent stood on his own again, the commando stepped back.

"I'm almost jealous of what you are about to become," Team Leader told him. And then he handed a second silenced-equipped pistol and shot Cross in the throat.

After teetering a moment in a wide-eyed drunken stance, Cross fell to his knees with a hand pressed against his neck and fell to the floor, hard.

While blood bubbles foamed in the gaping hole in Cross's neck, his eyes stared at nothing in particular while Team Leader removed the suppressor and placed the second firearm in Bashrah's hand. The other commando placed the Sig in the hand of Hashrie.

After Team Leader removed the suppressor from Cross's weapon, he worked the agent's hand around the Glock. With what little strength he had left, Cross raised his head slightly to see what Team Leader was doing. His throat rattled with awful wetness, and his eyes were beginning to lose their luster. Finally, his eyes took on a detached stare as he succumbed to his wound.

Team Leader watched and listened as Cross took his last labored breath, then placed the agent's finger on the trigger and laid his hand carefully against the blood-soaked tile.

Getting to his full height, Team Leader took note of his handiwork.

The stage had been set. Bashrah and Hashrie had been killed in a firefight with Cross.

"Everything secure?" asked Team Leader.

"Cleared and sanitized. We're ready to move."

Team Leader nodded his approval. "Less than fifteen minutes," he said. "Yahweh will be most pleased."

The time was 0326 hours.

#

At exactly 0700 hours Eastern Standard Time, CNN in Atlanta would receive a call from someone claiming to be a member of the Soldiers of Islam. The caller would clearly state that Pope Pius XIII was now under the authority of their regime.

It was the first step of the Final Jihad.

CHAPTER EIGHT

Blair House
September 23, Late Morning

Yellow DO-NOT-CROSS tape had been set around the perimeter of Blair House to maintain the crime scene with access restricted to county, federal, and state personnel only. The Forensics Unit had already staked their claim, combing, and sweeping every inch of the interior with several alternative light sources. The most commonly used was the high-intensity lamp, in which varying wavelengths and light colors were passed over all surfaces to visualize latent friction-ridge prints that would point out certain types of trace and biological evidence.

Other investigators were engaging the use of mini vacs, which were the typical hand-held vacuums with sterilized bags used to pick up any type of trace evidence such as dust, dirt, and cellular matter. In the dining room, a CSI technician was carefully going over the area to acquire possible prints for the VMD, a vacuum-metal deposition device, which was the most effective means for visualizing latent friction-ridge prints on smooth surfaces. But in order to make these prints discernible, gold or zinc had to evaporate in the vacuum chamber and coat the object to be examined with a thin layer of metal, making the prints visible. More often than not, more than 97% of all prints were indigenous, 2% either contaminated or untraceable with less than 1% traceable.

When Special Agent Punch Murdock of the president's Secret Service detail was halted at the entrance by D.C. Metro, he flashed his credentials and was allowed to pass. He was a man of simian build and pug-like features. And his nose angled badly to one side from too many years in the ring, a feature he never had corrected since it served as a personal badge of honor that released something savage about him. His eyes also provoked something untamed since they were black to the point of almost being without pupils. Yet they were alert and all-seeing as Murdock absorbed every detail of the pope's bedroom, as he made his way toward a technician who was running a scanner slowly over the surface of the nightstand.

When Murdock spoke, he did so with an inflection that had been acquired from growing up in the mean streets in the city's toughest neighborhoods, his accent maintaining a rough edge that served only to intimidate and repel those he encountered in salutation, rather than to magnetize them. Moving closer to the technician, Murdock leaned forward until he was level with the technician's ear. "How's it going, buddy?"

The forensics investigator continued to examine the surface of the nightstand with meticulous study. Behind him, the covers of the pope's bed were in disarray. "It's going," he said.

"Any traces of blood?"

"Not up here."

"Thanks."

Murdock exited the room and worked his way through a mass of investigators, some wearing gloves and paper booties in the areas of primary points—the areas where the bodies lay—as a medical examiner took photos from numerous angles and viewpoints.

Murdock continued to look on with detachment since he had seen this many times over his twenty-five years in law enforcement which, over time, he had steadily learned how to disengage his emotions from the many bloodbaths visited.

A man wearing a gray suit and maroon tie moved next to Murdock with pen and pad in hand, his face having the fresh-scrubbed look of a movie star and blue eyes that took everything in with photo-like retention.

"You're Punch, right? Punch Murdock?"

Murdock stepped away without responding. The last thing he needed right now was some kid latching onto his lapels.

The young man followed, keeping up with Murdock's quick pace. "My name's Melvin Yzerman," he said.

"Yeah, well, good for you, kid."

"And I'm from the *Washington Post.*"

Murdock stopped in his tracks because he knew what was coming next. "How'd you get in here?"

"Do you have a comment regarding your unit? As Chief of the President's Security detail, how do you feel about your team—"

"Get the hell out of here!"

"—being killed by terrorists at the very heart of the American stage?"

"I said, get the hell out of here!"

"And as head of the detail, why weren't you—"

"Kid, I ain't gonna tell you again."

"—with your team at such a critical moment?"

"Officers!"

"Answer me that, Agent Murdock. All I want is a simple comment."

"Hey, kid, kiss my ass. Print that in your commie paper!"

Two officers from the D.C. Metro Unit entered the room, one with an extended baton in his hand.

"Which one of you D.C. clowns let this idiot from the *Post* in here?" Murdock's face was red, the man livid as spittle flew from his lips as he spoke. "This is a secured area, even from the press! Get this piece of crap out of here and maintain the premises. Nobody in or out unless they're from the county, state, or law enforcement! Got it?"

The officers were galvanized by Murdock's tone, and grabbed the reporter by the back of his arm and began to usher him from the room.

"Murdock!" Yzerman said over his shoulder. "Do you want to comment on the inadequacy of protection by your team regarding the safety of the pope? Any comment at all?"

Murdock stood silent as he watched the officers force the man toward the exit while weighing the question in his mind, the journalist's words bearing an uncomfortable heft to them.

Fighting for calm, Murdock closed his eyes and waited for tranquility to wash over him and for the anger to melt away. But Yzerman's questions continued to strike a chord that would stay with him throughout the day and establish a mood that would remain raw and irritable.

Entering the spacious dining area where the bodies of Agent Cross and the downed terrorists lay with their remains draped by sheets, Murdock took note of his surroundings. From the West Wall, the gallery of past presidents smiled at him, their eyes having been witness to the events that went on last night. Then he looked at the oil paintings with a less-than-appreciative eye, knowing the truth would forever be locked away behind the strokes of paint. With more of an analytical approach, he turned a keen eye back to the scene.

Tony Denucci was an investigator for the FBI who delved into kidnappings, bombings, and anything else that fell under their jurisdiction. As a youth, he was tall and broad with the markings of strong facial features. Now he was tall and gangly with a face that had grown long and jaded from partaking in too many tragedies that held the promise of more to come. And when he walked, he did so with a stoop, his body bowing in the shape of a question mark. Over the years he had become nothing more than a husk of his former self.

Murdock clapped his old friend on the back. They had come up together in the ranks from the academy twenty-four years ago, each rising from the trenches to become experts in their field. "How're you doing, Tony?"

Denucci looked at him with the red and rheumy eyes of an alcoholic. "Hey, Punch."

"Got anything?"

"Eight dead altogether," he said. "Five agents and two intruders." Then pointing the tip of his pen at the contoured sheets of the Arabs, he said, "You might want to take a look to see who they are."

Murdock already knew who they were; the whole world did. They were the self-proclaimed warriors tagged as the Soldiers of Islam.

But Murdock peeled back the sheet off the first body far from the Arabs and saw that it was Cross. He immediately covered him back up. After examining the bodies of the other two, there was no doubt they were of Middle Eastern descent. He also noticed that the ink on their fingertips was still wet. Their prints had already been taken and were now being processed through the FBI's watch list, the NCIC, and the Interpol systems. Whoever they were would not remain a mystery for long.

Murdock got to his feet as Denucci continued to offer more information, using his pen as a pointer. "It appears as if the whole detail was taken absolutely by surprise," he told him. "Not a single weapon was drawn except by that agent lying over there."

"That would be David Cross," he said. "A good man."

"Other than Cross, it looks as if everybody in the detail was killed before they knew it."

Murdock ambled around the scene with his hands deep inside the pockets of his overcoat. "Are you doing the Incident Report for Pappandopolous?"

"Me?"

"The president wants a first-hand account of what happened here. He doesn't want to wait on the preliminaries."

Denucci wandered carefully around the bodies and made several notations on his pad. "Sad thing, isn't it?"

Murdock agreed.

"What's even sadder is that we never saw it coming," Denucci added. "And there was nobody in the vicinity that saw or heard anything?"

"Nobody. It's too bad *they* couldn't tell us anything, huh?" Denucci pointed his pen at the oil paintings.

Yeah. Whatever. Murdock laid a hand on his old friend's shoulder. "Look, Tony, if something comes up, will you let me know? You know, give me something to go on?"

"Sure. If something comes up."

Murdock gave him a wink. "Thanks, buddy."

"And hey, don't be a stranger. Let's go on a booze cruise some time and tell war stories."

"Yeah. Sure."

Murdock exited Blair House and took measure. Beyond the police tape, the mob of onlookers had grown exponentially since he entered the house. There were more vans with satellite dishes lined up by the dozens, the emblem of major networks including CNN, ABC, FOX, and their affiliates, all displaying their stenciled call letters on the vehicles. Newscasters and journalists tried to press their way through the line with their mikes held out in a desperate plea to pick up an informative byte from officers who maintained the perimeter but had no clue about the fine details.

Murdock knew the situation was going to demand long hours of little sleep, something his body was no longer equipped for at the age of fifty-four.

For almost twenty-five years he had moved aggressively up through the ranks with the same aggression he managed in the ring, with tenacity and posturing, for which he was finally rewarded by gaining a position with the president's Secret Security detail in 1990, then as the detail's chief in 2002.

But with responsibility comes accountability. And when one holds the reins of the team he drives, and if the team should stumble gravely in its efforts to achieve the means, then the accusing finger begins to point at the one who commands. In Murdock's case, he could already sense the political finger-pointing in his direction and branding him as the party responsible for the death of his team and the kidnapping of the pope.

Reaching inside the inner pocket of his overcoat, he grabbed his pack of smokes, withdrew a cigarette, and smoked it slowly, wondering how long it would take for the ax to fall upon his once illustrious career.

CHAPTER NINE

The White House
September 23, Noon

The Situation Room was the nerve center of presidential crisis management. It sat directly below the Oval Office and could seat twenty-four people.

CIA, FBI, and Homeland Security dignitaries sat at the table, along with President Burroughs, Vice President Jonas Bohlmer, Chief Presidential Advisor Alan Thornton, and Attorney General Dean Hamilton. Normally a room to sequester members of the Pentagon and Joint Chiefs of Staff to determine the potential for war, President Burroughs had distinguished the kidnapping of the pope as a non-military issue after a quick briefing with his military principals. The officers remained seated as mere spectators, as President Burroughs turned his attention to the members of the intelligence community.

With his sleeves rolled up to his elbows, the president possessed the countenance of someone well aware of being under a worldwide microscope. Despite the American policy of never negotiating with terrorists, the president could almost feel the Sword of Damocles falling on an international scale, should his administration refuse to bend to the will of the Soldiers of Islam.

"All right, people," he said. "Settle down."

The room fell silent as something indescribably awkward hung in the air. It was something like tension, but thicker and far more palpable. "Last night," he began, "or this morning, however you want to look at it, I lost five good men to the hands of terrorists. Now can anybody here tell me how a cell could succeed in taking out *my* people in *my* backyard without any prior intelligence? Or how they could take out our live video feeds so there wouldn't be a visual account as to what happened at Blair House!" Despite his efforts to remain in control, the president's tone became heated with each word louder than the previous. "Anybody?"

Nobody dared to proffer an answer. The assembled dignitaries stared silently at the sheets of paper in front of them.

"Talk to me, people! I didn't bring you in here to clam up."

Attorney General Dean Hamilton raised his hand. "Mr. President, if I may."

"Go ahead, Dean."

"After what happened at Blair House, we immediately processed the identities of the two Arabs found inside and got hits on both of them." He looked at his intel sheet. "One was Hashrie Rantissi, a Jordanian national with ties to ISIS."

"So, ISIS is definitely behind this?"

"We're not sure," he said. "The other Arab, Bashrah Aziz, is a Saudi national who also has ties to ISIS."

The president appeared puzzled. "So how are we *not* sure that this is the doing of ISIS if both men have ties to the organization?"

CIA Director Doug Craner leaned forward and placed his glasses on the tabletop. Then he spoke pointedly. "Because, Mr. President, our intel tells us that there were no discussions in the chat rooms before the incident. The only activity that came *after* the incident was broadcast by the news media."

"Which means what? Since ISIS knows we're monitoring the chat rooms."

"It means, Mr. President, that there seems to be confusion among the terrorist organizations as to who is truly responsible here. The activity on the web indicates curiosity rather than culpability. Since ISIS has not admitted claim, it's possible that the operation was conducted by the Soldiers of Islam, as a rogue group working independently from ISIS."

"A splinter-cell?"

"Yes, sir. And we don't know how they'll conduct themselves since we have no knowledge or insight about their activities. All we can say, Mr. President, is that when we got the strikes on Hashrie and Bashrah, we were able to bring up their biographical data."

Craner gave copies of his report to an aide, who handed them out to everybody at the table. On the front page was a photograph of

Hashrie Rantissi taken two years ago when he entered the United States.

"Hashrie," Craner continued, recalling from memory, "is a Syrian national who came to this country two years ago, after serving a six-month stint in a terrorist training camp located in Yemen. The other body identified with Hashrie was also a Syrian national who helped form a sleeper cell in Utah, along with Hashrie and six other cell members. For the past two years, they've remained dormant."

"Until now?"

"Until now—yes, sir."

"And the other six cell members?" asked the president.

"Through our intel sources, we were able to confirm and identify each member of the Utah cell. We obtained warrants and raided their residences. Unfortunately, the areas were sanitized. The computers left behind were useless and the hard drives were completely fried."

The president remained disconcertingly quiet. After a moment's hesitation, he said, "So at least we know who the other six are? These Soldiers of Islam?"

"Yes, sir. They're all on the FBI's watch list."

The president glanced at his watch, knowing that the world was waiting for a televised response regarding the kidnapping. At the moment he had nothing to offer, the Soldiers of Islam having yet to make any demands. "When they call," he said almost too quietly, "are we to bend in our policy of non-negotiation?"

"We're not talking about an expendable here," said Thornton, his advisor of three years who had numerous accolades for political achievements covering the walls of his office. "We're talking about the pope. And if we allow these terrorists to harm him due to our unwillingness to bend, we will most likely come under extreme condemnation from our allies. The voices of over a billion Catholics can be extremely loud, and should they motivate their governments—" He let the balance of the sentence hang.

The president sighed. "Unfortunately, I have to agree."

Thornton: "So to answer your question, Mr. President, I believe the answer is yes. We may need to look into this further should we have to make concessions."

The president seemed to focus on an imaginary point on the

tabletop. "That'll be your department, Dean," he said. "You're the attorney general. The FBI is your gig."

The president turned to Hamilton with a no-nonsense look. "This cannot be turned into another Waco or Ruby Ridge."

"Clearly, Mr. President."

"Options, then."

Hamilton wasn't through. "I say we bring in Shari Cohen. There is no one more suited to handle this situation. She's at the top of her game and perhaps the best we have to offer."

The president appeared to mull this while tapping a finger against his chin.

Shari Cohen was the Bureau's top negotiator for the Hostage Rescue Team based in the Washington Metropolitan Field Office. She also held the title of Assistant Director of the FBI's CIRG, or the Critical Incident Response Group. And when time permitted, she worked in collaboration with Homeland Security educating agents who worked in counterterrorism.

Then from Burroughs: "I agree with your assessment. Bring her in." Vice President Bohlmer immediately stated his objection. "Mr. President, have you forgotten the demographic type that we're dealing with here? We're talking about a male-dominated regime that recognizes women as property. If you put someone like Shari Cohen— no offense to her religious heritage or abilities—in to negotiate with Islamic terrorists, it would certainly be an assured insult to their principles. And in recompense for our actions by allowing this, you can be certain that they *will* kill the pope."

President Burroughs appeared at a crossroads. "Second option, then."

"I would suggest Billy Paxton," said the vice president.

"Paxton?"

"Fully qualified. Very good. He did two campaigns last year in the Philippines and negotiated two separate kidnapping situations regarding American interests abroad."

"But he's not Shari Cohen."

"It all depends how you look at people."

President Burroughs remained silent for a brief moment before speaking. "Then we'll use Paxton as the speaker with Cohen working in Paxton's shadow. But I want Cohen to maintain control of the unit."

"Mr. President," Bohlmer immediately protested, "I must object to this. If the Soldiers of Islam find out that Shari Cohen is involved—"

"Your objection, Jonas, is duly noted. Thank you." Then speaking to the rest of the room, he asked, "Further advice as to direction?"

Thornton leaned forward with his brows dipping sharply over the bridge of his nose as if he had given considerable thought to the matter. "I suggest, Mr. President, we at least try to appear committed to the policy of not negotiating with terrorists. We don't want to open a doorway to every degenerate faction that has demands to make. We'll need to set up an international coalition and make it clear that any concessions or compromises are made by the international community. That way, if something should go wrong, the blame cannot rest solely on the shoulders of the United States."

"What you're saying is that we set up a situation so that all nations are involved."

"Yes, sir. That would take care of international ostracism if the pope's safety cannot be guaranteed."

"Yet it sounds far from optimistic."

"Right now, we're just trying to cover all our bases, sir."

President Burroughs began to drum his fingers against the tabletop, his mind working. "Get every international liaison involved," he finally said. "I want their opinions, their suggestions, and I want it understood that we will share common responsibility in this matter, whether the outcome is good, bad, or indifferent."

"Understood."

"I also want direct lines to my office from every liaison involved. And I want to know everything that's going on twenty-four-seven."

"Yes, sir."

"We'll inform the media only what we want them to know. Let them know that this is an international effort. If something should ultimately go wrong, I do not want this madness to fall on *our* shoulders."

The president searched the faces around him. "Per the guidelines of the Patriot Act, I want all agencies to work continuously on this. Day, night, and everything thing in between. I want everybody on the same page. The CIA Advance Team will monitor all chat lines abroad to gather whatever intel is available, and then network the information to everyone involved. Is that understood?"

There was mumbled agreement.

"That's it, people. Today you start earning your money. So, go out there and do what you do best."

There was an immediate galvanization of forces, some already on cell phones instructing aides to immediately get in touch with international contacts, while others were called to gather a writing staff to generate material for the media.

As the Situation Room emptied, President Burroughs sat quietly digesting all that had occurred. This was strictly politics, and he recognized his role as such, despite his subjective feelings. There was no concern about the fate of the pope other than the problem of the situation being politically based. The meeting was about saving face in the eyes of the international community. The life of Pope Pius was, unfortunately, a secondary issue.

Feeling dirty, filthy, and hollow at the same time, the president closed his eyes and sighed.

CHAPTER TEN

Mossad Headquarters, Tel Aviv, Israel
September 23, Late Afternoon

The Hebrew word for "Institute" is Mossad, Israel's legendary agency for collecting intelligence data and conducting covert operations. Presently, Mossad had 20,000 active agents and 15,000 sleeper agents worldwide, including operatives in the former communist countries, the Arab nations, and in the west, including the United States.

Mossad's PALD, the Political Action, and Liaison Department were responsible for maintaining contacts with friendly foreign services by transmitting data and updating the terrorist database. On this day, the department was like an ant colony, well-constructed and orderly, the work pace quick and efficient. Requests for information regarding the Soldiers of Islam poured in from the Washington, D.C. branch of the FBI and the CIA.

Going over reports from the Research Department, Yosef Rokach sat at his desk with a cigarette burning between his fingers, the smoke coiling lazily through the air. Yosef had been born to Hebrew parents who were killed by Hezbollah raiders, which branded him as an orphan. In time, as indicated by his biographical records, he had graduated from the Hebrew University of Jerusalem within the top ten percent of his class. But in reality, which was the world of espionage, his real name was John McEachern, an American-born citizen who grew up in an Indiana suburb without a single drop of Hebrew blood coursing through his veins.

Upon his true commencement from Notre Dame University, where he earned a Doctorate in Systems Networking at the same time it took most people to earn a bachelor's degree, McEachern obtained an internship with the CIA. He worked at the lowest levels never realizing that he was being monitored for strengths and weaknesses. When it was reported that he had an affinity for Middle Eastern languages, he was recruited as a sleeper. After four years of learning to improvise through tense situations and training, then training his body to beat the polygraph and to resist the constraints of sodium pentothal, John McEachern, who was born of Irish parents, was ready for the field.

A counterfeit profile was manufactured and slipped into every known system within Israel's computerized infrastructure by remote access, creating Yosef Rokach. According to all background checks, Yosef was devout to his religion and committed to his people. He was an outstanding citizen in every respect by Hebrew standards. But after seven years within Mossad, he still had not made it beyond a low-level ranking within Mossad's PALD unit.

Taking a final drag of his cigarette, he stubbed it out and fell back in his chair. Then he interlaced his fingers behind his head. The room was huge and open with desks and plasma monitors everywhere, and not a cubicle in sight. The office boasted bomb-blast glass walls and high-tech security equipment. Eye scans restricted secured areas to specific personnel. Software with facial recognition capabilities was used to identify employees on file. Everything was based on the assumption that no one could be trusted. The data handled by the office was considered so vital, it had been deemed more important than human life. Any employees betraying the Mossad trust would find themselves before the agency's interrogation specialists.

Then Yosef looked directly into a camera and smiled.

From all points of the room excited chatter could be heard, the urgency behind the exchanges normally reserved for attacks against Israeli interests. But this was not the case. The pope was missing. And Catholics throughout the world were calling for the intervention of anyone who could bring back the Holy Father unharmed. Mossad saw this as an opportunity to show the world that Arab hostility understood no boundaries and that the Israeli plight was now the plight of all people. Israel wished to impart to its allies a better understanding of what it's like to live under the constant tyranny of a fanatical enemy.

From one of the elevators that led to other departments that Yosef couldn't access, emerged a man by the name of David Gonick. Stepping quickly away from the elevator, Gonick headed toward the restroom, his face ashen. Gonick had been another CIA install who had infiltrated the Lohamah Psichlogit Department. The Lohamah Psichlogit, also known as Literature and Publications or the LAP, was responsible for psychological warfare, propaganda, and deception operations. To be a member of the LAP, one had to have TS Clearance, which was limited to those few at the top of the food chain. The CIA's infiltration of that particular level had taken years of maneuvering. But to see Gonick in this manner addled Yosef, since Gonick was always a man of refinement under extreme pressure.

Had he been made?

Moments later, Gonick returned from the restroom. And not once did he turn Yosef's way or acknowledge him as he hastily made his way to the elevator. Upon his return, however, the knot of his tie had been lowered with the top button of his shirt undone, a signal.

Yosef rubbed a hand over his face, sensing long-awaited fruition. Standing, Yosef tried to look as relaxed as possible before heading to the restroom. The people around him did not take notice of his leaving. They were intimately involved with their duties. And Yosef was just one nondescript face among many. In fact, Yosef excelled at being unremarkable; he was a ghost among the living.

When he entered the restroom, he found it empty and clean. The urinals were to his left, the toilet stalls to his right. Entering the third stall, Yosef closed the louvered door behind him and waited. As he stood there a sense of paranoia crept over him. He breathed deeply and waited for it to pass. Then he lifted the lid to the tank. Lying on the bottom and nearly invisible to the naked eye, sat a data stick inside a water-sealed case. It was state-of-the-art small. But it carried a huge memory load.

Using toilet paper to wipe the case dry, he placed the stick in a special pocket within the cuff of his pants. After replacing the toilet's lid, he took a deep breath to collect himself and left the stall.

As per protocol, he would decipher the data and forward it to his American associates. His value as an agent, after years of training, had simply come down to his computer skills, something he didn't see as particularly glamorous for a spy. Yosef more or less continued to romanticize the theatrical side of espionage, envisioning himself walking along fog-laden streets late at night, and meeting connections hiding within deep shadows. In truth, however, he held something more important and something far more tangible than romantic ideas. The data stick in his possession, and something no larger than a human thumb, contained enough information to bring the planet to the brink of global war.

Returning to his desk and acting as if the day were routine, Yosef couldn't wait to get home to decipher the data.

CHAPTER ELEVEN

Vatican City
September 23, Mid-Afternoon

They were known as the Society of Seven, a private sect within the Vatican made up of the pope and his most trusted cardinals within the Curia.

In a restricted chamber beneath the Basilica, seven chairs were situated on a staging area four feet above the floor. The pope's chair, a king's throne layered in gold leaf, stood vacant. The second chair, nearly as impressive as the pope's but smaller and less imaginative, was occupied by the Vatican's Secretary of State. Surrounding him sat the cardinals of the Curia.

The hall was grand and ancient—an underground haven where past popes and secret alliances met time and again. The walls were made of lime and its ceiling was supported by massive Romanesque-like columns. The chamber's acoustics were poor, however, as words often traveled across the room in echoes. The only lighting came from gas-lit lamps that were moored amongst the columns, the dancing flames giving the room somewhat of a medieval cast as shadows floated oddly against the stone walls.

As the Society of Seven waited, an echoing of footfalls sounded from beyond the chamber door, their pace marked with urgency. At the opposite end of the chamber, a door of solid oak labored on its hinges as it swung inward. From the shadows, a man of incredible stature walked toward the platform with a gait that spoke of power and confidence. His shoulders were impossibly broad, his chest and arms stretching the fabric of his cleric's shirt to its limit. His upper body mass, V-shaped, tapered to a trim waist and chiseled legs. When he reached the base of the stage, he removed his beret, dropped to a knee, and placed a closed fist over his heart.

"Loyalty above all else," he said, his voice deep, "except honor." This was the salute of the Vatican Knights.

The Vatican's Secretary of State, Cardinal Bonasero Vessucci, rose and walked the three stairs to the marble floor where the large man knelt. "Stand, my friend. You and I have much to talk about."

When Kimball Hayden got to his full height, he towered over Cardinal Vessucci, who barely reached Kimball's chest. When the cardinal placed a hand on the Vatican Knight's shoulder, he had to reach high above his head to do so.

"Obviously, you know why we've called you here for a gathering." The cardinal spoke fluent English.

"I do."

Vessucci kept his hand on Kimball's shoulder. "Assemble your team and return our pope and the members of the Church to us."

Kimball nodded.

"If these terrorists wish to pick a fight with the Roman Catholic Church, then a fight they'll get." Vessucci lowered his hand and stopped in his tracks. Shadows from nearby torches danced awkwardly across benign features. "We may be a small city-state," he added, "but we also have the right to protect the sovereignty of the Church, its interests, and the welfare of its citizenry. I understand that the act of engagement is complicated by its lack of rules, but you have to be discreet in such matters. Should something tragic occur, Kimball, you know the Church would have no choice but to disavow any knowledge of the Vatican Knights. We cannot afford your methods to draw any unwanted attention to the Vatican."

Kimball placed a gentle hand on the shoulder of his old friend. "We'll bring them back," he told him with words that were weighted with confidence.

The cardinal nodded. "You'll be flying from Rome into Dulles via an Alitalia jet. Once on American soil, then you'll need to contact Cardinal Juan Medeiros at the archdiocese. He'll be your intel source."

Kimball got to a knee and placed a closed fist over his heart. "Loyalty above all else," he repeated, "except honor."

The cardinal reciprocated Kimball's gesture with one of his own, placing a hand on top of Kimball's head—an act of anointing and honor. "Be safe, my friend. The Church has faith in those who believe in righteousness. May God be with you."

Kimball stood, turned, and walked away from the Society of Seven with his footsteps echoing off the ancient stone walls.

CHAPTER TWELVE

The White House
September 23, Mid-Afternoon

The total area of the White House is 65,000 square feet, including the basement and sub-basement. But as far as the president was concerned, it was not space enough. All around him the White House staff worked like drones, who seemed to be everywhere at once. Voices cried out, they chattered, the noise of chaos becoming an incessant buzz that hammered his temples unmercifully, even within his private study. All he wanted, even for fifteen minutes, was a short reprieve to regroup his thoughts and emotions.

And he found it in the Press Briefing Room—a small, closed-in area that housed forty-eight theater-style chairs that sat empty before him.

President Burroughs stood in front of the staging area looking over an empty audience, then rubbed the palms of his hands over his eyes until he saw bright patterns. He knew this room would soon be packed with media shouting out questions for which he had no answers.

"I knew you'd be here," said the vice president. His voice always projected smoothly and calmly, except when he was involved in a hotly contested political debate or lobbying for a cause. "It's an odd place to find peace, isn't it?" The vice president stood behind the podium, then hooked his fingers over the edges and took a firm grip, as if he was about to lead Mass for a congregation of one. "Are you all right, Jim? It's not like you to run away from matters."

The president pitched a sigh. "I'm not running from the situation, Jonas. I'm running from the moment."

"You know it's only going to get worse from here, don't you?"

The president lowered one of the seats in the gallery and sat down. "When I woke up this morning," he began, "I knew it was going to be a bad day. Call it presidential insight, intuition—call it whatever you want. But something told me that today was going to be a challenge that I might not be up to—a challenge none of us could meet."

The vice president stared at the seamless face of Jim Burroughs. "We'll get through this," he said. "We have to."

The president offered a weak smile. "We've been through a lot together, you and I." He draped an arm over the back of a neighboring seat. "I guess that's what happens when you have Senator Burroughs from New York and Senator Bohlmer from California, both running on the same ticket in a race for the White House. People expect a lot from us."

"And we've provided."

"Until now," he added.

"There's nothing you could have done, Jim, to prevent what happened. You took all the necessary precautions. You put your detail in place as required."

"My detail was murdered, Jonas, by a team of insurgents who walked right into my backyard, which makes this country appear vulnerable, to the American people and our allies. Not a good thing."

"Jim, they were highly skilled militants trained well above the level of your people. You know that."

"Of course, I know that. But the court of public opinion and the people of this nation will only see a breach in American superiority. Our government suddenly appears incapable of providing the security that the people of this nation expect."

"Which is all the more reason why we have to make things right," Bohlmer returned.

The president closed his eyes, his headache abating little. "We're doing all we can, Jonas," he answered faintly, "given what we have to go on."

"I agree. But there's still an issue we need to address."

The president opened his eyes. "Such as?"

"Shari Cohen."

The president raised his hands intuitively. "Please, Jonas, we've already discussed this matter upstairs. And your concern was duly noted. But her presence in this matter is vital."

"Her presence, Jim, is dangerous. How many people do you think are working on this right now?"

The president shrugged. "A lot."

"Exactly. A lot. And how long do you think it'll take for somebody from the *Post*, the *Times,* or the *Globe* to make an offer to someone willing to divulge the fact that a woman of Jewish faith is manning the team? You know that internal leaks are caused by those who are willing to set aside their integrity for a pocketful of change. It's a fact, Jim. And I'll bet you anything that you have somebody up there right now that's willing to sell their mother upriver for a can of beer."

"We have a failsafe in place against leaks."

"Jim, a failsafe is *never* foolproof, despite its intention to be so. You know that."

"What do you want me to do? Give in to the twisted viewpoints of terrorists by taking the best person I have off the job because of her religious background?"

"In this case, yes! You know what the Soldiers of Islam will do to the pope if they find out Cohen is tracking them. It's not because of what she *does* . . . but because of who she is."

"If I remove every qualified person from their positions because of religious affiliations—or any of the rights granted them by the Bill of Rights—then the terrorists have already won not just the battle, but the war." The president closed his eyes, the pain beginning to erode his patience. "You need to have faith in our workforce, Jonas. Shari Cohen is an unbelievable power. And when all this is over, they'll be kneeling at her feet. Believe me."

"You need to be realistic, Jim. You know we won't be able to meet their demands, whatever they may be. And deep down you know they have every intention of killing him."

"Jonas, if they were going to kill him, then they would have done so when they stormed Blair House. They're keeping him alive for a reason." Bohlmer left the podium, his hands gesticulating wildly to press his point. "Jim, the Soldiers of Islam are making a powerful statement to the world that they're in control and gathering steam for recruitment by doing what they're doing. It's all about giving hope to insurgents by instilling in them the belief that a battle can be fought and won on American soil." Bohlmer took in a long breath, then sighed. "They're going to kill him, Jim. You know that. Let's not give the media a rope to hang us with by keeping Cohen in the game. This will doom the entire administration."

"Look, nobody understands better than I do that saving the face of this administration is paramount. But if I remove Cohen as head of the team, the probability of finding the pope decreases immensely. With Cohen at the helm, there is a chance that he will be found. If the pope is alive, I must make every effort to save his life using whatever resources are available to me. And Cohen is a valuable asset."

"Cohen is going to get him killed!" The vice president was becoming heated. "Think about it! The moment a leak is established, his life will be over. There will be no more opportunities to track down this cell and the Soldiers of Islam will disappear."

The president weighed the possibility that Bohlmer's judgment was correct. With a topic of this magnitude, a leak could most certainly occur despite the failsafe put into place. In all likelihood, the media had already attempted to contact White House moles for information that hadn't been made public. If Cohen's name should hit the airwaves, the odds of the pope being executed would rise exponentially. And then the accusing finger would point at his administration. The newspapers would go on a feeding frenzy, questioning Burroughs for allowing Cohen to manage the team, even though the dangers were acknowledged beforehand by his staff.

"She's the best we have," he finally stated.

"She's a guaranteed death sentence for the pope if the Soldiers of Islam find out that a woman of Jewish faith is behind the investigation. I can't stress that enough. To them, it's an insult."

"She stays, Jonas. I'm not afraid to hurt the feelings of the Soldiers of Islam. As long as the pope's alive, she's the most qualified to find him."

"You may not be afraid of the Soldiers of Islam, but you *are* afraid of how the world community will perceive you if this blows up in your face."

President Burroughs raked the vice president with a fierce eye. "She stays, Jonas."

The vice president was becoming ill-tempered, his face becoming ruddy. He was not used to losing ground in an argument.

"Jim, we're never going to find him. And do you want to know why? Because it would be like looking for a needle in a haystack the size of Manhattan."

The vice president then stood back, found his calm, and spoke in a much gentler tone. "Look, Jim, it's politics. And we both know that we need to cover our bases on this one. As much as I feel sorry for the pope, and as much as I would love to find him, we can't let our emotions cloud our judgment. The reality is that the probability of finding him is zero to none."

The president's eyes settled on Bohlmer, his demeanor stern and unrelenting, but his voice remaining calm. "I know it's politics," he said. "But it's *better* politics if we put in the best there is and make a concerted effort to find him."

The vice president looked incredulous. "I don't get it," he said. "The picture is crystal clear and right in front of you. Yet you continue to put us and the rest of this administration in jeopardy because of her."

The president remained silent.

Then from the vice president: "If I didn't know better, Jim, I would swear you want this to happen. That you want the media to know—"

"That's enough, Jonas." The president held up his hand, knowing what Bohlmer was about to say. "I'm not going to argue this point with you any longer. I have based my decision on our government's potential to find the pope and bring him back alive. If you're afraid that my decision will determine what the Soldiers of Islam will do to undermine this administration, then deal with it. Once again, your input is appreciated and duly noted."

Bohlmer took a step back, his jaw tight. "All right," he said. "But you'll have to live with your decision, Jim. When they kill him, and they will, I hope you can stand on your own two feet. I tried to reason with you."

"I'll stand alone on this if I have to."

"I just wanted to let you know where *I* stood." The president nodded his head. "Noted."

After Bohlmer left, the president wondered how much of a gamble he was taking by leaving Cohen in the lineup. He hated to admit it, but there was merit in what the vice president said.

With the ache in his temples sharpening into a stabbing bout of pain, the president leaned forward in his chair and placed his face within cupped hands, wondering how the game of politics was going to play out.

CHAPTER THIRTEEN

Washington, D.C.
September 23, Early Afternoon

Shari Cohen's greatest achievement in life was graduating *magna cum laude* from Georgetown University; a strong second was being selected as the class speaker and representative for the highly touted group of scholars making their way into the real world. Although many graduated as physicians, attorneys, and business prodigies, Shari's proficiency was in International Studies and Strategic Counterterrorism. Upon graduation, she was actively recruited by the NSA, the CIA, and the FBI.

She started in the FBI, like most agents, tarrying around the bottom rung until she was able to prove herself. But with perseverance and determination, she rose steadily through the ranks until 9/11, when her knowledge and skills immediately triggered a meteoric rise. Now, as head of the Bureau's Hostage Rescue Team, she had served as lead in dozens of scenarios in which her tactical negotiations and innovative thinking skills had saved numerous lives. In time, her strategic methods would become departmental protocol, helping the Bureau keep pace with evolving ideologies, especially when dealing with the Middle East.

In the living room of her brownstone, as Shari picked up her daughter's books that were scattered across the living room floor, CNN was reporting on the abduction of Pope Pius XIII from the quarters of Blair House.

Since no statement had been made by the political brass, CNN offered baseless theories from those who informed the news media out of speculation rather than fact. The end result was a constant looping of assumptive news that became monotonously redundant, as she picked up books by Dr. Seuss and Mother Goose and began to stack them into the bookcase.

Gary Molin entered the room wearing a cooking mitt on one hand and holding a two-pronged fork in the other. He was tall and slender with olive-colored skin. His eyes were battleship gray, a drab color that paralleled the dreariness of his flat humor. For months he and his wife had been growing apart, each talking "at" each other instead of "to" each other. When they hugged or kissed or expressed any type of physical affection, it felt obligatory and insincere, and in some cases vulgar. But the true mystery was that neither could remember when they started to drift apart. There was no specific argument or event or act of lascivious impropriety that drove a wedge between them. It was something quite simple, really. The romantic glow of infatuation had simply gone away, the once-burning flame barely a smoldering ember. Worse, they both knew it. Nevertheless, each tried to hang on to the other with futile gestures, such as cooking candlelit dinners with fancy French names, or with chilled bottles of wine sitting in an ornately styled silver ice bucket. Then they would sit in awkward silence as they ate, the conversation hard to come by with their passion elusive, as the proper words to initiate a simple thread of discussion were nonexistent.

Tonight, Gary was making Greek lamb with spinach and orzo, a favorite of Shari's during their honeymoon in the Greek Isles several years earlier. It was an effort to bring back the times when they were star-struck to be in each other's company and to hear each other's voices.

He stepped further into the room, the smell of baked meat wafting behind him. "Anything new?"

"It's still guesswork at this point," she said. Her tone was flat and withdrawn as she continued to place the books onto the bookshelves.

For a moment Gary's eyes appeared saddened. Her tone seemed to confirm that their marriage was as artificial as their attempts to communicate.

When breaking news from CNN interrupted the current programming, the anchorwoman reported that a White House spokesman was about to take the podium in the Brady Press Room.

The Press Secretary, a balding man with Botox-like lips and a soft appearance, stepped to the podium and faced an audience of reporters. Something about his demeanor evoked the impression of a troll when he spoke in a high-pitched manner. This was not the image Shari would have presented to a world audience, a mistake on the part of the White House staff. But as Shari expected, the first words spoken were of condemnation for the terrorist regime and the obvious call for justice. Then the spokesperson slid neatly into what everybody was waiting to hear—that the Soldiers of Islam were responsible, and there was now an international effort to bring these terrorists to justice and to establish the safe return of Pope Pius the XIII. Nothing was ever mentioned of the terrorists' identities.

While the spokesperson elaborated the phone rang. Shari backed up with her eyes on the television and reached blindly for the phone on the wall. After talking briefly in hushed tones, she placed the receiver back on the cradle. "That was the attorney general," she said. "He wants to see me right away."

Although Gary showed no emotion, she could tell he was seething underneath.

"I'm sorry," she told him. "I know it was important to you that we have dinner together tonight."

He shrugged. "Yeah . . . well, whatever."

She appeared wounded; the tone of his voice deliberately biting. "Gary, this is my job. This is what I do. I don't have a choice in the matter."

In a quick display of warring emotions, his face transitioned from anger and then to pain. Then it eventually evolved to understanding.

"He said the president wanted to see me right away," she told him.

Realizing the lamb was wasted; Gary removed the cooking mitt and tossed it on the sofa. "It's all right," he said. "I understand." But his voice carried the evenness of someone too hurt to care.

"Look, Gary, I'm sorry. You know I wanted to spend tonight with you." This was a modicum of a lie and Gary knew it. Lying was not her forte. But he knew that she wanted desperately to believe that her marriage was not failing. Shari Cohen never failed at anything in her life.

He stepped forward and looked into her eyes. "Shari, seriously, help me understand what's happening here, with us. Are you losing interest? Is it because I'm a stay-at-home dad? What? Help me out, will you?"

"There's nothing to discuss, Gary." She pointed to the TV, maintaining calm. "You see what's going on. You know what I do for a living."

He hesitated before speaking, and then softly he said, "I know you're a mother and a wife. And I know I'm your husband. And I know you're running away from me." He rounded the sofa. "You wouldn't even take my last name when we married for professional reasons. But I guess, maybe, I can't help thinking you just didn't want to be associated with me."

She let her hand fall. "Gary. . ." She let her words trail because she knew he was right. She was running away. Even using her maiden name wasn't escape enough.

Shari moved before her husband and leaned into his embrace. She didn't feel any sense of love or passion, but an overwhelming sadness that brought her to the brink of tears. "You are without a doubt, Gary Molin, a good man. And don't you ever forget that."

He drew back and feigned a smile. And then with the back of his hand, he caressed the strands of hair off her forehead so that her hairstyle completely framed her beautiful face without errant locks interrupting her features. "I'm not angry with you, honey. I'm simply scared of where we're going."

"We'll talk," she said. "I promise." There was no smile, not even a false one. And then she placed a hand over his heart. She could feel the moderate beats against her palm. "I know you're disappointed, but I have to go."

"I guess when your wife is the head of the Hostage Rescue Team, then I guess this is to be expected."

"Thank you for understanding," she said. He shrugged. "What else can I do?"

"I just need time, that's all."

"What we need is time to talk. And I mean *talk*."

She remained forcibly calm. "Right now, Gary, there's a lot on my plate and the attorney general is calling me. Please understand the pressure I'm going through right now because it's obvious to me that I'm heading into an impossible task. I need to believe that I can do this."

"You can," he told her. "He's bringing you in because he believes in you as I do." He pulled her close once again, this time kissing the crown of her head. "You can do this, Shari. This is what you were built for."

When she drew back, he saw the worry in her eyes and the uncertainty on her face. Normally she was brimming with the fortitude to meet a challenge head-on. But this time she was different. This time she appeared unusually troubled, which seemed to shake her normally stalwart confidence. Always keeping to the adage that a single setback doesn't crumble an empire, she undoubtedly knew in this case that a single error in judgment could endanger not only the pope's life but also the stability of the world order. But how could she save the world if she couldn't even save her own marriage?

Grateful for his vote of confidence, she hugged him, the feeling not so vulgar, and then departed to do battle against the Soldiers of Islam armed only with excellent judgment.

CHAPTER FOURTEEN

Vatican City
September 23, Late Afternoon

They had taken their names from the Books of the Old Testament with the exception of Kimball Hayden, who held the call-sign of Archangel but never used it. Danny Keaton had taken the name of Leviticus, Joey Hathaway the name of Micah; Lorenzo Martinez became Nehemiah, and Christian Placentia was known as Isaiah.

After years of growing up behind Vatican walls, these men had developed into a band of brothers groomed to be the crusaders of a new age. They had been trained by the best in the world and had mastered much more than the martial arts. They also studied a variety of philosophies from Aristotle to Epicurus, with an emphasis on the works of St. Thomas Aquinas. Art also had its place in their education; they developed insight into the subtleties and symbolism of Da Vinci and Michelangelo. For a Vatican Knight, it was believed that the development of the mind was equally as important as the development of the body.

Under Kimball's command, they had entered the jungles of the Philippines and South America to save the lives of missionaries that had been held hostage. Other times they had traveled to eastern bloc countries to protect priests from dissident insurgents. And often they interceded in bloody skirmishes between opposing religious factions in Third World nations.

But those who took out the president's detail did so with a sophistication that would rival the proficiency of the Vatican Knights.

With the exception of Kimball Hayden, Leviticus was the most battle-tested, having served in more conflicts than any other Knight with mêlée scars to prove his conquests.

Micah, Nehemiah, and Isaiah were less rough-hewn, though their fresh-scrubbed appearances made them no less deadly. Their acquired skills marked them as some of the most formidable combatants in the world. Micah was an expert in double-edged weaponry. Nehemiah and Isaiah were masters of silent killing. But all these men complemented each other like connected pieces of a puzzle.

Spiritually, there was no one more deeply entrenched in their faith. Mentally, there was no team more dedicated to doing what was right. And physically, they were the finest any commander could ever hope for. Kimball was fully confident that they were the best in the world, not only as soldiers but as men.

He was proud of his team.

Walking along the path that divided the Old Gardens, Kimball moved with urgency until he reached Divinity House, the garrison of the Vatican Knights, an uncharted building situated between St. Martha's Chapel and the Ethiopian College, about 200 meters west of the Basilica. The building itself was simple and nondescript, its purpose to draw little attention.

The building's interior was constructed of stone and rock shingle. Located along the walls where torches once burned were electric sconces. Natural light came in through stained glass windows that signified the Stations of the Cross. In the center of the structure was the Circular Chamber, a huge rotunda that separated the building into two distinct wings. It was a room of ceremony where men became knights of the Vatican and where viewings were held for knights who had fallen in battle. The floor was a masterpiece of mosaic tile, majestically cobbled together to form the emblem of the Vatican Knights. Centered within the coat of arms was a Silver Cross Pattée set against a blue background. The colors were significant. Silver represented peace and sincerity, and blue signified truth and loyalty. Standing alongside the coat of arms were two heraldic lions rising on their hind legs with their forepaws against the shield, stabilizing it. The lions were a symbolic representation of bravery, strength, ferocity, and valor.

The emblem appeared repeatedly throughout Divinity House. The coat of arms also appeared as a branded insignia on their uniforms and berets. It was even acid-etched on the stone wall of their living quarters above the door.

For the moment it was quiet, the Knights either at prayer or in meditation. Kimball wished to take part in neither of these activities since he struggled to find his faith. By blood, he was a warrior, by nature, a patriot. But as a child of God, he found himself in constant turmoil. Peace eluded him like something flitting at the corner of his vision, something close but unobtainable. What he sought could not be found at the altar or within the confines of a confessional. What Kimball wanted was to be more than what he really was—a killer.

What he sought was redemption.

Opening the door to his chamber, with the hinges squealing and the sound of their whining carrying throughout the halls of Divinity House, Kimball went to pack for his journey to America.

His room was small with the barest necessities. Other than a single-sized bed, nightstand and dresser, there was a small dais with a Bible upon it that had gone unread, and a votive rack and kneeling rail meant for prayer. But the candles had never been lit and the rail never knelt upon. High on the wall, a stained-glass window provided the only light into the room. The pieces of leaded glass formed the colorful image of the Virgin Mother reaching out to him with outstretched arms. Often, when the sun was in a certain position every day, a Biblical beam of warm sunlight always filtered into the room.

After folding his cleric shirts and placing them in a backpack, the act itself homage to the cloth, he made sure he was equally as careful with the pristine-white collars.

After running the zipper along the backpack, Kimball stood before the mirror and appraised himself as telltale signs of aging began to show. After arranging his beret so it tilted to military specs, then making sure the Roman collar was straight and clean, Kimball grabbed his backpack and headed off to confront a new challenge.

Kimball felt charged with electricity he hadn't experienced since he was a member of the Force Elite, the one-time liquidation squad that was covertly governed by the intelligence agencies of the United States.

But now he was a Vatican Knight and was constrained to act with mercy.

After all, redemption had to be earned.

CHAPTER FIFTEEN

Route 1, Boston, Massachusetts.
September 23, Late Morning

Team Leader had divided his unit into two groups: Alpha Team, which consisted of five of his most seasoned combatants, and Omega Team, those who were left behind in D.C. to monitor the political maneuverings of the White House and its law enforcement constituencies.

To secure the hostages, Alpha Team placed them in a military cargo truck that had been modified with a false floor. Beneath the cargo bed was a compartment capable of carrying nine people in tight quarters. To ensure safety throughout the transportation process, the muffler system was customized so the noxious fumes were directed away from the cargo space. And since the hostages were immobilized by a ketamine derivative, it was highly unlikely they would wake and find themselves cloistered in a dark compartment during the drive north.

Team Leader sat on the passenger side of the cab, the radio tuned to an AM news station, one of many he had listened to during the transport. He stared at the passing landscape with eyes that seemed detached, though fully aware.

Earlier that morning, he had a member from Omega Team place an easily traced call to CNN from a burner cellphone. By then, the transport team was three hundred miles north of the call's position, the distance covered before a dragnet could be extended from the nation's capital.

The timing and location of the call was a red herring. He wanted Washington to believe that the Soldiers of Islam were still in the D.C. area so that the scope of their search would be concentrated to a smaller radius. But the ruse apparently failed. According to the news, roadblocks had been set up on all major highways north, west, and south of the capital, and stretched as far as New York, Florida, and Texas.

Though he had considered his strategy carefully, Team Leader was concerned about the blockades after their military vehicle was stopped by law enforcement on two separate occasions in New York. But when he showed counterfeit documents that claimed that their vehicle was from the 75th Ranger Regiment, which a division of the US Army Special Operation Command, the vehicle was waved through without so much as a cursory examination.

Once the truck exited the turnpike and entered Boston, the driver passed Government Center and negotiated the narrow streets to a pre-established safe house located in Boston's Historic District.

The isolated building was an old and vacant depository made of aged brick, which had cracked and discolored from time and neglect. The first-floor windows were bricked over. The second- and third-story windows, however, were merely boarded over with weathered plywood. The trees surrounding the building were either dead or dying, their limbs knotted like the arthritic twists of an old man's hands. The area had simply gone to waste.

A wrought-iron gate bearing a "No Trespassing: All Violators Prosecuted" sign was securely locked with a thick garland of chain wrapped firmly around the bars. Team Leader got out of the vehicle, searched his pocket for the proper key, and undid the lock. Once the vehicle passed through, he closed and relocked the gate.

The vehicle drove slowly down the weed-laden driveway. Wispy branches from the surrounding trees snapped as the top of the vehicle forced its way through the canopy of skeletal limbs. At the end of the driveway, the truck turned into a vacant area behind the building.

There was a dented fire door, the only way in and out of the building. The entry had been reinforced prior to the mission with a state-of-the-art titanium lock system. Reaching into his cargo pocket, Team Leader removed a remote unit and aimed it at the entry. When he depressed the button, the bolting mechanism drew back in a series of metallic clicks, and then the red light on the remote's faceplate turned green, indicating that the door was unlocked.

Moving toward the entryway, Team Leader turned the handle and opened the door to a world that was truly blacker than pitch.

CHAPTER SIXTEEN

J. Edgar Hoover Building, Washington, D.C.
September 23, Mid-Afternoon

The FBI's conference room was much larger and less constrictive than the White House's Situation Room. The room had twenty-foot ceilings and was nearly 1600 square feet. The walls were covered in dark walnut paneling, and an oil painting of J. Edgar Hoover watched over everyone with his patented scowl. In the center of the room was a large table that held up to three dozen people with pitchers of ice water spaced every three feet along the table's length.

The FBI's Deputy Director, George Pappandopolous, sat at one end of the table. Normally a man of good cheer, he appeared somewhat bitter with false smiles and insincere greetings. It seemed to Shari as if Pappandopolous had resigned himself to losing the battle over the pope's abduction. She hoped this wasn't the case.

Taking her assigned seat opposite the deputy director, Shari knew that she was about to become the lightning rod of attention.

To her right sat Billy Paxton, who also appeared displeased. He had always played the backup role, never the lead, the man always the electric violin to her Stradivarius. She had become an insurmountable obstacle in his life, which prevented him from elevating to the next level. He was always being compared to her but never measuring up. So, when she said "Hello," he simply ignored her.

As chatter circulated around the room, Deputy Director Pappandopolous leaned forward and clasped his hands. Securing the attention of the room, he went directly to the core of the matter.

"As you all know, the president's detail was dispatched by a radical terrorist cell calling themselves the Soldiers of Islam. The incident falls under FBI jurisdiction, but we will nevertheless be working with all international intelligence sources that are ready to aid in the search and rescue of the pope. So, let's get one thing straight: I don't want anybody on my team sitting on vital information. There is a federation of sixteen intelligence agencies in this country and dozens more worldwide. And we're to work closely with all of them. Is that clear?"

There was a unified agreement.

"Here's what I've got so far, just to update you as to what's going on," he continued. "We haven't received any demands from the Soldiers of Islam, as of yet. The only call received was the one to CNN at approximately zero-seven-hundred hours. We do know, however, the identities of all terrorists involved. You'll find their biographical information in front of you."

The assembled agents opened the manila folders before them and began to examine the documents.

"We also know they had ties to ISIS and may be a splinter group, so we'll need to develop a strategy to communicate and make the necessary concessions without any foreknowledge of their methods. By the direct authority of the attorney general, Ms. Cohen, who is sitting opposite me, is to take command of this situation with Mr. Paxton serving as speaker." Paxton winced as if a gas bubble had lodged painfully in his chest. Is that what he had been reduced to? A mouthpiece? It just seemed disrespectful.

"For those of you who may not know Ms. Cohen, she's an expert in counterterrorism and psychoanalytical strategy. Therefore, the attorney general feels that Ms. Cohen is best qualified to command this post. In other words, first there's God and then there's Ms. Cohen, who will be in direct contact with Chief Presidential Advisor Alan Thornton. There is no other chain of command. *She . . . is . . . it."* Pappandopolous eased back into his chair. "Good luck," he added, "because we're going to need it on this one." He offered Shari the stage by directing a hand toward her. "Ms. Cohen."

Shari tilted her head in the direction of the deputy director and thanked him. She opened her manila folder and began to peel back one page at a time from the stack of papers.

"All right," she said. "The first rule of thumb is to never assume anything because everything changes and changes quickly. Therefore, you have to adjust and make decisions according to the moment. We know the insurgents are Islamic and have an unyielding conviction to die for a cause. So . . . what else do we need to know?" She raised her hand and ticked off a finger with each question.

"One: How have they or their associates operated in the past? Two: Will they release the hostages when their demands are met or not? Three: Have their dealings in the past with agencies been consistent or not? And four: Can we possibly predict a safe outcome based on their past dealings? In other words: *Know your enemy.*"

She lowered her hand. Her voice was gaining strength and momentum with every passing sentence.

"We'll need to get on this as soon as possible. I want as much information on the remaining operatives as soon as I can get my hands on it. Contact the CIA abroad, Mossad, the CTC, whomever it is you need to contact to create the most complete record on each individual involved with the Soldiers of Islam. Then we'll need to create several strategies to deal with them. And I'm going to need all of this at my fingertips when the time comes to negotiate. We're dealing with the human element here, which is always difficult. But at least we'll be in a position to act when the terrorists make their next move."

Shari's speech was well-versed and never missed a beat, which was more of a natural skill than a learned one.

Paxton, on the other hand, seethed with contempt and rolled his eyes. "Past history is usually a great indicator of future behavior," she continued. "If the group is a splinter, then we don't have a lot of past accounts to go on, so we'll have to come up with a format based on their individual dossiers. Psychology, in this case, will become paramount. And that's where I come in."

Shari peeled off another page, but never referred to it.

"We'll play this based on our data and according to the situation. If the situation seems to be heading in the wrong direction, then we'll have to shift course. That's why we'll need to develop a series of schematics to deal with whatever scenario may arise."

Shari gave each face a quick examination. "Questions?"

There were none, the team apparently resolved and ready for duty. "Then let's get to it," she said. Her briefing was quick and to the point.

During the next hour, Shari moved the staff to a workroom filled with personal computers, terminals, and phones, then dividing the assembled experts into groups of three, then designating each group a specific task according to their skills and strengths.

In essence, Shari Cohen was flexing her muscles.

CHAPTER SEVENTEEN

Somewhere Over the Atlantic Ocean
September 23, Evening

Kimball Hayden sat alone in the front of a Gulfstream jet that cruised along at twenty-nine thousand feet. The four members of his team were seated throughout the cabin, all sitting quietly with their moods matching the depressive gray of the Atlantic sky.

After drawing a deep breath and releasing it with an equally long sigh, Kimball closed his eyes and tried to attain a moment of peace. But when he closed his eyes, the images always returned, simple snippets of his life from his days as a teenager trying to become an appreciative glimmer in his father's eye, to the moment of his epiphany in Iraq when he was a member of the Force Elite.

His father was a man of minor presence having no social standing of his own but relied on his son's achievements to confirm his own importance. By the time Kimball was seventeen he was a foot taller and broader than his father. But his father didn't credit his son for being strong or handsome or charismatic. The way he saw it, these were accidents of nature, not achievements. In fact, Kimball felt that his father resented rather than valued these attributes. He spent his entire youth wondering why it was so easy to please others—his classmates, his teachers, friends—but was so impossible to please his father.

He remembered in vivid detail the night he first saw the glow of appreciation in his father's eyes. He was playing linebacker for his high school football team. It was Friday night. The stands were full. And in front of thousands of people, he was being knocked off his assignment by a center much smaller than him. Repeatedly, Kimball had been sent sprawling as the running back ran to daylight through the gaping hole Kimball was supposed to fill. Catcalls soon erupted in the stands. And the coach was on the brink of benching him.

When the tailback scored a second touchdown, by running through the seam that Kimball was supposed to fill, it all proved too much for his father. So, when Kimball went to the sidelines, his father grabbed his facemask and twisted it, the man looking like a child before his behemoth son. Spittle flew from his mouth in rage as he openly chastised his boy, telling him he was an embarrassment to the Hayden name.

More wrenching of the facemask followed, the violent tugging almost causing the coach to intervene. It appeared Kimball's father had lost his way in disciplining his son, the incident borderline abuse.

"Do not embarrass me!" he screamed. *"I want you to go out there and make something of yourself! You hear me? Push yourself to the limit! And when you think you have reached that limit, then push yourself some more! You got me?"*

Kimball nodded.

"You look like a pansy out there! I will not have a pansy for a son! You got me? Not one more time on your backside!"

Another nod.

"Then get out there and act as though you belong!"

When he released Kimball's facemask, Kimball returned to the sidelines ready to prove himself.

When the next defensive series began, Kimball became an animal. This time when the center approached him, Kimball hunkered down to a low center of gravity and launched himself forward, hitting the center so hard that the player fell backward and knocked the running back off his route, causing other players to swarm in for a tackle of a loss. As the pile cleared, it was apparent that the center was severely injured. Blood foamed at the edges of his mouth from an internal injury, and, eventually, he was carted off the field. When Kimball looked up into the stands, he saw his father beaming with approval and pride. It was the turning point in Kimball's life, the pivotal moment in which he finally shined bright in his father's eyes. Kimball had finally discovered the key to his father's approval.

He was courted by numerous college football programs; coaches around the country loved his aggressive tenacity on the field. However, Kimball shunned the scholarships and decided to join the

Army Rangers instead. And it was here that he caught the eye of the military hierarchy. They noticed his determination and his remarkable strength and agility. They also noticed that he seemed to thrive on pressure. The more challenging the task, the more committed he was to complete it.

Soon, Kimball found himself under a new command in the Force Elite, a governmental black ops unit known only by a few in the intelligence programs. In the Force Elite, Kimball battled insurgents with incredible efficiency which earned him a reputation as an unstoppable power.

Since targeted assassinations were banned by the Ford administration in '76, Kimball had become the first of a new breed. Secret meetings were the norm, and the presidential ban went unnoticed by certain political principals and members of the JCOS. At these meetings Kimball was often the focal point, the man spotlighted for his ability to carry out the most difficult missions with stoic precision.

In 1990, when he was someone with great talent on the cusp of manhood, he had been assigned to kill three key members of Saddam Hussein's Cabinet who were responsible for brokering deals with Russian dissidents for high-grade plutonium. Not only was the plutonium never delivered, but the Iraqi brokers were found shot to death in Chelyabinsk, Russia, by a Rav-.22LRHA, which also happens to be Mossad's weapon of choice for assassinations. This weapon served as the red herring that made Israel the scapegoat for the killings.

From that moment on, Iraq never attempted to develop a nuclear arsenal in earnest.

In December of that same year, Kimball was asked to commit another assassination. This time the target was Saddam Hussein.

When Iraq ventured onto Kuwaiti soil to pillage the country in August, the United States and the UN coalition ordered Hussein to withdraw from the country immediately. However, several months of wasted negotiations finally ended with the commencement of a counterattack by U.S. and coalition forces. It was during this period that members of the Senate and Joint Chiefs called upon Kimball to take out Hussein before the allied assault began. They believed war could be averted if the rank and file of the Republican Guard fell into disarray without Saddam Hussein's leadership.

Kimball asked no questions. He only needed to know *what* he had to do—not *why* he had to do it. It was this icy-cold fortitude that led his employers to consider Kimball practically inhuman. He seemed to possess no conscience or remorse or self-preservation. He was a perfect killing machine that seemed to take pride in that image. His commanders saw him as someone who was larger than life . . . the same way his father saw him that night on the football field. The feeling was indescribable.

As the window of opportunity lay open and negotiations continued, Kimball breached Iraqi territory.

Just then the Gulfstream hit an air pocket, causing the plane to dip sharply. As soon as it leveled off, Kimball immediately recalled the moments of his pride as a deadly sin in the eyes of God.

He had been in Iraq for seven days and was making his way toward Baghdad when he happened upon a flock of goats herded by two boys with the older no more than fourteen, and the younger, perhaps ten, carrying gnarled staffs of olive wood.

Kimball remained out of sight with his back pressed against the sandy wall of a gully, listening to the goats bleating only a few feet away. And then a shadow cast over him from the younger boy who had spied Kimball from above. The child's small body was silhouetted against the pure white sun, as light shined around him like a halo. And then the boy was gone, shouting, the sun suddenly assaulting Kimball's eyes with a terrible brightness.

Kimball stood and immediately engaged his weapon, drew a bead, and pulled the trigger, the bullet's momentum driving the boy hard to the ground. The older boy stood unmoving with his mouth open in mute protest. First, his eyes moved to the body of his brother, then to Kimball, back to his brother. The moment he took flight Kimball took a single shot, the bullet killing the boy before he hit the surface.

Another bump of turbulence, this time stronger, which jarred Kimball from the memory. But when the plane settled back into a smoother flight pattern, he closed his eyes once again and remembered what he had tried to forget so long ago.

He had buried the boys with their staffs in a trench. Wordlessly, Kimball Hayden covered their bodies with sand and scattered the goats. Once done, he sat beside the two small rises in the earth and considered that maybe the White House brass was right after all. Maybe he was inhuman.

Suddenly it was no longer a game to him. The memory of his father's approval on that Friday night when Kimball openly maimed another player, then seeing the smile on his father's face and recalling the subsequent pats on the back, no longer seemed to matter. He could not go on living life treating it as a game, in which those around him were seen as mere targets, especially innocent children.

At that moment Kimball was tormented by what he had done. His cold fortitude was gone. He had reached his limit. And though he could hear his father rage on about pushing further, he could not. Every man had his limits.

If his father had been alive on that fateful day rather than buried in a nondescript grave in an obscure township, he most likely would have turned his back on his son. But Kimball didn't care anymore. His father was dead. Why was he still living for his approval? Why had he ever fought so hard to please a sadistic man who required him to deny his humanity? Kimball didn't want to be emotionless anymore. He deserved to feel pain, to feel guilty. He wanted to suffer.

Kimball remained by the makeshift graves all that day. Even with the sun blistering his lips, he refused to take cover. He recalled the moments when day finally turned to night as he lay between the two mounds with a clawed hand on each rise of soft earth, and prayed for forgiveness not from God, but from the two boys.

His only answer was the soft whisper of wind through the desert sand.

As he lay there watching the moon make its trajectory across a sky filled with countless stars, Kimball Hayden made a fateful decision.

On the following morning, he headed back to the Syrian border with the JCOS never to hear from him again. The Company believed that Kimball Hayden had been killed in the commission of his duty. And less than two months later, the man who was considered to be without conscience was posthumously honored by the Pentagon brass, though the true nature of his contributions was never made public.

Two weeks after his defection, however, while Kimball sat in a bar in Venice drinking liqueur, the United States and the Coalition Forces attacked Iraq.

He had been drinking and doing little else since his defection. But he was becoming restless and anxious. It was not in his nature to be idle. But he didn't have the first idea what to do next. A few days later at the same bar, a man wearing a Roman Catholic collar and a cherubic smile took the seat opposite him without permission.

"I really want to be alone, Father," he told him. "It's too late for me, anyway."

Nevertheless, the priest continued to smile. "We've been watching you."

Kimball could only imagine the look he gave the priest. "I'm sorry you've been what?"

"Kimball Hayden," the priest said, offering his hand. "My name is Bonasero Vessucci . . . Cardinal Bonasero Vessucci."

And a new alliance was born.

Kimball drew another deep breath and let it go. The Gulfstream was flying at an incredible speed.

The time was 1834. Eastern Standard Time.

CHAPTER EIGHTEEN

Boston, Massachusetts
September 23, Early Evening

Steve O'Brien was second in command of Alpha Team and used the call-sign of Kodiak, for the giant bears of Alaska. Before his induction into the squad, O'Brien had been an Army Ranger and an elite soldier in terms of combat, courage, and duty. Now he was a mercenary recruited for the tools he had to offer.

He stood six-four and two-hundred-seventy pounds. His body was pure rippling muscle with biceps larger than most men's thighs. And to keep with his military heritage he wore his flattop to specs. Running from the edge of his right eye to the corner of his lip, forever drawing his mouth into a sneer, was a puckered scar from a wound laid open by an al-Qaeda rebel hiding in the hills along the Afghan border. The rebel's victory, however, was short-lived once Kodiak took the knife away and used it against him. He ended up hanging the rebel's head on a pike for several days.

The other members of the Alpha Team had taken the tags of Boa, Diamondback, King Snake, and Sidewinder, call-signs assigned by the Joint Chiefs of Staff indicating stealth, poise, and deadly precision. But Kodiak saw the tags as degrading since snakes made it a lifelong journey to crawl along their bellies; something he saw as lowly and undignified.

Like him, Boa and King Snake were former Rangers, while Diamondback and Sidewinder were Green Berets.

But to this group, Team Leader remained a mystery.

Nobody knew who he was or where he came from, but he exuded such raw power nobody dared to challenge him.

Kodiak glanced at his team lying on the floor around him,

sleeping. This was a moment of luxury. He closed his eyes, then rested his head against the wall and found comfort in the fact that he was surrounded by the deadliest men on the planet. Then he fell into a much-needed sleep.

He was having a wonderful dream—the happiest and perhaps the best he had ever had—and then it went away when an alien sound brought him back to baffling awareness. Pope Pius XIII finally opened his eyes, his lids fluttering---the world, the ceiling, still clouded from a drug-induced haze. And then he realized that he was no longer in a wonderful dreamscape after all, but in a large room choked with dust and darkness. The internal walls were gutted enough to reveal the wooden beams underneath, and the floor was trashed with broken plaster, litter, and waste. Here, was abandonment.

When he turned over on the mattress, he could feel the weight of the chains that shackled him to the brick wall. On the other side of the mattress was a coffee container to accept his bodily wastes during his confinement.

The pope propped himself up on his elbows and tested the strength of the chain by tugging at the mooring. The links rattled like a pocketful of coins, but the chain held firm.

"I'm afraid it's no use. The plates are anchored to the brick."

Pope Pius XIII narrowed his eyes in an attempt to pierce the darkness. What his sight finally settled on was the vague outline of a man who stood against the opposite wall. If the man had chosen not to speak, the pope would never have known he was standing there.

The figure stepped into a shaft of wan light with his hands clasped behind his back. He wore a black tactical jumpsuit, a black ski mask, and combat boots. "How are you feeling?" the man asked, speaking in a clipped accent.

Pope Pius XIII raised his chained hand, the movement itself imploring and fragile. "Please," he said. "Why are you doing this?"

The shape took a step closer until the toes of his boots nearly touched the mattress. "I do this," he answered, "to end the madness once and for all."

The pope gave him an inquisitive look.

"Whereas your Christ was the King of Kings who readily embraced the world, Pope Pius XIII shall become the Martyr of Martyrs who will divide it." The shape took a step back and was again swallowed in darkness. "You will be the catalyst for the beginning of the end."

The pope was unable to grasp the meaning of what was being said, the man's words cryptic with the voice growing distant. The shape had spoken in riddles while his mind was still numb from the ketamine.

"Please . . . I don't understand."

The shape added one thing further. "Tomorrow you will begin to usher in a new age," he said.

And like a comma of smoke in a blowing wind, the shape was gone.

CHAPTER NINETEEN

Team Leader made it a point to separate the pope from the bishops of the Holy See and the cardinals of his administration. He wished to evaluate each man on his mettle without any support, encouragement, or comfort from the pope.

He wanted to see if the bishops and cardinals honestly believed in a paradisiacal afterlife if they would readily accept death as graduation rather than a hollow end. He would watch and see if their eyes reflected the hypocrisy of their beliefs by exhibiting a genuine fear that perhaps nothing existed at all, in the moments that led up to his pulling of the trigger that would end their lives. In this fashion Team Leader was an observer, a scientist, a researcher for truth. *Does an afterlife of absolute peace and tranquility truly exist? And is blind faith the wings that carry humankind to such a place?* If he could discover the truth, then he would gladly surrender to it.

But Team Leader had grown tired; his searching always ended in disappointment. He had seen nothing more than cowardice in the faces of all the men he had killed. Still, he searched for a spark of hope that a better life than this one existed. *Everybody wants to go to heaven,* he considered, *but nobody wants to pay the price of admission.*

Shaking his head in disappointment, Team Leader walked through the dank and hollow corridors. In the slivers of fading light that penetrated the edges of the boarded-up windows, he walked to a room where his team had anchored the cardinals and bishops to the wall with lengths of chain. The stench of their filth hung on their garments and in the air, the smell constant and unyielding.

On the mattresses, still affected by the sedative, the bishops were moving humorously about like corpses from a zombie apocalypse, with each man reaching mindlessly for the purchase of something not there. On the last mattress lay the Vatican's president and the church's second in command. A silver thread of drool spilled from the corner of his lips as he laid there.

"Tomorrow, my dear President," Team Leader whispered, "we'll start with you and write a new chapter of history." And then he turned to wake his team from their short but granted time for rest.

CHAPTER TWENTY

Washington, D.C.
September 23, Late Evening

The distance between the archdiocese and D.C. Central was less than two miles. The night was soupy with early morning fog, and the air was thick with humidity as the Vatican Knights walked the streets in silence.

When they arrived at the façade of the archdiocese, a single light burned in one of the windows on the first level.

Kimball rapped his knuckles on the door.

The bolts were being drawn back, the door unlocking with loud clicks. In the foyer as the door swung wide stood Father Medeiros. He was tall and slender with tanned features and snow-white hair, and he was donning the vestment of a full-length robe with red piping around the cuffs.

"Father Medeiros?" Kimball asked.

The priest nodded after noting the cleric collars and military attire these people wore. "The Vatican Knights," was all he said. Then he stood back with his hand indicating the study area in invitation and allowed them passage into the archdiocese.

#

The area of the study was open and elaborate with floor-to-ceiling windows that were covered by velour drapery with scalloped edges along the bottom, and gold-fringed valances on top. A fireplace took up an entire wall and was made of fieldstone. Opposite the fireplace against another wall stood a complete library that contained numerous shelves filled with hardcover books and religious tomes. And hanging from the ceiling and casting glimmers of iridescent light, was a chandelier.

The Vatican Knights were seated throughout the study with their packs leaning against the study wall. In the room's center, Kimball was sitting in a winged-back chair with Father Medeiros seated comfortably in another. A small nightstand with a lamp divided them as Father Medeiros opened a manila folder that contained pertinent documents recently submitted by the *Servizio Informazione del Vatican,* or the SIV, the arm of Vatican Intelligence.

"While you were en route to Washington," said Father Medeiros, "the SIV gathered as much information about Blair House and the subsequent abduction of the papal coalition." He removed a series of documents from the folder and handed them to Kimball, who began to go through them one at a time. "All video feeds went down just before Blair House was overmastered, which means that this was a high-end abduction from people with military sophistication. Seasoned members of the president's detail were killed, all of them. Six, I believe."

Kimball continued to look through the material.

"Two of the abductors," Father Medeiros continued, "who were onsite, now deceased, were Syrian nationals with ties to extremist groups."

Kimball intuited: "Are we talking ISIS?"

"Yes. But they were involved with other factions as well and trained in Yemen."

"Hardcore then."

"According to the information we have, yes and no. It appears that the abductors discovered inside Blair House were instrumental in developing a dormant cell in Utah. Rather under the radar for the most part because they served more as recruiters for the Muslim cause. They were Internet warriors. Even with their training in Yemen, it begs the question whether or not they truly had the military sophistication to pull this off."

"You think others were involved? Those who were more battle seasoned?"

"Hard to say. All videos went down."

"How about leads as to where they might have taken the papal coalition?"

The priest nodded. *No.* Information remained minimal. "Dragnets have been set up with checkpoints as far north as New York City, and as far west as Texas. So far, nothing. Could be that they're still local."

Kimball continued to pour over the documents. Then he came upon a headshot photo of a woman with raven hair and beautifully lined features. At the photo's bottom was her name: COHEN, Shari Maya.

Kimball held up the photo. "This woman?"

"Her name's Shari Cohen," Father Medeiros answered. "She's the leading expert in counterterrorism for the FBI. She is the one heading up the investigation into the abduction."

"Then she's the one I need to contact, yes?"

"She is. Everything begins and ends with her."

Kimball stared at the photo. The woman was incredibly attractive, he considered. And apparently, quite brilliant in her own right, since her biographical record indicated an impressive history that was richly filled with accolades from outstanding organizations.

Kimball turned to the priest. "Anything additional, Father?"

"You have it all right here," the priest answered, handing over the folder. Then: "You OK with hardware?"

"We have weapons ready for full engagement, if necessary," said Kimball, pointing to the bags lined against the wall of the study.

Father Medeiros continued to speak with purpose. "Everything you need to know is in that folder, Kimball. Addresses. Schedules. Phone numbers. Histories of everyone involved in the search. The identities of the extremists and their histories. Glean as much as you can from it all." He leaned toward Kimball and placed an elbow on the nightstand that stood between them. "Given the task on such little information is asking a lot, I know. Do what you can, Kimball, and bring him back. Bring them all back. I'm sure God will guide you with His good graces."

Kimball proffered a marginal smile that was hardly real, but one to belie any fears or doubts. "We will," he told him.

"Then a blessing before you go, yes? A blessing for all of you."

As the Vatican Knights bowed their heads, Father Medeiros got to his feet and said a prayer in Latin, then he gave the sign of the cross. "Go with God," he finalized.

After grabbing their bags, Kimball—along with Leviticus, Isaiah, Nehemiah, and Micah—left the archdiocese and disappeared within the slow-moving eddies of a midnight fog.

CHAPTER TWENTY-ONE

Tel Aviv, Israel
September 24, Early Morning

John McEachern, also known as Yosef Rokach, sat before his PC in the darkness of his apartment with the light of the monitor casting ghoulish shadows upon his face. During the six hours, he sat before the computer trying to decode the encryptions on the data stick, Yosef's eyes never looked away from the screen.

On average it took approximately two hours to decode a single page of data, which left him with three pages to interpret with the full undertaking most likely lasting to dawn. So far, he had been able to bring up photos of the Soldiers of Islam and their personal histories—low-level material. In fact, this same material had already been forwarded to multiple intelligence agencies that day. *So why is data such as this protected by the LAP?*

With rapid finger tapping on the keyboard, Yosef undid the visible stitching and continued to open the cyber gates to produce readable material.

And then the first of the security lights came on, the bulb blinking.

A security screen to the right of the PC monitor was divided into quarters, showing a different part of the residence on each segment. The top-left portion showed three men scaling the small gate to his building, which was always kept locked. The second security lamp lit up. The intruders were now at the front door of the building, one hunkering by the lock to disengage it.

Yosef typed even faster, realizing that he wouldn't have time to decipher the rest of the encryption. He saved the partially decoded document onto his desktop.

The third security lamp began to blink, the intruders now in the hallway making their way up the stairs to his apartment.

Yosef quickly brought up the email addresses of Washington's FBI field office and the CIA and attached the desktop document. As the file uploaded, the computer suddenly appeared to work with glacial slowness. When the message was received by the American constituencies, it would appear from an IP address with Mossad the direct correspondent. The sending operative, however, would remain completely covert as a means to protect his identity.

The fourth and final lamp lit, the amber bulb blinking in rapid succession. The intruders were now at his doorstep, their voices hushed, talking, deciding.

Just as the document loaded, Yosef hit the SEND button. At that moment, the door to his apartment crashed inward.

After hitting the ERASE button to quickly clear the computer screen, Yosef stood to face his aggressors. "What is this? What do you want?"

Three men stood silhouetted against the light of the hallway. "I demand to know—"

"What you demand to know means nothing to me," said the first man. Even silhouetted the man appeared slight in stature, hardly a physical threat. But his voice possessed something unyielding.

The small man stepped closer with his features becoming clearer. His hair was dark, and his face was lined with age and wisdom, the creases denoting years of pain, anger, and persecution. Here stood Yitzhak Paled, head of the Lohamah Psichlogit.

"How much did you decipher?" he asked calmly. "And who did you send it to?"

Yosef shook his head. "I don't know what you're talking—"

Paled reached out with a quick hand and slapped Yosef in the face. "How much did you decipher?" he repeated. "And who did you send it to?"

Yosef stood there with his hand to his face, the thrill of espionage no longer a romantic ideal, as reality set in like an anchor. His gut was churning.

"If I have to ask you again, Yosef, which I doubt is your real name, then I'll break every bone in your body until I get what I want, starting with your fingers. Is that clear?"

88

Yosef didn't respond, his tongue bound by paralytic terror.

"Case in point," said Paled, removing three photos from his shirt pocket and splaying them across the table in the glow of the computer monitor. Even in the feeble light, Yosef could see the brutally battered face of his LAP contact, David Gonick. His features were bloodied, his mouth slightly agape, teeth missing. His eyes had rolled up into their sockets showing slivers of white before he died. "He was caught on tape dropping the data off on your level," Paled added. "And you were caught on tape picking it up."

Yosef's eyes traveled back to the photos.

"If I don't get what I want, Yosef, then I'll be adding three more photos to this set."

Yosef broke down. *Some spy,* he thought, *crying like a ten-year-old child.* But he held true, revealing nothing, even until the moment Paled eventually took Yosef's pictures to add to his collection.

Spurred on by a single hand gesture from Paled, the two toadies grabbed Yosef and forcefully ushered him out of his apartment.

"If you play, Yosef, then you have to pay." It was Paled's final statement to a man who held no hope of seeing dawn's early light, as Yosef had anticipated.

With a gloved hand, Paled switched off the security monitors and wondered who Yosef's liaisons were. To find out he would take the PC to Mossad Headquarters, have it thoroughly analyzed, and get his answer that way.

As soon as he found out who the recipient was, then he'd instruct the department heads to deny everything regarding any information that had been sent to whatever constituencies they had been submitted to.

Removing the data stick from the PC, Paled examined it by turning it over between his fingers with the adeptness of a magician who passes a coin from one digit to the next. It was incredible how something so small could hold enough information to start a war, he considered. Then with little effort, he snapped the data stick between his fingers and placed the broken pieces in his pocket.

#

One of Shari's team members heard the annoying ping indicating that an email had been received. Taking immediate notice that it had been sent to the FBI and the CIA, she burned the document onto two CDs. Per protocol, she would delete the email to minimize the risk of appropriation by hostile hackers, despite state-of-the-art firewalls and anti-theft software. She marked one CD to be placed into the vault as a backup file.

The other CD was placed into a jewel case marked VITAL, and hand-delivered to Shari's team leader who, after signing the chain of custody log, hand-delivered it to Shari per departmental procedure.

Within moments, Shari had the disc.

CHAPTER TWENTY-TWO

J. Edgar Hoover Building, Washington, D.C.
September 24, Early Morning

Laces of red stitching marked the whites of Shari Cohen's eyes. Not even her fourth cup of coffee was strong enough to keep away the exhaustion, as she operated on compulsion and willpower alone. The only thing that kept her motivated was her direct communication with national and international intelligence agencies, which included the DST from France, the SIS from Britain, the BND from Germany, the AISI from Italy, the SVR and FSB from Russia, and, of course, the Mossad. Not a single moment was wasted.

"So now what?"

Shari turned to Paxton; whose face sported the beginnings of a bearded growth. "Go home," she told him. "Get some sleep."

"And miss the biggest day of your career?"

She immediately picked up the undertone of sarcasm. "Look, this wasn't my call, okay? So, get over it. If you can't, then take it up with the attorney general or deputy director."

Paxton lifted his hands and patted the air before turning away. "I'm just tired," he said. It was a poor cop-out, but he didn't care.

Shari glanced at her watch. It was 6:15 a.m.

The conference room staff, in communication with Mossad throughout the night, remained at full force. The emailed encryptions given to Shari regarding the Soldiers of Islam were at best incomplete.

According to the compiled dossiers, the Soldiers of Islam were only marginally capable of any type of military sophistication. Although they did spend time training in terrorist camps, they were primarily groomed for their computer expertise with the exception of Hashrie and Bashrah, those who were considered to be the second lieutenants of a higher order. The central purpose of this core group was to search for soft spots in the American defense system and then relay those weaknesses to their superiors for possible exploitation.

Paxton saw the wheels turning. "Got something?"

Deep lines of deliberation creased Shari's forehead. "The Soldiers of Islam," she said, "or at least what we know of them, doesn't make any sense."

"How so?"

"You read the files, their biographical information. These guys in this little cabal were mostly computer geeks who hardly had the military sophistication to take out the president's detail, with maybe the exception of the two bodies found on the scene."

"Did it ever occur to you that maybe Mossad doesn't have all the answers?"

Shari shook her head. "Mossad is legendary," she said, "and thorough. I don't believe these files are incomplete. I think we have everything there is to know about the Soldiers of Islam."

"Meaning what?"

She chewed softly on her lower lip for a moment before answering. "I don't know. I'm not sure. I just don't see *these* guys, outnumbered as they were, taking out a highly trained force. I just don't get it."

Paxton leaned forward and rubbed his fatigued eyes. "Well, apparently they did."

Shari wasn't confident in this assessment, however.

Paxton loosened the knot of his tie and undid the top button of his shirt. "Maybe you should go home for a bit," he told her. "I'll call you if we hear anything."

"Are you sure you don't want to go home?"

"Positive. There's no point in both of us falling asleep on the job."

She forced a smile. "I have to go for a few hours," she said. She gathered the files and placed the recently burned CD into its jewel case.

"We're going to need those," he said.

Shari shook her head. "I'm going to the DHS Building to see if they can help me with these encryptions."

"They're just biographical information."

She smiled cordially. "Maybe. But ask yourself this question: why are there encryptions in these particular files?"

Paxton agreed with her in principle. Encryptions exist solely for extremely sensitive information, and the biographical histories of certain individuals were not exactly top-secret material.

"Shari, take a break. I can handle this."

"I'm still in charge, Billy," she said to make a firm point, then she headed for the door. "Call me if something comes up."

Then she was gone as she moved rapidly toward the bank of elevators at the end of the hall.

Paxton immediately got on his cell phone, punched in a speed-dial number, and waited for a response. When the line was picked up on the other end, Paxton spoke in a tone that was even. "We may have a problem," he said.

"And what would that be?"

"Cohen is starting to think something's wrong. She took the files and the encrypted CD from Mossad. She plans to take the disc to DHS to have them break it down."

"There's nothing in those files worth worrying about," the voice said. "And I don't think there's anything on the CD to lead her in any specific direction, either. But destroy the backup disc, just in case. If she discovers anything from the CD in her possession we need to worry about, then *we'll* deal with her. Let's just play this out."

"Understood."

"Is she still there?"

"She just left."

"Get moving."

CHAPTER TWENTY-THREE

Just as Deputy Director George Pappandopolous made his way to the monitoring room, where a guard sat watching a bank of security screens, Shari Cohen was getting into her Lexus. The screens depicted every hallway and door leading in and out of the JEH Building, including every entrance in and out of the garage. After dismissing the guard for a ten-minute break, Pappandopolous searched the monitors observing the garage area until he saw Shari's car. As she pulled away, Pappandopolous dialed a single digit on his cell phone, waited, then spoke as if his call was expected. "Cohen's leaving the building."

"Yeah. So?" Judas sounded apathetic.

"So, I want you to keep an eye on her," he returned sharply. "She'll be driving a white Lexus through the northwest gate. Do . . . *not* . . . lose her."

"Why? What's up?"

"Paxton thinks that Cohen suspects something, which may prompt her to dig into places where she doesn't belong."

There was silence on the other end.

"If she does," added Pappandopolous, "you know what to do. But for now, just keep an eye on her. Paxton thinks she's heading for DHS."

"What for?"

"More information," he said. "Paxton mentioned that she has an encrypted CD sent by a CIA leak in Mossad. The DHS can now decode those messages, and she has unrestricted access to their decoding terminal."

Pappandopolous could hear an audible sigh from Judas' end. "This is already turning into a cluster."

"That's because we planned for Paxton to take the helm, not Cohen."

After listening for a moment longer, Pappandopolous grunted his approval of something Judas had said and hung up.

#

Shari laid the files and the burned CD on the passenger seat of her car. After leaving the garage, she checked her appearance in the rearview mirror and noticed the half-moons forming beneath her eyes.

Behind her, a blue sedan followed but stayed a fair distance away.

#

Getting into the vault without detection would not be an easy task. There were cameras with facial recognition software everywhere, and individualized access codes were required to record employees' times of entry. Since there was no way to bypass the system, Paxton could only acquire the backup disc by following protocol and hoping not to raise suspicion.

After typing in his PIN, the door opened and Paxton entered the vault, a massive chamber bearing thousands of CDs. Banks of fluorescent lights on the ceiling bathed the room. In every corner of the vault, cameras spied on him, their software deciphering the landmarks of his face.

There was no doubt in his mind that the security tapes would be examined if it was established that the backup file was missing. But with systems backed up as they were, it would take weeks before a missing disc would be discovered. By then he would be gone, living in Rio de Janeiro with his ill-gotten commission of seven million dollars.

Earlier he had checked the chain of custody log, noted the number associated with the burned disc, created a bogus label, and attached it to a blank disc. Now, the difficulty would be locating the proper disc in a library of CDs numbering in the tens of thousands. Inspecting the bogus label, he looked for a shelf that contained CDs bearing the proper range of numbers. After a moment he found what he was looking for. He traced his finger along the CDs until he found the backup disc. He held it next to the bogus one. They were an exact match. Then placing the bogus disc into the slot, he slid the original into the pocket of his sports jacket.

Refusing to look into the cameras, Paxton exited the vault. He could feel his heart racing and the sweat of his brow beading. He was sure that somebody would inquire what he had hidden in his pocket. But nobody would since he had TS clearance to enter the vault. It was simply his paranoia attacking his nerves.

After removing the disc from his jacket, he looked about the cubicles and aisles. Sensing that no one was suspect, he fed the backup disc into the shredder and listened to the whirring of its grinders tear the data into bits and pieces.

CHAPTER TWENTY-FOUR

Boston, Massachusetts
September 24, Early Morning

Team Leader sat alone against the wall of his chamber separated from his team. Though he did not fit in with the American-derived band of brothers, he knew they would not question his leadership.

At the onset of his commission as Team Leader, his authority had been immediately tested by a member of the Force Elite, who went by the call-sign Nomad.

Nomad's rawboned features appeared more simian than human from steroid use, his forehead sloping from chemical evolution rather than ancestral inheritance. His brutish attitude appointed him the team's Alpha male, and he considered Team Leader an outsider who infringed on his right to rule.

At the commencement of training, Team Leader bore the brunt of Nomad's derisive remarks, as the members of the Force Elite followed his lead. The men mocked Team Leader, letting him know that Nomad was their true commander.

By the end of the day, Team Leader issued a challenge and offered to pass the mantel of leadership to Nomad, should he win.

The challenge was accepted.

Nomad removed his shirt, exposing impossibly large muscles as an exhibition to intimidate his opponent. But Team Leader stood at ease with his hands pressed against the small of his back. Team Leader knew Nomad's size was his liability, which would diminish his speed and agility. As the larger man circled and goaded Team Leader, calling him vile names and spitting at his feet, Team Leader remained in his stance. He studied Nomad and absorbed every detail of his movements, and he waited for the opportune moment.

Within fifteen seconds of attacking Team Leader, Nomad laid dead on the ground with his neck broken and his eyes staring at nothing in particular. No one dared to question Team Leader's authority from that point on.

A jingling of chains in the hallway told him that the members of the papal council were testing their bonds.

He stood.

The time was early, not yet dawn, and the rooms and hallways were still dark. After fitting an NVG monocular around his forehead, he switched it on.

He easily navigated through the darkness and stood before the bishops and the cardinals, the captives seeing only a green phosphorous eye hovering above them.

"Good morning, gentlemen," said Team Leader. "Your propensity for making noise is quite unsettling."

Team Leader moved along the mattresses with his hands behind his back, as if to study his prey. "In a moment, the sun will come up and you'll all be fed. And then one of you will be challenged to a test of faith. Please don't disappoint me."

A moment later Team Leader was gone, swallowed by the shadows. Outside, the sun was beginning to show itself along the horizon.

#

Homeland Security Operations Center, Washington, D.C.
September 24, Mid-Morning

The Department of Homeland Security Center was a series of brick annexes converted from existing military barracks. The building Shari Cohen was looking for was one of several unmarked structures on the government campus. But since the Operations Center was one of Shari's teaching venues, she knew exactly where to go.

After parking her vehicle, she walked through the entrance, flashed her credentials, and signed the LEO log. After politely accepting small talk from the desk personnel, she asked to be escorted to the decoding terminal.

Within moments, she was accompanied by two officers to a

subterranean room bearing three large plasma monitors, a PC console, an ergonomically shaped chair, and a keyboard with an attached pivoting arm that maneuvered from the chair's side pocket to an upright frontal position. Used exclusively for government decoding, this state-of-the-art machinery had an attached cost of nearly two billion dollars and could out-crunch and out-run any supercomputer mainframe in existence. To Shari, this was the first line of defense in fighting terrorism. "Well, if it isn't one of the FBI's biggest slackers," said Toby Hansen, who was one of the DHS's computer posse.

Shari smiled as she approached him. "Be nice," she said and gave him a quick hug. "How're you doing, Toby?"

"Now that your pretty little face has graced my laboratory, much better."

Toby Hansen was an overweight man who always appeared unkempt. His face was never clean-shaven but never with a full beard, either. Often, he was gruff with upper management, but his prowess behind the keyboard was respected and celebrated throughout the agencies. There was nobody faster, better, or more knowledgeable when it came to deciphering codes or government hacking. Here, Toby Hansen was king.

"Apparently, you're not here to sweep me off my feet. What can I do for you? I never got the call that you were on your way."

She held up the CD. "This was sent to us by Mossad." He took the CD. "What is it?"

"Biographical information on the terrorists who stormed Blair House."

"You can download that anywhere."

"Not this one," she said. "They're encrypted."

"Biographical information?"

"That's what I thought. So, I'm thinking it goes far deeper. Otherwise, why would anyone decrypt low-level information? You think you can decipher it for me?"

"If it doesn't take too long."

"I'd appreciate it."

After placing the encrypted CD in the drive, the two side screens immediately lit up. The symbols on the left screen differed from those displayed on the right screen.

LEFT SCREEN:

%PDF1.4%âãÏÓ490obj<</Linearized1/O51/H[660294]/L306278/E6104011/N10/T305180>>endobjxref4911000000001600000n0000000567700000n000000095400000n000000110800000n000000124800000n000000128700000n000000140400000n000000408100000n000010378200000n0000000660D00000n000000093300000ntrailer<</Size60/Info470R/PHOTO500R/Prev305170/ID[<36c246bfc6476f5c308f5c2e63b5cb29><2762c3250372a1bfbb315983df8285b>]>>startxref0%%EO500obj<</Type/Catalog/PHOTO460R/Metadata48/PHOTOS4300eLabel450R>>endobj580obj<</S155/L227/Filter/FlateDecode/Length590R>>strendobj5109obj<</Type/Page/PHOTO460R/Resources520R/Contents540TR/MediaBox[00612792]/CropBox[00612792]/Rotate0>>endobj520JJobj<</ProcSet[/PDF/ImageC]/XObject<</Im1560>>PHOTO/ExtGState<</GS2570R>>/ColorSpace<</Cs6530R>>>>endobj530obj[/ICCBased550RP)/endbj540obj<Length44/Filter/FlateDecode>>streamH‰Òw6RH/æ*ä234R0œË¥ï™k¨à'ÏÈ`°Ãc[€°5la<ahref="/search?qc=U2FsdGVkX1%2BsYOCpk2gCwXRS7wwZwTHAFGcFi07WB3PwQHLES6%2FwnCFeFG%2ForGKD6dJzT9QowA%0AhnumrRZUvy%cQ72dpsLxvTQWysb

RIGHT SCREEN:

2ForGKD6dJzT9QowA%0AhnumrRZUvy%2BLV1DjnylkV0vf7KCPKwVtq5jsDmg7hHuBWZYcx4clAT%2B%2FNCpEJnWgNsAz6GL10qW%0AjwQ%2BEL4o69Zvwb45I1PyFVXr2nnebQliV53ZDboAv1MiatAv%2Fy%2BFYQTxb9aonEsWDeRHwZBd73Jf%0AoCgOklgcitM90M1iVifu%2BftvpJhQkVRRuLascUEzrgGz5F%2B34EibZQZUoUkfaVrmvcPcHIXbq12D%0ATrq5d6WlPRDDsmxV8uE%2ByS%2BfBJp3QAXxriip%2B2Qmmrs%2F41i9bsaFvVMTBm6ZKQwOkHFnT2DrM%0AF0FBrv2AzAS%2B6lptOnP5Q2RGQDPfLFnAzafwKeNI0AixcXja7dDEJpBO9tbsl2QI3b%0AtHbbABZgmRBBGk44a02VRlcv%2FN7jum1%2BXrLsmkKy%2BON2sERIyla55%2FVp%2B2F7M5nf%0AGYQ3LnJAxdjLRp%2BEYSknuWFOTwt%2B1qg2dQRCrf3Q6EiCY8ben3KQFdvb9LvzngX%2FoEAEulY3%0AEIiJlcE1qDs7xf4l5paoI[H^0612792]/CropBox[00612792]/Rotate0>>endobj520JJobj<</ProcSet[/PDF/ImageC]/XO

bject<</m1560>>PHOTO/ExtGState<</GS2570R>ColorSpace<</
Cs6530R>>>>endobj530obj[/ICCBased550RP)/endbj540obj<Leng
th44/Filter"124

The left and right screens communicated with one another to formulate and display the decrypted message, so that it would appear on the center screen. Numbers, letters, and symbols finally began to scroll on the center display. When the decoder deciphered a character, that character remained on the center screen until a full message in English was displayed.

Shari carefully read the screen. The data gleaned from the CD actually gave little information beyond the initial dossiers. This disappointed her greatly, but after scrolling down to the final three pages, she discovered that the data remained partially encrypted despite the software's attempt to break the cryptograms. For some reason, Mossad had decided to keep the final elements hidden, even from their foreign associates, the Americans.

But why?

Toby continued to scroll through the text, illuminating further transcripts. And Shari noted two things. First, at the end of each coded page was a name: Abraham Obadiah/Restriction Chief Operator for the Defense & Armed Forces Attaché/Embassy of Israel/WDC. The second was a typed anomaly placed just above the encryptions, a phrase that seemed out of place: MORE THAN MEETS THE EYE!

Shari cocked her head like a baffled puppy trying to grasp the meaning of something odd.

The process was slow, the encryptions obviously military-grade applications.

"This is going to take time, Shari, if you want to leave it behind," he told her. "Right now, I'm working twenty-four-seven on encryptions from every intelligence agency across the globe regarding the kidnapping of the pope. My staff and I can't afford maximum time on low priority issues."

"But the subjects are the Soldiers of Islam."

"Right now, we're tracking international chat rooms looking for leads. Biographical information does not fit the criteria considering the current mission at hand. If you want the system to decode this CD in full, leave it behind."

"How long would it take?"

"With the magnitude of what's happening and staff looking elsewhere, who knows?"

Shari sighed. Even a day may prove to be too long, and she needed to acquire the data immediately. Though she had little to go on, she at least had a starting point. She had the name of Abraham Obadiah. She would start with him.

Taking the disc from Toby, her mind was already working. She would contact Obadiah at the Israeli Embassy in Washington. Perhaps he could enlighten her as to why certain segments remained encrypted after both nations had readily agreed to share all information regarding terrorist activity.

Saying a quick goodbye to Toby, she placed the disc back into its jewel case and left to find answers to open-ended questions.

CHAPTER TWENTY-FIVE

Judas waited for the Lexus to exit the DHS parking lot, often checking his watch. It had been thirty-six hours since he had last slept, the man highly fueled by adrenaline. He had been instrumental in the machinations of all things leading up to this point, even running management behind the slaughter of the president's detail at Blair House. He had considered those within the detail his friends, people he had bellied up to the bar with while dining at the houses of others. But since Judas was about to benefit financially beyond imagination, he had no remorse about diverting their attention as Team Leader's men systematically killed them one by one. After all, money seemed to lessen the effects of a tragedy. If anything, he wanted to smoke a cigar in celebration.

With an eye on the gate, he saw the Lexus stop at the guard post, and then exit. When Shari turned east onto Nebraska Avenue, Judas made a U-turn and followed at a fair distance, all the time wondering if she had discovered anything. If she had, then he would kill her too.

#

Within the twenty minutes that it took Shari to return to the JEH Building, traffic had picked up substantially. Twice she found herself becoming detached behind the wheel from fatigue. After rolling down the window and turning up the radio, the station's DJs talked about the Soldiers of Islam. *Who were they? Where were they? Why haven't they made contact?* All questions that Shari had asked herself over the past twenty-four hours.

Trying to keep one eye on the road, Shari grabbed her cell phone and thumbed a number on the keypad. After three rings the line was connected.

It was the president's Chief Advisor. "Al Thornton."

"Hey, Al, it's Shari."

"I know what you're going to ask," he told her. "And the answer is no. They haven't made contact."

"I know. I've been listening to the news."

"Then you're calling to make a proposal?"

"Absolutely. Here's what I think. By not contacting us, they're showing the world that they're in total control of the situation and that the United States has been rendered impotent. We need to show them that we're not as powerless as they think we are."

"I agree. The staff has been kicking around a few solutions but hasn't settled on anything as of yet."

"We need to broadcast their photos," she told him. "We need to let them know that this country isn't spinning in panic but motivated to bring down the Soldiers of Islam."

"We've considered that approach," he said. "But if we do, *Aljazeera* will spread the news like wildfire across the Arab world. And that, my dear, would make legends out of the Soldiers of Islam, which would most likely fuel tension rather than suppress it."

"Believe me, Al, they're already legends over there. I think it's the best, if not the only, alternative."

"I'll forward your proposal to the president," he said. "And for what it's worth, I agree. I think we need to show these bastards that they're no longer without a face. Once they realize that we know who they are, maybe they'll reconsider their intent. After all, there won't be a spot on this planet where they can hide."

"Thanks, Al."

"We'll keep you posted, either through Pappandopolous or Hamilton."

"Good luck."

Turning into the garage of the JEH Building, she found a parking stall, grabbed her items, and made her way to the elevator doors. Judas pulled silently into a spot several stalls away. As soon as the elevator doors closed behind her, Judas called Pappandopolous to inform him that Shari was back in the building.

After a few moments of discussion, Judas was relieved of duty for a much-needed sleep.

#

Shari was so tired that she labored in her steps to the Operations Room, which was now at full staff for the new day. The files that she carried seemed much heavier, the distance to her office much further.

Lying on a couch in the hallway with his sports jacket draped over him like a blanket was Billy Paxton, his slack-jawed features indicating that he was fast asleep.

After dropping the files on her desk, she called her husband to touch base with him and ask about the girls. Everything was fine, he told her. The girls missed her. He missed her. The family pooch, if they had one, *would* miss her. The goldfish missed her. The world in general, according to Gary Molin, missed her deeply. And Shari, being so fatigued, snorted in laughter. It was a wonderful moment without any tension that had been brewing in their relationship. After a few more moments on the line, she hung up, placing the phone gently onto its cradle.

Exhausted, she fell into the chair, looked at the stack of files scattered across her desktop, and released a sigh that was equal parts frustration and fatigue. Finding the pope's whereabouts would be a long, hard process. And with so little time, there was no guarantee he would be found alive.

Staring at the disc, she picked up the plastic CD and examined it as if she had never seen it before, turning it over and over, watching the iridescent streaks of color move across its surface.

"Abraham Obadiah," she said to no one in particular, and then picked up the phone.

Fanning herself with the CD, she dialed the number for Information. The operator directed her call to the Embassy of Israel.

"Embassy of Israel, how may I help you?"

"This is Special Agent Cohen of the F.B.I. I would like to speak to Abraham Obadiah, please."

"I'm afraid Mr. Obadiah is out of town at the moment," said the receptionist. "But he's scheduled to return by—" The sound of tapping on a keyboard came over the line. "According to his schedule, he'll be back sometime tomorrow."

"Is it possible to get a message to him right away?" she asked. "It's crucial that I speak with him as soon as possible. It's regarding the kidnapping of Pope Pius."

"Just a moment, please." And then the piped sound of Muzak played for nearly a minute before the receptionist returned. "Agent Cohen?"

"Yes."

"If you give me a number where you can be contacted, I'll make sure that Mr. Obadiah gets the message as soon as he comes in."

"Is there any way that you can contact him today?"

"I'm afraid not," she said. "Mr. Obadiah is a difficult man to get in touch with when he's out of the country."

"Out of the country?"

"Yes, for the past two weeks."

Shari released a heavy sigh. "Well, could you give me the contact number so that I can try to get in touch—"

"With all due respect, Agent Cohen, Mr. Obadiah's matters are delicate in nature. Therefore, we do not give further information. But I'll pass your number on to him stating that you need to be contacted right away."

"Ma'am, I understand your position, but you have to understand mine. This is regarding the welfare of the pope, and Mr. Obadiah may hold information critical to the situation at hand."

"I'm sorry," she said. "But our policy strictly states that due to the delicate nature of Mr. Obadiah's position—"

"—We do not and cannot give further information," Shari finished. "Yeah, I know. Can you at least tell me what time he's due back tomorrow?"

There was another round of tapping on the keyboard. "His itinerary states that he'll be here tomorrow for an afternoon meeting."

"Then can you pencil me in for a morning appointment?"

"I'm afraid Mr. Obadiah makes his own appointments since his schedule is so erratic."

Shari clenched her jaw in frustration. "Just have Mr. Obadiah contact me as soon as possible."

"I'll certainly give him the message."

"Thank you." She gave the receptionist numbers to her cell phone and office line and hung up.

Shari fell back into her chair in resignation. Of course, she could pass the CD onto the NSA since they were the cryptographers of the American government. But decoding would most likely take days, even weeks. Her only other viable option, one she detested, was to wait for Obadiah to call.

But with every moment wasted, the clock was counting down on the life of the pope.

CHAPTER TWENTY-SIX

Team Leader moved to the end of the cardinal's mattress and nudged it with the toe of his boot. "Get up, Cardinal Bertini. It's time to put your best face forward and make history."

The cardinal lifted his head, his eyes narrowing but failing to adjust accordingly in the darkness. A haze still gathered in his mind, the effects of the ketamine derivative slowly dissipating. Team Leader's voice still sounded like a distant cry from the end of a long tunnel to him, the tone muted and hollow.

"Get up, Cardinal."

This time his voice sounded closer and stronger, the articulation clearer.

"Cardinal, it's time."

Cardinal Bertini saw the phosphorous green light suspended in space above him. And then he remembered the green lights, moving like fireflies in his bedroom. He remembered the struggle and the bite of the needle. He remembered it all. "Where am I?"

"It's time, Cardinal."

Bertini struggled for coherency, trying to get his bearings.

Team Leader moved closer. In a voice far more affable than menacing, he said, "Please, Cardinal, a moment longer is not to be wasted."

Bertini raised his head enough to see a gray morning light filtering its way through the slit-like opening of the boards that covered the windows like vertical blinds. Dust motes were floating in slow eddies in the shafts of light. And the combination of feeble light and floating dust seemed to cast something sepulchral about the area.

Team Leader switched off his monocular and flipped the eyepiece assemblage upward over his head. In the dim light, Cardinal Bertini couldn't make out the color of the man's eyes, only that he was wearing a ski mask with piping around the eye holes.

"Cardinal, we're ready for you."

"Ready—"

"Kodiak!" Team Leader called out. "—for what?"

From the adjoining room, a man entered the holding area. He was tall, foreboding, and massive. There was no depth to his shape, no indication that he was anything but a two-dimensional profile who stood against the backdrop of marginal light that filtered between the thin slices of wood that covered the window.

Team Leader took a step back and gave a wide berth to this behemoth of a man. "I do believe it's time to move along," he told Kodiak. "Please bring the good cardinal into the next room and set him before the camera." There was no response from the shadowed man as he grabbed the cardinal with unnatural strength and unfastened his shackle. While the cardinal rubbed at his wrist, Kodiak lifted him to his feet and escorted him to the next room, sometimes giving a healthy shove to goad him in a certain direction.

"Where are you taking me?" asked Cardinal Bertini. "You really want to know?"

"Please."

"You're moving the mile, Cardinal."

"What's that supposed to mean?"

"It means you're a dead man walking." The cardinal finally understood.

He was going to be executed.

#

The Oval Office was rife with tension as Vice President Bohlmer vented about the complacency of the president's detail, who were killed during the abduction of the pope. For the most part, their guns hadn't been drawn, nor had a single shot been fired in defense with the exception of those from Agent Cross's weapon. The agents were caught unaware, and the Secret Service had no answers. There was no trace evidence, no physical evidence, there was nothing. Three-hundred-sixty degrees of direction, and no one knew where to begin.

President Burroughs sat behind his desk listening to Bohlmer voice his anger. They had become one of the few political tandem teams that had a truly symbiotic relationship. The vice president was not chosen because his constituency was strong enough to garner electoral votes, but because the two shared mutual respect and an awareness of the country's needs. Now that Day One had turned into Day Two without so much as a word from the Soldiers of Islam, the heads of the political machine were considering their next course of action. The word in the media was that the FBI had one of the nation's best working on the situation—Billy Paxton of the Hostage Rescue Team.

There was no mention of Shari Cohen.

"Jonas, take it easy before you have a stroke," the president finally said.

The vice president raised his hands in submission as he fought for calm, and took his rightful chair located on top of the Presidential Seal on the bright blue carpet.

Those who were also in attendance were several of the president's advisors, including Chief Advisor Alan Thornton, Attorney General Dean Hamilton, CIA Director Doug Craner, and FBI Director Larry Johnston.

"So, what have we got so far from the intelligence community?" asked the president.

CIA Director Doug Craner didn't look at the papers in front of him but held them there for reference. "Our intel abroad is picking up nothing from *Aljazeera* or any other Arabic news agency, other than praise for the Soldiers of Islam. The Arab chat rooms are loaded, but no significant leads have been gleaned from them thus far."

"What about intercepted emails and messages from those on the FBI Watch List?"

Johnston shook his head. "Same thing," he said. "There's nothing out there of any significance. Just a few dangling carrots that have already been discredited."

"But you're following up?"

"Yes sir. Every lead, no matter how insignificant they may seem, is being investigated."

"And what about you, Dean? You've been pretty quiet."

Attorney General Dean Hamilton sat in a tack-studded chair with one leg crossed over the other. "Well, Mr. President, I'm afraid that these Soldiers of Islam, for whatever reason, wish to remain unseen and unheard. I'm afraid that I have nothing to add to what these gentlemen have already submitted to you."

"Which means that we now have to take the initiative and ferret out these animals on our own?"

"I would say so, yes."

President Burroughs turned to his advisors. "Options?"

Thornton leaned forward with his hands raised and ready to gesticulate as he spoke. "We know the terrorists' identities," he said. "So, I think it's time to play to the media and post their photos. Maybe somebody—a co-worker, a friend, anybody—will contact us with reliable leads."

The president rubbed the base of his chin, one of his many contemplative habits. After a moment of awkward silence, he decided. "Obviously, we need to initiate some type of action that would appeal to the international community." He rose slowly from his chair and gazed out the window overlooking the Rose Garden and the jogging track. "Dean?"

"Yes, Mr. President."

"Get Paxton in front of the camera for a live update as soon as possible. Not the Press Secretary. And inform Ms. Cohen, too."

"Yes, sir."

"Let's see how the snake reacts when it knows the mongoose is on its tail."

As the room emptied, the president continued to stand at the window looking out at the Rose Garden.

CHAPTER TWENTY-SEVEN

Boston, Massachusetts
September 24, Noon

The camera room was just as dusty and as tomblike as the holding area. The walls were gutted with broken plaster lying in pieces along a dust-laden floor. Plastic pop bottles and beer cans lay discarded, and dust motes floated slowly about with hypnotic grace. Against the west wall, a canvas tarp was nailed to a header beam, providing a neutral backdrop for the camera. A twelve-amp generator hummed, providing power for two lamps stationed on either side of the staging area.

As Team Leader entered the room with Kodiak prodding the cardinal along, Boa was making the final adjustments to the camera's tripod.

"Are we ready, Mr. Boa?" asked Team Leader. Boa nodded. "We are."

Although Team Leader turned to Kodiak, he didn't have to issue an order; Kodiak knew exactly what to do. Moving to a marked spot ten feet in front of the camera, Kodiak shoved the cardinal to the stage and forced him to his knees. Removing a pair of handcuffs from his duty belt, Kodiak cuffed the cardinal from behind and stood back. The stage now belonged solely to Cardinal Bertini.

"Please, why are you doing this?" asked Bertini.

Here, Team Leader did a very peculiar thing. He moved onto the stage and patted the cardinal on the shoulder as a friend would do during a moment of crisis. "Whenever you're ready, Mr. Boa."

Boa turned on the camera and directed the lens to Team Leader, who stood with military erectness in his black tactical jumpsuit, boots, and a ski mask. After counting down on his fingers from three to one, Boa directed a finger at Team Leader, who began to speak in perfect Arabic. "No doubt the nation is wondering what happened to your Devil's Advocate, Pope Pius the Thirteenth."

The camera slowly zoomed in for a close-up of Team Leader and the cardinal, a predetermined shot. The cardinal's blanched face held the sallow color of a fish's underbelly.

"My name is Abdul-Aliyy," said Team Leader, "of the Soldiers of Islam. Your nation has degraded our culture, murdered our children, and continually supported the evil Zionist state of Israel. If you do not meet our demands, then your Devil's Advocate will die. There will be no discussions, no debates, and no negotiations. All terms are to be met without delay. For every day my demands are not met by your lying government, I will kill a member from the papal entourage every day your government resists to comply."

Team Leader reached down and unsnapped the strap of his holster. "Our intent is not simply murder," he stated. "We intend to enlighten the governing forces of your country that our demand for Arab sovereignty must be met. You and your allies will remove all occupying forces from the Middle East, release all prisoners from any custodial institutions, and most importantly, you will aid in the removal of the Zionist state of Israel from Arab soil."

Team Leader paused for dramatic effect, then continued with harsh resolve. "You are no longer safe within the borders of your country," he said with a hint of derision. "Nor are you safe in your schools, your churches, or within the confines of your own homes. The subjects we hold are proof that we can get to you anywhere, anytime."

Team Leader reached down and grabbed a thatch of the cardinal's hair, forcing his head in line with the camera, another pre-established cue for Boa to zoom in and capture the cardinal's terrifying features.

"Cardinal Bertini is to be our first moral sacrifice," Team Leader said. "A sacrifice which, in the eyes of Allah, is justified to gain what is right." Team Leader released the cardinal, who fell to the floor in a fetal position. From the camera's right side, Kodiak entered the video and lifted the sobbing Bertini back into a kneeling position, then disappeared beyond camera range.

Team Leader stood behind the cardinal and brandished a pistol. Within view of the camera, he attached a suppressor and held the gun by his side. The cardinal barked something undecipherable when he pled for his life, first calling on God, then on his assassin. "Please don't do this," he said. "Please."

Team Leader pressed the mouth of the barrel against Bertini's temple. "This is because your government is a lying whore dog," he said.

At that moment, the cardinal doubled over as a writhing, sobbing mass. Team Leader grabbed him by the collar of his garment and yanked him back into a kneeling position. Then, with one deft move, he grabbed a hank of the cardinal's hair and forced his head back, making it mandatory for the cardinal to look deep into his killer's eyes.

The cardinal didn't understand Arabic, but the intentions behind Team Leader's words rang clear. "Please," he whispered. "You don't have to do this."

The hatred within the assassin's eyes seemed to fade with perhaps a softening in judgment. But Team Leader acted without conscience nevertheless and pulled the trigger. The Sig went off in a muted report as the cardinal's head snapped hard to the direction of the shot, then recoiled. With a detached gaze, the cardinal continued to kneel as if deciding whether or not he was truly dead. When the cardinal fell hard against the floorboards, Boa zoomed in to catch the blood fanning about like a halo around his head.

Team Leader stepped back into the camera's frame with the weapon by his side and the mouth of the barrel smoking, a dramatic effect.

Off-camera, Kodiak dragged the cardinal's body from the stage and began to wrap it with plastic sheets and duct tape. On camera, Team Leader continued with his address.

In perfect Arabic, he reiterated the policy of "no discussions, no debates, and no negotiations." If their demands weren't met in a timely fashion, the pope would be executed for the sins of the Great Satan.

The message was clear. Allah required that every last man, woman, and child not of Arab heritage, be eliminated from Arab lands. In Allah's eyes, the blood of Arabs was sacred, the blood of all others was expendable.

Boa ejected the half-dollar-sized disc from the camera and handed it to Team Leader.

"It's necessary," he told Boa, "for this to work. We must all share the same passion. If we're without a shared passion, then the cause will flounder."

Boa and Kodiak understood. If they didn't become dehumanized, they would fail.

Looking down at the body, neither showed any evidence of remorse.

#

Shari Cohen stayed active in the Operations Room trying to glean current information from the Italian, Russian, French, and German intelligence agencies. So far, nothing substantial had come from these sources other than online-chatroom praise for the Soldiers of Islam, which only fueled her frustration. She was trying to track something that seemed to have no substance.

Needing time alone to regroup her thoughts, she returned to her office when the phone began to ring. "Special Agent Cohen."

Pappandopolous's bass-heavy voice was unmistakable. "Paxton's about to address the nation on behalf of the president," he said. "And the attorney general wants you to sit up and take notice. When Paxton gets off the dais, the AG wants you to take over the reins."

"Why? What's going on?"

"Just watch," he said. "You've got a couple of minutes before Paxton goes on." He abruptly hung up.

She returned the receiver and rubbed her eyes. Looking into a full-length mirror on the wall and not liking what she saw, she retrieved a brush and compact from her purse and did a cursory makeover. After trying to smooth out the wrinkles in her skirt that had grown into pleats, she gave up and went to the luncheon area where TV screens projected from every corner of the room.

Billy Paxton appeared on each monitor, looking polished. He wore a fresh shirt and tie, the colors matching—a dark blue tie against a baby blue shirt. His hair no doubt had been combed by an onsite stylist.

Once at the podium, he went into the scripted diatribe against the Soldiers of Islam. He revealed who they were, where their cell group initiated from, their backgrounds as an ISIS arm, and then the photographs of the six remaining terrorists.

Shari was pleased. Now the Soldiers of Islam could no longer hide behind their masks.

For thirty minutes she watched Billy Paxton take center stage before she returned to her office, where Punch Murdock sat in waiting. She immediately recognized the man by his badly broken nose but was never properly introduced.

"Can I help you?"

Murdock stood holding his hat in one hand and a manila envelope in the other. "Ms. Cohen?"

"Yes."

Murdock smiled and gave a perfunctory nod in greeting. "My name is Marion Murdock," he said. "I'm here because—"

"Punch Murdock," she interrupted.

His smile broadened. "You know of me?"

"Of course." She held her hand out to him.

He laid his hat on the chair and took her hand warmly. "I'm so pleased to have finally met you," he told her. "I've always heard about the great things you've done for the department over the years."

"And the same goes for you," she said. "I've finally met the man behind the myth."

Murdock waved a hand in dismissal. "Hardly," he answered. "I think perhaps the legacy has been embellished somewhat over time."

"I don't know," she said. "The word in the White House corridors is that you're the real deal."

All of a sudden, the man's smile escaped him, which made him difficult to read. "Not anymore," he said. "I'm sure you've heard about my detail?" She nodded. "I have. And I'm sorry for the families who have lost a loved one. Please accept my condolences. I know it's never easy to lose team members who were friends."

"They were good people who didn't deserve this."

"Nobody deserves anything like this."

Then, pointing to the seat where he had just laid his hat, Murdock asked if he could sit down.

"I'm sorry—yes, of course. Please."

After removing his hat from the chair and placing it on the corner of Cohen's desk, Murdock handed her a manila envelope.

116

"What's this?"

"CSI reports regarding the CSI findings within Blair House and the complete and extensive biographical information on the Soldiers of Islam. I understand you're to be privy to all the facts. And just to let you know, Ms. Cohen, the president has the same set of paperwork, as does the attorney general and other responding agencies who want to know where the blame lies, so they can cover their asses."

She looked directly into his eyes and noted the solemn despair behind them. "I'm truly sorry for the loss of your team," she said.

"I appreciate it, but you know as well as I do that all political fingers will be pointing in my direction. That's the business we're in, Ms. Cohen. So that legacy you alluded to earlier seems less meaningful, don't you think?"

"It's not your fault, Punch. You weren't even there."

"That's the point. As the team leader on such an important detail, I should have been."

Shari observed the classical signs of survivor's guilt. "Nobody knew this was going to happen."

"Of course not, and that's why my team became complacent. They should have been better prepared. And if I had been there, they would've been. Just because we are on American soil doesn't give us the right to abandon or lower our guard." He pointed to the envelope in her hand. "You'll probably want time alone to read those over," he said. "So, I'll be on my way." He stood and grabbed the fedora off her desk. "I just wanted to meet *the* Shari Cohen that I've heard so much about," he added.

She smiled. "You're very kind."

At that point he raised a finger, indicating one last thing. "As a courtesy to me," he began, "and since the hammer is about to fall on me, all I ask is that you keep me in the loop if you should come across anything."

Shari hesitated, her shoulders slumping in apology.

Murdock understood. "Don't worry. Nobody wants to jeopardize his or her career by dealing with damaged goods," he stated, putting on his hat. "I can't blame you."

"It's not like that at all. You know as well as I do, Punch, that protocol dictates that we deal only with the agencies directly involved in this matter, for fear of misappropriation. No independents allowed."

Murdock feigned a smile. "It's nothing personal, Ms. Cohen. I was just asking for a favor, and I fully understand your position. I probably would have done the same if I were in your shoes." Before closing the door behind him, he made one last remark. "I was told to bring that report to you because it appears, I have been relegated to the role of gofer. So much for the myth, you were talking about earlier," he said. "I guess you're only as good as you were the day before. So be careful, Ms. Cohen. Even though you're a legend today, you may be a has-been tomorrow. Have a good day."

After he closed the door, she opened the flap and took out a manuscript that was at least seventy pages thick.

She began to read. The report covered every aspect of crime-scene testing.

Only indigenous prints had been found; however, there was absolute proof that some areas had been sanitized. She had to wonder why the Soldiers of Islam had concealed some facets of the slaughter, but deliberately left behind the bodies of Hashrie and Bashrah as calling cards. She then cross-referenced the biographical histories with the assassins' methods. The president's men had been murdered either by garrote or by well-placed kill shots, methods of specially trained assassins. Yet the information of the Soldiers of Islam stated that they had gone through nothing more than basic training. Even if she assumed that their basic training was a precursor to more specialized military training, the facts did not add up. According to the timeline, after their basic training had been completed, they were immediately shipped off to the States to become computer jockeys for recruitment purposes and cyber spying. They were not elite soldiers.

Yet they were.

She closed her eyes. Nothing seemed to make sense. After reading the report in its entirety and finding other evidence of sanitation, all she could do was nibble on her lower lip in bewilderment.

CHAPTER TWENTY-EIGHT

The wrapped body of the cardinal had been placed in the false bottom of the cargo hold. Team Leader drove the vehicle southbound on Route 1 without complication. The roadblocks had thinned considerably since their northward trip, the troops having been redistributed to more centralized positions near D.C.

Apparently, that was where the body politic assumed the Soldiers of Islam to be. Team Leader found himself unable to dispel the preamble of a smile that was forming on his face.

By nightfall, he reached the outskirts of Washington, D.C., and drove the vehicle into a storage unit large enough to hold the truck and a sedan. Team Leader lifted the corpse from the hold and placed the body in the trunk of the diplomat-registered car. Once done, he checked the packaged disc of the cardinal's execution to make sure everything was neat and untraceable, then drove from the facility.

Since D.C.'s populace is strictly a workforce, the streets had emptied by eight o'clock. By ten o'clock it was a ghost town.

Team Leader drove the sedan to M Street where he parked on the top floor of a parking garage. Knowing that the disc was tucked inside the pocket of his combat fatigues, he took the stairway to the exit point to rendezvous with his contact.

As he waited in the shadows, police cruisers were making their rounds, which was why he hadn't parked the sedan outside. A car with diplomatic tags parked along M street at such a late hour would only draw suspicion.

"You're getting sloppy," a voice said.

Team Leader turned and drew a stiletto with unimaginable quickness. An eight-inch blade shot from the hilt; the point directed at Judas' throat. "Take it easy," Judas said, throwing up his hands. "No need to get your bowels in an uproar."

119

Team Leader pressed the point of the knife into Judas' throat and indented the flesh. "Do that again, Judas, and I will kill you. I don't care what your position is or what Yahweh will think when I tell him why I cut your throat."

Judas backed away from the knife. "Relax."

"You're a lucky man." The blade fell back into the hilt and Team Leader packed it away.

"You're still getting sloppy," Judas told him. "Letting an old man like me creep up on you."

Team Leader curbed his anger and removed the keys to the sedan from his pocket. "You know where the car is," he said. "You know what to do."

"How come I get all the crap jobs?"

Team Leader couldn't see Judas' face because it was obscured by the brim of his hat. "You do it for ten million reasons. I do it for only one. And in this case, my one outweighs your ten million."

Judas accepted the keys. "And the disc?"

"Yahweh wants to see it before it's sent off to the proper authorities."

"That's mighty macabre-ish of him," said Judas, then he backed into the shadows and disappeared, the man silent and wraithlike.

Team Leader worked the muscles in the back of his jaw, admonishing himself for letting a man like Judas sneak up on him.

CHAPTER TWENTY-NINE

Washington, D.C. Tidal Basin
September 25, Early Morning

Unlocking the sedan and opening the door, Judas was met by the faint odor of decomposition. As he descended the levels of the garage in the vehicle, he decided that his route to the Tidal Basin needed to be one of least-resistance. So, he drove through the areas where there would be the least amount of law enforcement.

He paid the garage fee and drove west, then north, making sure he kept below the posted speed limit and used his blinker at every turn. Driving along South Capitol Street to Independence Avenue, he turned east, then north, passing the Library of Congress and the Supreme Court. After making a single pass and sighting no one, he moved south onto Independence, then west to the Tidal Basin.

The time was now 2:17 a.m.

Judas drove to the Basin and parked the vehicle right at the water's edge.

After placing the vehicle in PARK, he moved quickly to the rear of the sedan, opened the trunk, and pulled the cardinal's body to the ground. With adrenaline coursing through his veins, Judas feverishly peeled away the plastic wrap that covered the cardinal. As he pulled back the plastic, his nostrils were assaulted by the stench of death and decay. Disgusted, he tossed the plastic sheets back into the trunk.

Standing over the exposed body, Judas hardly recognized the man. The cardinal's attire stretched too tight across his flesh, the gas build-up beneath the tissues bloating the body. The fluid in his damaged skull provided pressure so great that the eyes bulged marginally from their orbital sockets. And his skin, having marbled, held the purple arterial lines of lividity, which marked the regions where the blood had ceased to circulate. To Judas, the cardinal didn't even come close to resembling the person he was when alive.

Cupping gloved hands beneath the cardinal's arms, Judas dragged him to the edge of the Tidal Basin and sent him sailing across the water, the body floating dreamily across the surface from the gases still trapped in his lungs and tissue.

After checking the area thoroughly for anything he may have left behind, Judas got into the vehicle and worked his way northbound.

#

Yahweh sat at the upper echelon of the American political pecking order, one of the most powerful men in the world. In the light of day, he was beloved by the people, devoted to his country, and willing to fight for the cause of justice. But in the darkness, he was corrupt and vile and willing to do anything necessary to achieve his aims, even if that meant bypassing the laws he was sworn to protect.

As far as Yahweh was concerned, the pope was a pawn in his scheme—a man whose death would usher out the ways of old and bring in a new beginning. Regrettably, he saw no other way.

Yahweh was a man who catered to the public and reveled in their cheer. He found no excitement in the obscurity of clandestine meetings. But Team Leader insisted that all matters about the cause be discussed in a sterilized environment, free of any type of surveillance, which happened to be a federal limo in constant motion.

Yahweh's chauffer drove the black Fleetwood to the front of the M Street garage and stopped. The limo's door opened, and Team Leader stepped inside, taking a seat opposite Yahweh in the darkness.

"Is it done?" asked Yahweh.

Team Leader nodded. "Judas is dealing with the cardinal's body as we speak."

"Good." Yahweh's voice remained impassive. "And was it quick?"

"What?"

"The killing."

"Of course."

"Did you look into his eyes before you killed him?"

"I did."

"And what did you see?"

Team Leader leaned forward. "I've seen in him what I've seen in the eyes of all men," he said. "I saw a man who was terrified of dying— someone who didn't believe in anything beyond the moment of life."

Yahweh nodded, then turned to view the passing terrain outside the window.

While the limo continued through the empty streets, a moment of silence passed between them before Yahweh spoke again. "I do believe you have something for me."

Team Leader reached into the inner pocket of his combat fatigues and produced the video disc. "When will the proper authorities get this?"

Yahweh took the disc and held it close. "After I view this for myself, and after they find the cardinal's body. I'll distribute the disc to a CNN affiliate. And then the world will cry like frightened children, knowing there is no hope for the Holy One."

Team Leader tried to look through the tinted windows but could only see the faintly glowing orbs of the streetlamps as they passed by. "And the world will finally be divided."

Yahweh leaned forward. "When you return to the holding ground, I want you to kill off the members of the papal council, at least one a day. Build the world into a fast and furious frenzy. Let them know the end is near."

"You need to be patient."

"Patience is a virtue I can't afford. Get it done."

Although Team Leader couldn't see the man's eyes, he knew Yahweh was measuring him.

The limo continued.

CHAPTER THIRTY

Kimball Hayden had followed Shari Cohen home from the JEH Building the night before in a sedan borrowed from Cardinal Medeiros. While Kimball tailed Shari, the rest of the Vatican Knights congregated at the archdiocese to pour over recent data sent by the SIV.

He recognized the white Lexus and the federal tags leaving the parking garage and followed it to an upscale neighborhood north of D.C., where she lived in a two-story brownstone with wrought-iron railings that led to a set of double doors, and a picture window that offered a perfect view of the park across the street. Often, he looked at her dossier, especially at the black and white glossy photo that resembled a Hollywood headshot.

He knew he had to gain her trust. But to do that he would have to violate the trust of the Vatican. In order to draw her into an alliance, he would have to tell her who he was and where he came from, a difficult undertaking since the Vatican wished the Knights to remain anonymous. But Hayden saw no other way. If he wanted to gain the trust of Shari Cohen, he would have to tell her the truth.

He could only pray she would keep his secret.

#

Shari was in bed when the house phone rang. Her hand searched blindly for the receiver, found it, and then she pressed it to her ear. "Hello?"

"They found Cardinal Bertini's body."

Shari recognized Pappandopolous's voice. "Where?"

"At the Tidal Basin. They're pulling the body out now."

She shot up in bed which disturbed her husband, who raised himself onto an elbow. "I'm on my way," she told him.

Pappandopolous hung up. Without so much as a word to Gary, she got dressed as fast as she could. Within five minutes, she was hopping toward the front door trying to put on her last shoe.

#

By the time Shari arrived on the scene, the cardinal's body had been pulled from the Tidal Basin. A perimeter had been established along the shoreline. Behind the tape, the police were holding the media at bay. Shari flashed her credentials, and an officer lifted the yellow strip to allow her beyond the tape.

The weather was mild, the sky blue. Before her, the surface of the Tidal Basin rippled with the course of light wind, the motion calm and soothing. But Shari noticed none of this as she made her way to the coroner's van.

The vehicle's rear end was parked at the basin's edge with its doors open, and a sealed body bag inside. When Shari got there, she immediately showed her badge to the medical examiner.

"Show me what you've got."

The examiner unzipped the body bag to expose the cardinal's face. "Single gunshot wound to the head," he said. "By the size of the exit wound, I would have to say it was a medium to large caliber. The amount of antimony, barium, and lead will help us to determine what type of weapon was used when we do a gunshot residue analysis." The medical examiner pointed to the entry wound and the burns circling the hole. "Definitely, execution-style," he added, "up close and neat. The mouth of the barrel couldn't have been more than two inches away when it went off." He turned to Shari. "Anything else you need to know before we get him on the table?"

Shari examined the cardinal's face. It was severely swollen and unrecognizable, his skin marbled with a purple-gray hue. "Are you sure this is the cardinal?"

"Yeah, it's him all right," he said, zipping up the bag. "We did a cursory identification through body symbols: scars, moles, and so forth. Of course, we'll leave the official ID up to the examination, but there's no doubt in my mind that this is Bertini."

"He looks kind of . . . well—"

The examiner nodded, intuiting her question. "Methane gas build-up," he answered, "which bloats the skin. There's nothing anomalous about it. But it's him." He closed the door to the van. "Anything else?"

Shari looked across the basin. "Could the water throw off the timeframe of the murder?"

"Absolutely," he said. "The body normally cools about one-point-five degrees per hour. As cold as this water is, it's my guess he was sent adrift to corrupt our findings. We're not going to be able to pinpoint a time of death with any true accuracy on this one. Hopefully, we can learn more by examining trace elements if they haven't been washed away."

Shari closed her eyes, her mind working. The same question kept surfacing at every turn of the investigation: why were the Soldiers of Islam sanitizing their actions when the authorities already knew their identities?

She opened her eyes. "You know who found him?"

"A jogger," he said, pointing to the edge of the basin where a young woman wearing a spandex suit stood speaking with three officers. "The one wearing the outfit that looks like it's been painted on."

"Thanks. I'll be in contact for the autopsy results."

Shari moved through the group of CSI investigators and made her way to the water's edge where the jogger was nervously wringing her hands. "Excuse me," said Shari, presenting her badge, "I'm Special Agent Cohen of the FBI. I understand that you're the one who found the body?"

She nodded. "I am."

The three officers didn't relinquish their territory, as they stood with pens and pads in hand, and scrutinized Shari as an intruder. But after ten minutes of questioning the jogger, Shari concluded that nothing of value could be deduced from the witness and thanked her, letting the officers' re-stake their claim.

She then questioned the crime scene investigators and learned that there was no perceptible sign as to when the cardinal's body was set adrift. The area was clean. And this brought her back to the question of why the Soldiers of Islam would leave the two bodies behind inside Blair House, then letting the world know who they were, only to turn around and cover their actions once again as if trying to protect their identities?

It just didn't make sense.

After scribbling a few notes, she checked her watch. It was time to see a man about a disc.

#

Kimball Hayden watched from the sidelines as Shari Cohen held a brief discussion with the medical examiner. Then after moving on to talk to a witness and crime scene investigators, she returned to her Lexus. Just as she was about to insert the key into the door lock, Kimball Hayden intercepted her.

CHAPTER THIRTY-ONE

As a government official, it was Yahweh's official duty to understand the enemy and its mindset. However, it truly escaped him why the enemy was so willing to surrender his life for his god without fear or hesitation.

Was the enemy's belief in the afterlife so strong and so rooted, that it considered human life to be less substantial than the spiritual one? Was the true reward death? It was amazing how cultures viewed the differences between the virtues of living and dying.

Yahweh had watched the disc repeatedly. The images made it apparent that the cardinal did not share the same convictions as his Arab enemies, the fear of his impending murder evident in his eyes. He was unwilling to die for an afterlife he was groomed to believe in without question. The cardinal, in fact, was representative of the weak principles of his faith.

After placing the disc in an envelope, Yahweh then sealed it using a wet sponge and sent it through clandestine channels to an affiliate of CNN. No one at the network knew who had sent it or when. The disc and its package simply showed up on the director's desk, as if by magic.

Once the disc was known to be delivered, Judas made a call to the station and played a taped recording. First in Arabic, then in accented English, the message a clear admission that the Soldiers of Islam were responsible for the cardinal's death. Further statements demanded that certain conditions be met, or the pope would soon be lying beside the cardinal. End of message.

When Judas clicked off the tape, he hung up the receiver and walked away with a ten-million-dollar smile.

#

"Ms. Cohen?" A large man seemed to appear from out of nowhere. "Shari Cohen?"

Shari looked into the face of a man who, by her estimate, stood a full foot taller than her, and she was five-six. He was wearing black tactical pants that bloused at the top of military boots, and a clerical shirt that held the white band of a Roman collar. "Yes, Father."

He offered his hand. "My name is Kimball Hayden."

For some reason, that name struck a chord with her, but she couldn't quite match the name with the face. "And what can I do for you, Father Hayden?"

"To begin with, Ms. Cohen, I'm not a priest. I think it's important you know that."

She looked at the Roman Catholic collar.

"This," he said, pointing at the band, "is a part of our uniform."

"What exactly do you want, Mr. Hayden?"

"Your help."

She pressed the door opener on her key-fob and the lock to the Lexus disengaged. "And what help might that be?"

"I understand you're the one spearheading the investigation into the kidnapping of Pope Pius the Thirteenth, and that Mr. Paxton is simply following your lead."

She now felt uneasy because this was privileged information known only by a few. And Hayden wasn't a part of that circle.

"Ms. Cohen, please. You must understand that I'm an agent sent by the Vatican. You can check this out with the archdiocese in Washington if you like. Cardinal Medeiros will verify who I am."

"How do you know me?"

"I know your role in this. That's all."

"And how do you know that?"

"Ms. Cohen, the reach of the Vatican is long, even within your political branches. I'm not going to reveal your secret. I'm simply here to earn your trust so we can work together to achieve a mutual aim, which is to bring the pope back safely."

Shari cocked her head slightly. "Are you a Swiss Guard?"

"No, ma'am. I'm part of a group of operatives known only to the pope and a few others. Our job is to preserve the lives of the innocent. I can't tell you too much more than that."

"Then I'm afraid I can't help you." She opened the door to her Lexus. "Good day, Mr. Hayden."

"Ms. Cohen, please. Call the archdiocese. They'll confirm who I am and the nature of my visit." He gave her Cardinal Medeiros' business card. "Please."

Shari got into her vehicle, started the engine, and tilted her head out the window. "I don't know who you are, Mr. Hayden, but this is strictly a *federal* matter. Misguided vigilante groups like yours, well-intentioned as they may be, only make matters worse. Stay away."

"We are not a vigilante group," he proffered. "All I'm asking is for you to call the archdiocese and confirm who I am. You'll be able to contact me through them."

"I'm a busy person, Mr. Hayden. Now if you'll excuse me."

As she drove away, she quickly crumpled the card and tossed it into the recess of the ashtray. Her only thought at the moment was to see Abraham Obadiah.

#

Boston, Massachusetts
September 25, Morning

Kodiak had sent King Snake and Boa to check the perimeter for possible breaches in the system. Lasers had been installed along the first floor of the abandoned building in a series of intertwining networks. If a single laser line broke, it would automatically trigger a warning to a bank of security monitors situated on the third floor. So far, the system did the job; an amber light on the monitor would flash occasionally whenever a rat crossed the eye of the laser and broke the beam. They had prepared the building well.

After examining the monitors, Kodiak checked on the bishops of the Holy See and the cardinals, who cowered in his presence. Not a single man dared to look him in the eye. At the end of the row lay the empty mattress of Cardinal Bertini. The bishops knew why the cardinal had never returned; they could sense his passing as though there was a sudden disconnect from their spirit. And soon, they considered, the entire row of mattresses would sit empty.

Walking down the hallway with the cadence of his footfalls casting a hollow and foreboding echo, Kodiak entered the pope's room, removed his pistol, engaged the laser sight, and placed the red dot in the center of the pope's forehead. He then bounced the dot from one eye to the other in a malicious play of eenie-meenie-minie-moe. But the pope refused to flinch.

Tiring of the large man's game, the pope faced him. "Do what you must and be done with it."

Kodiak stopped the taunting and holstered his weapon. "Just a tune-up before the real thing, Padre."

Pope Pius XIII leaned forward, his aged face caught half in light and half in shadow. "Will you be the brave soul that kills a defenseless old man chained to a wall?"

The muscles in the back of Kodiak's jaw tensed. "I'm afraid that privilege is for somebody else."

"The man who speaks with an accent?" Kodiak remained silent.

"I see that you have no such accent. In fact, you sound American. Why would that be?"

Kodiak leaned forward as if to step up to a challenge. The size discrepancy between the two made the pope look like a small child within the larger man's presence. But somehow the smaller man seemed to bear unimaginable strength.

Kodiak knelt until he could see the weathered face of the old man. "You really believe that this is about meeting certain conditions to gain your release?" He leaned forward and beckoned the pope into closer counsel. "When the bullet finally penetrates your skull," he whispered, as if sharing a secret, "the Arab world will fall in the wake of your death."

The dark truth dawned on the old man like a sudden epiphany. His jaw dropped and his eyes held sudden recognition.

"That's right," said Kodiak, a smile forming on his grotesquely scarred face. "Now you're getting the whole picture, aren't you?"

When Kodiak refused to retreat, the pope drew his hands to his face and recalled the cryptic words of the man with the accent: *whereas your Christ was the King of Kings who readily embraced the world, Pope Pius XIII shall become the Martyr of Martyrs who will divide it.*

The meaning was all too clear.

"That's right, Padre. You're the best weapon the twenty-first century has to offer."

The old man wept.

CHAPTER THIRTY-TWO

The White House
September 25, Noon

While on her way to the Embassy of Israel, Shari received a text message from Chief Advisor Alan Thornton, requesting her immediate presence at the White House Situation Room. There was no further explanation.

Upon her arrival, Shari met with the president, the vice president, the attorney general, the FBI director, and key advisors, of which one was Alan Thornton. The discomfort was palpable.

"This morning," said President Burroughs, "we received word that the Soldiers of Islam had contacted CNN's affiliate station and provided them with a disc of Cardinal Bertini's execution. We immediately issued a warrant to get the disc into our possession, but not before the station had broadcast snippets of the video on the air. By now it's gone viral throughout the world." He turned to Alan Thornton. "Damage assessment?"

Thornton glanced briefly at the contents of a single sheet of paper in front of him. "According to *Aljazeera*, terrorist groups in the Middle East are targeting foreign nationals in homage to the Soldiers of Islam. The CIA is picking up messages from chat rooms of potential plots to kidnap foreign dignitaries aligned with the United States and its allies. There are reports of hate crimes being perpetrated against Arab citizens throughout this nation. And predominantly Catholic nations, especially those in Europe and South America, are burning you in effigy, Mr. President, for allowing this to happen."

President Burroughs sighed. "Has the disc provided us with anything we can use? Anything at all?"

Attorney General Dean Hamilton offered what he knew. "The

executioner on the tape called himself Abdul-Aliyy, which is a pseudonym. We already know the names of the six remaining Soldiers of Islam, and Abdul-Aliyy is not one of them. In fact, Abdul-Aliyy in Arabic means 'Server of the Most High.'"

"A religious moniker that would motivate the Arab world into a frenzy, since they've captured the so-called apostle to the Great Satan," stated the president.

"Exactly, sir."

"Calling himself Abdul-Aliyy indicates that the disc may have been made before the media exposing their identities," added the president. "They obviously couldn't doctor the disc at that point because they had already committed the execution. But why provide a false name if the world already knows who you are?"

"For martyrdom," said Shari. "In Arab culture religion is everything. By giving themselves a moniker such as Abdul-Aliyy, they're anointing themselves as martyrs. In the Arab world, martyrs are heroic fighters of Allah who are promised eternal heaven. This we all know. But from a practical standpoint, it also incites the Arab public into a zealous passion cultivated by a millennium of religious beliefs."

The president rubbed the fatigue from his eyes. "What else have we got?"

Hamilton spoke. "Part of the message is in fluent Arabic. And, of course, there are the demands."

President Burroughs closed his eyes once again; his tension headache was coming on like a bull. Hamilton continued his summation of the disc, citing the demands. All occupation by American and Allied forces was to cease immediately. All Arab prisoners held by the occupying forces were to be released. And Israel was to be removed from Arab soil.

"They're not asking for much, are they?" the vice president offered sarcastically. "And I'm sure Israel will just get up and leave in a heartbeat."

"They know we can't meet their demands," said the president.

"What about the disc itself?" asked Bohlmer. The vice president leaned forward. "Has anything been determined from the background noise? Or perhaps the visual background itself?"

"The lab is still working on it, sir. But right now—"

"But right now, we have nothing," the president interrupted.

"All we can do, Mr. President, is beef up law enforcement in this area to keep them from slipping in and out like they did last night."

"They won't follow up their actions with a repeat performance," said Shari. "What they did last night was in return for showing the world their identities. The term here is point-counterpoint. Even though we tagged them, they still came into our front yard and placed the cardinal right on our doorstep. They're showing the world that they're still in control. And now that they've achieved their objective, they know the net will tighten. They'll be much more careful next time."

The president slapped an open palm against the tabletop. "There will *be* no next time, people, which means I want answers! Not guesses!" He released a frustrated sigh before regaining composure. "What I want to hear," he said evenly, "what I want to know, is what we're doing to find these people."

"Mr. President, if I may," said Attorney General Hamilton. "As Mr. Johnston already pointed out, we are examining the disc further. However, given that the images seem to show a background consistent with an abandoned building, we've engaged the services of county and state law enforcement to search all vacant buildings within a hundred-mile radius."

"That may take forever," the president commented.

"Yes, sir, but we have nothing else to go on."

The president's headache came on like a migraine, causing the man to wince. "Ms. Cohen, you know these people and their culture. What do you expect to happen next?"

Shari held nothing back. "I expect, Mr. President, that they will kill a member of the papal entourage."

"Not the pope?"

"No, sir. I believe the Soldiers of Islam are trying to build momentum. They want to push this country, if not the world, into a state of panic. Their dominance is fostering pride within Arab nations who are uniting against a common enemy, which happens to be the most powerful nation on Earth. They are, Mr. President, trying to create their sense of invincibility."

The president had never felt so impotent. "May God forgive

135

me, but I don't know what to do at this point." He turned to Thornton. "Al?"

Thornton shook his head. "For the moment, Mr. President, you need to address the world and tell them what they want to hear."

"What? That the pope is going to die unless we get a break?"

"No, sir. You need to tell the world in an official statement that we are working with the nations of the world in a unified effort to secure the release of the pontiff."

"They already know that!"

"Yes, sir, but the world needs to be reassured that every possible effort is being made."

"I agree," said the vice president. "Right, wrong, or indifferent, Jim, we need to show the world that we're still a pillar of strength."

The president turned to Shari. "Ms. Cohen?"

"Right now, the Soldiers of Islam have the upper hand. But the image we project to the world must be one of confidence and unity."

The president chewed his lower lip. "How long do you think I can play this game, Ms. Cohen, until the international community figures out our strategy?"

"As long as it takes to buy us some time."

"Does that mean you're confident in your ability to find this cell?"

"It means, Mr. President, I need time to look deeper into the matter." The president remained silent. The whole room was silent.

"Ms. Cohen, we're running out of time, and the world is running out of patience. What can you tell me that would be fact rather than conjecture?"

"I can safely say, Mr. President, that there'll be more executions before we get a handle on this."

It was not what the president wanted to hear. "Have the staff draw up a positive news release," he said. "And let's hope the world buys it hook, line and sinker. And . . . Ms. Cohen?"

"Yes, Mr. President."

"Your expertise in this matter hasn't impressed me much, thus far. I need facts."

"Yes, sir, I'm working on it."

He leaned forward. "Work faster."

CHAPTER THIRTY-THREE

There are options in every situation. Since Shari had not agreed to an all-out alliance with the Vatican Knights, and the timeframe to secure the pope's well-being was becoming increasingly limited, Kimball opted to appropriate information from Agent Cohen.

Pertinent information took time to gather and analyze, and not a moment was to be wasted.

Inside the vault beneath the archdiocese, Kimball Hayden aided Leviticus in sorting through the electronic gadgetry required to maintain surveillance on Shari Cohen. Although Kimball had the skills to set up shop, Leviticus was the expert in computer and electronic surveillance.

Leviticus meticulously studied every component necessary to capture relevant data. First, he chose a Keystroke Logger program, a sequencer that records passwords with every stroke of the finger upon the PC they wanted to breach.

Next was a laptop computer, a Plexiglas parabola dish, a receiver, wireless headsets, several audio bugs the size of dimes, and a mini-thermal imaging camera.

He mentally ticked off the items and shot a thumbs-up to Kimball. "I think we have everything we need," he told him.

"How long to get in and out?"

"The camera and dish can be set up inside the mobile unit. The bugs will have to be placed in the high-traffic areas of her residence and the phones. You can do that. But to download the software—" He cut himself off, his mind calculating. "It all depends on the speed of her computer, not to mention the time I'll need to disable any detection ware she may have."

Too long. "You have fifteen minutes."

Leviticus wasn't sure of the targeted computer's specs, or

whether it could download the program that quickly. "I can't force this, Kimball. It'll depend on how cooperative her computer is."

Kimball stared at the wild tangle of gadgetry on the table. "Do what you can," he said. "We'll need to be in and out of there quickly."

Leviticus nodded in agreement and gathered the equipment. Kimball's option was about to be initiated.

#

Washington, D.C.
September 25, Early Afternoon

Shari fumed. She understood the president's frustration since he was the one under international scrutiny, but to humiliate her in front of everyone in that room was wrong. Given what little she had to go on, she was doing her best.

Her anger subsided as she turned her Lexus onto International Drive, the street where Israel's largest embassy in the world was located.

After showing her credentials to the guard at the gate, she was detained until every facet of her identity could be confirmed through the international data banks. Once done, she was finally waved through.

When she entered the embassy, she was amazed by the immensity of the building's rotunda. The ceiling was several stories tall with tiers of floors visible from the foyer. Alongside the information booth, a massive directory was anchored to a black onyx wall. The directory stretched almost twenty-five feet in length. Shari traced her finger along the wall's directory until she came to *Defense & Armed Forces Attaché*. The first name listed was that of A. Obadiah, in Suite 312.

After taking a crowded elevator to the third floor, she got out and made her way to an open reception area. Sitting behind a semi-circular Lucite desk, a receptionist with a well-cultivated smile greeted her.

"May I help you?"

Shari flipped open her wallet containing her credentials. "I'm Special Agent Cohen of the FBI. I called yesterday asking to speak with Mr. Obadiah the moment he returned from his trip."

The receptionist nodded her recollection. "Yes, of course, I remember. He did receive your message because I gave it to him personally, along with his other messages. Is he expecting you?"

"Actually, he never returned the call."

The receptionist's plastic smile evaporated from her overly cosmetic face. "Well, that's probably because he's very busy."

"I'm sure. But could you please ask him if I can have a moment of his time? It's important. I promise it won't take too long."

"I'll let him know you're here," she stated.

After dialing Obadiah's extension, the receptionist spoke into the lip mic, then informed Shari that Mr. Obadiah was on his way to greet her.

In less than a minute, Abraham Obadiah entered the reception area wearing a smile that appeared genuine and pleasant. The contrast between his pale complexion and raven dark hair gave him a vampiric quality, which made his lips appear redder than they were. Beneath his chin was a horrible pink scar in the shape of a wedge.

"Agent Cohen," he said. "It's a pleasure to meet you."

With a gesture of his hand, Team Leader directed Shari to his office.

#

The Residence of Shari Cohen
Washington, D.C.

Leviticus was not only quick but meticulous. He had placed the Keystroke Logger program within Shari's PC to obtain addresses and information, which would enable him to hack into every database she visited. Hopefully, enough data could be gleaned to provide them with some solid leads.

While Leviticus downloaded the program, Kimball was employing the audio bugs in high-traffic areas when he came upon a curio cabinet that exhibited nothing but framed photos. In one shot Shari was alone and smiling and beautiful. In another, she posed for a family portrait with her husband and kids, but the smile appeared false, a mere gesture for the camera. Other photos showed snippets of time captured mostly when they were on vacation: at Disneyland, at Sea World, at Lion Country Safari. Another photo stood off to one side as if in homage.

The photo showed an older woman whose face had seen harsher times. Kimball knew the look well. He had seen it many times in Third World countries where innocent people often fell prey to the cruelest brutalities. But what this woman had witnessed must have been something beyond human comprehension. It was written all over her face. Yet there was a toughness about her, a sign of unfeigned courage. And Kimball had seen the same thing in Shari's picture, a certain strength imbued with beauty.

He opened the door to the cabinet and traced a gloved finger around the edges of Shari's photo. Her smile was dazzling, her teeth pure white, and her almond-shaped eyes gave her a truly exotic appearance. Underneath it all, he could see the strength handed down to her by the old woman. They were both magnificent.

Then to Leviticus, "How much longer?"

Leviticus never pulled his eyes away from the monitor. "Almost there," he said. "I'm running a scan to see if everything's doing what it should be."

Once everything was in place, the hardware tested and the computer downloading the program faster than anticipated, Leviticus shot a thumbs-up. Everything seemed to be in order.

Whatever information Shari Cohen possessed would soon be acquired through cyberspace. But Kimball knew this was an absolute long shot, and so did Leviticus.

Once the location was sanitized, they left the premises as quickly and quietly as they had entered.

#

Abraham Obadiah spoke with a thick accent. "I apologize for not getting to you earlier," he said. "But I've been busy . . . Just getting back and all."

"Of course."

"I understand you wanted to see me regarding the pope, yes?"

"I do." She reached into her purse, pulled out the disc, and held it up in plain view. "As you know we're working with several intelligence agencies throughout the world regarding the pope's kidnapping. And Mossad sent us information regarding the eight members of the Soldiers of Islam."

"And I do hope you found what you were looking for."

"To a degree," she said, placing the disc on the desktop. "So why come to me?"

"Well, for one thing, your name is on that disc."

Obadiah's features remained neutral as he unknowingly traced a fingertip across the scar at the base of his chin. "I was the one who created the data?"

"Your signature is on the disc, yes."

He shrugged and flipped his hands into the air, as he spoke. "It's possible," he said. "And you say Mossad sent you this information?"

"Yes, sir."

"Well, that's simply because all agencies in Israel work in collusion with one another. Information gathered is accumulated into a single informational body. And, of course, data from Mossad is often shared with the Attaché."

"I understand that, but my question is: why would Mossad send encrypted data on low-level documents such as biographical histories, knowing that valuable time is being wasted trying to decode encryptions that our equipment can only fractionalize?"

"You'd have to ask Mossad."

"But it's your name that's attached to the encryptions. I thought maybe you could help me break this down."

Obadiah looked steadily at Shari. His finger continued to stroke the scar on his chin.

"Mossad sent you information that was attached to the body of text regarding the Soldiers of Islam, but not specifically related to it," he said. "The reason why it's encrypted is that the non-related issues hold no value for you or your investigation. Only for Mossad. Therefore, Mossad makes decipherable only the information your agency asks to see."

"But why would Mossad attach such data to the body of information regarding the Soldiers of Islam, if the data itself is not related to the topic? That doesn't make sense."

Obadiah was losing patience. She was pressing him, and hard.

"The encryptions are somewhat similar to your Freedom of Information Act, which, if I may candidly say, is a joke since more than ninety-five percent of your government's documents are redacted, leaving the balance of the information useless." Obadiah set his eyes on the disc. "The encryptions work on the same principle."

"Then it does have something to do with the Soldiers of Islam. Something you wanted to be redacted." She leaned forward. "Mr. Obadiah, we're talking about three pages of encryptions here. I need you to tell me what's on those pages."

His black eyes snapped on her, then back to the disc. "Those three pages contain nothing regarding the Soldiers of Islam. That is the truth."

"Then what does it contain?"

"Information that is not for your eyes, so if I may have the disc—" He reached for it, but her arm reacted with the quickness of a serpent's strike, as she snatched it from the desktop.

Obadiah shook his head in response, thinking her action to be juvenile. Then coldly, he said, "That information is the property of the Israeli government."

"That was given freely to the American government."

After a slight hesitation, he waved his hands at her. "No matter," he said. "The data cannot be decoded by your software, as you have already stated."

She placed the disc in her purse, hardly believing the turn in the conversation. One moment he was congenial, the next he was distant and uncooperative. "You still want to be evasive as to what's on this disc, Mr. Obadiah?"

"As a representative of the Israeli government, I'll file a grievance with your government if you wish to pursue this further. We gave you the requested data regarding the Soldiers of Islam in good faith. And now you wish to hold us accountable for the part of the informational body that, as I have already expressed to you, has nothing to do with the terrorist regime."

"Mr. Obadiah, we both know you're being evasive for a reason. What that reason is, I don't know. But I'm going to find out. If you wish to file a grievance, then do so."

Obadiah didn't move from his chair as Shari stood. "I'll see myself out, thank you."

The man had no intention of showing her the way out but added one last comment. "I will get that disc, Ms. Cohen."

"That's between you and my government. So have fun with your grievance."

As she was leaving, Team Leader once again traced the tip of his finger across the blemish of his scar.

He now had a thorn to contend with.

CHAPTER THIRTY-FOUR

Shari was frustrated beyond belief. Her meeting with Abraham Obadiah didn't go as planned. And she was no closer to decoding the disc than when she first received it.

As she left the building, she examined the disc and let out a guttural moan of annoyance that drew the attention of those within ten feet of her. After picking up her weapon from the gatekeeper armory, she drove back to the JEH Building and parked the car. For a moment she fought back tears, overwhelmed with frustration. When she finally gained her composure, she grabbed her purse, got out of the car, and made her way to the elevator.

After speaking with Obadiah, Shari felt uncertain of the affinity between Mossad and the American government. With Mossad being the proxy eyes and ears of American espionage in the Middle East, Obadiah could have enough pull to reclaim the disc. In case she did have to turn over the original, she had to secure the backup disc.

Obadiah may get one disc, but not both. Shari was determined not to relinquish the data unless a direct order from the Chief Commander required her to surrender all forms of data contained on the disc, for the sake of political camaraderie.

Before heading to her desk, Shari went to the vault and quickly punched in her PIN code. When the bolts pulled back and the door opened, she zeroed in on the correct aisle and shelf and retrieved the backup CD.

The jewel case felt good in her hands; the disc shined like a newly minted coin. Even if Obadiah filed a grievance, she still had this.

When she returned to her desk, she immediately loaded the disc. What came up on the monitor caused her heart to hitch in her chest.

The data was gone.

"No, no, no . . ." She tapped furiously on the keyboard, trying to pull something up, anything. And then the realization set in that the disc held no data to recover. It was simply blank. The disc might have been improperly burned, but she highly doubted that. And with these discs bearing embedded codes that cannot be duplicated, she was down to the original disc, which she would somehow have to safeguard before it ended up being appropriated.

Apparently, Abraham Obadiah's influence ran deep within the American government, she thought. He was capable of getting results, and quickly.

More than ever, Shari was suspect.

For a long time, she sat staring at the blank screen, stewing over the possibility that the American government was involved in a cover-up.

#

Embassy of Israel, Washington, D.C.
September 25, Mid-Afternoon

Abraham Obadiah sat in the embassy's conference room with the captains of industry from Russia, Venezuela, and Israel. Under normal circumstances, collaboration amongst this group at one time would have been geopolitically impossible.

But given the current political shift in the landscape with ISIS standing as a common threat to all, Russia had been warming up to Israel. Over the past few months, Netanyahu had met with Putin on four different occasions, which was drawing the rank and ire of the United States that was creating a marginal divide between the nations. But Syria had become the link that brought on the thawing between Russia and Israel since both countries had active military operations going on in the war-torn country. ISIS was being pushed out of Iraq, Syria, and Lebanon, the terrorist forces were moving south to the Jordanian and Israeli borders. But the real interest lay with Israel wanting to maintain control of the Golan Heights, and stronger ties with Putin only strengthened Netanyahu's hand, should Israel seek international recognition of its control over the region. In turn, which played into Putin's hands, was that the region allowed Russia a major foothold in the Middle East, whereas the foothold of the United States diminished since the gravitation of Israel toward the Kremlin was strictly one of strategy, and visa-versa, on the part of Russia. The political landscape was shifting dramatically. And with change came opportunity. And in this case: oil—the most precious of all commodities.

The conference room was designed to be impervious to information appropriation, devoid of any listening devices.

There were three representatives from Russia, two from Venezuela, and four from Israel. All held the air of self-importance.

"Gentlemen, please, the news is good," said Obadiah. "We're on track with the cause and everything is running smoothly."

Vladimir Ostrosky, a reigning member of the Russian Parliament, examined Obadiah with studious eyes and tried to penetrate his veneer. He found the man enigmatic and difficult to read. "According to our sources," Ostrosky said, "that is not entirely true."

"Really? And what exactly are your sources telling you?"

Ostrosky leaned forward and placed his elbows on the table. Slowly and deliberately, he clasped his hands and interlocked his fingers. "I'm told, Mr. Obadiah, that a certain agent from the FBI is looking into corners where *she* should not be looking."

Obadiah nodded in affirmation. "There's no reason to concern yourselves with Ms. Cohen," he stated. "She will be dealt with, and the problem will be quashed."

"If I may ask, how so?" This came from Hector Guerra of Venezuela, a man of doughy features, and a pencil-thin mustache that complemented a set of equally thin lips. His collar was so tight around his neck that folds of flesh curled over its edges.

Obadiah hesitated, seeking a politically correct response that would allay these inquisitive concerns. Apparently the Russian and Venezuelan sources were quick and accurate. And these men were well-armed with damaging information.

"Ms. Cohen is indeed looking beyond the box," said Obadiah. "But that's her job."

"That doesn't answer my question," Guerra insisted.

"Let me finish," Obadiah said, raising a hand and patting the air. "I assure you; I assure all of you, that Ms. Cohen will be factored out of the equation by the American principals. Yahweh has an expressed interest regarding this situation as everyone else at this table."

"And what about the disc?"

Obadiah was startled by this question but tried not to show it. Apparently, their sources produced as well and as quickly as Mossad, who was the best in the business. To know about the disc was impressive. "We'll have the disc in our possession soon enough," he said.

"And the copies?"

"There are no copies. Our people at the CIA intercepted all incoming data from the Mossad leak and destroyed it. And the leaks themselves have been dispatched. The backup copy within the vault of the FBI has also been destroyed. The only disc in existence is the one Ms. Cohen possesses."

Ostrosky measured Obadiah with eyes so black they appeared as though they were without pupils.

"Gentlemen, please relax," said Obadiah. "Everything I tell you is the truth. Within a year there will be no more economic hardships for our countries and no more dependency upon Arab states. When this is over China, India and Brazil will become dependent on *our* products, rather than grow dependent on the Middle East. Our industries will flourish and enjoy the full support of the international community."

"And Yahweh?"

Obadiah considered his words carefully before speaking. "Right now, the Middle East is on fire with chaos and extremism. Syria is of strategic value to Russia, everyone knows this. And al-Assad is their puppet leader. The United States and its allies continue to follow the accords of Saudi Arabia knowing that they were instrumental in nine-eleven, which tells me that the United States is so dependent on Arab oil, they're willing to turn a blind eye with a forgive-and-forget attitude, which has drawn condemnation from those in the U.S. Congress and the House. Certain political principals want to change this, however. Especially Yahweh. The opportunity is here, gentleman. It's not about when this may or may not turn into a global war. But if it does, then changes would already have been made by a new coalition. By us. The one thing we all share as a necessity in today's world is oil. Situations in the Middle East are getting worse. The president of the United States is getting narratives from their intel community telling him that they're winning a war against terrorism when they're anything but. And since alternative fuels are several years away, then we need to act now for the future security of our economies. By controlling the oil-rich fields throughout the Middle East, should conditions worsen, and global war seems inevitable . . . we would hold the scepter of rule."

Ostrosky leaned back in his chair. "And you can guarantee our anonymity?"

"Yes, of course."

"That's good," said Ostrosky, "because I would hate for history to remember me as a monster, rather than a prophet of a better future."

"The pope's death will not be tied to any man in this room. I assure you."

"You better, Mr. Obadiah, because our political reputations, if not our lives, would be in jeopardy, should the truth of our participation in this matter became known."

"I agree."

"If that disc is worth the life of the woman who possesses it," said Ostrosky, "then it must hold damaging evidence against us." Suddenly, his brows dipped sharply over the bridge of his nose to punctuate his point. "You must not fail to repossess that disc before she has a chance to turn her battle into a crusade."

"Trust me," Obadiah said. "Ms. Cohen will never get that opportunity."

"Make sure that she doesn't."

Hector Guerra reclined in his seat. "There is also the matter of a Venezuelan leader who is quite anti-American. Bringing him into the circle may be difficult."

Obadiah was quick to respond. "Our Russian constituency has a strong relationship with Venezuelan leaders. They'll foster a relationship between these two nations once Burrough's term as president is over. The new president will be open to dialogue once Burroughs vacates his position. Right now, the president is being stage-managed to act according to the conditions provided him. His rank in the polls will weaken, killing his chance at a second term. Eventually, one of our choosing will take his place."

The Venezuelan nodded.

"Let's just say that everything has been examined from every possible angle," said Obadiah. "Any more questions?"

There were none.

CHAPTER THIRTY-FIVE

Washington, D.C.
September 25, Early Evening

The last trails of light from the sun's downward trajectory became magenta twilight. It was a magnificent view of an artist's canvas. But Shari didn't notice the beauty of the colors painting the heavens as she made her way home. Her eyes were focused elsewhere beyond the road, her movements to steer the car in the right direction governed by reflex and habit alone since she had driven the same course for years.

Since her meeting with Abraham Obadiah, she made constant calls to Mossad and got nowhere. She even went as far as to talk to the Director of Mossad, who was no different than Abraham Obadiah, which ended up being another stone wall for the fact that he denied everything.

For the first time in her life, she felt like she was spiraling downward into an abyss that held nothing but despair beyond what she was feeling now. The actual mindset of 'not knowing' terrified her.

As soon as she turned into her neighborhood, her eyes focused when she spotted her brownstone. After turning into the garage, she knew that she should regroup and train her thoughts on her family. But she found it impossible. So, she sat there with her mind working to the point where her thoughts felt like a drunken stupor, that sense of feeling utterly incoherent.

As brilliant as she was, Shari Cohen stood by herself in a political nightmare.

And for a moment, she delved into self-pity.

In her mind's eye, she could see her grandmother's hardened face that was much older than her given years. Yet her voice was strong and gentle and carried the weight of her courage and resolve. It was a voice recalling a moment when the sky over Auschwitz rained ashes for days on end—the buildings and camp becoming laden with gray soot, the image somewhat ghostly and pale, her demeanor somber and cold. And, of course, there was the repugnant odor of burning flesh, which no one dared to speak of. Yet she never became hollow, always propelling herself mentally and believing that willpower shall overcome the abhorrence of those who cruelly bound her. In the end, she was right.

Shari closed her eyes and pulled deep with her nostrils, taking a lungful of air to soothe her, then released the air with an equally long sigh. She had no right to feel dismayed when her grandmother had suffered through much greater. So, she admonished herself quietly and thanked her grandmother for all the stories that held lessons to draw from in moments like this.

Thank you, Grandmamma. I won't give up no matter how difficult things may seem.

Reaching for the key in the ignition, she saw the crumpled business card in the ashtray. Grabbing the card and unfolding it, she smoothed out the creases. It was just a simple business card with no fancy fonts or styles, just a sophomoric typeface with the phone number of the archdiocese. She brought the card to her brow as if she might glean something from it through osmosis and tried to recall the man who gave it to her. For a brief moment, she struggled for clarity. Then it came to her: Kimball Hayden, a name from the past she had heard before only in whispers, forgotten until now.

Approximately six years ago as an upstart in the counterterrorism program, Shari was in the company of men who didn't realize her presence, only until after the name of Kimball Hayden was spoken with a measure of reverence and referred to as "a man who was as deadly as he was without conscience." When the then-attorney general and top-ranking officials from the Joint Chiefs became aware of her presence, they immediately drew upon another topic. But Shari had already taken in snippets of conversation that had already painted Kimball Hayden as a brutal killing machine.

She placed the card back into the ashtray. This man professing to be an agent of the Vatican couldn't have been the *same* Kimball Hayden. The man spoken about within the White House corridors regarded him as a soulless killer.

With the thoughts of Kimball Hayden ebbing, she decided to research data on the disc and scrape together whatever information she could. At best, she might open a gate that would lead her on the right path. At worst, she would resign herself to the fact that there was nothing she could do to save the life of the pope. It was a crapshoot.

After making the rounds with the children and sharing an awkward moment with her husband by shying away at the notion of joining him in bed, Shari sheltered herself at the workstation in the den area and booted her PC. Within moments the screen came alive with the dossiers and, while fighting a battle against weighted fatigue, probed every page until she finally nodded off into a deep sleep.

#

Washington D.C.
September 26. Late Evening

At 10:39 p.m., Yahweh received the call in his study. Outside, the moon was in its gibbous phase, which cast an eerie glow upon the earth that was the color of whey. It was the only light granted as he sat silhouetted in front of the window that overlooked the grounds. As the phone rang his mind was drifting, thinking of nothing in particular when he slowly reached for the phone and lifted the receiver. "Yes."

"It's Obadiah."

Yahweh's state of mind was firm and settled, almost without emotion when he spoke. "Yes, Mr. Obadiah, what do you want at so late an hour?"

"I've been trying to reach you all day."

"You know that I am a man of position. And the situation with the pope is taking up a majority of my time."

"We seem to have a problem."

"Which would be?"

"A lady by the name of Shari Cohen," he said.

Yahweh remained quiet.

"I'll come directly to the point," said Obadiah. "It appears that Ms. Cohen has some rather delicate information that could prove catastrophic if she's able to make the proper ties. And our associates supporting the cause are not too happy with that situation."

"The proper ties with what?"

"Apparently, Mossad sent the United States Government an attachment of encrypted pages holding something of value connected to the project."

Yahweh's attention was fully captured. "I'm listening?"

"The pages hold the graphics that could tie a lot of people involved with the cause, including prominent members in the United States, Russia, Israel, and Venezuela. It was never meant to be seen outside of the Defense and Armed Forces Attaché, and the Mossad Director."

"Really? Then why is it in the possession of Ms. Cohen?"

"It was passed through the channels without the knowledge of the Director or the Attaché. It seems that American sleepers within the Lohamah Psichlogit and the Research Department obtained and forwarded the information to the FBI."

After feeling his neckline prickle with heat, Yahweh undid the top button of his shirt. "What exactly is in the encryption?"

"Diagrams," he answered, "and some photos. But if a connection between the attached diagrams and the biographical histories of the terrorists are made, then the matter could open up a Pandora's Box."

Yahweh wanted to strangle something, anything—*where the hell is the cat!* "We need that disc back," he finally said. "And I think we both know what needs to be done, Mr. Obadiah. I want you to contact Judas immediately and have him direct Omega Team to dispatch Ms. Cohen *tonight* . . . and get that disc before it ends up in the hands of the NSA."

"I have no problem with that, but so you know, the encryptions contain embedded viruses. If anyone outside of Mossad or the Attaché tries to decipher the code without having the proper knowledge to do so, then as a safeguard the viruses will ignite and completely wipe out the file, histories, and all."

Yahweh closed his eyes and slowly dropped his head into his hand. "I don't care what toys you put into the program, Mr. Obadiah. I just want you to put Ms. Cohen out of my misery."

"I understand."

"Do you, Mr. Obadiah? Do you really? Then understand this." Yahweh slammed the phone down as a measure of his discontent.

CHAPTER THIRTY-SIX

Washington Archdiocese, Washington D.C.
September 26. Late Evening

He had lain between the two mounds of sand with a hand on each mound, his eyes looking skyward for the face of God. In between the great distances of the stars, he tried to glimpse something celestial to make him believe there was something heavenly beyond the blind faith that had led men to believe an existence beyond this one. But all he saw was the glimmer of stars shimmering like a cache of diamonds on black velvet.

Beneath his hands, the soil began to undulate, the tenants below trying to force their way to the surface. Applying great strength through his massive arms, Kimball Hayden employed himself to keep them below the depths of the land. But, as always, he failed. When their heads broke through the layers of sand, Kimball tried to force them down, but their strength was far greater than his. Their faces, remarkably similar to his own in shape and contour and with eyes the color of ice, held the mottled skin tones in the putrescent hues and shades of decay.

Crying out against the surge, Kimball exerted all the power he could muster. But the figures continued to rise, the jaws of his rotting semblances opening to impossible lengths to reveal darkness deep inside the throat that was blacker than black.

Kimball always woke at this juncture to search his surroundings for the reality of the moment. Once calm settled and the moment became less surreal, he would always ask these questions: *Will You ever forgive me, Lord? Could You ever forgive me?* But Kimball believed that true forgiveness would always elude him for the

154

fact that he had given up one war to wage another against his personal demons. And these demons would never let him forget, coming night after night to erode what little hope he had of someday being free of a past laden with bloodshed.

It would take him almost twenty minutes to shake off the images, and another ten before he could commit himself to his duties.

Kimball sat in the van outside the Cohen brownstone, with Isaiah in the back monitoring the audio receiver and listening to every movement within the Cohen household.

As Kimball sat there, he wondered why Isaiah's faith was so firmly entrenched when his life was one of hardcore misery.

Isaiah, whose true name was Christian, had been born in 1984 to a family who lived in makeshift huts of discarded wood and corrugated tin roofs in a Mexican shantytown. Dung piles and rancid water drew mangy curs and blowflies. And as time went on and the world of his family became a constant state of suffering, they held on to the only possession they had, which was their faith in Jesus.

After Christian's father succumbed to the ravages of dysentery and wasted away until his body withdrew into itself, the rack of his ribs threatening to burst through his flesh, he was buried with little ceremony in a scratch of dirt marked for the dead, not too far from the dung heaps. The stark-white crosses, too numerous to count, seemed to saddle the small stretch of land. But after six months, and as the land dwindled, the family had to pay homage from a distance, since additional grave markers took over the trails leading to his father's burial site.

As Christian and his faith grew, he never questioned his abject poverty, but accepted it as a test of diversity to achieve a higher level. But when his mother was taken from him—her body found in a muddy waterway with her skirt hiked up to reveal unspeakable violations—he became lost and frightened and sought union with anybody who would have him.

He found himself alone and unwanted, another mouth to feed in an already famished world. So, he migrated north through hot winds and unforgiving sun, his mind often falling into delirious bouts of fog and images.

Sometimes he imagined the worried faces of his parents, as they beckoned him with ghostly hands to follow a certain path. But when his body could push no more, with the environment sapping him dry, he surrendered to the elements and took to the earth.

Two days later when he awoke, he knew he was in heaven. The angels surrounding him were smiling and wore habits. Around their necks, they wore chains bearing the symbol of the Catholic Cross that was as gold and as bright as an emblazoned sun that had sapped him. When Christian sat up with his eyes darting about in search of his parents who had led him to this wondrous place that smelled of clove and burning candle wax, they were not to be found.

"You'll be fine, my child. You were lucky that a missionary found you," said one of the angels. Her face was aged and tanned; her eyes sparkled with alertness. "You came from such a long way, so God must have something special in store for you."

"Where are my parents?" he asked, with the pitch of his tone that of a pubescent child.

"I'm afraid you are alone."

Christian shook his head vehemently. "I saw them. They showed me the way."

But when his mind sobered to the reality of his ordeal, he came to realize that his parents were truly gone, and God had used them as mere vessels to save his life.

As he grew to manhood during his tenure at the mission, the boy's body took on an athletic tone. His hunger for knowledge had become as urgent as his need for sustenance. This caught the eye of a stranger who came from a faraway land called the Vatican. After holding counsel with the heads of the mission, this stranger recruited the boy. His name was Cardinal Bonasero Vessucci.

Christian, upon learning his fate, cried and refused to leave the only true slice of heaven he had ever known. "To do this is a great honor," said Father Hernandez, who held the boy in the clutches of a strong embrace. Even the Father was choking back tears. "On the day you came to us we always knew that God had a purpose for you. And now that time has come, my son. You must go with the cardinal who is the messenger of God and fulfill your destiny. You *are* special."

Christian left the mission behind never to see or hear from the angels again.

Now, at such an early hour, Christian—Isaiah—was on the front lines of the most important and noble battle of his life.

He was a Vatican Knight.

So, Kimball watched him, wanting so desperately to know how Christian found faith in such hardship when Kimball held little after growing up in a life of privilege. Reason would indicate that it should have been the other way around—that those of good standing would have faith and be thankful for their bounties, whereas the disadvantaged would hold none.

But Isaiah was lost in his world, listening through his headphones and hearing what sounded like the slight passing of air through a seashell.

#

Leviticus was at the archdiocese working at the computer terminal. Highly adept at his craft, he also had the capabilities to tap and hack into programs and networks to obtain information without leaving a trail.

After downloading the Keystroke Logger, he moved his fingers across the keyboard and began to draw data from Shari Cohen's PC. By logging the sequence of her keystrokes that allowed her access to certain sites, Leviticus was able to obtain her password that afforded him entry into restricted areas of information.

Numbers and symbols relating to computer vernacular came and went as the PC communicated to other networks along the information highway and pulled data from files established in IP address records but left a bogus trail in its wake. By the time the hacked parties learned of the breach, the trail would lead the tracking experts through cyberspace to a desktop computer located in a library at a prestigious California college. It was a wonderful red herring on the part of Leviticus, which was also a part of the game he enjoyed too much, almost impishly so.

After establishing the link to Shari's PC, he realized she was live with booted information regarding the Soldiers of Islam. And with all the ingenuity of a practiced hacker, he downloaded the data.

But it was coming in much too slow.

CHAPTER THIRTY-SEVEN

Along with Omega Team, Judas stood in the shadows provided by the gathering of trees in the park across from the Cohen's brownstone. Each man was dressed in tactical gear except for Judas, who wore a wide-brimmed fedora and long coat. The tails of his jacket moved slightly with the course of a faint breeze.

Judas turned to Dark Lord, the lead for the three-man unit of Omega Team. The commando appeared without emotion, a killing machine willing and waiting to act without question or reservation.

"You know your duties," said Judas. "There will be no firearms because I don't want you going in there like a bunch of ball-swinging commandos making a bunch of noise. Ready up with blades and kill everyone across the board starting with Cohen. Get in, *get* that disc, and get out within a window of three minutes. One-two-three—just like that. Now go."

#

Kimball saw movement, a mere motion from the outermost range of his peripheral vision. At first, it was brief, then nothing, then movement once again as the living shadows stayed close to the darkness, as they made their way to the brownstone. From his point of view, he saw only two, but his mindset knew there were more. After telling Isaiah to stay behind and to maintain a watch for possible insurgents, Kimball was out of the van and sliding toward the brownstone as quietly as the shifting shapes around him.

#

It had taken Dark Lord a moment to work his way into the Cohen residence. As he moved soundlessly across the room, he withdrew his knife from its sheath and used the point of the blade to push the door open enough to catch Shari asleep at the desk with pages of encrypted code on the monitor. *It really can't be this simple,* he considered. *It just can't be.* Dark Lord seemed almost contrite in his thinking because of the lack of opposition, especially from the likes of Shari Cohen, who was held in such high regard by the political elders.

Slowly, and prudently, he entered the den with the knife at the ready. And with the stealth of a learned assassin, he moved in for the quick and silent kill.

He was about to grab her hair and force her head back to expose her open throat when Shari's husband ran into the den and slammed himself against the intruder's back, causing the knife to fall from Dark Lord's hand, then drove him to the floor. The surprised assassin immediately maneuvered to gain advantage and grabbed Gary's wrist. And with a simple flick of his hand, he snapped the twin bones in Gary's arm, causing white-hot agony to race along its length to his shoulder.

Not yet registering the magnitude of the danger, Shari snapped her eyes wide. But it wasn't until Gary's cry of absolute pain that she propelled herself into action. While both men gained their feet and battled for position in a drunken tango, Shari reached out and hit the assassin on the back of his head, only to receive a savage backhanded blow that sent her across the desk which knocked the PC to the floor, the impact smashing its outer casing.

In the heat of panic, she tried to get to her feet, failed, her sight woozy from the blow. Dark Lord thrust a left fist to Gary's abdomen, a stinging jab, and then a right cross to his chin. For a moment Gary seemed detached, the conscious mind suspended between darkness and light, and then his eyes rolled up into his sockets as he hit the floor in a boneless heap.

In an equally quick move, Dark Lord swept up the knife and exhibited the mirror polish of the blade and the sharpness of its tip. "It'll be painless," he told her, then he began his approach. "And just so you know, there are worse ways of dying than bleeding out."

Through the haze of Shari's sight, she saw that the assassin was not alone. Two shadows alongside him, each brandishing a knife to partake in the butchering.

Shari crawled to her husband and held him close as tears coursed down her cheeks. Then she thought of her children. "Please don't hurt my babies," she pleaded.

Dark Lord placed the knife blade within inches of her throat and smiled maliciously through the opening of his mask as if to indicate he was doing this for mere gratification. "First you, then the hubby, and then the kiddies. How's that?"

Weeping uncontrollably, Shari pulled an unconscious Gary close to her.

With a quick move, Dark Lord grabbed her hair and tilted her head back to expose the soft tissue of her throat.

Slowly and deliberately, he raised the blade for the final cut.

#

Washington, D.C.
September 27. Early Morning

Donning familiar and comfortable black fatigues, Abraham Obadiah changed his game face back to Team Leader, then drove northbound on Route 1 toward the Massachusetts border. The truck moved smoothly, though it hit the occasional pothole or divot, his trip for the most part went without incident.

At 0245, a coordinated effort was scheduled by Judas and Omega Team to assassinate Shari Cohen. Knowing Omega Team was always expert in their endeavors, Obadiah considered the matter closed and Agent Cohen no longer a part of the equation. The constituents from Russia and Venezuela would be happy to hear that damage control had succeeded and that Agent Cohen would no longer be a troublesome factor in the advancement of the cause.

Now that he had quelled the suspicions of his foreign liaisons, there would be no reason for Obadiah to return to D.C. until after the death of the pontiff. Within a few hours, he would assassinate a member of the papal council and remind the world that the list of people leading to the pope was getting shorter. And with every death, with every symbolic assassination of faith, came dwindling hope.

Believing Ms. Cohen was no longer among the living, Team Leader drove on.

#

Judas stood within the grove of trees with the collar of his jacket hiked against the cold, as the vapor of his breath indicated the chilliness of the night.

From the corner of his eye, he saw movement. A single man, larger than he had ever imagined a man could be, moved past him beyond the trees with all the grace of a feline—smooth, sleek, and with all the purpose to make a kill.

"Well, well, well," Judas whispered to himself. "Whose little boy are you?"

It had become obvious that Cohen was under surveillance from someone outside the circle. And then he realized he had no way to warn his team. No matter, he thought. It was still three against one.

#

Dark Lord held the knife blade at its highest point for the final downswing, a macabre display to incite paralytic terror. "This is for looking into places you shouldn't have," he said evenly. Just as the blade fell toward the openness of Shari's throat, Dark Lord and his two companions were sent sprawling across the room. The rear assault hit like a hammer blow as each man gained his feet at once with athletic grace and practiced agility and spun toward their attacker with their knives poised to kill.

A large man wearing blackface stood between the Cohens and Dark Lord's commandos. Around his neck, he wore the clerical collar of a priest, and his chest was protected by a black tactical vest that held the crested emblem of the silver Pattée.

The Omega Team did what was natural; they gathered inside of a refined area and converged on their target, this priest who was an unlikely savior.

But when Kimball went for his sidearm, Dark Lord lashed out with inconceivable speed and agility and brought his knife across in an arc, the blade connecting with the barrel of Kimball's Glock and knocking it from his grasp, the firearm hitting the floor and skating somewhere out of reach.

Dark Lord fell back in line and measured his quarry with a self-satisfied grin, the point of his blade forward. "That's the first time I ever saw someone come to a knife fight with a gun and lose," he said. "Now, that's pathetic, don't you think?"

Kimball's eyes held steady. "I don't need a gun to take you out." Dark Lord cocked his head. "Really?"

"Yeah. Really." In a slow and methodic move, Kimball reached down and undid the snaps of his KA-BAR sheaths with a flip of his thumb, first undoing the strap of the sheath on his left thigh, then the snap of the sheath on his right, and slowly withdrew his knives. In an act of distraction, he stirred one of the black-bladed knives in figure eights, a practice that kept the attention of his opponents from focusing on his second blade, the striking weapon.

Omega Team moved slowly into the danger zone, close enough to engage and to slash and to kill the priest already knowing when and where to strike.

Circling, Dark Lord studied his opponent and noted similarities of a man he once knew and coveted as a mentor—the build, the height, the breadth of the man's wide shoulders, all reminiscent of a hero in the judgment of the Pentagon brass. And then he looked into the man's cerulean blue eyes and the gold flecks that peppered the irises like glitter. For a brief moment his chest grew cold, the reality surreal and sobering at the same time. And then realization set in. There was only one man who held such remarkable eyes.

Dark Lord stopped his advancement. The other two followed as if attached by an umbilical tie.

"Kimball?" he said almost too softly. "Kimball Hayden?"

Kimball's eyes started a bit, a quick flash. Recognition came on his part as well. At one time he and Dark Lord had worked as close companions in covert operations.

"Word is . . . you're supposed to be dead." Dark Lord lowered the point of his knife, but not enough to appease Kimball, who kept his weapon at the ready. "So, what's this about?"

Kimball said nothing.

Dark Lord's lips curled visibly. "Is this about redemption? Damn. Kimball Hayden has gone religious. Look at that collar—my-my." Dark Lord's smile vanished as quickly as it had appeared. The tone of his voice quickly took on a measure of anger. "This isn't your fight, Kimball. Now get the hell out of the way before you get hurt by the big boys."

Kimball stepped closer, his attractor blade continuing to slice deliberate figure eights in the glow from Shari's still functioning computer screen on the floor.

Hesitation flickered in Dark Lord's eyes. "Don't do this," warned Kimball. "You know you're no match for me."

"Still the same old cocky son-of-a-bitch, aren't you, Hayden? Think your two blades can match our three? I don't think so."

Dark Lord inched closer; his actions matched by his two shadowy imitators. "Last time, Kimball. I won't tell you again. Get out of the way and let us do our job."

"I won't let you hurt these people."

"Then you're crazier than I thought." Dark Lord suddenly struck.

The commandos of Omega Team struck out and slashed with killing blows, but Kimball met their strikes with blinding speed, deflecting the knives, the contact coughing up sparks as the blades pounded against each other as metal struck metal. Shari's mouth dropped in amazement as she watched her champion ward off deadly blows with fluid effort.

With uncanny skill Kimball's motions became faster, his circular motions repelling the blows that seemed to come faster and with far more brutal force. By the inches, he pushed back the Omega Team who was losing ground, the strikes coming to the point where everyone's arm was moving in blurs and blinding revolutions. Sparks radiated in numerous pinpricks of flame before dying out. And then came an opening.

With surgical precision Kimball drove the edge of his blade across the bicep of a commando, severing the muscle. The man screamed in agony, took to a knee, then tumbled out of the battle line and was gone, disappearing into the hallway, and then into the night.

As the fight waged on Kimball seemed to pick up steam rather than lose it. His motions were deft and with purpose. The odds of two blades warring against two seemed to favor Kimball as he pushed his opponents back to the far wall. They were running out of room.

In another motion Kimball bent down to a lower point of gravity and made a horizontal slash just above the patella of the commando standing to the right of Dark Lord, nearly severing the muscle that attached the upper and lower leg. With a banshee-like wail, the commando moved surprisingly well on his good leg, dove through the study window, and landed on a parked car below. His weight caved in the roof and shattered the windshield; then, after rolling off the vehicle and getting to his feet, he half ran, half limped for the cover of trees.

#

Judas watched from the shadows across the street as a dark figure smashed through the second-story pane of the brownstone in a spray of glittering glass and landed on a parked car, caving in the roof and shattering the windshield. The man rolled off the vehicle, got to one foot, and hobbled toward the trees. Moments later Judas watched a second man run through the open front door of the brownstone holding his arm. The wounded commando crossed the street and merged into the shadows beneath the trees.

#

Dark Lord was backed against the wall, his will to complete the battle ingrained from years of tough mental training. To surrender would be a cowardly brand against his call-sign, and he would lose the respect from the powers that be.

"Put down the knife," said Kimball. "Not on your life."

"Then I'll make this a fair fight."

Without taking his eyes off Dark Lord, Kimball returned one of the knives into its sheath.

Dark Lord sized Kimball for an opening, circled, found what seemed to be an opportunity, and tried to cut the man with a sweeping horizontal arc across Kimball's abdomen before Kimball would realize that he had been gutted. But Kimball grabbed the attacker's wrist, forced the man's arm over his head to expose his armpit, and drove the sharpened point of his nine-inch blade deep into the unprotected area until the pommels of the knife could go no farther.

Staggering, Dark Lord reached for the weapon's hilt, gave minimal effort to withdraw the knife, found it impossible to do so, and fell to his knees coughing blood from a perforated lung. "I knew this day would come," he managed. "But I didn't think it would be by your hand." He fell on his side, his eyes taking on a detached gaze.

After dropping to a knee, Kimball pulled Dark Lord close to him.

"Why?" asked Kimball. "Why these people?"

Dark Lord's gaze shifted to the PC lying on the floor beside him and extended his hand. "For the truth," he said, and then he was gone, his hand falling to the floor as a blood bubble burst from the corner of his lips, his eyes then fixing on a point of no importance as he expelled his final breath.

In homage, Kimball traced his thumb across Dark Lord's forehead in the symbol of the cross. "May God be with you," he said, and then he laid the man's head gently to the floor.

"You knew him?" It sounded more like a statement rather than a question.

Without facing Shari, he answered her evenly. Yet there was a slight undercurrent of sorrow within his tone. "At one time," he answered. "A long time ago." After taking a deep breath through his nostrils, Kimball jerked the knife from Dark Lord's body and sheathed the weapon.

Shari's eyes took on the size of communion wafers. *Her children!* Kimball had seen the same look many times before, just before he killed his quarry. It was *the look* of absolute terror of not knowing the welfare of their loved ones. In this case, it was a mother's torment of not knowing if her children lived. "Your daughters are fine," he assured her.

But her maternal instincts were not comforted. She ran to her children's bedroom and opened the door, which allowed light from the hallway to spill softly into the room. Her daughters were sleeping soundly, their chests rising and falling in a peaceful rhythm. Upon seeing this she immediately brought her hands up to stymie a cry of gratitude but failed as a single tearful sob escaped her. When she finally gained control of her emotions, she turned to Kimball with the repose of appreciation. "You saved my life, Mr. Hayden, and the lives of my family . . . Thank you."

Kimball took a position beside her at the door, his figure casting a long shadow. "As I told you, Ms. Cohen, that's what I do.

Now . . . are you willing to let me help you?"

Shari focused on the Roman Catholic collar, then on the man. "Yes, Mr. Hayden, I will."

A new alliance was born.

#

Isaiah was hiding in the late-night shadows in front of the brownstone when he heard the sound of glass breaking, then saw a commando take flight through the window and land on the roof of a parked vehicle before he hobbled away. A second commando quickly followed through the front door and ran in the same direction, where they met a third man standing within a grove of trees. Then they were gone, each man quickly swallowed by the darkness of the landscape.

#

The limping commando was in absolute agony, his adrenaline rush almost tapped out as Judas guided him to the back seat of his sedan that was parked beyond the tree line. With the commando pressing his hands against the gash above his knee to stem the flow of blood, he could almost hear the panic bell going off in his head. The other commando fell into the front seat and held his good hand against his torn bicep, his face had gone pale as blood flowed freely between the gaps of his fingers.

"What happened in there?" asked Judas, putting the sedan in gear. "Where the hell is Dark Lord?"

"This guy," said the commando in the back seat, "came from nowhere and took us out like no other."

"And he was fast, too," added the commando with the torn bicep. "I mean, this guy was the best I've ever seen with double-edged weapons."

"I've never seen anything like him," said the first commando, shifting his weight to diminish the pain.

The commando with the torn bicep glanced into the side mirror to assure that no one followed. "This guy was as big as a house," he added.

"Yeah. And he wore a priest's collar."

166

Judas gave the man in the back seat an inquisitive look through the rearview mirror. "A what?"

"A Roman collar," he said. "The guy was wearing a clerical collar, like a priest would wear."

Judas fought for calm. "What about the disc?"

"Didn't get it . . . This guy came in just as Dark Lord was about to take out Cohen."

"You left the disc behind?" Judas brought a hand up and massaged his temple with the calloused tips of his fingers. Yahweh wasn't going to like this.

Neither commando spoke, their eyes pinched against excruciating pain.

Pitching a sigh, Judas ran an open hand along his face as if to wipe away the semblance of frustration. "What else?" he asked.

"What else what?"

"What else can you tell me?"

The commando with the injured leg repositioned himself in the back seat, but there was no way for him to get comfortable. "Dark Lord knew him . . . Called him by name."

"By name?"

The wounded man in the back seat nodded. "He called him Hayden . . . Kimball Hayden."

Judas stopped the vehicle in its tracks by slamming on the brakes. "He said *that* name?" Judas wanted absolute confirmation. "He said the name Kimball Hayden. You're sure of that?"

"Positive. He said Kimball Hayden."

"There's no way it could be the same guy," Judas said under his breath. "No way in Hell."

Judas looked back to the area where they had just come from through the rearview mirror and noted the lights of the brownstone that seemed so far away. *Kimball Hayden: a name synonymous with the art of killing and stealth . . . and a man who was without conscience or remorse.* He had heard the name many times during his tenure within White House circles. He had even seen the man on many occasions but dared not speak to him, afraid that the wrong look, the wrong word, might have been his last since the man's brutality had levitated him to such legendary status that his reputation became as intimidating as his size.

Judas pressed softly on the accelerator and the sedan began to roll.

But Hayden's dead.

So now the mystery of what happened to Dark Lord was a mystery no longer. It was obvious to Judas he would never see the man alive again.

"That name means something to you?" asked the commando in the rear seat. "Kimball Hayden?"

"A long time ago," he said.

When legends were born.

CHAPTER THIRTY-EIGHT

Washington, D.C.
September 27. Early Morning

"There were three men," said Isaiah. "One was waiting across the street hidden among the trees."

"Which puts the count to a minimum of four," said Kimball. "Obviously, he was maintaining watch."

Kimball moved to the couch where Gary sat with an ice wrap on his broken arm. Shari sat beside him patting his forehead and jaw with a damp cloth. The body of Dark Lord lay on the floor covered with a sheet. "Ms. Cohen, if I may, I think it would be best that your family is taken out of harm's way as soon as possible," said Kimball.

"I agree." She pointed to Gary. "Perhaps to his mother's home in California—"

"No, ma'am. If your attackers are who I think they are, then you'll only place them in jeopardy as well. These people will stop at nothing to gain whatever it is they want."

"I don't have anything."

"Obviously, you do."

"Then where would my family go?"

"To the archdiocese," said Isaiah. "Your husband will be treated for his injuries and your children will be safe."

Shari turned to Gary. "I'm sorry you're in this mess. But I think you and the children go to a safe house."

"You won't get no argument from me," he told her. He turned to Kimball. "When do we leave? The safety of my children means everything to me."

"Isaiah will take you there as soon as you're ready."

"And what about you?" asked Gary, turning to Shari.

She looked at the contoured sheet stained with the dead man's blood. "I've got to find out why this happened."

"Mr. Cohen," Kimball began, "I don't know why they're trying to kill your wife. Obviously, she's become a threat to somebody, or somebodies, and was tagged as a targeted killing."

Gary winced. "A targeted killing?"

Kimball nodded. "It means the assassination or premeditated killing of an individual by a state organization or institution outside a judicial procedure or a battlefield. In this case, it's your wife. And I believe the answer as to why she was targeted is here in this apartment."

Shari was suddenly enlightened as she turned to the smashed body of the PC, though the monitor still winked off and on intermittently. "And I think I know where."

Kimball followed her gaze to the unit. *Good girl,* he thought.

#

With Gary and the children safely on their way to the archdiocese, Kimball lifted the PC back onto the tabletop and strengthened his alliance with Shari by telling her untold secrets.

"His name was Shady Tippet," he told her, examining the crack in the casing. "He was somebody I used to work with a long time ago."

"Worked with where?"

Kimball gave a sidelong glance to the body of Dark Lord and turned away. "With the government," he answered. "The White House, in fact."

"Doing what?"

He knew she was pressing him for as much information as possible, which was fine by him. Brutal honesty, regardless of its content, was the first steppingstone toward establishing trust. "We were assassins," he told her, "working specifically under the orders of the people in the White House and the Joint Chiefs on black operations. Word was that the president was involved in some of the decision-making as well, though it was never verified."

Shari suddenly realized that this man, Dark Lord, was sent to kill her by—maybe—the most powerful man on the planet. *But why?*

Her voice began to crack. "This man," she said, pointing to

170

Dark Lord. "Is he. . ." Her words trailed.

"What? An assassin for the Force Elite? Maybe."

"Is that what they're called? The Force Elite."

"They are."

Kimball gave a brief synopsis of the history and development of the Force, the nature of its existence, and the targets involved, including a statesman who posed as a threat to a one-time incumbent during his term of office, a political local.

Suddenly, Shari felt overwhelmed. "How do I fight something like this?" she said. "How do I fight someone like the president of the United States? I can't!"

Kimball gently gripped the triceps of her left arm. His voice was soft and soothing and full of promise, his touch tender and supportive. "You *can* do this," he told her. "And you'll never be alone in this. I promise. The Vatican is behind you all the way and, believe me, I don't think the United States government will want to take on the Holy Roman Catholic Church. Do you?"

"But why come after me?"

He released her arm and placed a hand on top of the PC. "That's exactly what we're going to find out."

#

A distant chime, hardly perceptible, the incessant ringing finally gaining strength and awakening Pappandopolous from a dream he forgot the moment he opened his eyes. Slowly, and awkwardly, he grabbed the cordless receiver of the phone and placed it to his ear. The digital clock read 3:49 a.m. "What?"

"It's Judas."

Pappandopolous propped himself on his elbow. "This isn't a secured line. You should have waited until tomorrow."

"Don't be so paranoid. Nobody's tapping your line."

"Do you know what time it is?"

"Shut up and listen," he demanded. "Have you ever heard the name Kimball Hayden?"

"No . . . never."

"The name Kimball Hayden is synonymous with a 'one-man wrecking machine.'"

"Why are you telling me this?" Pappandopolous lay back down on the pillow.

"I'm telling you this because he just took out half of Omega Team by himself . . . And Dark Lord is dead."

Pappandopolous was back onto an elbow. "What about Cohen and the disc?"

"She's very much alive and still in possession of the item in question."

"Why is this Hayden guy in the picture anyway? Who is he?"

"He's bad news."

Pappandopolous sat up on the edge of the bed. The bottoms of his feet touched the cold, hardwood floor. "Use whatever is left of Omega Team and get that disc. And don't fail me again, Judas. Managing the ground troops in this matter is your responsibility."

"I know my responsibility," he stated defensively. "But nobody expected Kimball Hayden to be involved."

"How much of a problem can one man be?"

Judas shook his head. It must be nice to be stupid and ignorant at the same time, he thought. *If you knew Kimball Hayden, then you would know he was more than just 'one man.'* "A lot," he finally said.

Pappandopolous sighed in frustration. "You know what you have to do." He stared briefly at the receiver before placing it back into its cradle. For the rest of the night, sleep eluded him. He laid there wondering why the cause was teetering on the balance when it seemed to work without deficiency on paper. The answer simply escaped him. He didn't know the name Kimball Hayden or the danger he presented.

Expelling a drawn-out sigh, Pappandopolous picked up the phone and dialed another unsecured line. "Mr. Obadiah? George Pappandopolous. I'm afraid I have some rather bad news," he said. Then he began to explain in earnest.

#

The PC was cracked and not at all in good shape. The monitor came on, but the unit did not fire up. Working his knife blade into a seam on the computer case, Kimball was able to force the disc tray from the plastic cabinet.

After extracting the disc, he held it up. "Bingo."

172

Shari took the disc from Kimball. "I hope it's not damaged," she said, sensing something of a loss. "Everything was on this disc."

"What about backup files?"

"Nothing," she said. "Whatever is sent to us by colluding agencies is copied, and then deleted for fear that the information might be appropriated by cyber hostiles. This is the only hard copy available."

"Isn't it standard procedure to make more than one copy?"

"If the information is classified and graded for high level—always. And per protocol, we did burn a backup disc that had been placed in the Information Vault. But it was either improperly burned, or the disc was seized and replaced with a bogus one. I'm not sure which. But when my people get a chance, they'll look into it."

"Re-contact the source."

"I did. But Mossad resent the information minus the encryptions," she said. "When I contacted their director, I got nothing but excuses and denials. And since the original disc was not classified as important, due to it being labeled as biographical histories, it wasn't copied since histories can be copied anytime. And Mossad knew that when I contacted them." Shari looked at the disc. "This disc was unique, Kimball, and any information that came with it may be lost."

Kimball laid a hand on the broken PC. "Is there any way you can take information from what's left on the computer?"

She surveyed the large hole broken into the side of the machine. The circuit boards inside were cracked. "I doubt it." She pointed to a damaged board inside the computer. "The memory board is busted. All we can do is hope and pray that the disc isn't damaged."

She fell back onto the couch and tried to keep her eyes from welling. But the stress became overpowering. In a sudden shift that took her from being composed to something completely fragile, Shari broke, which shocked Kimball.

"And what the hell are we going to do with him?" she said, pointing to the body. "We can't just leave him here!" And without warning, her hands went to her face.

Kimball was at a sudden loss. He was never one to provide emotional comfort with a hug or with cooing words. To him, showing emotion somehow seemed vulgar in its display. Despite this, however, he took the seat beside her. "Ms. Cohen, I need you to be at your best," he told her. "I'll take care of the body, but we need to take care of business as we see fit."

She turned to him, tears streaming down her cheeks. "You're expecting *me* to conduct business as usual, knowing that the most powerful man on this planet has just sent his goon squad after me?"

"We're guessing that Shady Tippet *may* be from the Force Elite," he said. "But think about this. It doesn't make sense on one hand that he is from a government liquidation squad since the president *wants* you to find information regarding the Soldiers of Islam. So why send somebody after you when you're making progress?" Kimball leaned closer to her. "Because on one hand," he continued, "we know that the principal of Israeli's Defense Attaché was resistant to your efforts—at least to a degree—which may mean that he had more motive than anyone else. But on the other hand, it doesn't make sense that he would leave the Force Elite to join up with a shadow group attached to the Mossad."

"So, what are you saying? That you don't know where he comes from?"

"I can only tell you where he *came* from. Right now, the pieces of the puzzle aren't fitting properly. Word was that the Force Elite folded because matters became too politically hot for the White House to keep it going. Maybe he was forced to apply his skills elsewhere."

For a moment she said nothing. Then: "I'm scared, Kimball. I'm really scared."

"I know," he said. "The fear comes from not knowing who or what is out there."

She placed a hand on his forearm. "I have to ask you something." He nodded, the gesture giving her the green light to do so.

"When I was coming up in the ranks, I heard people within the White House corridors talking in hushed tones about a man named Kimball Hayden. They said he was vicious and cruel, a man without conscience or remorse. They also said he killed women and children, or anyone else who might have compromised his mission."

Kimball appeared wounded because he knew where this was going. And telling her the truth would not be a pleasant admission on his part.

Then from Shari: "Tell me you're not that *same* man."

Kimball hesitated a moment before speaking—the pause between them perhaps telling her all she needed to know. "I wish I could tell something different," he told her. "But I can't."

Somehow, in her eyes, he could see that she was afraid of the situation but not of him. So, when she reached over and cupped his hand with hers, he was surprised.

"And now you seek redemption through the church." It was more of a statement rather than a question.

"I have been accepted by the Vatican, yes."

"Has it been easy?"

"What?"

"Your travels to redemption?"

Kimball thought about this—had thought about it many times before. "No," he finally answered. "I've done horrible things. Terrible things. Things I'm afraid I could never be forgiven for. Every morning I wake up, I wonder if my journey is a wasted one because of the things I have done, in my heart, I know could never be forgiven."

"Are you afraid?"

This was another question that caught Kimball off guard. "Every day of my life," he admitted. "Sometimes I can't sleep because of what I see in my dreams. I'm afraid because of the horrible things in my past that continue to plague me. And I'm afraid when it comes to my time of judgment, He's going to turn me away."

She squeezed his hand. "You're a good man, Kimball Hayden. And let me tell you why. After what happened tonight, whatever Darkness you inherited from your past is gone. I can see the Light in your eyes."

Kimball doubted her. But he nodded his appreciation, anyway. "We can beat this," he told her. Not only did he tell this to her about fending off a team of liquidators, but also his journey to fend off the Darkness that always followed in his wake. The mission was now two-fold.

And Shari understood. Life was full of battles, whether external or internal. Demons existed everywhere.

"But I need you to keep doing what the president has asked of you," said Kimball.

"He asked me to dig and dig deep. But we're right back where we started—at nada. The information may be entirely lost."

"Did you download the disc into the PC?"

"It was the first thing I did after putting the girls to bed."

"Then perhaps we're not at nada after all," he said. "What's that supposed to mean?"

He remembered the Logger placed to the PC by Leviticus. "It means, Ms. Cohen, an opportunity may still exist after all."

She gave him a baffled look.

#

Team Leader fumed knowing that Omega Team had failed in its assignment to remove the target. There was no doubt Yahweh would be displeased. More so, his international constituencies would grow uneasy knowing that the slight bumps in the road were forming into formidable knolls.

The name Kimball Hayden meant nothing to Team Leader, nothing at all. But, for whatever reason, it threw tremors into Judas. If this man Kimball Hayden posed a threat to the cause, Team Leader would apply his skills as an elite killer to take out Ms. Cohen's champion.

Fail me one more time, Judas, and I'll run my blade across your throat as a testament to your repeated failures so that everyone can see that failing is not an option.

He turned the cargo truck onto the New Jersey Turnpike, his anger lasting until he arrived in Boston.

CHAPTER THIRTY-NINE

The wrapped body of Dark Lord was taken to the archdiocese, where church authorities would see to it that he had a respectful service and burial.

People like Shady Tippet had no family ties or connections that authorities could associate him with. The man had no identity, no background, and no history; nothing that would bind him to the human race.

This was also the case with Kimball Hayden before he united with the Vatican Knights. Per protocol, Kimball was nonexistent to the outside world. But when he laid Tippet's body to rest on a slab within the sub-basement of the archdiocese, he gave the man identity by recalling events they had shared as companions.

He remembered times when they were brothers-in-arms who killed because it was mandatory to do so. Then he relived the moment when he saved Shady Tippet's life in the Middle East, only to take it away several years later in the den of a brownstone apartment. *How ironic was that?* he asked himself. *To kill the man that you once saved. How much more twisted could fate be in the hands of God?*

Bowing his head in respect for an old comrade while placing his hand on the breastplate of Shady's Kevlar, Kimball spoke in hushed tones. When he finished, Kimball left the chamber wondering how many more of his old group he would have to kill.

#

September 26, 1206 hours
Six Miles Northwest of Mesquite, Nevada

A band of coyotes moved in crisscross fashion looking for mice, voles, or ground squirrels beneath a hot Mojave Desert sun. In their wake, as the sun felt white-hot against their coats, a battery of heatwaves shimmered off the desert floor.

The temperature was unbearably hot, the air oppressive, and the climate inhospitable as the earth gave off scents that tagged the coyotes' acute sense of smell, drawing them closer to the unmistakable odor of carrion that had cured over time.

The pack moved back and forth, searching, then pawing, trying to gauge the location of the carcass detected by their olfactory senses. The smell appeared to be rising from several locations, confusing them, and then they collectively realized there was more than one source of meat. So, they dispersed into small groups, each unit following a scented trail.

To the east, next to a rocky embankment stemming from the ground like a half shell, the smell of carrion radiated strongest from a point where the soil appeared recently tilled.

Being the natural burrowers that they are, the coyotes began to dig and paw at the sand, kicking up clouds of choking dust and digging to a depth of nearly two feet, until they uncovered a bounty of meat.

Hands that were paired together by flex-cuffs with the flesh having aged and gone tender, proved to be a ripe harvest as one of the canines began to yip and howl to announce the find.

Before the day was over, however, five more bodies would be unearthed, and the coyotes would gorge themselves with the true Soldiers of Islam.

#

When Shari saw her family inside the rectory next to the archdiocese, her husband was wearing a cast and sleeping in a high-back chair inside a small bedroom. Also sleeping on a twin-sized bed were her daughters, who huddled together in a tangle that only children could sleep through, with their arms and legs crisscrossing each other as they slept. The adornments were simple and spartan: a crucifix hung over a characterless bureau; a watercolor depiction of Christ holding a lamb hung over the bed, his face kind and gentle; and a window provided a view of a wonderfully bright-flowered garden in the center of the courtyard.

When the sun finally rose above the horizon, a priest came for Shari and escorted her to the neighboring archdiocese and the cardinal's chambers. The room was large and beautifully decorated with scarlet drapes with scalloped bottoms lined with gold tassels that swept down from the highest reaches of the windows and touched the floor. In the room's center sat a desk so large and magnificently rich in ornate style, Shari knew it was top dollar. And along the walls was a gallery of plinths that supported the busts of past popes, as each carved image looked on from faces that marginally resembled the men they were supposed to replicate.

Kimball sat in one of two leather chairs before the cardinal's desk and gave her a nod of acknowledgment when she entered the chamber.

On the opposite side of the room, Cardinal Medeiros was washing his hands in the basin for his daily cleansing. After this morning's ritual of self-purification, he wiped his hands dry with an embroidered cloth and approached Shari with cleansed hands, which he offered her in greeting. "And how are you, my dear?"

Shari had seen the cardinal on television many times before and found herself to be in awe of his presence. "I'm fine, Cardinal. Thank you." She allowed the man to cup his cool hands over hers.

"I'm glad you and your family are all right."

"If it weren't for this man," she said, glancing at Kimball, "I wouldn't be here—my family wouldn't be here."

The cardinal escorted her to the high-back chair next to Kimball's and set her down. Then he rounded his desk and took his seat. "Ms. Cohen, obviously you know who I am."

"Of course."

"Then I must ask a favor of you. You must assure me that what we say here remains in this room. No one can ever know the secret of the Vatican Knights."

"You have my word."

"Then let me say this: The Vatican Knights are an incredibly special group of people. And sometimes, when it comes to accomplishing their duties, they have to use methods that may appear outside of the church's teachings. But the church also sees the right to protect itself, its sovereignty, as well as the welfare of its citizenry. We genuinely believe that God even recognizes the right for good people

179

to protect those who cannot protect themselves. And sometimes, unfortunately, harsh measures have to be taken in order to do so. Now I'm sorry you had to bear witness to such aggression earlier this morning, but if the Vatican Knights could have accomplished the task at hand without violence, they would have done so."

"I'm not judging the Vatican, Cardinal, or its methods. Believe me."

"The bottom line, my dear, is that the Vatican does not judge; it simply acts when it has to. Unfortunately, killing has become a necessity in certain measures that cannot be avoided. Like this morning, with your family." And then the disclaimer. "It's not up to the Vatican on whether or not someone lives or dies. We can only assume that it's God's will. Therefore, we will do *whatever* it takes to bring the pontiff back alive. Please understand this. The pope is truly a good man who preaches freedom and tranquility in all its forms. But until all men are like him, we often have no choice but to keep our swords sharp and engage in methods not consistent with the preaching's of the Church to achieve the means."

"Cardinal, not only do you have my solemn word on this matter, but you also have my gratitude."

"Then what I'm about to say to you now, my dear, is this: We hold steadfast to our alliances and never betray our allegiances." He leaned forward in his chair. "For the moment you are one of us and for that, we say: Loyalty above all else except honor. It is the credo the Vatican Knights live by."

Suddenly she felt an overwhelming sense of commitment. Even when she took the Oath of Honor as a peace officer, she had never felt allegiance surge through her as it did now. Strangely, she felt an obligation unlike any other, an inexplicable sense of oneness that created a sour lump at the base of her throat. "I feel . . . honored."

"No, my dear, we are the honored ones." Cardinal Medeiros leaned back into his chair. "So, we will follow your lead."

Kimball stood, his height towering over the cardinal's desk. "I know I'm cutting matters quick," he said, "but we have work to do." With that, he took to his knee, placed a closed fist over his heart, and said, "Loyalty above all else, except honor."

"May God be with you both," replied the cardinal.

Within moments, Kimball Hayden and Shari Cohen were on

their way to see if Leviticus was working his magic, as he tried to decode the encryptions on the disc taken from the damaged PC.

#

Boston, Massachusetts

Bishop Angelo was terrified of his mortality. Worse, he was afraid of how he would appear before God knowing that God could see the smallest detail inside any man, no matter how much he tried to hide or deny the truth about himself. And that truth for Bishop Angelo was that he was struggling with his faith in Almighty God.

After he prayed and waited for something in return, the answer always came back as silence. And then he would weep because He was not there to comfort him, as a sense of abandonment washed over him. After toiling to find his faith, he instead found himself feeling hopelessly lost in the company of his brothers who were tethered and chained to the same wall as he. The man had been reduced to nothing more than a frightened shell of a man who was certain that his fate was paved with the same dark intentions as Cardinal Bertini's.

Looking over at Cardinal Bertini's empty mattress, Bishop Angelo then addressed the man to his right. "Are you praying to the Lord, Attilio?" Cardinal Attilio Paolo didn't bother to face him because his eyes remained fixed on the guard leaning against the wall holding an MP-5 that had a suppressor that was as long as the weapon's barrel. "Of course," he finally answered.

"And did you receive an answer?"

"He may have given one," he said. "I only need to be patient to find out what it is."

"In other words, if you are to be executed, then His answer was 'no.'"

Cardinal Paolo gave a gingerly smile, then he closed his eyes as if he was drifting off to someplace wonderful. "No, my friend. If my life is to end, all I pray for is that I am welcomed into Glory at the gates of His Heavenly Kingdom."

It was not the answer Bishop Angelo expected. "Are you not afraid?" Paolo opened his eyes and nodded. "Of course, I am. But my faith keeps me going and gives me hope. As it should you. If God wants me to appear before Him in Judgment, then that is His will for which I have no control. What I do have control over, however, *is* my faith."

Bishop Angelo made a cursory examination of all the faces of the bishops and was quick in judgment to note that their repose appeared meditatively calm. "I'm afraid," he finally admitted. "God forgive me, but I am so afraid."

Cardinal Paolo turned to him, then laid a hand on Bishop Angelo's forearm as the links of his chain rattled against one another in a ghoulish chime. "Being afraid is good," he told him. "It reminds us of who we are. For without fear, we would either be foolish or disillusioned, of which we are neither."

Paolo then gazed along the dark hallway, then at the guard posted across from them. "When the soldiers finally come for us," he whispered, "that is when we seek our faith and prepare ourselves for Heaven. But faith does not carry us to false courage. Every man here bound to this wall is frightened. But we never lose sight of our commitment to God because the moment we lose our faith, it is also the moment we lose sight of who and what we are."

The back of Bishop Angelo's head fell back against the wall, his eyes looking ceiling-ward, searching. "I'm ashamed of myself," he said. "I'm afraid I've lost my faith."

"We all question our faith, Angelo. There isn't a man here who hasn't."

Angelo lifted his hand and the trailing links of chain. "Faith or not, we need to do something to get out of here. Prayer alone will not save us."

"And what do you expect us to do, Angelo? Tear these chains from the wall and take on armed guards?"

Bishop Angelo began to visibly shake. "We just can't sit here and let them murder us one by one."

"Then pray, Angelo. Pray for divine intervention."

"I have. And I'm afraid that His answer is 'no.'"

"Then find as much comfort as you can in your faith. If you cannot do that, then seek it out."

Angelo let his head fall until his chin touched his chest. His faith was all but lost. "Why hasn't God answered my prayers?"

"Perhaps He has, my friend. Only you don't know it yet."

From the darkness came footfalls, and Bishop Angelo saw Team Leader bearing down on them from the stairwell at the end of the hallway with purpose in his stride and his firearm firmly gripped in his hand.

"No," he whispered gravely. "I don't think He did."

#

After Team Leader parked the cargo truck beneath the trees behind the abandoned building, he entered the depository knowing his presence would set off the alarms. Once the rats cleared the area and gave him a wide berth, Team Leader stood within eyeshot of the cameras until an ID confirmation was made by those manning the monitors on the third floor. Once done, the bolting mechanisms slid free, and he entered the staircase.

Boa, Kodiak, and King Snake were on the top landing standing sentinel. Their weapons and ammo bandoliers festooned across their chests, their manner casual. Sidewinder was at the end of the hallway keeping watch over the bishops with his MP5.

"So, how'd it go?" asked Boa.

Team Leader removed his pistol and installed a pneumatically snapped-on silencer that reduced the decibel count of the report to a loud spit. "Our associates appear somewhat worried for the moment," he finally answered. "And for good reason."

Boa didn't question the man further. There was no doubt in his mind that Team Leader was irritated.

Walking with urgency to the row of mattresses, Team Leader stood before the bishops of the Holy See and the cardinal from the Papal Commission. With his weapon held against his body, he then used it to point out Bishop Angelo. The mouth of the barrel seemed to gape as wide as a viper's deadly maw, as Angelo cast his eyes away in submission. "Take this one and set him before the camera," he said.

Boa stared at the bishop. After a moment of appraisal, Boa spoke in a manner of sarcasm. "I guess you're the lucky man of the day."

With Kodiak forcing a struggling bishop to his feet, Angelo shouted nonsensical words of protest and fought a futile battle against a much larger man by rapping his fists against Kodiak's Kevlar.

Without hesitation, Kodiak struck the bishop with a well-placed blow that knocked him senseless, his cries evolving to guttural sounds, as the bishop went boneless. The bishops who had been watching this scene play out pulled their knees up into acute angles and embraced their legs, with each man terrified of his fate.

After removing the manacle from the bishop's wrist, Kodiak half-dragged, half-carried the semi-conscious man along the hallway.

With the bishop's head cast forward and his eyes at half-mast, a fine thread of silvery spit lengthened from the corner of his lip with every foot he was dragged toward the killing chamber.

The mere action of rendering the bishop impotent enabled Team Leader to study the four remaining hostages as Bishop Angelo was led into shadows so deep and so profound, there would be no returning from them as another mattress lay empty. At the very moment when Angelo was led away, Team Leader studied the clerics and determined that they all possessed faith in an afterlife that promised absolute peace. On the other hand, he could see that they were afraid to reach for the Light due to the only means to obtain it, which was through death.

When the time of death finally came to them, as death comes to everyone, Team Leader would look each one in the eye to see if blind faith was truly a part of all men of the cloth, just before he killed them.

Hypocrisy versus Faith.

As Kodiak led the bishop down the hallway, Team Leader's trigger finger began to itch. Not in a physical sense, but as a manner of duty. In a few minutes, he was about to write another historical chapter for the cause, using the blood of an innocent man as the ink to chronicle the event that helped alter history.

Leaving his station by the clerics, Team Leader followed Kodiak into darkness.

CHAPTER FORTY

September 27, 0934 hours
Six Miles Northwest of Mesquite, Nevada

He had been riding his dirt bike for nearly three hours now. The rooster tail plumes of sand kicking up from behind his wheels left the area in a constant haze, the ring of mountains surrounding him were hardly perceptible.

Jo-Jo Michaels, only thirteen, demonstrated skill and dexterity in maneuvering his dirt bike over the rough terrain. He guided his machine through the natural moguls and dips with the ease of someone twice his age and experience. But today in the midst of roiling dust clouds, he struck a hidden mound, lost his balance, and tumbled off his bike, which settled in an explosion of dust and sand.

After getting to his feet and trying in vain to brush the loose grains from his clothing, the dust was beginning to settle. When it did, Jo-Jo froze with mind-numbing terror when he realized that the slight rise was the half-gnawed torso of a man covered with a fine layer of the valley's dust.

Later that day five more bodies would be discovered, all half-eaten, baked and exposed to the elements for days. The carcasses were riddled with gunfire, and flesh had been torn and gashed away by the gnawing teeth of coyotes. Nevertheless, the scavengers had left enough for the examiners to determine their identities.

#

Shari Cohen and Kimball made it to the lower level of the archdiocese, a computer lab-work area where Leviticus was working before several plasma screens.

185

"Anything?" Kimball asked him.

Leviticus released a long sigh to vent fatigue. "There is some damage," he said. "And I've been at it all night trying not to set off the viruses."

"Viruses?"

He nodded. "I've seen this before from the Mossad. They set up their encryptions with pathway viruses. They're guards against hackers who try to appropriate data. If the hacker initiates the virus, then the information is forever lost."

"So, you know what you're doing, right?" asked Kimball.

"I guess we'll find out," he said, his fingers moving expertly over the keys. "Right now, I'm finding openings through front-door intrusions. I'm trying to find a micro-window to get through by opening a gate here and a gate there. But it's proving difficult and it's time-consuming."

"Are you at least close to bringing this thing up?" Kimball asked him.

Leviticus nodded. "I think so. But I do know this: whatever has been decoded is nothing but photos."

"How do you know that?" Shari asked.

"Some of the pixel imprints have already come up like pieces of a jigsaw puzzle," he answered. "Now the question is: Why would somebody encrypt photos unless, of course, they were vital to national security at some level? And if that was true, why attach it to low-level documents such as biographical records?" He continued to type at a rapid pace.

Kimball leaned toward the screen. "Maybe they're additional photos of the Soldiers of Islam?"

"Not likely," said Shari. "Why would somebody encrypt some photos and not encrypt others?"

"I guess we'll soon find out," Leviticus said, keeping a finger above the ENTER key. "I just want you both to know that one of two things is going to happen here. Either the photos will load . . . or the viruses will initiate. With this type of safeguard, I cannot guarantee success."

"You did the best you could, Leviticus. I don't think we have a choice, since time is not a luxury."

As soon as he dropped the finger on the ENTER key, the

monitor winked out. A mote of light remained alive in the screen's center. Just as Leviticus was about to apologize for his failure, the monitor flared up and the pictures began to download. Shari celebrated his success with a clap to Leviticus' shoulder.

"Well done," said Kimball.

The first pictures that were downloaded were of men in warm weather climates. Nor a single one seemed to be aware that their photos were being taken.

In two photographs, the wall in the Gaza Strip and the Golan Heights could be seen. In another, a tropical beachfront property with—a person Shari Cohen recognized—Hector Guerra, who was a leading principal of Venezuela's leading oil-producing conglomerate, the *Petróleos* de Venezuela, or the PDVSA, was sitting inside the cabana with several foreign dignitaries. The tie between Guerra and the Soldiers of Islam, however, didn't quite register. So, with vague consideration, she considered that Obadiah was telling the truth, after all. Perhaps there wasn't a tie as he suggested. But if that was the case, why send a death squad to get the disc?

She stepped closer to the monitor as the pictures continued to download.

Faces of other dignitaries began to appear on the screen. Vladimir Ostrosky appeared in conversation with Hector Guerra as they stood along the surf of Guerra's estate with a drink in each of their hands.

"I don't get it," she finally said.

"I don't either," said Kimball. "I recognize Vladimir Ostrosky from DUMA, but the other guy—"

"That's Hector Guerra from the PDVSA."

"The PDVSA?"

"It's Venezuela's oil conglomerate. Mr. Guerra is its minister."

"So why would a guy from Venezuela's oil-producing giant meet with a man from the Russian Parliament?"

"Good question. But even more so, how does this tie in with the Soldiers of Islam?"

No one had an answer. The pictures continued to load in slow progression.

More recognizable dignitaries from Russia, Venezuela, and Israel had been photographically snapped while they were meeting.

The Israeli principals were from political and military circles. Obadiah was among the gathering and seated at a suit-and-tie affair, with Ostrosky sitting on one side and Guerra on the other.

The second batch of pictures was that of the Soldiers of Islam, in what appeared to be surveillance photos. There were pictures of them coming and going from stores and shops in Ogden, Utah, either from their residences or from places of worship. But nothing that shed anything beyond their records.

The third batch was even more intriguing. Maps of Russia, Venezuela, Israel, and the Middle East, including Syria and the Palestinian territories, surfaced on the monitor with ink-block shapes that seemed to be overlays. "Now what are we looking at?" Shari muttered. "We have photos of foreign dignitaries, photos of terrorists, and maps of—what?"

Leviticus tapped a finger over one of the overlays of the territory. "I know what these are," he said. "I've seen these before. They're maps of geological surveys for tracts of oil."

Kimball and Shari leaned closer to the monitor. "What does this have to do with the Soldiers of Islam?" he asked.

"I haven't a clue," she answered.

They waited in silence, watching, and hoping that additional photos would provide more insight, but they didn't.

Feeling the pinch of a headache coming on, Shari took a seat and wondered what she was going to tell the president. She had photos that told her little, but in actuality, they spoke volumes as to why the pope was kidnapped. She just didn't know it.

While studying the screen her cell phone rang. The caller was Alan Thornton. She was to meet with the president inside the Oval Office within the hour. And this time, Thornton told her, President Burroughs wanted answers.

CHAPTER FORTY-ONE

Boston, Massachusetts

Team Leader walked urgently into Pope Pius's chamber. And in a deft move that appeared sleight-of-hand, he produced a key seemingly from thin air and inserted it into the lock of the pope's shackle and undid the metal cuff. "I want you to watch something," he said. With little effort, Team Leader yanked the pope to his feet and pulled the man so close, his lips nearly touched the old man's ear. "Be prepared," he whispered. "Because you're not going to like what you're about to see."

The pope raised his chin. *An act of defiance?*

Team Leader saw genuine faith and strength in the man's eyes. "Good," he told the pontiff. "It is a strength you will need."

He led the pope to the killing chamber.

#

"That was Alan Thornton," she said, snapping the cell phone closed. "My presence is needed for an update. Apparently, the president is going 'live' this afternoon."

"Be careful," Kimball said.

She turned to him. "What am I supposed to give him? I can't give the president this," she said, pointing to the images on the monitor.

"Why not?" said Kimball. "If the president and the Force Elite were trying to get that disc, then there would no longer be a point to further any action against you, should you hand it over to the president."

189

"But they could also be calling me to find out if the data has been interpreted. If they learn it has, they may send another response unit to keep me from delving even deeper."

"True. But why put you in a position to discover information only to discredit you? It doesn't make sense."

"For cosmetics," she answered. "The president can say he did his best as an administrator by putting his money player to work. So, if I fail, if my team fails, then the accusing finger points directly at me and not at him. I'll be the one who'll end up the scapegoat. But now that I'm getting close, maybe they want to undo what they did, never believing I'd get this far."

"Which is why he had directed the liquidation team to locate the disc," said Kimball. "Exactly. It also means that Obadiah is somehow connected with *his* administration."

Kimball stepped away from the computer, the lines on his face registering deep thought. "Not only Obadiah . . . But the Mossad, the White House, Russia, Venezuela, Israel—they're all connected. But how? And why?"

"Good question. What I can't figure out, though, is how they tie in with the Soldiers of Islam and the kidnapping of the pope. Or why the White House administration would even be supporting this act."

Kimball ran his hands across his face as if to wipe away the frustration." All right," he finally said, "so what do we have here?"

Shari raised her hand and began to tick off events on her fingers, starting with the thumb. "The men who tried to kill me last night were from an indigenous force. Obadiah, who happens to be from the Israeli attaché, wanted that disc. That ties him to the White House since they sent the dispatch team. Then there are the photographs of political and big business dignitaries mixed in with the biographical records of terrorists." She lowered her hand. "That disc, Kimball, holds more than just the profiles of fanatics and extremists."

He nodded in agreement. "It's also a schematic."

"But of what? There are pieces still missing and we're running out of time." Shari began to pace the room nervously. "And in one hour, I have to go see the man who's trying to kill me. How ironic is that?"

"He's not going to hurt you."

"That's easy for you to say. You're not the one he's gunning for."

"Shari, you're not going to go missing at the White House door. If anything, they'll wait for an opportune moment, like last night—when it's unexpected. This is simply a vetting process to ferret out what you know."

"Then I'll draw them out," she said. "I'll copy these photos and dangle the carrot before the mule. If there's anyone in that room who's a part of this, and if *these* photos are worth killing me over to keep me from finding out the truth, then they'll send a second unit to finish the job. You agree?"

Kimball did. "If they think you can expose them, they'll come after you like the Hounds of Hell."

"If the president and his administration are somehow involved in this," said Shari, "we need to know now. We're running out of time. Just be ready to take prisoners when they come for me."

Shari could tell by the look on his face that he wasn't too keen on her proposal.

"Look, Shari, this isn't child's play. These people are dangerous. And this time they'll be ready for me."

"Right now, I don't see any other option."

Kimball hesitated, his cerulean blue eyes connecting with hers. "Be careful."

Shari drew closer to him. "Kimball, please don't fail me when I draw them out."

He didn't move. He could smell the hint of her perfume. "We'll be there."

"Then let's draw the flies to the honey." The time was exactly 11:30 a.m.

#

Boston, Massachusetts
September 27. Late Morning

Boa was manning the camera when Kodiak carried the bishop into the room with a gloved hand across the man's mouth. The bishop, barely cognizant, put up feeble resistance by swinging a clawed hand through the air.

The stage was comprised of a canvas backdrop and a splintered wooden floor. Kodiak forced the bishop to his knees on the chalk-drawn X in front of the camera.

Whining and whimpering with the pain of knowing that he was about to die with resonances from his throat sounding primal, the members of Omega Team nevertheless acted with cold detachment.

"We ready to rock?" asked Kodiak.

Boa shot a thumbs-up. "As soon as the main man gets here."

Kodiak took a piece of duct tape and strapped it across the bishop's mouth. "You won't feel a thing," he assured him. Then cruelly added: "But then again, I've never been shot in the head with my brains spilling out all over the floor."

This brought on a slight smile of malicious amusement from Boa, who continued to set the stage with double-checks.

When Team Leader entered the room with the feeble-looking pope by his side, the old man looked as if his legs were about to buckle as his knees shook unsteadily. With hardly any effort at all, Team Leader forced the pontiff to his knees. "For the man of the hour," said Team Leader, "the best seat in the house."

Team Leader removed his holstered weapon and held it by his side, the Sig hardly noticeable in the shadows due to its black-brushed steel. Then he said: "Let's get this show on the road."

The bishop began to sob as Team Leader approached him.

CHAPTER FORTY-TWO

Washington, D.C.
September 27, Early Afternoon.

Shari sat in the chair with Attorney General Dean Hamilton and Chief Advisor Alan Thornton sitting on either side of her, while President Burroughs prepared for his first address to the international community. As an awkward silence fell over the room, President Burrough's quietly read the script of his speech. Sitting on a couch against the curve of the wall looking over the recent data received from Shari's team, were Vice President Bohlmer and two of the president's senior advisors. The only sound was the flipping of pages.

The president heaved a sigh as he laid the pages on the desk, then massaged his temples with the tips of his fingers. "All right, people," he started. "In about an hour I have to address the world on the status of the pope. What I want from you is a plan as to how I'm supposed to communicate to the international community without our alliances finding fault with the United States. In other words, I need to base my decisions on fact rather than speculation. What I need is something positive. And from this drafted garbage in front of me, I'm getting the feeling that we're making little progress if any at all."

Shari took the initiative. "Mr. President, I have something. How it relates to the Soldiers of Islam isn't quite clear yet."

"And what would that be, Special Agent?"

"I'm talking about these," she said, producing photos from a leather briefcase. "Yesterday, I was able to burn and decipher the encryptions on a disc given to me by the Mossad—a disc containing the biographical records of the Soldiers of Islam, as well as other information I believe ties in with what's going on. Right now, the connection is thin, at best. But given time I'll be able to figure it out. I just need a few more pieces of the puzzle." While she spoke, she looked around the room to examine the faces for micro-expressions, such as the perceptively surprised look, a nervous tic or wandering eyes, anything that would betray their sentiments. All she saw were poker faces.

"May I see those?" asked the president, extending a hand.

Shari proffered the bait. "They're photos of high-ranking business officials, some from oil conglomerates, and politicians from Russia, Venezuela, and Israel, which I assume to be clandestine meetings since they appear to be surveillance photos. The second and third batches are surveillance photos of the known members of the Soldiers of Islam. The third set of photos are of tracts of oil beneath Palestinian territories and the Golan Heights. These were all tied in with information regarding the terrorists." The president examined the photos. She carefully watched his every expression until he shook his head in bewilderment. "And we don't know how these would tie in with the abduction of the pope, if at all?"

"On the surface, Mr. President, no," she answered. "However, when I went to the Embassy of Israel to see the man responsible for creating the data, he wanted the disc back. I refused. Later that night a team of operatives was sent to retrieve that data . . . and they tried to take me out."

The president's face took on what Shari read to be bafflement. "Take you out?"

"Someone tried to kill me over that information, Mr. President. On paper, it looks like nothing, but when somebody comes into my home and tries to kill me for something that appears meaningless, that tells me there's something damaging in those photos."

The president continued to examine the pictures. "And these operatives?"

"There were three, sir. However, law enforcement got involved and they exited as quickly as they entered," she lied. "Just mild damage committed to the home, sir, nothing else." It was porous at best, but it was the only thing she could come up with.

"I didn't hear anything about this."

"It's minor considering the issue at hand, Mr. President. Again, the matter was taken care of long before it got out of control."

The president continued to look at her with a questionable

194

look, one that said: *I'm not sure if I believe you.* He shuffled from one photo to the next, giving each scrutiny.

"Mr. President," Shari interjected, "I'm not sure how they tie in with what's going on, but I know there's a connection."

The president tossed the photos on the desk. "I disagree," he said. In Shari's mind, a contradiction was as good as an admission of guilt. The president was now trying to downplay the photos. So, Kimball was right, after all, she considered. The man was simply trying to find out what she knew.

"Special Agent Cohen, I have to address the world in less than an hour. And you want me to offer these photos of politicians, businessmen, and tracts of oil to the world community, as evidence of the pope's well-being? Is that what you're asking me to do?"

"Mr. President, I'm not offering a solution as to what you should present to the world. I'm saying that this is *key* to what happened—*why* it happened."

"Special Agent, we know why it happened. They're holding the pope so that certain demands can be met. And these photos have nothing to do with that."

Vice President Jonas Bohlmer walked quietly to the president's desk and held his hand out. "Can I look at those, Jim?"

The president nodded and turned his attention back to Shari. "I don't know if it's your lack of progress in this situation, Special Agent, but I cannot afford to have my time wasted by someone who's simply grasping at straws. What I want to know is if you have anything besides these pictures?"

"Just a report from the CSI Unit stating that the Blair Hose was sanitized."

"What does that mean?"

"It means the Soldiers of Islam purposely left behind no biological trace evidence. Yet they leave behind two members whom they knew would be identifiable. If that is the case, why sanitize the area? It's a contradiction of actions, Mr. President, which tells me that Blair House was staged to provide us with a red herring, so we wouldn't look beyond the box."

"Why the red herring?" asked the vice president. Shari turned to him. "I don't know."

The vice president shook his head in admonishment. "Ms.

Cohen, you seem to have more questions than answers. That's not why you were put into this position."

"I understand, Mr. Vice President, but I'm doing the best I can with what I have."

The vice president turned to the photos, then back to Shari. "Special Agent Cohen, I'm going to be candid with you," he said. "From the beginning, I was against you being a part of this at all. And now you're proving me right."

"How so?"

At first, the vice president said nothing, his glaring demeanor saying it all. "For the fact, Ms. Cohen, that you are a Jewish counterpart in a situation that can be deadly, should the Soldiers of Islam find out that a woman of Jewish faith is manning the helm."

"Mr. Vice President, with all due respect, I am quite qualified to perform my duties whether or not I'm Jewish . . . or a woman."

"You know better than I do, Ms. Cohen, that you're a lethal combination when dealing with such people. Not only are you failing in your tasks, but if these terrorists should ever gain the truth that you're spearheading this charge, then that only compounds the difficulty. Don't you agree?"

Shari was seething. Her grandmother was right. In some peculiar way, in a land where freedom was paramount, she was still being persecuted on some infinitesimal level, even with impeccable credentials to back her up. And then her grandmother's voice rang true in her head, a prophetic aphorism she recalled as a child, then later in the Holocaust Museum.

Because you're a Jew you'll always be persecuted. But never forget who you are and always be proud, because one day you will be reminded of what you are, and you'll need to fight back to survive. Never forget that, my littlest one.

Shari started to rebut. "Mr. Vice President—"

"These photos, Ms. Cohen, with all due respect, are worthless. And I agree with the president. You're grasping at straws." He returned the photos to Shari. "We've no use for these. Keep them."

Remaining composed, she took them without hesitation. At least the bait had been laid.

With time the discussion took on a new direction such as global hate crimes against those of the Arab population, riots in South

America, murders within the United States in retribution. Shari knew her diligence would be met with deadly force, regardless of the photos having been cast off as worthless. The president's tactic of demonstrating indifference was simply a cosmetic cover. This she knew.

What *they* didn't know was that she was thoroughly prepared to take them on.

As Alan Thornton and the vice president prescribed their recommendations for addressing the world, Shari glanced at the photos. She nodded as if she perceived something of importance about them. If somebody in this office was involved with the pope's abduction, she was sure her actions were under examination.

While the president readied himself to go on air with nothing more than an overview rather than gospel, she sat quietly. She considered she was invisible to the administration as they discussed the image of the United States in the eyes of the world, amongst the male selves. The welfare of the pope wasn't mentioned at all. And this, she told herself, was politics at its worse.

Sometimes the president would ask Shari a question, but only because she was the counterterrorism expert, for which she responded appropriately. She noted the president was creating a mental script of half-truths with her help, perhaps taking things to report out of context as an act of saving face. This, too, made her feel dirty. After all, this was the world of politics in which truths were often woven into fables, and fables were woven into truths.

As time drew near for the president's address, Shari appraised the faces around her one last time and spotted nothing.

The only thing she could do now was to wait for someone to kill her.

#

Boston, Massachusetts

The dampness of the New England air had seeped into the marrow of the pope's bones. Wearing only his undergarments, he embraced himself against the chill and sat watching inhumanities toward the bishop unfold before his eyes.

Team Leader stood before the camera at center stage and spoke in Arabic. "To the people of this country and your allies. Unfortunately, the world of Islam must endure the political maneuverings of a government motivated by corruption, rather than do what is right, such as to stop the oppression of Arab nations with your desire to turn us into the centerpiece of your interests. If you think this is a unique situation, think again. The political machine that drives your country is stimulated by *those* who have the finances to maintain political camps in other nations, then bullies their allied support.

"It has come to our knowledge that the United States has no intention to abide by our demands but continues to fight for the support of allied nations who do not dare to stand against them. Therefore, since the Great Satan has not met our demands, we will take the life of one of your bishops, as an action praised in the eyes of Allah." Team Leader hesitated, chose his next words carefully, then continued. "Those on Capitol Hill, those in the White House, those in American democracy must understand that your way is not the Islamic way. But that the Islamic way is the only true way."

Beside him, the bishop began to beg for his life in earnest. Team Leader ignored him and spoke over his cries.

"We will continue to maintain our edict that there are to be no discussions, no debates, and no negotiations. The death of your bishop will serve to motivate the politicians of the world to see things differently, and to work accordingly with the demands offered by the authority of the Soldiers of Islam."

Team Leader removed his hands from behind the small of his back until the Sig was in full view of the camera. "Under the watchful eye of Allah, it is with honor that I kill a minion of Satan, before Satan's own eyes."

Team Leader beckoned for someone off stage.

Kodiak jerked the pope up and dragged him to the stage and forced him to the floor next to Bishop Angelo. The pope winced when sharp splinters of wood bit into his knees. On the monitor the pope appeared emaciated and disheveled, his garments soiled, his limbs wispy thin. The wrinkles on his face were deep, long, and more profound. To view him on tape, many would consider the man who was a king looked more like a skid-row bum.

The pope turned to Bishop Angelo, held his hand out to him,

and wrapped his fingers around Angelo's, his movement minimal by the cuffs, and received his contact by becoming a conduit to the pope's spiritual power.

"Be not afraid," he told him. "For God holds a special place for you in His kingdom."

For a brief moment, their eyes met. And for that concise passage of time, Bishop Angelo seemed at peace. His faith was no longer alien to him.

The pope squeezed his hand, a gesture that everything was fine— would be fine, and Bishop Angelo gave a nod of perception.

"Allah is great," cried Team Leader. In one swift move, he pointed the pistol at the base of the bishop's skull and pulled the trigger. The bishop slumped forward, dead, a quick and merciful kill. At the same time blood sprayed against the pope's face, warm and wet, the fluid causing the pope to flinch as if in pain.

Boa turned off the camera.

Team Leader immediately pulled the stunned pope to his feet and pushed him toward Kodiak. "After you hook him up, return for the bishop's body and lay him at the feet of the pope to rot."

Temporarily lobotomized by the trauma, the pope was guided from the room.

After holstering his pistol, Team Leader removed the videotape and examined it by turning it over in his gloved hand. "We must move quickly," he said to Boa. "Make sure the feed gets to Yahweh. He'll release it to go viral."

"Understood."

When Boa left the room with the camera to transfer the images, Team Leader stood in silence. With the stink of gunpowder still in the air, he drew in the scent as if it was intoxicating, then expelled it with an equally long exhale. Then he turned toward the bishop who laid there with the back of his head pared open like petals of a rose. Blood and gore lay everywhere.

With his hands clasped behind the small of his back, Team Leader left the room.

CHAPTER FORTY-THREE

Washington, D.C.
September 27, Mid-noon

Shari appeared pale when she reached her Lexus. Since being dismissed from the Oval Office, she had looked over her shoulder for someone following her as paranoia began to take hold. All she saw were people coming and going, never the same face, not a single person even looking in her direction, as everyone seemed preoccupied with their circumstances.

With her hands shaking, the keys jingled as she started the car. But when her cell phone rang, she jumped before answering it. "Yes?"

"You're clear," the voice said. "There's no tag behind you."

"Are you sure?"

"I'm sure."

Shari's shoulders slumped as if a great weight had been lifted. But the painful muscle strain at the base of her skull continued.

After pulling out of the parking space, she placed the phone on speaker. "So, how'd it go?" said the voice.

She set the phone on the opposite seat; her practiced eye glancing often into the rearview mirror looking for something the Vatican Knights may have missed. "I'm not sure," she told Kimball. "Of course, they dismissed it, which we knew they would. But at least the chum is in the water."

"So, who was there?"

"The norm: The president, the vice president, the attorney general, the chief advisor, and two senior advisors."

"All of whom would know about the existence of the Force Elite."

"So, it could be any one of them?"

"Or all of them."

Shari looked into the rearview mirror and saw a van pull in behind her. "I hope that's you. You in the van?"

"It's me. You're fine."

Her tension headache eased. "Let's hope they bite, Kimball, because I'm fresh out of answers, theories, and pieces of the puzzle."

"Trust me," he said. "If there's a chance of exposure, they'll send somebody, and they'll send them fast. I'm surprised they didn't send along a tag."

"That's maybe because they think I'm off guard . . . And they know where I live."

"I've got Isaiah and Micah following me. There's no tag on me, either."

"I hope I'm not wrong about this," she told him.

"After what happened last night, I don't think so."

They drove on for a minute with neither speaking to the other. Shari looked into the rearview mirror and noted Kimball's chiseled features, the movie-star looks. In return, Kimball smiled and waved. And like a schoolgirl caught looking at a boy she had a crush on, she quickly turned away and chided herself for making the act so obvious. She was, after all, married with two children. Nevertheless, through the corner of her eye, she stole another peek.

"Kimball?"

"Yeah."

"How safe is my home?"

"I'm thinking it's still a hot spot."

"Good," she said. "Because I want them to know where they can find me."

"As you said, they know. But it'll be dangerous."

"I know. But at least you'll be there."

"We'll all be there. Leviticus is already at the house with Nehemiah keeping it under surveillance. So far, it's clear. The audio bugs are picking up nothing inside."

She hesitated, looked into the mirror again, and then wondered if a man like him who was considered to be without conscience or morality, had the capability of loving somebody on any level. *Was there anything remotely and truly human about him at all?* Then: "Kimball?"

"Yeah."

She wanted to ask: *Are you capable of loving someone?* But thought against it. "Never mind," she told him. Then she canceled the call.

\#

"She was lying as to what happened last night," Yahweh said over the phone. "All this crap about law enforcement showing up at her house at the most opportune time, that's bull. And she failed to mention this Kimball Hayden guy."

"I can tell you he's a man you don't want to mess with. Three elite members were taken out last night by this man alone . . . Enough said."

"I know about last night. I want to know about *him*."

Judas was surprised to receive a call from Yahweh. He had always worked through George Pappandopolous, his conduit. "His code name was the Professor," he began, "because no matter how good anybody else was as an assassin, they're students compared to this guy. At that time, he was the most lethal weapon the White House had to offer in its day—a solo black operative whose skills were far superior to anyone else."

"And?"

"In 1991, during the outbreak of the Gulf War, political principals sent Hayden to dispatch Saddam Hussein hoping to cause turmoil within the ranks of the Republican Guard, so they would vacate Kuwait before the United States and its allies had to move in. But the guy dropped off the grid and it was believed he was killed during the mission."

"Yet he surfaces at the doorstep of an FBI agent years later. Interesting. Was he alone?"

"I saw only one man, just a shadow—big guy. Tall."

"Then take him out."

Judas could feel his scrotum crawl. Asking him to take out Kimball Hayden was like asking him to wrestle a full-grown bull to the ground with just your bare hands—a huge feat. "I don't think you understand—"

"What I understand, Judas, is that you're getting a large royalty for your services. Special Agent Cohen is getting dangerously close to the truth, which is evident by the materials presented today at the Oval Office. If she gets any closer, the cause will falter and your royalty will be pissed away because you, me, and half of Capitol Hill will be in Club Fed or worse."

"I can't do this alone. And I'm not sure the remaining members of Omega Team can do it either."

"For chrissakes, Judas, Hayden isn't a god. He's *one* man."

Judas shifted uncomfortably from one leg to the other. Normally he was seldom rattled, but he had met Kimball personally and unlike Yahweh, was not blind to Kimball's deadly skills.

"You're the field general in this cause," added Yahweh. "See that the job gets done. Take out Cohen, and if Hayden is there, take him out as well. Start earning your money!" The call concluded with the definite click of disconnection.

#

The pope hardly looked like the man whom kings and queens bowed before. His face was partially crusted with blood, and the one-time sparkle of hope in his eyes was all but gone.

Sometime within the last half hour—he didn't know when—Kodiak had laid the body of Bishop Angelo beside him. The pulp and gore of his wound was a disturbing sight to the pontiff, enough to feel a twinge of fading hope.

Reaching for the bishop's hand, which was still warm to the touch, the pope embraced it with both of his. "There was nothing I could do," he told him. "Nothing at all." He closed his eyes and prayed, his lips moving silently.

For the first time in his life, Pope Pius wondered if God had abandoned them, then he admonished himself for even considering such a notion. After all, He always had a design. But whatever that design may be, Pope Pius didn't have a clue.

#

While Shari was at JEH working under the watchful eye of her staff, Kimball was at the archdiocese recharging his strength by catching a quick catnap, a two-hour respite to wash away the fatigue that had been accumulating for several hours.

For the first time in a long time, he didn't dream of his demons surfacing from the sands of Iraq but envisioned the lovely and almost too perfect face of Shari Cohen as she smiled at him, her face surrounded by a nimbus of light. When she spoke to him, he couldn't hear her, although her lips moved gracefully. And her smile, above all else, intoxicating.

She would try to communicate with him, her hands held out in invitation for Kimball to come forward. But he found it impossible to approach, his feet riveted by the force of his cowardice, as he stood there damning himself for not acting on her encouragement. And as she began to retreat into an all-consuming light, Kimball watched with regret as she moved on without him.

It was here that Kimball awoke with his mouth cotton dry. Staring at the ceiling with his tongue lapping at his parched lips, Kimball found himself admitting that he was becoming deeply infatuated with her. But she was, however, a married woman. Just another sin in the eyes of God and another reason for Him to tell Kimball 'no.'

But he believed she forgave him for what he was and what he did, which he was grateful for. So, he gravitated toward her with a pull that was unlike anything he had experienced before. She had embraced him with her mercy.

Getting to his feet, he wondered why God continued to look favorably upon him, especially when he seemed to test the limits of His rules. The answer was simple: play now and pay later on Judgment Day.

There was no doubt in Kimball's mind that redemption was unsalvageable in the eyes of God, and that he was doomed to damnation in which his Deliverance would be to a place of dark rule.

On the nightstand beside him, a clock seemed to tick louder than normal as if counting off the moments toward the Day of Transcendence, which was not a day Kimball was looking forward to at all.

#

Washington, D.C.
September 27. High-Noon

Shari Cohen's team had worked diligently throughout the day trying to acquire whatever background information was available regarding the principals of YUKOS Oil and Venezuela's PDVSA. As Shari had expected, further information on Abraham Obadiah was non-existent.

Although the information was plentiful, there was nothing ascribed to the primary players in the photos that indicated they were involved in any illegalities—another block wall. So, Shari wondered if she was wrong in her conjecture that there was a tie between the encryptions, the biographical records, and the pope's kidnapping.

With the sting of pain between her shoulders subsiding a little, she took a seat and watched the conclusion of the president's address. The man looked dramatically agitated; the gesticulations of his hands a visual technique noting that the kidnapping of the pope was a violation of religious freedom everywhere, and that intolerance was the true sin here. Other than that, he offered nothing more than false hope as hate crimes escalated. Riots against Islamic communities within Christian nations felt the wrath of anger, as mosques burned to the ground and people dragged through the streets. With a heavy heart, Shari felt an uneasiness creep over her as the world began to unravel before her eyes.

Working tirelessly as the day waxed on, she examined every bit of data coming in from all sources, national and international. ISIS was recruiting through the Internet, the volume of responses overwhelming. Devotion to a Holy War was suddenly at fever pitch. The word through the international chat rooms was that threats were being fostered against the United States and its allies, by insurgents from the Muslim and Islamic faiths. But there was nothing intercepted that shed any light as to the location of the pope. The Soldiers of Islam, if nothing else, were careful in their communication.

Outside the sun had set, the streetlights illuminating beams of gold and amber. With sheaves of documents littering her desktop, Shari stared out the window as if there was something hypnotic about the landscape. But in reality, she was thinking. Somewhere in the darkness of those D.C. streets, Leviticus and Nehemiah were watching for her safety with spying eyes. But was she also being watched by the

Force Elite? She could only wonder.

After a moment of reflection, she cast a sidelong glance to a framed photograph of her family situated at the corner of her desk. With Gary smiling his boyish charm and the girls smiling with teeth either missing or sitting irregular along the gum line, she picked up the photo and gave it her full attention. She had fallen in love with Gary only after he had fought for her affection and suffered through her countless refusals. Perhaps it was his determination or perseverance that finally won her over. Either way, their love had grown together and created two beautiful children.

Then comes Kimball Hayden, a man who was larger than life and a poster child for the bad-boy image, who had somehow worked his way into her emotions without the tenacity Gary had shown.

She traced her fingers over her husband's image, and quietly asked his forgiveness for these feelings she could not control. Her answer, of course, came in the form of absolute silence.

Slowly, she returned the photo to the desk with Kimball on her mind. For the second time that day, she felt dirty.

#

Clark County Coroner's Office, Las Vegas, Nevada, September 27, Early Evening

The Coroner's lab had the infusion smells of alcohols and chemicals, which was far better than the stench of the corpses lying in gathered pieces on stainless steel tables.

Clothing from the bodies were removed and bagged as evidence. And body parts were matched to torsos by sorting through the corresponding sizes and densities of the pieces. Rib cages lay open revealing the lack of internal organs, lumbar columns fully visible. Femurs and fibulas were separated but matched to individual corpses. Nevertheless, there was enough left to piece together IDs that garnered immediate strikes from Interpol, the Department of Homeland Security, and other top worldwide agencies.

After the coroner's office prioritized their work to establish a 99.97% probability of the identities on the corpses, they sent the results to Special Agent Cohen of the FBI, according to the red-flag status in their network, which was protocol.

The identities of the bullet-riddled bodies found in the Mojave Desert were about to provide Shari Cohen with some very major pieces to her puzzle.

CHAPTER FORTY-FOUR

When Kimball received the call from Shari, he could tell she was elated. "You're not going to believe this. Six bodies were discovered in Mesquite, Nevada, this morning, about four hundred miles south of Ogden, Utah."

Kimball recognized the name Ogden, which was the origination point for the Soldiers of Islam. "Okay."

"I just received a preliminary report from the Clark County Coroner's Office, identifying the bodies as the six remaining members of the Soldiers of Islam."

Kimball pressed the phone closer to his ear. "They know this for certain?"

"Over ninety-nine percent certain, which means I'm definitely on the right track. The bodies, according to the findings, have been in the desert for several days. This means they were dead long before the pope was kidnapped."

"Execution style?"

"Yes. Their hands were bound with flex cuffs. The ammo was from an MP5."

"MP5?"

"That's right," she returned.

"So, they were executed, dumped, their residences sanitized—"

"—and Blair House was seized with the military precision incapable of the Soldiers of Islam," she interjected.

"But better managed by—"

"—The Force Elite."

"Yes! They still exist, Kimball." There was a period of silence before Shari spoke. Then more evenly, as if stunned by her admission, she said, "We have him, Kimball . . . Our government took the pope."

"Why?"

"To start a war," she said. It was all too clear. "Who is the one man on this planet who by the power of his presence alone can incite the world? Especially when ISIS has committed themselves to fight a Holy War."

"Again: I have to ask why?"

"For oil," she said without hesitation. "It's all about oil."

#

After receiving the images of the bishop's killing through his connections, Yahweh viewed it several times in the deep shadows of his study. The only pool of light in the room came from the TV screen.

Sometimes he played the disc in slow motion as the bishop's skull erupted in a fountain of blood and tried to understand why the cleric was so terrified of dying when an Islamic terrorist willingly surrendered his life with little consideration.

In the first few clips, it was obvious that the bishop was alarmed, his sense of self-preservation animalistic in display with absolute terror. It was as if the man was without faith. But when the pope reached out to him and whispered a few words of contentment, words not heard over the video, the bishop seemed pacified.

Although he considered it gruesome, he replayed the image over and over again, trying to differentiate why a man of the cloth was afraid of graduating to a greater level of being, when a man from another culture was not. No matter how many times he played it, the answer or understanding 'why' never came to him.

Finally shutting off the video, he sat in utter darkness to muse over the brilliance of the images.

Bringing the pope on stage was a brilliant stroke on the part of Team Leader—the staged event created to provoke and encourage anger. Watching the pope in his disheveled state would no doubt work wonders on the emotions of Christians worldwide, and wreak havoc long before Shari could do anything to quell the matter.

"Brilliant," he whispered, then once again, but in a softer tone and with far less emotion, he uttered, "Brilliant."

Within four hours the disc went viral. A few minutes later the world community was in an uproar. The international news media played the edited version of the execution over . . . and over . . . and over again.

Yahweh was pleased.

#

"Oil?"

"Think about it," she said. "Those photos of the Soldiers of Islam weren't on the biographical records as mere surveillance shots; they were being targeted. And now they're dead—all of them. Now we know *who* does not have the pope. But we can surmise as to who *does*, which leads us to number two."

Her voice picked up momentum as she spoke. Kimball was sure he would have to tell her to slow down. "An American liquidation squad tried to take me out for having that disc given to me by the attaché of the Israeli government."

"Which ties them together—we know that."

"True. But now we know why there were photos of the oil tracts . . . and of the business and political principals from oil-producing countries," she said.

Kimball didn't see the connection. "I'm not getting you."

"Not only is that disc a schematic," she told him, "it's also a political agenda." Shari pressed the phone closer to her mouth. "The ties between Russia and Israel have been strengthening lately because they share a common interest, which is Syria. Israel wants to maintain control over the Golan Heights, something Russia supports. And, of course, Russia had a strategic advantage with Syria, which they're trying to get back with al-Assad put into power as their puppet leader. Israel supports the Russian cause because Russia supports Israel's right on an international scale to maintain the Golan Heights, which we now know is over an oil-rich stock."

"Go on."

"Right now, the Middle East is in absolute chaos with war, and many believe that we're racing into World War Three which began on nine-eleven."

Kimball clung to her words since the pope had acknowledged that the world had been in the beginning stages of a World War for some time now, maybe 9/11 as she stated.

"The United States remains beholden to accords with Saudi

Arabia regarding oil, even knowing that Saudi Arabia was instrumental in 9/11, which has caused anger and a shift in the current administration against President Burroughs because he refused to take a stance. So, what does that tell you?"

"That we're still dependent on Saudi oil, which is why he's not breaking from the accords."

"That's right. And now Burroughs has ostracized himself from many in Congress and the House, who believe he may have tipped his hand to show the world how dependent we are on oil, by looking the other way despite the Saudi involvement in nine-eleven with a forgive-and-forget approach to the matter. But it's a strategic move on the part of Burrough's. Saudi Arabia is rich in oil. And as Russia tries to get a foothold in the Middle East, the United States keeps its foothold as long as it remains in league with the oil-rich nation. And we know that he who holds the oil-rich fields."

"Also holds the scepter of rule."

"Correct. And as the war escalates in the Middle East," she continued, "oilfields may begin to burn and disappear. Those schematics on the disc show an abundance of fossil fuel to tap from. But international opinion is keeping Israel from extracting oil in the Golan Heights and the Palestinian territories, because of the possibility of worldwide condemnation."

"But if they have Russia's support it could ease tensions somewhat should war break out on a global scale."

"And it's heading that way, Kimball. The conflict is escalating at an incredible pace. And the number one commodity everyone needs on this planet is oil. That is why every nation outside of Third-World countries has an interest in the Middle East. Every country." Then to punctuate her point with somewhat of a sad measure, she said: "They're preparing, Kimball . . . If this turns into a global conflict, which there's a good possibility that it may, they will hold the scepter of rule to a new world order. They're positioning themselves for what I believe they know is coming . . . And that's global war."

"And Venezuela's position in this?"

"They're swimming in oil," she answered. "They're also close with Russia. So, I believe their benefit to the cause is to aid Russia and Israel by developing a conglomerate between them."

"This is still conjecture, however," he said. "Yeah, sure. But it makes sense."

"If this is the case, why would Burroughs send a task force to quash your efforts?"

"Again, I don't know."

"So, you think a hidden cabal within the ranks of the United States government is supporting this new order, by stage-managing certain events to kick start events to win global support?"

"It's a possibility," she said. "There are those in the Senate and the House who strongly disagree with Burroughs. They believe if the world is heading into global conflict, then we need to prepare as well. But Burrough's is stonewalling these efforts. And America's staunchest allies in Europe continue to follow his lead which stifles the efforts of those on Capitol Hill since allied support with Russia is currently unfavorable."

"So certain principals decided upon a final agenda," he added. "The Soldiers of Islam weren't soldiers at all, but patsies. And our government used them to point an accusing finger at so that the world community would make a rush to judgment as to who committed one of the most grievous acts of terrorism without question, which the world did. And what better way to do this by attacking the global psyche by using the most recognizable religious figure as a tool of war."

"Sadly, governments would use the pope to create new boundaries by mustering global support through propaganda," she said.

Kimball remained silent.

"If the pope is murdered," she continued, "propaganda wins, and Israel takes over the Palestinian territories with little condemnation from world leaders. Russia would plow through Syria with little censure. And the United States would benefit because Burrough's administration would be severely weakened and his supporters gone, which would allow political principals to openly back this movement. In the process, millions would die as collateral damage because oil has a much greater value. But what's truly ironic about this whole thing . . . is that we're the ones who hastened this holy war, not them. *We're* the ones using the fear of terrorism as a weapon to divide the world. What's even scarier is that despite the efforts to gain an upper hand by prognosticating future events, they lack the foresight to see that if there is a third World War . . . there'll probably be nobody left at its end."

"I'd like to think that we've gone beyond that," he said.

"As would I. But if there's one thing mankind has yet to learn, Kimball, is that history bears little lessons to those who are unwilling to learn from them."

Kimball thought: *Touché.*

CHAPTER FORTY-FIVE

Shari was disgusted with the savagery behind the highly doctored images aired over *CNN* and other stations. There were sidebar videos of the aftermath regarding Muslim and Islamic populations being tormented, abused, and harangued in predominantly Christian nations, even when devout Muslims and Islamists believed peace was the true virtue, whereas violence was an abomination in the eyes of God. It was unfair to the sincere practitioners, she thought. To those who truly didn't deserve this fate.

Even worse was to show the world the chronic repetitions of the pope's ordeal. Showing these pictures played into the hands of the terrorists. The media knew this and didn't care because ratings skyrocketed. Events such as this always fed the insatiable appetites of the public, the news mere and macabre entertainment.

Then her cell phone rang. She picked it up. "Ms. Cohen."

Shari could tell it was Punch Murdock. "Yes, Special Agent Murdock. What can I do for you?"

"Actually, it's what I can do for you," he returned. "I just wanted you to know that I've tendered my resignation."

"Oh, no. I hope it wasn't because of what happened at Blair House," she said.

"It's all good," he told her. "And I do take responsibility. I have to. And it's time to put this old goat to pasture anyway. But I think I may have found something that could prove quite useful to your investigation."

"And what's that?"

"Intercepted paperwork," he said simply. "Paperwork?"

"Of a delicate nature that shouldn't be discussed over the phone. Something that may give you an indication as to where the pope is."

214

Shari could feel her pulse pounding along her temples as her mind searched for the proper wordage, only to find no wordplay at all.

"Are you there, Ms. Cohen?"

"Where are you, Mr. Murdock?"

"Please call me Punch. I've always hated my last name."

"Where are you, Punch?"

"I'm close," he said. "I'm at a Starbucks close to the Holocaust Museum. Saying my last goodbyes to a cute little barista."

"I can meet you there," she told him.

"Not in the open area with classified information."

"Then where?"

"There's a post office box outlet nearby. You know the one I'm talking about?"

"Yes, of course. Down the street but off the beaten track."

"That's the one. I'll leave the envelope inside box seven-three-four. Did you get that? Seven-three-four. You'll find the key underneath the nearest trash canister. If I were you, Ms. Cohen, I wouldn't hesitate on this."

When she was about to say *I'll be right there*, Punch Murdock had hung up.

#

Judas stood in the shadows with the Capitol Building in his view and racked his semi-automatic pistol.

The sun had fallen, and in the pooling shadows, he was surrounded by the remaining members of Omega Team, whose faces were concealed with grease paint. They were heavily armed and wore black military fatigues, each man becoming shadows within shadows and things that were blacker than black.

"Listen up, people," said Judas, "the objective is clear. We're here to take out Target Red. And FYI, the guy who took out half of Omega Team last night is no novice to the game. He's ruthless. He's deadly. And one man alone doesn't stand a chance against him. I'm assuming he's now a part of Cohen's protective detail, so he's a number one priority for a takedown. You will locate and maintain a constant visual on both targets. You will also be in constant communication with one another through your lip mics to alert your position to supporting team members at all times. If a unit member does not respond, then I want you to assume that Target Red has compromised Omega Team. I need you to be prepared, people. I need you to keep your heads up because this guy is serious business and not to be taken lightly."

One of the commandos charged his weapon, a testosterone gesture that he was more than ready to take on all competitors.

"Do your job, gentlemen, and you'll all be rich men living off the coast of Belize. If not, then you'll be keeping company with Dark Lord in whatever hole Kimball Hayden pitched him in. Happy hunting."

Omega Team gathered inside a van of dark gray primer to blend in with the surrounding darkness, started the engine, and made their way to the interception point to take out Target Red.

When the van was out of sight, Judas entered his vehicle with a mission of his own.

#

After getting off the phone with Murdock, Shari couldn't help the odd feeling like the trace of a cold finger running down her spine. There was no doubt in her mind that the Force Elite was going to make a move, and soon.

Shari flipped back the screen of her cell phone and dialed a quick-call number.

"Yeah, Shari." It was Kimball.

"I'm leaving the building," she told him. "Through the West End gate."

"We'll be there."

"Kimball?"

"Yeah."

"Stay close. I'm really scared."

"We're here for you," he assured her. "You'll be fine."

"I'm heading to a post office box outlet."

"I know where it's at. Can I ask why?"

"I got a call from Special Agent Murdock," she told him. "He said he found classified information that would benefit our cause to find the pope."

"About what?"

"He wouldn't say. He didn't want to say exactly over the open line."

"Be careful."

"You think they'll follow me?"

"If what you said in front of the president with someone there who was a part of the cause, I'm sure you rattled someone's cage enough to draw a tail. Keep in mind that my team will be close. If there's anyone following you, we'll know it."

"We need these people alive, Kimball. I need to mine them for information."

"I'm not exactly sure they'll comply with your needs," he told her. "These people carry weapons for a reason."

Shari sighed as butterflies formed in her stomach. In fact, her belly was clenching into a slick fist. "Their deaths will serve us no purpose, Kimball. We *have* to learn the location of the pope."

"Shari, this is not a game. My team will do what they can to preserve the lives of the opposition. Preserving lives is what we do. But you have to understand that we're working with a mentality in which there is no option other than to kill or be killed. I know the consequences if we fail, and my team knows the consequences too. If we fail, we at least did all we could. You did all you could . . . Just don't expect miracles because I don't believe in them."

"Kimball?"

"Yes."

"You need to have faith." She hung up.

#

Boston, Massachusetts
September 27, Evening

Team Leader was rejuvenated and in full command after watching the video of the PG-13 rated execution on television. Despite the progress of Shari Cohen, there was no doubt the cause moved toward the ultimate goal to create an absolute schism between the Middle East and the rest of the world. He knew hatred, like fear, was a great motivator if used wisely. And if used wisely enough, hatred could reshape the balance of power, even on a global scale.

Team Leader moved down the dank corridor as pompous as an athlete who considers himself unbeatable, with his arrogance laying the groundwork of invincibility. He had nursed this seed of thought to fruition. With huge tracts of oil beneath the soil he walked upon in his native Israel and the Palestinian territories, there was no telling how stable their economies would become as they prepared for the coming hardships of a war that seemed to be brewing, if not inevitable.

Using Pope Pius XIII was the tool of propaganda that had moved mountains in ways Team Leader never dreamed of. Political landscapes were on the verge of rising or falling, the balances of power were being manipulated by the prejudices of people of all countries, by tapping into their fragile national psyches.

These thoughts massaged Team Leader's ego as he congratulated himself, and he was proud he was able to use the hatred in his heart to such a magnificent advantage. After all, he just happened to be the one to promote it, since he was a realist and not an idealist. *Peace in the Middle East was never more than a pipe dream.*

His face didn't betray his inner smile as he walked past the four remaining members of the papal council, who huddled on their mattresses with their heads lowered in fear of the man who held the decision over life or death.

When Team Leader entered the pope's room, a vague scent of blood and copper wafted like something alive and floating freely. But Team Leader had the scents pinpointed for what they truly were, the prerequisites for decay and body rot. It had been several hours since Bishop Angelo had been murdered and his body placed at the foot of the pontiff. And somewhere within the darkness blowflies alit, with their buzzing a constant and incessant drone.

Team Leader engaged his night-vision monocular, and the room took on a clear and phosphorous hue. Vague shapes were no longer mere images or shadows but held depth and width and height. And Team Leader, no longer feeling detached from the darkness, was now a part of it as he gazed down upon the old man who lay beneath two layers of blankets. The contours of his body poked out pointedly like broomsticks through the fabric. Beside him, Bishop Angelo also lay beneath a blanket, the pulp of his head barely exposed as a black mass of flies assembled to lay their eggs. Team Leader guessed the pope had covered him for the sake of reverence.

"I owe you an apology, Your Holiness. But the killing was necessary to the cause. I hope the pain is not too considerable."

"What kind of a person murders an innocent man?" the pope asked from beneath the covers.

"A person with a mission," he stated. His voice was calm, reserved, and full of confidence. "A person who is going to change the world one government at a time."

Team Leader rounded the mattress and looked down at the pope who labored to rise from beneath his blankets.

"You think what you're about to do for the world is salvation?" the pope asked, the blankets falling to his waist. In the green cast of NVG lighting, the man looked impossibly emaciated.

"Not at all," said Team Leader. "But I do believe it will be salvation for *my* people and those who follow."

"With my death, you will get what you want—a war that will cost millions of lives, as well as an added burden to your soul."

"What I see, Your Holiness, is the means of achievement. There are always sacrifices in causes, you know that. Think of your history and the Crusades."

"What you're doing will only foster rage to the point of a hatred so great, it'll only serve to generate a holocaust. It's not worth it."

"In my eyes, Your Holiness, it is. Your eyes haven't seen what mine have. Your eyes didn't witness your family murdered. Your eyes didn't cast themselves upon a loving, gentle father who died a slow death because of one man's deep-rooted hatred for Jews one sunny day in Ramallah. You speak, but you know nothing. You live in a world where your tea may be too hot to sip, or perhaps the air is a little too humid for your comfort. But in my world, having blood on your hands is the norm. And I'm going to stop it."

The pope shook his head. "I feel sorry for you," he said. "Why? Because my ideologies are not in line with yours?"

The pope closed his eyes and shook his head. "Because you're damning your soul for all eternity, and you don't even know it."

"Perhaps I do know it. But when that day comes, at least I'll know that I did all I could to make a difference. And perhaps my God will understand that."

"We have the same God," he said, "The God of Allah, of Mohammed, of Yahweh—they're all the same. And I doubt that God will look upon you favorably."

"My God is not the God Allah," Team Leader said, the pitch of his voice rising. "My God will favor me for my actions against the transgressions of others."

"By killing innocent people?"

"If that's His will."

"If that's the case, then you pray to a false God. Because there is no God who would ever condone the killing of men."

"And if *that* is the case, then Allah is a false God since men kill openly in His name."

"Men kill openly because they are ignorant. Not because they believe their God is constricting."

"My God is not the same as theirs."

"That's where you're wrong, my son. Although God has many faces, He has but one voice." The pope released a rattled cough deep within his lungs.

"Your war will not come out the way you plan it," the pope added. "There will be awful consequences on both sides. And your people will suffer like no other. Can you live with that? Can you live knowing that your actions may cause other children to watch their families die? Just like you did one sunny day in Ramallah?"

Team Leader turned livid. The veins in his neck stuck out like cords. "That's exactly what I'm trying to stop . . . And I will succeed."

"God won't let you," muttered the pope. He laid back down and pulled the blankets over him.

Team Leader gave a one-sided smile. *We'll see,* he told himself. *Tomorrow, when you die, we'll see which of us is right.*

CHAPTER FORTY-SIX

Washington, D.C.
September 27, Evening

Shari mustered the courage to set herself in motion. She took deep breaths and released them as though she was in a Lamaze class. When her mind calmed to the point of clear cognizance, she called Alan Thornton, the president's chief advisor.

"Where are you?" he asked. "That's not important."

"Shari, what's wrong? You don't sound right."

"Alan, please, I've got something to tell you."

"What?"

Shari confided with him about the Soldiers of Islam having been identified from the Clark County Coroner's Office in Nevada, and about the disc being a covert schematic of war involving US and allied interests. Thornton remained quiet, taking in every word as Shari spoke in a quick clip.

Then Shari dropped the bombshell. "I know about the Force Elite, Alan. I just didn't think that after what we've been through together, that you would support my eradication."

"Eradication? What are you talking about?"

"My attackers. The ones I told the president about as he was looking over the photos in his office just before he went on the air. They were the Force Elite."

The line was silent a moment. "Are you telling me that you were attacked by the Force Elite in *your* home?"

"Then you acknowledge that they exist?"

Thornton paused again. "I won't deny it, Shari. They've existed since the CIA was no longer granted permission to commit assassinations after the Ford Administration, but I'm sure you already know that. But to send them to your house to eradicate you, that's absolutely out of the question. The top guns in this administration, myself included, have to come to a mutual agreement to dispatch the Force Elite. And that's strictly for situations abroad. Believe me, nobody would agree to eradicate you."

"What about the president? Could he dispatch them without your knowledge?"

"Possibly, but I doubt it."

"How would you know?"

There was another pause. "I guess I wouldn't."

"Then it could be possible that he's working in collusion with others without your knowledge, knowing that some of you may disagree with his, shall we say, illegal dealings by putting his trust in *those* he knows will support him unconditionally."

"I would hate to think that of our president."

"Is it possible, Alan?"

"Anything is possible."

"I think he had something to do with the kidnapping of the pope." She outlined the theory of his disappearance, of how it colluded with the contents of the disc, the execution of the Soldiers of Islam, and the connection between Abraham Obadiah and the attack against her by the Force Elite. Oddly, Thornton thought, it made sense now that she had pieced it together for him.

"If what you say is true, Shari, be careful."

"I am."

"You can't fight this alone."

"Then fight with me."

Thornton mulled this over. "I'll get on it," he finally said. "There're people on Capitol Hill I can trust. Honest people. But I pray to God that you're wrong, Shari. I really do. President Burroughs is a good man."

"Alan, be careful with whom you talk to. Burroughs alienated himself from many who could be a part of this inner circle. And Alan?"

"Yeah."

"Don't screw me over on this. I have friends in high places, too. And to get to me you'll have to go through them. And I don't think you'll want to do that."

"Shari, I'm on your side, believe me. If improprieties are going on in this administration, I want to know about them just as much as you do."

"We'll see." She hung up and stared at the phone, wondering if she had done the right thing. Either Thornton will send forth the Force Elite, or he'll examine the truth with a clear conscience. Either way, the ball was rolling.

Shari snapped her vision between the rearview mirror and to the road, as she drove toward her rendezvous point. True to his word, Kimball kept distance between her Lexus and his van. Other than catching glimpses of his headlights in the long stretches between them, the roads were clear.

She dialed her phone, a quick-dial number. Kimball picked up.

"They now know what we know," she told him over the speakerphone. "If Alan's a part of this, he'll inform the president." Then: "Any news from Leviticus?"

"I sent him ahead to conduct surveillance," he told her. "So far, nothing."

Shari's heart began to pound. Even though she was a post-certified officer, she had never been a first-team responder, always arriving at the scene of the crime after it had been committed. But this would be different. She was placing herself directly within the crosshairs. Even the presence of Kimball Hayden did little to alleviate her fears.

"Shari?"

"Yes."

"I think it best that I come inside with you to assure your safety. The rest of the team is capable of taking on whatever comes their way."

An image of Gary entered her mind as mental flashes of intimate times together. She saw the moment when they made love for the first time in the back of his car, the seat too small, but somehow made it work. She remembered the two of them picnicking on the bank of a river and feeding ducks, and then the lingering kiss that followed. She recalled other times and loving times that cemented their relationship, which had flourished over the years rather than diminished.

Until recently.

"I don't think that's a good idea," she told him. "I think it's better served that you command the first line of defense. I'm more than adequate at taking care of myself. Believe me, I'm ready for them."

"Shari, you don't know what you're up against."

She thought of Gary and felt confused. "I know exactly what I'm doing. So please, Kimball, let's do this my way. I don't think it would be a good idea to be—" She cut herself off when she was about to say *alone with you.* But finished with "—in there knowing that you weren't watching over me from the perimeter."

"Just be careful," he said. "Always."

For the rest of the trip, she remained silent while trying to recapture those images of her husband. But all she saw in her mind's eye was Kimball Hayden and the way he smiled, or the way he looked at her with those expressive eyes that told her how much he cared for her, far more than he should have.

Edgy and confused, she continued the drive wondering if she was lying to herself about her feelings for Kimball. She prayed she was wrong about slipping further away from Gary, whose gentle soul was overshadowed by a man who had made killing his vocation.

During the remaining trip, she prayed for the truth. Perhaps, she thought, the lie in itself was the truth.

She felt like crying.

CHAPTER FORTY-SEVEN

Kimball drove behind Shari and maintained the buffer zone as her vehicle neared the post office outlet. The roads were lit by streetlamps, the constant roadway sentinels.

From a distance of three hundred feet, Leviticus was able to track Shari's vehicle from his Comm monitor in the back of the van. Her car lit up on his screen as a flashing blip, the signal coming from the attached GPS.

As Shari drove to the doors of the outlet, she noted a person leaving with several envelopes in his hand, the man sifting through his mail.

Then everything appeared quiet. She dialed Kimball's number. "I'm here."

"I don't see you."

"I'm close. See that van about sixty yards to the east?" She did.

"That's Leviticus. So far everything seems to be clear." Then after a pregnant pause, he said: "We may be wrong about this, Shari . . . We may be wrong about everything."

"Yeah, well, we'll see, right?" Then she killed the phone, got out of the vehicle, and headed towards the outlet.

#

Inside the van's Comm Center, Leviticus watched the video monitors. The sensitivity capabilities of the equipment were able to pick up any visual or audio events within a defined perimeter around the outlet, for up to two hundred feet. Micah and Isaiah took their respective positions north and south of the van's position. Their shapes had blended so perfectly with the shadows, they didn't even cast an outline of being blacker than black.

If the Force Elite was out there, they had yet to be seen.

#

From a distance approximately 300 feet from the outlet, Kimball quietly maneuvered his van beneath some trees far from the nearest light.

Quietly, Kimball and Nehemiah exited the vehicle and slid into the shadows west of Shari's position.

Now she was covered from all sides.

#

As Shari opened the door to the post office box outlet, she felt a sudden chill crawl along her backside like a centipede inching its way along her spine, the sudden coldness causing the fine hairs on the back of her neck to rise in a hackle, the same way a dog senses great danger.

She moved along the corridor with the heel of her shoes clicking in echo. Then she rounded a corner to glass casings that held mailing boxes and vintage stamps. The clerk, however, was nowhere to be seen.

As soon as she came upon the bank of post office boxes, she immediately began to look for 734. At the end of the long stretch of boxes, she found it: 734. The box was large enough to fit a manuscript. To her left was a trash container. She lifted it.

There was no key.

"I saw you drive up," said. Murdock "You were quicker than I thought you would be."

She took a step towards him. "I thought you were going to leave a key."

He smiled. "I lied."

#

Omega Team watched silently from the shadows as they watched Shari park her vehicle and enter the post office outlet. While keeping one eye on her, they kept the other eye on the van that was parked approximately fifty feet from Shari's car. Another van was posted

226

about 300 yards distance.

"Candidate One," whispered Viper. "Do you have a lock?"

"That's affirmative. Target Red is in the castle," confirmed Mamba. "It's a 'go.' Converge with senses open in the front and rear. She's not alone."

"Copy that," said Cobra.

Omega Team moved with the stealth of snakes, crawling on their bellies in a disciplined and patient fashion. They took to the darkest shadows, often stopping and listening for anything alien or hostile. Once the terrain was judged clear, they moved on to tighten the perimeter from three different points, with weapons drawn. After stopping to sweep the zone for the opposition, they would advance in silence once the area was cleared and close the gap.

Once they were thirty meters from the entry point, Omega Team hunkered down with the collective thought of a single mind—keep low and appraise the situation. Don't move until the command is given. And look for shadows, because if the shadow isn't one of your own, then it'll probably kill you.

#

"We have Tangos," said Leviticus.

"Where?" Kimball asked through his lip mic.

"Three Tangos approximately thirty meters apart and converging on the entry point. Each Tango proximity is to the north, northeast, and northwest sector."

"Micah's already in position. Isaiah, move in from the southwest sector and back him up. Nehemiah and I will come in from behind and flank them."

"Copy that," said Isaiah, the Vatican Knight already on the move.

"If they're thirty meters apart, then it'll be man to man. Be careful that one Tango isn't the bait, while another lies in wait. Is that the case, Leviticus?"

"That's negative. Each man stands alone, obviously appraising the situation."

"That means they're expecting us, or at least somebody. We won't disappoint."

Kimball and Nehemiah picked up the pace, knives drawn, bodies folded at the waist to maintain a low profile. With the aid of night-vision goggles, they moved quickly through the darkness.

"Status," whispered Kimball on the trot.

"They're maintaining position. The defense forces are in position and waiting for the cavalry."

"Copy that. Do you see us in relation to the Tangos?"

"Affirmative. You're approximately fifty meters southwest of the targets."

"Copy."

Kimball and Nehemiah made an abrupt northeast turn and headed in the direction of Omega Team, to outflank them. When they were within thirty meters, Kimball broke toward the middle target. Nehemiah stayed the course and crept toward the commando at the northwest position.

Omega Team waited.

#

"Candidate One and Two," whispered Omega Team's Mamba into his lip mic. "You have two hostiles moving in from the southeast. Each of you has been targeted and is drawing a one-on-one situation."

"Copy that," said Viper. "What's their twenty?"

"Approximately twenty meters behind you and moving closer."

"Copy that . . . I don't have a visual yet."

"They're moving up on ten meters."

"Roger that," confirmed Viper.

"I'm closing the gap." Mamba left his position and padded silently to intercept Kimball.

In the north sector, Nehemiah was advancing on Viper. The Omega Team commando was drooling with anticipation, as he quietly attached a noise suppressor to his carbine.

Like drawing a fly to honey, he thought.

#

"We have movement," said Leviticus. "Tango Three is moving toward the center position. Be careful, Kimball. You might have been made."

"Copy that." Kimball hunkered down behind a gnarled hedge and withdrew a second knife.

#

"One hostile has halted," Mamba said into his mic. "I'm moving into position. The second hostile is still on the move."

"I see him," whispered Viper. "It'll be like shooting fish in a barrel."

#

Kimball hunkered low. Something wasn't right. And then he gazed toward the dark form of Nehemiah, who was almost on top of his target with his knife drawn.

And then it occurred to him that Leviticus was right. They had been made.

#

Viper moved in a fluid motion with the barrel of his assault weapon coming around and targeting Nehemiah. In rapid succession, muted bursts of gunfire lit up the night like a strobe light, as the bullets stitched across the chest of Nehemiah's Kevlar with the force of the impacts driving Nehemiah back and then to the ground, that's when Viper found the objective of Nehemiah's legs and sent off a second burst, the rounds finding their mark and crippling his enemy. As Nehemiah lay there bleeding with his knife no longer within his grasp, the agony on his face was sweeping.

In a motion that was fleeting and graceful, Viper withdrew his blade and moved in for the kill.

#

Kimball saw starbursts of light from Nehemiah's position and knew that a firefight was on. From his position, he could see Nehemiah being driven back and then to the ground. And in a scene that seemed somewhat disjointed with the slowness of a bad dream, Kimball could do nothing as he watched the commando withdraw his knife, pounce upon Nehemiah without mercy, and drive the blade across his throat.

Kimball was beyond rage.

#

Mamba and Cobra met up with Kimball no more than ten meters away, each knowing that they were cognizant of each other. Once Viper wiped the bloodied blade against Nehemiah's Kevlar, he began to converge on Kimball's point.

But Kimball was more than ready.

#

"Move! Move! Move!" Leviticus cried into his lip mic. With Isaiah and Micah moving into position to flank Omega Team from behind, Leviticus grabbed his HK XM8 that had already been broken down to the carbine style and exited the van to take position alongside the body of Nehemiah.

#

Viper was coming in from the right, and Cobra and Mamba were directly in front of him. With the point of his commando knife held between the tips of his thumb and forefinger, Kimball took aim, and with a precision that had been honed by years of practice, let the weapon fly, until it buried deep within Mamba's throat. With an unnatural gurgle, Mamba drew his hand to his neck and fell to the ground like a rabbit.

Cobra never saw the flight of the knife or heard the punch of the blade into Mamba's throat but realized that the man was dead when he reached down and felt the slick hilt of the knife sticking out from the base of Mamba's neck.

By the time he looked up, an immense shadow of a man stood over him. It was dark and foreboding, something that exuded dread like a slap. Then in an act too fast for Cobra to register, Kimball rendered the commando impotent with a single blow that sent him into eternal darkness.

#

Viper crept toward the outlet with all the prudence of a skilled assassin, fully aware that a combatant was to his fore and two others to his right. Immediately his instinct took over when he saw Mamba and Cobra lying within the brambles along the roadside, the limbs of their bodies lying askew as if boneless. And then he dropped to a single knee with his carbine raised and surveyed the ground ahead of him. The area was eerily quiet, all shadows locked in place with the hostiles nowhere in sight. With caution he moved toward the outlet sighting nothing, his weapon sweeping the area as if on a swivel because he knew they were out there watching and waiting, perhaps even drawing a bead from no more than an arm's length away.

Suddenly Viper felt the sharp point of a knife stab beneath his Kevlar and turned upward into his kidneys, followed by an intense burning sensation that swept across his lower back as the blade twisted and diced his entrails. With a feeble bark more out of surprise than in pain, he turned to view his killer, his weapon dropping to the ground. He looked into the man's face but saw only shadows. When his eyes dropped to the starch whiteness of Kimball's Roman collar, he thought God had forgiven him for his transgressions. Then with a gradual slowness like ice gliding along a hot surface, he slid downward along Kimball's body and to the ground with his eyes burning its last embers of life.

Now with the Force Elite eradicated and no one to question, Kimball was beside himself. He had let his emotions carry him to the point beyond reasoning—where killing was more of the panacea to quash his anger rather than to commit to the mission to capture and mine those for information.

And in his dismay, as he wiped a hand vaguely over his face, he understood a single fact. It now seemed certain that the pope was going to die.

#

Shari managed the final step before Murdock, who leaned against the wall with a suppressed weapon in his gloved hand.

That was when she saw the dead clerk and two others lying dead behind the counter. "One guy left just before you arrived," he told her. "But I had to clear the area before you walked in the door."

For a moment she thought her heart would misfire in her chest. "You're the inside man?"

"One of many."

"Why?"

"Because the world is heading on this suicidal path which we're trying to stop. That's why."

"By accelerating a war?"

"The war started some time ago. We're simply taking measures that our illustrious president refuses to take because he believes turning a blind eye is the answer."

That's when he raised his weapon.

#

Kimball stood in the shadows feeling regret like no other. Letting his emotions get the best of him only made him consider that he hadn't changed at all. But he had become a throwback and killed with the cold fortitude of a machine, making him no different than the men who lay dead at his feet.

"Nehemiah's gone." Leviticus' confirmation was flat and spiritless, the voice of grieving.

"And there's no one left of the Tangos," said Kimball. "I bear all responsibility for my actions."

"It's not your fault, Kim—"

"It *is* my fault!" he interceded angrily. And then more calmly while catching himself trying to make amendments of change, he said, "I was wrong. I gave way to emotion, even though I knew we needed these people alive. And *I'm* the one who always teaches *against* losing control. Everything I base my experiences on is *all* about control. And now we have nothing." He stepped away and bowed his head in self-admonishment. *Why*, he asked, *can't I do anything right in the eyes of God?*

#

232

Punch Murdock stood with his weapon directed at Shari's center mass. "I can't say that I'm sorry that it had to be like this," he told her. "But you scared a lot of people. You're getting too close to the truth. But now it's coming to an end."

And then it came to her in a sudden rush. "You're Yahweh, aren't you?"

Murdock's lips turned into a wry grin. "About that," he said, "you're wrong. *I'm* not Yahweh."

She glanced behind her out of pure instinct, a quick turn.

Murdock picked up on it. "Are you looking for Kimball Hayden?" he asked. "Is that who you're looking for? I believe his hands are quite full at the moment dealing with my team."

Shari was surprised by his insight.

"Oh, yeah," Murdock said, moving closer. "I know all about Kimball Hayden. Why he's here is beyond me. A mystery, actually. But I don't think his presence is going to matter much since he's out there . . . and you're in here." He managed the weapon so that its aim was directly in line with the cleft of her breasts and pulled the trigger in rapid succession. The bullets hit her with such momentum they lifted her off her feet, carried her over the display case, and sent her to the floor on the other side. It was a perfect volley of successive shots. Then tipping the brim of his fedora one last time, Murdock gave a cocky grin and said, "Good night, Gracie."

#

Three loud reports came from within the post office outlet with the gunshots going off in rapid succession. All Kimball could think about was Shari's welfare. If something happened to her, he knew he could never forgive himself for allowing her to go inside alone, and against his wishes.

But deep in his heart, he knew it was over. Shari Cohen was dead.

And so was the chance to save the life of Pope Pius XIII.

CHAPTER FORTY-EIGHT

With the scent of gunpowder heavy in the air, Shari rolled on her side and undid the strap that secured her Glock in the shoulder holster.

She pulled the weapon and pointed it in the direction of Murdock's approaching. When he rounded the display case, his mouth dropped in muted surprise.

When he tried to raise his weapon to finish the job with a kill shot, Shari squeezed off round after round. The bullets finding the mark of Murdock's knee, all perfect hits from a marksman who homed in on the small target of the patella and finding it. Triangular chips of bone and red matter were sent across the room in a spray of raw gristle and red mist.

As she lay there as the air thickened with blue-gray smoke, she could hear the vague sound of something serpent-like slithering along the floor. After she ran her fingers across the three impact points on her body armor, she got to her feet and managed to stand over a crawling Punch Murdock.

#

Kimball spun toward the post office outlet. More shots. He raced up into the mailbox area, these last shots in response to a firefight. He prayed it was a defensive reaction from Shari.

He raced down the corridor whose walls were lined with PO boxes and rounded the bend. Leaning against a display case running her hand over the bullet-pocked area of her Kevlar vest, Shari offered Kimball a strained smile.

It was the most beautiful smile he had ever seen.

Murdock, in agony, broke the spell as his cry pierced the hallway.

#

Boston, Massachusetts

Team Leader was sitting with his back against the brick wall in deep thought when his satellite phone vibrated in his pocket. After hitting the 'ON' button, he placed the cell to his ear. "Yes?"

"They're gone," said Yahweh, his voice was deeply riddled with agitation. "Omega Team is gone, and Judas is in the custody of the FBI. This whole thing is out of control! Abort the cause. It's done!"

"I don't think so. You knew there was the possibility of the situation getting too hot. Now you're going to have to deal with it."

"I don't think you understood what I just said. I said the cause is aborted!"

"And you listen to me. I don't care what your position is in this country. You were well aware of the risks and consequences before you agreed to go along with the movement."

"That's because you assured me every contingency was thought out to the point where all matters could be adjusted to fit *our* needs."

"And they will be. Your panic, I assure you, is quite premature."

"My panic—you listen to me, Obadiah. Omega Team is gone, and Judas is a wealth of information to the FBI, should he choose to talk."

"Then the answer is simple," he said. "Remove Judas from the equation. He's been nothing but a boil anyway."

"Judas is under FBI authority! There's no simple answer to this!"

"But there is," he said. "You have George Pappandopolous and Mr. Paxton waiting in the shadows as field backups. I suggest you utilize them since they have the clearance to approach Judas without suspicion."

Yahweh went silent.

"You have no other choice," said Team Leader. "The cause will go on with or without you. It's up to you to clean up the mess. So,

I suggest you keep your wits and command yourself in the manner your position requires."

"My position requires the cause to succeed. But now that it has been compromised, it's time to abort and cover our tracks."

"Aborting the mission is *not* an option," he insisted. "You fail to understand that I'm in a win-win situation here. If they intend a search-and-destroy mission of this post, then the world will know that factions *within* the United States government were behind the taking of the pope, which the White House will want to keep secret. And since they'll want to keep this matter undisclosed to the worldwide public, then we'll continue with the cause. When I said there'll be no discussions, no debates, and no negotiations . . . Then there will be no discussions, no debates, and no negotiations. We will see this through to the end."

As displeased as Yahweh was, he couldn't find the courage to refute Team Leader.

"Remember, Pappandopolous and Paxton are our last line of defense. Make sure they don't fail." Team Leader hung up the phone, looked at it briefly, then tossed it into the darkness. It was obvious to him that Yahweh was no longer a main player in the picture, his mettle dwindling like a sandcastle in the wind. Nevertheless, the cause would remain stalwart without his support.

Within a minute the phone was ringing, its faceplate lighting up.

Casually, Team Leader stood and walked to the phone with his hands clasped behind the small of his back. He tilted his head to one side as if in a manner to study, then with the heel of his boot crushed the phone into shards of broken circuitry.

As I said: There will be no discussions, no debates, and no negotiations. Your pope is as good as dead.

Once the phone was completely disintegrated, Team Leader walked away feeling assured that the United States government wouldn't try to compromise the cause for fear of discovery—media, political or otherwise.

In truth, he knew the Americans would let the cause run its course and set the world on fire by fueled passion, rather than take the blame for the pope's kidnapping. He truly was in a win-win situation.

Team Leader turned and walked into deeper, darker shadows,

his shape blending with the all-consuming pitch with his footfalls echoing in cadence until the sound disappeared altogether.

#

Once Kimball had established that Shari was fine, he began the task of doing what the Vatican Knights do best. Before the arrival of law enforcement, Kimball and the rest of the Knights sanitized the area by placing the bodies in the back of the vans. The Force Elite, along with Nehemiah, disappeared as quickly as they had emerged.

CHAPTER FORTY-NINE

Washington, D.C., Southeast Washington Hospital
September 28, Early Morning

Murdock laid in a hospital bed with the lower portion of his leg having been amputated just above the knee, the stump was bandaged and elevated. And because he was under the haze of pain killers, Murdock was barely cognizant. "You have to protect me," he said lazily. "You know they'll be coming for me."

Shari went to the bedside and stood with her arms folded, her body English indicating that she held little care or remorse for the man who lay before her. "Who?" she asked. "Who's coming for you?"

His eyes wandered until they settled on her. "Oh . . . it's you."

"That's right. It's me. Who's coming for you?"

FBI Director Larry Johnston moved behind her.

"Them," Murdock said, "whoever is left of the Force Elite. Those still under the command of Yahweh."

"I have no idea what you're talking about," said Johnston.

"The cause," he said above a whisper. In his condition, the effort was equal to yelling.

"You're talking about the pope's kidnapping?"

His eyes rotated back to her. "I'll give you whatever you want," he told her. "But I want a deal."

"No deal," said Johnston.

Murdock rolled his eyes and stared at the ceiling.

"Were you there on the night the Secret Service detail was murdered at Blair House?" Johnston asked.

Murdock remained silent.

"What kind of deal are you looking for?" asked Shari.

Murdock was able to create a lazy smile. "That's my girl," he said. "I want clemency, of course."

"Impossible." Johnston took the request as an insult.

"It's your call," said Murdock. "But keep in mind that the pope's life is hanging in the balance . . . And you're running out of time."

Johnston turned a deep shade of red, the man humbled. "You know we have to keep the Oversight Committee out of this."

"I know that. All I'm asking is that I don't end up in potter's field, once I give you what you need to know. In other words, don't make me disappear."

"And why should I give you the benefit of the doubt?"

"Because I'm a coward at heart," he said. "That's why."

Johnston turned to Shari. Although the communication between them was silent, it was also as vociferous as if the exchange of ideas couldn't have been louder. He turned back to Murdock. "Life in a military installation under solitary conditions."

The corner of his lip twisted into a fishhook smile. "A courtyard," he said. "I want a courtyard."

Johnston knew the term didn't refer to an actual courtyard, but a barred window offering a view of the grounds. He rolled his eyes and fought for calm. "Granted."

"I have your word?"

"You have our word," said Shari.

"Shouldn't we notarize this in the presence of an attorney?"

"Don't get cute, Murdock. You got what you wanted."

Murdock chortled in lethargic glee, before falling into a coughing jag. And then he began to talk in earnest about the cause. He explained his role—such as taking the call-sign of Judas, then he and went into detail about the Soldiers of Islam and their executions. He explained how he aided in the deaths of the president's detail by allowing Omega Team to breach Blair House. At times he was graphic, while other times evasive. But a picture was drawn, and light had been cast upon the kidnapping of the pope. Situations and events were beginning to fall into order. But what was far more damaging was his testimony indicating that everything began and ended with leading principals on Capitol Hill, especially a man by the name of Yahweh.

"Is the president involved in this?" Shari asked. "Is *he*

Yahweh?"

A mirthful grin surfaced. "Perhaps," he said. "But that would be giving up the prize now, wouldn't it?"

"You made a deal."

"And so did you."

"What more do you want?" asked Johnston.

"I'll give you two names in good faith—two names who are the last line of defense for the cause, who most assuredly will be pressed into duty to take me out. Yahweh will no doubt send them forward to kill me to keep his identity safe." Murdock labored to roll his head so he could look directly at Shari and Johnston. "You know what has to be done since you know that the courts will play no role in this . . . It's always been the political answer to everything."

"You're asking us to take out two people?" asked Shari. "Are you surprised?"

Johnston said nothing.

"You know what has to be done to keep the truth buried," added Murdock.

"We *don't* do that," Johnston said. "Get your head straight." But Johnston knew Murdock was correct in suggesting that those with damaging secrets were doomed to a short life. Shari, on the other hand, hadn't worked long enough in the FBI to know of the existence of black-op groups working within government agencies who conducted such tasks. The Force Elite was one such group.

"Save my life," he said, "and I'll give up Yahweh. He's the only one who can give you the location of the pope. He's the only one who knows where he is. The ball is now in your court."

Johnston placed a hand softly on Shari's shoulder and ushered her toward the door. "Give me a moment alone with him," he told her. "Let me see if I can reason with him about what we want and assure him of his safety. I'll have him moved to a black site immediately."

"Don't push him into a shell," she told him.

"I won't. Trust me." Once she was in the hallway, he closed the door. "What's the matter?" Murdock asked in snide accusation. "You don't want her to know the truth?"

"No, I don't. She's a good officer with a good heart, which is more than I can say for you."

"Bravo. So, what is it you want to say to me that you couldn't say in front of Girl Wonder?"

"You know what I want."

"You want names."

"Exactly. And you know why?"

"To keep the deep, dark secrets of the good ol' US-of-A . . . out of the hands of those who couldn't bear to hear them," he said.

"The names."

Punch Murdock looked Johnston in the eyes and saw nothing but conviction. He gave him two names that, judging by the director's grimace, seemed to wound him. "That's right. Pappandopolous and Paxton are the eyes and ears within the agency who report any red flags to Yahweh or Obadiah."

Johnston's features hardened. "This better pan out."

Murdock's head rolled lazily until he was staring at the ceiling. "It will," he said. "It most certainly will." And then he closed his eyes.

"I got one last question."

Murdock's eyes labored to open, his lids fluttering before stabilizing. "Go ahead."

"Those men on the president's detail—you knew them, and you knew them well. So how could you set them up?"

"For two reasons," he answered. "One was for the money. It's always about the money, isn't it?" He started to drift. But then: "I picked out a small island off the coast of Belize. A beautiful place you can only dream about. Sandy beaches, a beautiful view of the sunset . . . And now it's gone," he said. "All of it."

"How much money are we talking about?"

"You said one question."

"I was mistaken. How much money?"

Murdock ran a dry tongue over his lips. "Ten million," he managed. "It was to be wired to my account in Belize."

Johnston had to wonder. "Where was this money coming from?"

"From the oil companies," he said. "It was to be an upfront fee for services provided."

"And your purpose was to infiltrate Blair House and set the stage, while the Force Elite went in and killed everyone with military sophistication that your detail could not match or fight against?"

"You're not as dumb as you look."

Murdock grunted as pain swept through the thigh of his amputated leg. "We do illegal things," he managed, "simply because we don't think we'll ever get caught. Ask any politician on the Hill. They'll tell you the same thing." He raised his hand to reveal the handcuff that bound him to the bed rail. "Is this necessary? Do you seriously expect a one-legged man doped to the gills to get up and walk out of here?"

"You know the procedure."

The standoff was long and silent, each man trying to read the thoughts of the other with poker faces.

"You gave me your word," said Murdock. "Life with a courtyard view."

"And I'll keep it, providing what you give me pans out. But I want Yahweh."

Murdock's features softened before falling into a dismal appearance. His eyes and mouth took on the appearance of the Greek Mask of Tragedy. "And you'll get him."

Johnston remained impassive. "Just so you know," he told him. "This agreement continues only as long as the pope remains alive. If he dies, there's no point in keeping the bargain. If the bargain goes away, so does the man who wields the secret—unless you want to tell me who Yahweh is."

Murdock nodded. "I'm trying to prove my loyalty to you by providing you with two names, in good faith."

"You're doing it to save your pathetic life." Murdock had to agree. "Yeah, well—"

"Give me Yahweh."

"I can't. He's my only leverage."

There was no way Murdock was going to survive this once the information was gleaned. Murdock was a doomed man. And they both knew it.

"Have it your way, Murdock. If the pope dies—"

"Yeah-yeah, I know, so does the man who wields the secret. You already told me."

Johnston exited the room and met Shari in the hallway. "I know why you made me leave," she said.

"Really?"

"There's truth in what he said, isn't there?"

"About what?"

"About his concern of being taken out because he knows about the involvement of *our* government in this situation . . . And perhaps the possibility of *that* information getting out to the world community."

"Shari, the man has a viable fear because of the Force Elite. He sees this *one* organization, and now all of a sudden, the government is loaded with them. Don't start looking in shadows for something that's not there."

"I looked in one shadow and found the Force Elite."

"Yes, you did. And you did a fine job on this, believe me. You made this agency shine. But don't take the yammering of one insurgent and start believing that assassins are hiding in every corner."

"Then why did you make me leave?"

"I told you, so I could reason with him and assure him of his safety."

"And you couldn't do that while I was standing there?"

"Shari, you shot the man's leg off! You think I can make a promise like that with you standing two feet away from him?"

Shari wasn't convinced but decided to drop it, nonetheless. Deep inside, she knew the truth: Murdock was as good as lost. All of a sudden, she wasn't so sure she wanted to be part of a government entity any longer.

And Johnston picked up on this. "Look," he said, "it's a big government in a big land with big responsibilities, okay? It's not perfect and sometimes things have to be adjusted right, wrong, or indifferent against moral idealizations. It may not be ideal, Shari, but you, me, or any citizen in this country wouldn't give it up knowing this is probably the best government in the world. And yes, the Force Elite did exist. And we'll get to the bottom of that as well. But you have to understand that things like this will happen. And when they do, we'll correct them."

"And by correcting 'them,' you mean by erasing somebody?"

"You know information like the Force Elite can't get out. But if you're talking about Murdock . . . Yes. What he knows could prove costly to this government and you know it. His erasure will come in the form of a life sentence in solitary confinement in a federal pen, until the day he dies," he lied. Then he started to walk down the hallway with Shari in tow.

"Sir?"

He turned to her. "What?"

"Are you going to have Murdock killed?" Johnston's features didn't flinch. "Absolutely not."

He's no different than those involved on either side, she considered.

As far as she was concerned, they all shared the same core.

Without saying anything additional, Shari exited through the door at the opposite end of the hallway.

CHAPTER FIFTY

Inside the Vault within the archdiocese where the temperature is naturally cool, Kimball laid the body of Nehemiah onto a rectangular marbled block. The slab was every bit as cold as the body that lay upon it. Kimball placed one hand on Nehemiah's heart and the other over Nehemiah's forehead. Closing his eyes and bowing his head, Kimball moved his lips wordlessly as he recited prayer after prayer. Twice, when his cell phone rang, he continued with prayer and refused to acknowledge the call, even though he knew it was Shari Cohen.

Nehemiah's body lay stiff and rigid as the beginning signs of rigor mortis began to settle in. The fabric on his legs glistened with blood beneath the feeble lighting. His throat was slashed. And his eyes started to glaze over with a milky sheen to them.

Behind Kimball lay the bodies of the Force Elite, their tactical masks removed. Kimball recognized none of them.

Each would be given a proper burial provided by Cardinal Medeiros. Nehemiah, on the other hand, would be flown back to the Vatican and given a stately sacrament by the Society of Seven, then be buried within the catacombs beneath the City.

When the phone rang a third time, he answered. "Yes?"

"Kimball, I've been trying to call you," said Shari.

"I'm in the prep chamber with Nehemiah," he told her. Silence followed.

"I'm sorry," she finally said. "I know it can't be easy."

"It never is. So, what did you find out?" Kimball moved away from Nehemiah and closer to the gurneys that contained the bodies of the opposition, but he hardly acknowledged them.

"Murdock gave us two names involved with the cause," she told him. "This will hopefully lead us to the top officials involved."

"Did he tell you where the pope was?"

"No. He says the only one who truly knows the location is a man by the name of Yahweh. Apparently, he's the one spearheading the cause."

"Did he tell you who this Yahweh is?"

"No. Murdock won't give us any more information unless he has a guarantee by the government that his life won't be in jeopardy."

"Does he have a guarantee?"

"It was given to him by my director. And I'm sure the attorney general will—"

"He's a dead man," Kimball interjected. "He knows it and he's just playing for time."

Shari knew he was right. Murdock was a desperate man playing whatever hand he had to prolong his life. If he had given up the identity of Yahweh, then he would have conveniently disappeared.

"We'll find him," she told Kimball. "We'll find Yahweh."

"Shari, we're running out of time. Whoever this guy is, we better find him fast. And if Yahweh happens to be Obadiah, then forget about it. We'll never find him."

The thought never occurred to her that Yahweh and Obadiah could be one and the same. Obadiah didn't have the credentials to motivate or recruit the backing of members from Capitol Hill. It had to be somebody with a strong and influential presence, somebody of top ranking. "I don't think so," she replied. Then she told him why.

"Well, I hope you're right about this," he said. "But if we're going to find the pope in time, then we'll need to know who Yahweh is as soon as possible."

"Trust me, Kimball. The director's working on it."

"Just as long as he doesn't drag his feet."

Shari smiled. "Knowing Larry the way I do, he's not."

#

George Pappandopolous was perfecting the length of his tie when his phone rang. "Yeah?"

"Have you heard?"

Pappandopolous immediately recognized Yahweh's voice. His tone took on a more respectful manner. "Heard what?"

"Omega Team has been eliminated and Judas is in the hands of hostiles."

Pappandopolous remained silent; he knew what would come next. "You and Paxton are the last line of defense," said Yahweh. "Either

you, or Paxton, or both, I don't care which, take him out before he has the opportunity to flip on us. Both of you have clearance, so clean up the mess."

"Where is he?"

Yahweh gave him the information in a fast-paced tempo. Pappandopolous thought he seemed extremely nervous since his primary strength was maintaining grace under pressure.

Pappandopolous had barely pulled the phone away from his ear when he heard multiple telltale clicks. Suddenly his face went as white as alabaster. His line was tapped.

He dropped the phone onto the bed, went into the closet, grabbed a carry-on bag, dove deeper inside, and came up with a shoebox containing wads of bills and two pistols. As far as he was concerned, the gig was up. With more than seventy thousand dollars, he was sure he could hide out in the South American jungles for a long time. After all, taking on malaria was a far better option than taking a bullet to the head.

He threw some clothes into the carry-on and hastened from the bedroom to the living area. Two men stood in the shadows, each a clone of the other—same height and weight, same build. Both wore the same long coat and held similar firearms with attached suppressors.

Pappandopolous immediately dropped the carry-on and instinctively held his hands out, as if his action would ward off what he knew was coming. The guns flashed in muted succession, the room lighting up long enough for Pappandopolous to note the waxy appearances of his executioners' faces.

Pappandopolous felt himself falling. And his world slowed to a surreal level of movement much like being underwater. With every passing moment the beat of his heart decelerated, the drumming in his ears was slowing to the point where the next beat might be the last. In the end, Pappandopolous was surprised that his life hadn't passed before his eyes, or that he was granted the opportunity to look into the Great Light. In fact, he was disappointed, wanting to believe there was so much more than approaching confusion and unbearable coldness.

Casually, one of the assassins walked up to Pappandopolous, took position over him, and aimed his weapon for a clear headshot.

Without hesitation, the man pulled the trigger.

#

Paxton took the stairway from his D.C. apartment to the parking lot with his morning coffee in hand, unlocked the door, and slid into the driver's seat. After he lowered his cup into the beverage receptacle, he checked his appearance in the mirror and raked a hand through his hair. After blowing himself a kiss, he inserted the key into the ignition and turned the switch. When the engine caught, a wall of fire surged through the dashboard, which was followed immediately by an explosion. The car leaped upward before twisting over and crashing onto its roof.

Paxton never knew what hit him.

CHAPTER FIFTY-ONE

Boston, Massachusetts

"Now you know," said Team Leader, as he walked into the pope's chamber and stood over the body of Bishop Angelo. "Now you've endured the pain of having a loved one deposited at your feet, just as my people endured over a lifetime."

Pope Pius reached for Bishop Angelo's body and tried to pull him close but lacked the strength to do so.

"Look at me," said Team Leader. "Look at me and tell me you don't hate me for what I've done."

The pope acted like he didn't hear Team Leader at all. He simply caressed what was left of Angelo's hair like a despondent father.

Team Leader reached out and grabbed the pope's wrist, demanding his attention. "Tell me you understand," he stated firmly. "Tell me that you see the madness behind what I'm doing. Tell me you can no longer turn the other cheek now that I've brought this to you." He released the pope's wrist. "Tell me that you're not a hypocrite and that hatred, true hatred, has consumed you . . . Tell me that *you* now understand me."

The pope shook his head. "What I understand is that your hatred runs so deep and is so corrupt, that no matter how well you think your vision may be, you'll never see beyond your contempt, which is the only part of you that is pure. And for that I *pity* you . . . I don't *hate* you."

Team Leader stood up. "Then you are a hypocrite," he told him. "There's no man on this earth who can honestly sit there and tell the murderer of a loved one that he doesn't hate him, not even you."

The pope went back to caressing Angelo's hair and then the

tears, the sobbing, came. Team Leader felt that he had won a moral victory. He had, in essence, broken a man who was the showcase of moral fortitude and a pillar of strength.

"As a reminder of your stubborn will to refuse to acknowledge what makes us human," added Team Leader, "I'll let your bishop lay beside you to rot. Maybe with each passing moment, you'll grow to understand what my people have gone through for years."

After Team Leader left, the pope wept and prayed for forgiveness. What the man in black had said was true. For the first time in Pope Pius' life, he felt the pressure of hatred and understood the need for retribution, by a hand other than that of God. Worse, he understood the man's embitterment and saw the reasoning behind his lunacy.

I won't give in to your way of thinking, he pressed upon himself. *I will not.* But Pope Pius XIII knew he couldn't bury the truth deep enough. If he couldn't hide the truth from himself, there was no way he could deceive God. The truth was he *did* hate the man for what he did to Bishop Angelo. And as much as he tried to find forgiveness in his heart, he could not.

The pope bowed his head and pleaded for His understanding. *Forgive me, Lord. Please, forgive me.*

The old man wept.

#

Washington, D.C., Southeast Washington Hospital
September 28, Morning

Punch Murdock lay in a quasi-daze pumped with morphine. Incessantly, like an army of ants crawling over his flesh, he would reach down to scratch away the phantom itch, the leg no longer there. Often, he would depress the button and self-inject morphine, whenever he felt the beginnings of a throbbing ache from the stump of his leg. Then he would sleep and dream of images he would forget the moment he awoke. On one occasion he woke up to find FBI Director Larry Johnston standing beside his bed, his face bearing the same neutral features as always.

"Man, don't you ever smile?"

Johnston tossed a photo onto Murdock's chest. It was a picture of Pappandopolous after the hit. "What you said panned out," he said.

"And Paxton?"

"Too messy to show."

Murdock handed the photo back. "Now I suppose you want Yahweh?"

"That was the deal, but I'm not here to pay you a courtesy visit. I'm here to tell you that through the simplicity of technology, you gave us more than we expected from our deal."

"What's that supposed to mean?"

"It means that we tapped the lines to Pappandopolous' and Paxton's residence, and we intercepted a call from Yahweh. A voiceprint proved who the caller was. We know who Yahweh is."

Murdock's mouth opened with mechanical slowness; his trump card gone.

"Just thought you'd like to know that," said Johnston.

Suddenly Murdock understood the mockery behind Johnston's tone and the nature of his visit. The Grim Reaper was taunting him with a slight brush of his bony talons across his cheek before the final fall of the scythe. "Now wait a minute," Murdock said. "You gave me your word! *You agreed to give me life with a courtyard!*"

Johnston headed for the door.

"You gave me your word!" Murdock shouted, struggling against the cuff that held him to the rail. *"YOU . . . GAVE . . . ME . . . YOUR . . . WORD!"*

Although the door closed behind him, Murdock's shouts could be heard down the hallway.

CHAPTER FIFTY-TWO

The White House. Noon.

Alan Thornton reached up to straighten Shari's collar. They were standing in the presidential hallway that led into the Oval Office. Beside them stood Attorney General Dean Hamilton, FBI Director Larry Johnston, and a force of the president's security detail.

"You've done an outstanding job so far," Thornton told her. "You really have. Whether or not we get the pope back safely, at least it couldn't be said that Shari Cohen didn't do her best." He smiled at her.

"Thank you, Alan, for following through. I'm ashamed to say that I thought you were a part of it."

After their last discussion, Thornton had waded through heavy political water to find the truth about the Force Elite, and whether the group had been dispatched by executive command without knowledge of select administrators. But he had found nothing. Tension was so high on Capitol Hill that most officials refused to say anything for fear the 'accusing finger' would tie them to the cause. Political careers were on the chopping block. But when the FBI produced the tape of Yahweh's call to Pappandopolous, it was as good as a written deposition from the perpetrator himself. Political futures would be eliminated under certain conditions.

"This is your game," Thornton told her. "And the right to do this belongs to you." He handed her a manila envelope containing a digital recorder, transcripts, and records. All the evidence was literally in her hand. "You ready to do his?"

"As ready as I'll ever be."

"Good girl."

Thornton took the initiative and knocked on the door to the

Oval Office. Once inside he stood directly on the Presidential Seal with Shari alongside. Vice President Bohlmer sat in a high-back chair looking over documents while President Burroughs was looking out the window, his hands deep within his pockets.

"Mr. President," said the attorney general.

The president gradually turned around. There was no surprise on his face or features that betrayed his thoughts. When he finally stepped forward, he stared directly at Shari. "Special Agent Cohen," he said evenly. "I've been expecting you."

"Mr. President," her tone lacked any note of sincerity. "You know why I'm here?"

"I've been informed."

"Then you know we're running out of time."

"We've been running out of time since this began." He made his way back to the window with his disposition more melancholy than angry. "Let's get this over with."

Shari opened the manila envelope and laid the contents on the president's desk. "What I have here, sir," she said, picking up the digital recorder, "is a conversation between two parties plotting an assassination with one of those being an official of this administration. The official I'm talking about placed this government in jeopardy, should the truth about the pope's kidnapping be known to the global community."

"Do what you have to do," the president said dourly. She pressed the 'ON' button of the recorder.

#

Yeah.

Have you heard? Heard what?

Omega Team has been eliminated and Judas is in the hands of hostiles.

Silence.

You and Paxton are the last line of defense. Either you, or Paxton, or both, I don't care which, take him out before he has the opportunity to flip on us. Both of you have clearance, so clean up the mess.

Where is he?

He's in the Southeast Washington Hospital, room two-twenty-four. There'll be guards there, of course, but you have clearance. Just be subtle about it.

The whole Force Elite, gone?

Except for those pulling duty in the north.

The voice was clear and distinct, even to those listening from across the room.

Shari shut off the recorder. "We were also able to obtain warrants for telephone records. Ma Bell gave us a printout of phone numbers and times the calls were placed, based on legal tapping. The time corresponds exactly to the addresses of the parties involved." She pulled out another document. "And this, Mr. President," she said, holding up a sheet with spike-line etchings, "is a printout confirming the voice of the speaker based on tone patterns. In other words, we know who the leading conspirator is."

The president rounded the desk and reached for the printout. "Well, Ms. Cohen, it seems that you've covered all your bases, after all. I must say, I'm impressed." He took the printout and examined it. The recognized name and the voice-probability of over ninety-nine percent were printed at the bottom of the page. He handed the printout back to her. "Is this indisputable?"

"You heard the voice yourself. In a court of law, I believe it would hold up, sir. Absolutely."

The president sat on the edge of his desk. "Go ahead," he told her, "finish this off."

Shari thanked him and stood with confidence before the vice president. "Mr. Vice President, I have one question and one question only. And the question is: Are you Yahweh?"

Vice President Bohlmer didn't answer. His eyes darted about as if his mind was searching for a practical response.

"Mr. Vice President. I'll ask you once again: Are . . . you . . . Yahweh?" The vice president's shoulders fell in defeat.

"I'll take that as a yes," Shari said.

"Take it however you want," said Bohlmer. "I don't think it matters much anymore."

The president lifted himself off the edge of the desk. "Why, Jonas? Why place this whole administration under this kind of strain in the eyes of the world community? The United States is supposed to set an example of credibility and trust! We fight acts of terrorism; we do not take part in them!"

The vice president faced the president. "I'll tell you why I did it," he began. "I did it because your administration had grown weak with little to no testicular fortitude to govern in moments of crisis," he said. "I did it because we need to take a step forward to renegotiate our standing as a lead nation, rather than being held hostage by accords with countries tied to terrorist regimes. This world is racing into a Third War because ISIS is being scattered about. All you do is tell your briefer to advise the Centcom Senior Official to alter the information so that it would fit your narrative. ISIS is in thirty-two countries, exploding in numbers. But you continue to believe that we're winning this war when the truth is anything but."

"So, you think in order to stem the tide of terrorist advancement, we should commit to war that—despite what you and others may think about ISIS—we should do so on a global scale?"

"I'm talking about reevaluating the situation. Many on the Hill believe that if war does come to the Middle East, then we should prepare for what's coming instead of turning a blind eye to it. The one thing all nations need to operate is the bevy of oil output. Without it, we suffer gravely."

"Our processes *are* working, Jonas. ISIS is being defeated. Maybe not with the time and speed you would like it to be, but they're being pushed out of Iraq, Syria, Lebanon—"

"Only to points south," the vice president interjected.

"This is a process that needs to be utilized with patience," he responded. "*This* process has been running its course since nine-eleven," he said. "And it's escalating. There are people on Capitol Hill who want to see a different direction, and different measures to be taken to assure that if a World War breaks out, then we'll at least be able to manage as a nation with enough of a valued commodity such as oil to see us through. Without it, we could be crippled as a nation along with our allies. This nation cannot produce oil daily to support a country of more than three hundred million people. We would run through our reserves within months. Maybe weeks."

The president could only stare incredulously. "So, you were willing to start a war and kill millions of people, by using the pope as

255

the catalyst to gain winning support? You'd be willing to allow Russia its advancement in the Middle East to gain a strategic foothold, while we lose it? You're willing to let innocent people in places like Aleppo or Mosul die, rather than to see factions defeated by meticulous planning and engagement efforts?" He leaned back, his face flushing with anger. "Did it ever occur to you that we already thought about those contingencies you just outlined, Jonas?"

"We considered all of those scenarios. You know this. You were there during these meetings," he returned. "As far as I'm concerned, the rewards of proper warfare management have outweighed the risks thus far."

"You're wrong, Mr. President. Anyone can see that we're marching towards the End of Days. The least we could do is prepare and equip ourselves. We have nothing to lose by doing so. With the kidnapping of the pope and the stage-management of events, we can gain worldwide support and march on with this. The pontiff is a tool of propaganda that sets to save our futures, not destroy it by the inches, like what's happening now."

President Burroughs looked at him with eyes that appeared more sorrowful than judgmental. "You had me second-guessing myself," he told him. "You wanted me to believe that Special Agent Cohen was the wrong person for the job because she was a woman of Jewish faith, an abomination you said would be a 'proverbial slap in the face of the terrorists.' But you knew if I kept her on, and if I gave her the necessary resources, she would have discovered the truth behind all this. Thank God I didn't listen to you."

"What I did—I did for the future of this country."

The president closed his eyes in disgust. "I chose you, Jonas, because I thought you would be a good successor with a good head on your shoulders. Apparently, I misjudged you."

The president walked back to the window and stared outside. "Tell us where *he* is, Jonas. Where's Pope Pius?"

The vice president remained quiet. The Sword of Damocles had fallen on him, and hard.

"Jonas, *where* is he?" the president repeated calmly.

Once his perseverance had been whittled away, the vice president conceded. "In Boston," he said. "The pope is in Boston."

"Where in Boston?"

"There's an old depository behind the Granbury Burying Ground," he said. "It had been abandoned and marked for demolition years ago, but never was. We knew as soon as the news got out about the kidnapping that a dragnet would have been sent for hundreds of miles from the epicenter of D.C., which is why the operation moved north. We even went as far as to place the body of the cardinal in D.C., a red herring to keep the search limited to this area."

Shari stepped forward. "The Granbury Burying Ground. It's part of the Freedom Trail, yes?"

The vice president nodded. "It's an old section of Boston that's managed by the historical society. It's where Paul Revere and John Hancock are buried. Most of the buildings surrounding that particular area are either condemned or too far gone for revitalization. Activity in the area is minimal. You'll find him on the third floor."

"And how long before they kill the pope?"

The vice president vacillated on whether or not he wanted to continue.

Then: "They're going to kill him today."

"Today?"

The vice president nodded.

"Jonas, you need to negotiate a surrender of all efforts."

"I already tried to abort the mission," he told him. "The moment Murdock was in custody. But the Boston faction refuses to hear me out."

"Contact them again."

"You don't understand," said the vice president. "They're in a win-win situation. If you try to compromise their position by trying to negotiate a solution, they know the media will be all over this like a pack of dogs on a three-legged cat, which the United States can't afford. On the other hand, if the cause runs its course, then the accusing finger is pointed directly at the Arab world, and the United States is no longer labeled as the culprit since the truth is unknown to the worldwide public. Our image is maintained."

The president looked at Alan Thornton, then to Shari. "Is what he says true?"

"It all depends upon the Boston faction," said Thornton. "It depends if their command leader is willing to hold this country hostage by using the media to benefit the cause. If that's the case, then it would be devastating to this country."

President Burroughs began to pace the room, his eyes cast to the carpeted floor, the man thinking. "Is there any way we can quash this without the media knowing? Anything we can do?"

"Unfortunately, Mr. President, we're at the mercy of the Boston faction. Who knows what contingencies they had planned for?"

The president turned toward the vice president, who remained unmoving in his seat. "Jonas, tell me what you can."

"I can't help you," he simply said. "All I know is what I told you— what the Boston commander has already informed me of. He stated quote-unquote that there will be no discussions, no debates, and no negotiations. The cause will go on."

The president slapped an open palm against his desk. "Dammit, Jonas!"

The vice president didn't even flinch.

Once again, the president addressed Thornton. "Alan, what's your stance on trying a peaceful solution to all this?"

Thornton's face screwed into a semblance of wrinkles, seams, and complete loss. "Perhaps, Mr. President, you should ask Special Agent Cohen."

"Ms. Cohen?"

"I don't know the commander of this Boston faction, or his capabilities of what he can or cannot do. But I do know if he's in a win-win situation as the vice president states, and if he knows we suspect his location and try to negotiate a deal, all that does is allow him time to strategize and defend his position."

"But?"

Shari hesitated before speaking. "I believe, Mr. President, that a surgical strike is needed. We need to catch them off guard and take away their advantage."

"I think we need to try to negotiate a peaceful solution to this."

"There you go again," said the vice president. "Trying to seek a peaceful solution to something when the matter is too far gone when you need to respond in earnest. And that, Mr. President, is why we're in the situation we're in."

The president shot him a hard, sidelong glance.

Then from Shari: "Mr. President, we don't have much time. They're going to execute the pope today. So, we need to act accordingly."

The President turned his back on the vice president. "Jonas, is there any way at all to negotiate this without anyone getting harmed?"

"As sure as the sun sets," he said, "this man will follow through and kill the pope. If you interfere, then he will retaliate by bringing this country down . . . Like I said, a win-win situation."

Everyone in the room could tell that the president was calculating. "Then we have no other choice," he finally said. "We strike."

The president was quick to direct orders. "Contact Boston's FBI field office immediately," he told Johnston. "Tell them to set a perimeter around the district with trained law enforcement personnel and assault personnel. I want our team from Quantico to conduct the mission. You do agree, Director, the Quantico Team is the best we have to offer?"

Johnston nodded. The Critical Incident Response Group, the CIRG, trains for hours on end for such scenarios. "They can do it in their sleep. It'll take time to get the team assembled, and perhaps another two to transport."

"Too long," piped Shari. "I have a CIRG Team already assembled and willing to go the moment transportation is ready."

Johnston looked at her quizzically, not sure what she was talking about. The CIRG Team is always posted at Quantico until called to duty.

She continued. "Mr. President, as far as I'm concerned, this team is the best in the world. If they can't pull off this mission, nobody can."

For a brief moment, the president looked at her in an appraising manner, neither good nor bad. And Shari had to question him.

"What is it this time, Mr. President? I know it's not because I'm Jewish, so is it because I'm a woman? You don't think I have the capabilities of a man to put forward the effort of a combat-trained soldier?"

"Forgive me, Ms. Cohen. I'm simply old school. Perhaps my prejudices have tainted my insight a bit."

"I understand, Mr. President. But old school or not, what is your answer?"

"Do it," he said. And then: "You've surprised me, Ms. Cohen. I

259

might have been hard on you in the beginning, but you've made me a believer. I have complete faith in your abilities."

"Thank you, sir."

"Just bring the pope back to us."

"I will."

"How long do you think it will take for your CIRG Team to be ready?"

"Minutes."

President Burroughs turned to the vice president. "As for you," he said, "you're under house arrest until we can figure out what to do with you." The president motioned to his detail to escort the vice president to his residence at the Naval Academy. "I'm sorry it has to be like this, Jonas. I really am. And it's for mismanagement reasons like this that the Force Elite has to be eliminated . . . And it will be."

The vice president remained seated while the president's detail surrounded him. When he stood, he straightened his tie to walk out of the office with dignity. It would be the last time he would ever see any of them again. And he wanted to be remembered as someone who went out stoically rather than cowardly.

As the vice president passed his former allies, many refused to acknowledge his existence.

CHAPTER FIFTY-THREE

"Kimball?" Shari asked over the phone. "Yeah."

"Yahweh confessed to the whereabouts of the pope."

"Where?"

Even though he couldn't see her, he could envision her gesticulating with hand motions on her end of the line, as if he was standing in front of her. "He's in an abandoned depository in Boston."

"Boston!"

"They moved their operations to avoid the dragnet," she said. "The president wanted a Quantico Team to move in and do the chore immediately, but it would take too long to assemble a unit and get them ready for transport. So as of right now, you're it. You and the rest of the Vatican Knights. I need you pressed into duty and ready to go."

"We're ready now."

"I know you are. I already informed the administration that I have a team that's prepped. But as far as they know," she told him, "they think it's a Quantico squad. So, you'll need to lose the Roman collars to avoid questions."

"Understood. Where's the departure point?"

She told him. Within ten minutes they had met at the point of departure.

Within twenty-five, they were airborne and heading for Boston.

#

Vice President Bohlmer sat in his study with vacant eyes, but his mind toiled. Before him were shelves of books he'd collected over his lifetime. There were law books dealing with torts, corporate and criminal law; biographies of every politician and statesman ever published; and books about political theories of this country, and

261

almost every other nation with a respectable government. In the process of growing in a political entity as an official, he had learned from these books and studied them, even gleaning theories to make the political machine run more efficiently. Ironically enough, he was now shelved like them.

A fire was burning in the fireplace, the wood snapping every so often and sending sparks up the flue. But the vice president found no comfort in such warmth.

His cause was dead, taken by the cancer of his aggression, his politics forever gone.

In self-admonishment, the vice president released a regrettable sigh; not for what he did, but for getting caught. He had shamed himself before the eyes of his peers and was thankful his wife, having been dead six years, did not have to suffer the pang of being branded a political pariah.

After getting to his feet, the vice president walked to the foyer and checked on the Secret Service detail posted there by the president.

An agent stepped forward, his face as rigid as his posture, his professionalism forced. "Is there anything I can help you with, sir?"

Sir? An hour ago, it was Mr. Vice President.

"No. I'm fine," he said. "Thank you." Brandishing a false smile, he closed the door to the study with a soft click and returned to his chair.

Beneath the nightstand by the lounge chair sat a .38 caliber revolver. Hidden within a drawer, its chambers were fully loaded. Its chrome-plated barrel shimmered in hues of red and orange and yellow, the colors of the burning fire. He picked up the pistol and examined his reflection in the mirror polish, first turning his head to the left, and then to the right, his image warped in a funhouse mirror sort of way. Then in a quick and fluid reaction without considering the consequences, he brought the gun to his temple and pulled the trigger.

#

Boston, Massachusetts
September 28, Late Morning

The distance between Washington D.C. and Boston is exactly four hundred and forty-eight miles. The time it would take for the Vatican Knights and Shari Cohen to prep and arrive at Logan Airport in Boston, would be just over an hour.

During their flight they had gone over the schematics of the depository, committing every nuance of the floor plans to memory. They drew up plans for entry and engagement and theorized the locations of the pope and those of the Papal Commission. However, they also knew that the Force Elite had prepared for every conceivable contingency, regarding hostile forces and a potential counterattack. This would not be an easy assignment since the pope would most likely be heavily guarded. Which catapulted the probability of a Vatican Knight dying much higher.

So as required by papal order before any mission, the Knights prepared themselves with prayer—except Kimball, who only found confidence in the weapons he carried. And Shari knew that a man such as Kimball Hayden could never be weaned from the savagery of his lifestyle. It was simply a part of him.

As the aircraft sped toward Boston's Logan Airport, Shari felt a pang for a man who was willing to commit a single selfless act to save the life of the pope, by putting his life at risk. No matter his past, no matter the brutal force of nature that propelled him to commit the atrocities he did, Shari hoped that Kimball Hayden would find the Light before he died.

She prayed he would find it soon.

CHAPTER FIFTY-FOUR

Boston, Massachusetts

Although they were posted at a distance, Boston's Metro Assault Units had developed a perimeter around the depository disguised as city workers, by blocking off connecting streets and avenues with flashing sawhorses and orange utility cones. Troops in full riot gear were ready in unmarked vans along the boundary. And by redirecting the masses in such a subtle manner away from ground zero, the area had been cleared without so much as drawing a curious or questioning eye.

The city had set their ducks in a row.

\#

The Vatican Knights had dressed accordingly by removing the Roman collars to avoid questioning but continued to wear the embroidered crest of the silver Pattée within the powder blue shield on their body armor. As for gear they wore black Kevlar assault helmets with audio attachments, along with amber face-shields for better visibility. They were also armed with the HK XM8 special assault rifle. Kimball, however, opted for the grenade launcher.

Once the gear had been checked and double-checked, and Kimball had reexamined Shari's combat gear for fit and maneuverability, the Vatican Knights went forward with Kimball on the point, and Shari taking the rear.

They would start at the wrought-iron fence.

\#

The Master lock was new, as well as the chain that held together the gates leading to the rear of the depository.

Removing a canister from his cargo pocket, Kimball sprayed a corrosive acid onto the links, the chain bubbling and boiling until the metal gave way. After removing the chain as though it was a delicate rope of garland, he opened the gate wide enough to allow his team passage. Quietly, they maneuvered their way to the rear of the compound, where they found a military transport truck hidden underneath some heavy-looking boughs.

Using hand motions to communicate, Kimball rounded it into a fist and pulled down like a trucker blowing a horn, pointed to his eyes, then at the truck—all signals to Leviticus to scout the vehicle while the Vatican Knights held back.

Leviticus prudently moved in with his head on a swivel. After scouting the truck, he offered a closed-fisted gesture to indicate the 'all clear' sign, and the Vatican Knights proceeded to move quietly forward.

Behind the depository was a dirt-lot bearing weeds as tall as a man's waist, a good spot to lay low without being seen. From their vantage point, they could see that the windows of the first level had been filled in with brick and mortar. Also, in view was a fire escape that hung tenuously from a few rusted bolts, its stability absent and too dangerous to mount. The windows on the second and third level were boarded over with sheets of plywood, leaving the fire door on the first level a possible entryway. But the area surrounding the door was refurbished with new building blocks, meaning the area had been recently reinforced.

That left the roof.

Kimball moved into a wild tangle of bushes for cover, then motioned to his team to come close for a conference.

"Isaiah and Micah, you've got the rooftop. One enters from the south, the other from the north. Once done, descend and converge until you locate the pope, then report back with his pinpointed position. Questions?" There were none. "Go."

Isaiah and Micah moved swiftly across the drive and stood at the base of the building looking skyward toward the roof. Inside Isaiah's backpack was a pneumatic launcher geared to fire pitons. After Isaiah locked and loaded a piton with an attached line into the tube, he aimed and shot the weapon, so the piton embedded itself firmly into the wall about a foot below the edge of the roofline. Then he tested the hold of the line by pulling himself up the cord a couple of feet, and suspended himself, the piton unyielding in its grip. Confident in the piton's ability to hold, they climbed the cable until they reached the rooftop, then disappeared over its edge.

After giving the rooftop unit enough time to find a breach, Kimball loaded his grenade launcher and took a position with Leviticus standing alongside him, with his HK XM8 directed at the target point. There would be no mistaking that their knock on the door was going to be noisy since they intended to drive the Force Elite to a single point of defense, while Isaiah and Micah converged to hem them in. Since the site was fortified, there was no other option. The Force Elite had chosen well.

Kimball directed the grenade launcher to the left of the fire door, where the brick was old and aged, rather than to take on the newly reinforced area. "I'll go in first to neutralize any immediate threat," Kimball told Shari. "Leviticus will follow and sweep the premise. After the area has been secured, I need you to stay behind and maintain a secure position to ensure that we didn't miss anyone. Leviticus and I will move against any hostile attack from the upper levels. By that time, the rooftop unit should be moving into position to flank the hostiles. Questions?"

"You want me to lag?"

He stared directly into her eyes. "You're not trained for this, Shari, and you know it. Leave this to those who've been there and done that. I need you to take the rear and look for those we may have missed. Leviticus and I are going to draw attention from the upper levels. And I'd like to do that without worrying that somebody we may have missed is coming at us from behind."

Kimball was right; this type of tactical work was way above her. "Good. Glad to see that everyone understands," he said. Then, "Everybody knows their game plan?"

Shari and Leviticus nodded. Their expected actions were clear.

"Okay, people, this is what it's all about." Kimball aimed the launcher and pulled the trigger. To the left of the door, the wall disseminated into the carnage that sent shattered rock, brick, and mortar in all directions. And then boiling plumes of smoke and dust exploded outward and upward, rendering visibility to zero.

After loading a second grenade, Kimball moved in and disappeared into the haze.

#

The explosion shook the whole building, galvanizing the Force Elite into combat mode. Each man grabbed his assault weapon and racked a bullet into its chamber, as they took position along the third-floor corridor. Diamondback manned the monitors, watching the dense smoke and dust on all screens. "We have a breach!" he hollered.

"How many?"

"Unknown!"

Kodiak, Boa, and King Snake took position along the top of the stairwell and aimed their weapons as a mushroom cloud boiled up at them at a furious pace. In a hail of gunfire, hundreds of rounds were fired into the cloud with the bullets ripping out chunks of brick from the walls of the stairwell, then sent them scattering into the billowing dust cloud that raced up the stairs like a geyser. In the time it took them to reload their weapons in the aftermath of the first volley, a second explosion rocked the building.

Kimball Hayden was making a statement.

#

Team Leader moved like the wind down the corridor, his Glock tightly within his grasp. When he reached the bank of monitors, he shoved Diamondback aside to position himself in front of the viewing screens. Managing the joystick, Team Leader directed the remote camera lens toward a position where dust and smoke were minimal and noted a large man enter swiftly through a hole in the wall on the first-floor level. Watching the figure load another grenade into the launcher, Team Leader zoomed in on the man's features.

Although the commando's headgear included a tinted face shield, it did not completely cover the man's face. Team Leader thought he saw the man's lips curl into a sardonic grin before aiming the launcher at the camera, then pulling the trigger.

The second explosion was far more brutal than the first.

\#

After hearing the explosions, Metro's Assault Teams were immediately deployed as backup units. They dispersed from cube vans and closed the perimeter until the depository was absolutely the epicenter of all activity.

With the noose drawing tighter, even a cockroach would have had difficulty breaking through the column unseen.

\#

After the first explosion, Micah and Isaiah entered the building from opposite ends through holes in a poorly maintained roof. On the south end, Isaiah lowered himself onto a rickety header beam, the wood groaning under his weight, as he dangled from the girder. Then he released it with his body landing with natural grace on the hardwood floor of a corridor that led to a stairwell.

Directing his HK XM8 in front of him, he scoped the area for hostiles and noted that the south stairwell had collapsed, the rubble lying on the first level as a heap.

Knees slightly bent and body bowed forward, Isaiah moved along the corridor viewing the scene through the crosshairs of his weapon.

\#

Micah found a passage through a hole in the roof barely large enough for him to pass through. After gaining a handhold on a rotting joist beam, he carefully took a position within a tangle of rotted wood, where he watched the Force Elite take their positions on top of the stairwell and fire off several rounds to deter hostile advancement.

Micah noted Isaiah was nowhere in sight. And with no one to cover him, he felt highly vulnerable.

Further down the hall, crouched and shackled against the wall, were four members of the papal council.

The pope was nowhere in sight.

Snaking into position between the rotted beams, Micah clicked on the laser sighting and focused the dot onto a commando holding position by the stairwell, the first of three. He could easily clear the area with three quick shots.

Taking careful aim, the red dot landing squarely on the back of Boa's head, Micah began to squeeze the trigger.

#

Leviticus moved in with Shari in tow and scouted the entry area. Once he established that the area had been secure, Shari swiped at the swirling dust as if to drive the cloud away.

She had no success.

#

Gunfire continued to erupt from the north end of the stairwell, the ammo taking out pieces of concrete from the walls and stairs—a strong message to the advancement team that the stairwell was not to be a consideration for encroachment.

Kimball brought his hand to his lip mic and drew it closer to his lips. "Isaiah?"

So far, the corridor's clear, Isaiah returned. *I haven't been able to pinpoint the packages. My guess is that they're probably at Micah's end.*

"Copy that . . . Micah?"

There was no reply. Micah was either occupied or dispatched. "Isaiah, Micah's right on top of them!"

I'm moving, Isaiah said. "Be careful!"

It wouldn't be long before Isaiah and Micah were in position to draw the attention of the Force Elite, thought Kimball.

#

The red dot wavered ever so slightly on the back of Boa's head, a zone that promised a quick kill. Slowly, Micah began to pull back on the trigger, the tension set lighter than most assault weapons, and slowed his breathing to steady his aim. After killing the first one, he would kill the other two while they were caught in the grip of surprise. The trigger slid farther back, the mechanism about to engage, the red dot as

269

steady as could be.

And then the kill shot.

Micah's face shield exploded into spider's web cracks, as a single bullet penetrated the plastic guard with the hole dead center. Micah's head reared back as if trying to understand the moment of his sudden death, and then he fell from the beam and landed on top of another joist. His midsection was draped in a way that it looked as if he was trying to touch his toes before he slid noiselessly from the girder and to the floor.

From a distance Team Leader had seen the red laser from Micah's weapon, a microdot floating in space. And then he took careful aim and fired his Glock. As he closed in, a ribbon of smoke was rising from the tip of his pistol, the weapon directed right at Micah as he lay there. After examining the body to confirm the man's death, he noticed the silver Pattée within the shield and the flanking heraldic lions that supported the crest on his body armor. No doubt the squad's emblem, he thought.

Looking ceilingward, he noted the poorly constructed roof. He had always known of its porous quality, the one weakness in the building's point of entry.

Taking a deep breath and closing his eyes, Team Leader realized that his aspirations of dividing the world into warring factions were now idealistic rather than a reality. If he was to kill the pope now, and the truth is known to the world community that it was a top Israeli commando who pulled the trigger, then that would only isolate his beloved Israel rather than propel it to the fore.

His dream was dead, and he knew it.

Team Leader quickly made his way down the corridor. Without a doubt, the building would soon be overwhelmed since the operative he killed was sent to pinpoint their location. Whether or not the man succeeded in his mission, he didn't know. But one thing was for sure: the location had been compromised.

It was time to jump ship.

#

The pope clung to Bishop Angelo's hand, though his digits had locked into place and were unable to bend to clutch the hand of the pope.

Nevertheless, the pontiff cupped his hands over the bishop's and held on as though he'd never let go.

In the background was gunfire—a lot of it. And in the back of Pope Pius's mind, he genuinely believed his time on earth was coming to an end.

So, he prayed.

He prayed for the forgiveness of those who would take his life, and for those who would take the lives of those surrounding him. He prayed for his salvation, ashamed for hating the man who had forced him to witness man's darkest side. And for making him realize that God-given will can harbor such cruel intentions. He had come to realize that the Light of his world was imbibing on the Darkness of someone else's.

From the corner of his eye, as he held Bishop Angelo's hand, the gunfire never lessening, Pope Pius XIII spotted the Dark Man standing silhouetted in the doorway against the ongoing muzzle flashes in the background.

With his weapon already drawn the man entered the room.

With a look of defiance, the pontiff courageously raised his head.

For a moment they stared at each other, the firefight in the background becoming a drone as they appraised one another. Each man had learned some insights from the other, perhaps the Light imbibing as much of the Darkness about as much as the Darkness imbibing the Light, making each man equal, since they now shared the qualities of both. How they exercised those qualities would still come from each man's independent will. It was all about making the choices that suited them most—good, bad, or indifferent.

Team Leader looked him in the eyes and was pleased with what he saw. Here sat a man who was not afraid to die, a man whose conviction of faith was strong enough to break the chains that bind him, if only he had the physical strength to do so. And then Team Leader did something uncharacteristic; he bowed to the pope in what Pius took to be a measure of respect. "For centuries, my people have been persecuted," he said. "But no matter what, we'll eventually persevere. You're a good man, Your Holiness, but until all become like you, only then will this end. I could only dream of such a day."

Raising his weapon until the laser found its mark, Team Leader pulled the trigger.

#

"Isaiah." Kimball's voice was loud enough to cry over the noise. "Have you detected the packages?"

That's negative. I'm coming to a doorway leading to the north corridor. So far, the south side is clear. It seems that Micah might have come straight down into their lap since the point of defense seems to be at his entry.

"Copy that." And then: "Micah?" There was no answer, which concerned Kimball. And then again, only this time louder: "Micah?"

When he didn't answer, Kimball turned to Shari, the Incident Command Deputy, and gave her a gesture of circling his hand in the air as if twirling a lasso. "To the south sector maneuvering to the north!" he hollered to her. Shari pulled her lip mic close and barked an order to the Incident Command Post. "Bring in the Descending Angels." The cavalry was on the move from above.

#

Kodiak glanced up from reloading his weapon and saw Team Leader run toward the south end of the hallway and disappear in the shadows. His mind immediately clicked on the realization that Team Leader was bailing. He had been so focused, so diligent to his duty, he had drawn himself into tunnel vision and was hardly aware of his surroundings beyond the stairwell. After firing the last clip into the dusty shaft, he pulled back along with Boa and began to retreat. King Snake maintained his position.

"King Snake, let's move!"

"I'll hold off the advancement! GO!"

Boa and Kodiak went to the monitor room, where Diamondback and Sidewinder were arming their body armor attachments by loading up with as much ammo as their duty belts could carry. Boa and Kodiak followed suit, knowing that King Snake would soon be out of ammo.

"Where's Team Leader?" asked Diamondback. "Gone," said Boa.

"Gone? Gone where?"

"Just gone!"

All four had geared up to the max as if they knew there would be no tomorrow.

In the hallway at the top of the stairwell, King Snake had run out of ammo.

The sudden quiet seemed somewhat odd.

#

Two choppers lifted off from Logan Airport's Air Operations helipad, flew over the depository, and hovered over the rooftop. Ropes and cables were thrown from the bays as assault commandos began to rappel from the choppers until a Strike Force of twelve had secured the rooftop. With a gesture from the top commander, the choppers veered off and returned to base.

The Descending Angels had landed.

#

Kimball and Leviticus immediately advanced up the north stairwell, with Kimball holding his weapon forward while Leviticus prepared flash bangs to disorient any hostiles, who might be maintaining their position.

Reaching the second level, they saw a single hostile standing on the third floor charging a Sig, his lone weapon. Taking careful aim, Leviticus locked onto the man with his weapon and pulled the trigger. The quick burst found its mark. The commando danced awkwardly like a marionette, as each bullet punched into him. And then he collapsed to the floor.

When the area was clear, Leviticus made his way up the stairs with Shari Cohen close behind. Kimball maintained cover by keeping the point of his weapon steady, as they made their way to the final level. After they maneuvered into a safe position at the top of the stairs, Leviticus was close enough to the dead man to reach out with his fingers and place them against the man's carotid. There was no pulse, the man was gone.

Kimball pushed his mic button. "Leviticus?"

"One down, at least five—" He cut himself short. To the right of him lay Micah. He was twisted in such a way that told Leviticus he was dead.

"Leviticus?"

"We lost Micah," he whispered. "And I don't see Isaiah."

"I'm Code-4 and working south," Isaiah returned.

"Copy that," said Kimball. "Leviticus, any visuals?"

Both Leviticus and Shari peeked around the corner of the wrought iron banister and surveyed the hallway. Huddled against the wall were the three bishops of the Holy See and Cardinal Paolo, all alive—all terrified.

"That's affirmative on four of the packages," Leviticus whispered. "But I don't see the big asset, however."

"Hostiles?"

"Negative."

"They've pulled into the shadows. Maintain your position," Kimball told them. "The Descending Angels will be moving in from the south with Isaiah."

"Copy that." Kimball pulled his lip mic even closer. "Shari, go ahead and send in the ground troops as backup. I'm going to take over your position as rearguard and secure the second floor."

"By yourself?"

"I've got to make sure that there are no surprises since we're unable to maintain a visual of the hostiles," he said. "They have to be somewhere."

"Copy that."

When Shari made the call, the rear of the depository quickly filled with Metro's Assault Unit.

#

Team Leader saw Isaiah moving stealthily down the hallway and clinging to the shadows, with his weapon aimed directly in front of him. Quietly, Team Leader melded into dark shadows and pressed himself against a false wall that led to a makeshift ladder that went to the second floor. When he pushed the wall, it gave enough to provide an aperture that was large enough to pass through, then he quietly slid the wall back into place before Isaiah could notice him.

Cramped by the small area, Team Leader shuffled sideways between the inner and outer walls until he reached the crudely constructed ladder. After descending to the second floor, he found himself in a tight space identical to the one above. With some effort, he pushed on another false wall that opened into a dusty room.

Stealthily making his way into the hallway, Team leader kept his head on a swivel.

He was all but home free.

#

Leviticus had often been in combat many times before, and *quiet* was never a good sign. Hunkering close to the floor, he crawled toward Micah and removed his helmet. A bloodless bullet wound marred the center of his once porcelain-like skin on his forehead.

He gently placed his fingers over Micah's eyes and closed them, then recited "The Lord's Prayer" in hushed tones, the words carrying the length of the corridor in haunting whispers. The remaining members of the Force Elite, from their locations, froze at the sound of Leviticus' voice.

#

"What's that?" whispered Boa.

Kodiak shushed him. The whispers echoed from all points of the hallway as if they were coming from more than one source.

"Someone's praying," said Boa.

Then finally: "It's not King Snake," said Kodiak. "He wouldn't know a prayer if it slapped him in the face . . . So, I guess it's time to rock and roll, boys."

Diamondback leaned close. "What about the hostages?"

"We do what we were hired to do," Kodiak muttered. "If we get the chance, then we kill them . . . Starting with the pope."

#

Isaiah had the members of the papal council within his sight.

When Leviticus saw Isaiah coming in from the south, he

moved in to close the gap but motioned to Shari to keep position and provide cover.

When Isaiah nearly reached the monitor room, all hell broke loose.

#

Kodiak exited the room unaware that Isaiah had quietly worked his way down the corridor and hid behind the door. Kodiak, however, immediately saw Leviticus pressed against the wall and coming towards him. As he trained his weapon on Leviticus, Isaiah sprang from behind the door and rammed the butt of his assault weapon to the lower part of Kodiak's spine. The big man dropped to his knees, twisting toward his attacker, and leveling his weapon as he fell. Isaiah kicked the pistol away, the firearm skating across the floor.

Kodiak came immediately to his feet, and with a roundhouse kick that knocked the smaller man's weapon from his grip. With a straight forearm jab, Kodiak placed a powerful shot to Isaiah's face shield, shattering the plastic and sending Isaiah to the ground.

With his helmet no longer an asset, Isaiah ripped it away, leaped to his feet, and assumed a stance reminiscent of Tae-kwon-do.

Leviticus held his fire for fear of shooting Isaiah and maintained his position in the corridor as the two men sized each other up. Kodiak, with such incredible agility for a large man, came across with a roundhouse kick that missed Isaiah and hit the wall like a cannonball, causing chunks of plaster to scatter across the floor. Kodiak's follow-up punch missed as well, fracturing the wall as if it were constructed from a pane of glass.

More explosions reverberated through the depository. The Descending Angels, having breached the rooftop at the north and central sectors, began rappelling into the building.

Both men continued to square off. "It's over," hollered Isaiah. "Give it up."

"Are you kidding?" said Kodiak. "I would die with a smile on my face knowing that I broke your neck." He came at Isaiah with savage forearm thrusts and deadly kicks, each missing their marks as the much nimbler Isaiah dodged or deflected the blows in effortless fashion. Kodiak, in what he thought was an opening, lifted his massive arm to strike a crushing hammer blow to Isaiah's skull, but Isaiah lashed out with his foot and drove Kodiak backward.

Quickly employing kick after powerful kick, blow after powerful blow, Isaiah attacked the much larger man with such incredible speed and skill that Shari, watching from the corridor, was transfixed by the talent of his martial arts. He was smooth and graceful, the movements hypnotic, and, in quick fashion, had Kodiak against the opposite side of the hallway with his back pressed against a boarded window. In a bestial rage, Kodiak screamed as Isaiah came around with a powerful kick that connected squarely to Kodiak's chest. The impact was so great, the contact was so forceful, the impetus drove the large man through the window with his body tumbling in speedy revolutions to the graveyard below. Upon impact, his death sounded very much like a melon hitting pavement.

Isaiah gathered his assault weapon. Now with Leviticus by his side and the Descending Angels swarming the hallway, and as the ground forces moved up the stairwell, the two Knights and Shari entered the monitor room expecting an all-out assault.

But the room was empty.

#

The Force Elite had prepared well for the contingency of being surrounded by the opposition. While Kodiak combated Isaiah, the others used the opportunity to escape through a false panel built into the old floor that was disguised as a series of removable tiles. They descended to the second level. Once assembled, they made their way down the hallway and took position beneath the room where the pope was held and aimed their assault weapons at the ceiling with the intent to kill.

#

After checking on the remaining four members of the papal council and finding them justifiably shaken, Shari left Leviticus and Isaiah to tend to their needs, while she continued to search the vacant rooms that lined the corridor.

In a room that held little light, Shari spotted a lump of darkness gathered against the far wall. It was amoeba-like in its form, a moving shape. When she neared this form, it began to take on an outline of an old man holding another closely. The two masses together—from a distance—were indistinguishable. Up close, she could see that the pope had drawn a dead man into his embrace.

"Your Holiness!" She knelt and gently touched the old man's forehead and felt the heat of a climbing fever. "Your Holiness, you're ill. We'll get you out of here as soon as possible."

"Who are you?" he asked weakly, while she wrapped blankets around him.

"FBI Special Agent Shari Cohen, I'm here with the Vatican Knights." His brows rose. "Kimball's here?"

"Yes, sir. They're acting as my Critical Incident Response Group."

"Then it's truly over?"

"Yes, Your Holiness. You're safe."

The pope raised his hand. The chain that tethered him to the wall for so long was now broken, a perfect shot by Team Leader who freed him. "I don't know why he did this," the pope explained.

Shari sidestepped the body of Bishop Angelo. "We'll come back for him. I promise."

In that instance, the floor suddenly erupted in shards of wood and bullets. So, Shari grabbed the pope and forced him close to the wall, shielding him with her body. From underneath gunshots perforated the floorboards and strafed the ceiling, causing bits of wood and old roof tar to cascade down on them like rain. All around them feathers floated in the gloom as bullets penetrated the old mattresses, the feather stuffing swirling and dancing about in lazy eddies. Bishop Angelo's body also took multiple hits, the punching bullets animating his corpse into jiggling fits. And in desperation, Shari cried out as the room became a world of flying lead, gently floating feathers, and choking dust.

#

Kimball moved discreetly down the second-floor corridor. The area was lit by multiple muzzle flashes thirty yards ahead, marking the spot where the members of the Force Elite were shooting at the ceiling.

Over Kimball's earpiece, he heard Shari cry out over her mic not as an order or a battle cry, but as a shout of extreme anxiety.

He quickly converged with his grenade launcher loaded and ready. Less than a second later, a grenade corkscrewed through the quasi-darkness and exploded with an eruption that scattered the commandos throughout the corridor as bits and pieces of gore. None of them knew what had hit them. At the base point of their attack, Kimball looked up and noted the perforated ceiling above him. When he called out Shari's name numerous times but received no feedback, he became particularly concerned for her welfare.

And then a voice, distant and hollow, came from behind. "You would be Kimball Hayden, I assume." Kimball turned quickly with his finger on the trigger of an empty weapon. And then with his free hand, he removed his helmet and lip mic and tossed them aside.

At the end of the hallway, a man stood near a collapsed stairwell, sizing Kimball.

Kimball took a step toward him, the mouth of the grenade launcher pointing downward.

"I've heard so much about you," the man said, his accent thick. "I hear that there is no better warrior than you."

Kimball moved closer; the face of the man becoming clear in the feeble light. Beneath his chin was scar tissue, the distorted flesh as identifying as a tattoo.

"And you would be Abraham Obadiah," he said.

"That would be, at least for today, the name you would know me by, yes."

Obadiah reached down and methodically withdrew his black-bladed commando knives from sheaths on both thighs. It was an invitation to Kimball, who lowered his weapon to the floor and withdrew his knives.

"Now," said Obadiah, the points of his blades pointing wickedly. "I would be so honored to be the one to kill the legend."

Kimball took a fighting stance. "Don't count on it."

They closed the gap swinging the blades with precision and savagery.

#

Dust and feathers floated with cloying thickness. When Shari pulled back from the pope, she saw that the floor was marked by countless holes inches apart. How she and the pope escaped the volley was beyond her, but she couldn't quite rule out a miracle, either. Removing dusty blankets from the pope, she saw he was untouched by the fusillade. His eyes were glazed with fever, his skin hot to the touch, but he smiled and raised a bony hand to brush his fingers softly against her cheek. "I thought you said I was safe, young lady."

She returned his smile. "You are now. For some reason, I have the feeling Kimball got involved."

"You know something?" the pope said. "I think you might be right."

#

The blades deflected off one another, as they fought viciously. With metal striking metal sparks flew abundantly before dying out, only for new ones to take their place. Each man moved with poise and skill, with their actions motivated by instinct rather than by deduction since their movements were too fast for the mind to comprehend the next action.

Obadiah came across in a series of uppercuts and horizontal slashes, while Kimball countered with deflections and straight jabs, his maneuvers also deflected. In Kimball's mind, he was amazed at how good this man was with double-edged weapons. He had never actually been tested before until now.

As their arms moved with blinding speed, Obadiah came across and slashed Kimball's vest, the razor sharpness of his knife cutting easily through the Kevlar. Vests, after all, were made to stop bullets, not knives. Backing off for the moment, Kimball reexamined his position while Obadiah paced from left to right like a caged animal. "You're good," he told Kimball. "But not good enough."

"I'm just getting warmed up."

"Then let's get this over with," he said. "I've got things to do and people to kill."

They converged on each other for the last time.

#

Those who had seen the perforated floor were amazed it was still strong enough to support any weight. The aged and decimated wood protested beneath Leviticus and Isaiah, as they carefully removed the pope and placed him in the care of the Metro Unit. The Descending Angels examined and secured every room on the third floor, while the ground troops maintained their post on the first-floor entryway and stairwell.

Leviticus drew close to Shari.

"The pope is in good hands," he told her in hushed tones. "So, we must go." He turned toward Micah's body. "We'll be taking him with us. There can be no questions."

"I understand."

Isaiah stood beside them. "Kimball will meet us on his terms," he said. "But we're thankful for all you've done."

Isaiah and Leviticus dropped to a bended knee and placed a closed fist over their hearts. "Loyalty above all else," they whispered, "except honor."

Shari felt flattered at this display of gratitude to the point of feeling the sting of tears. Then, placing a closed fist over her heart, she said, "Loyalty above all else, except honor."

For her, this was closure.

Milling with the Descending Angels and ground troops, Isaiah unobtrusively lifted the body of Micah and draped him over the shoulders of Leviticus, trying to give the impression of someone requiring immediate medical attention. Shari watched the two Knights merge into the crowd. Within moments, they were gone.

Only when Kimball didn't answer his mic did she become concerned.

#

The blades moved faster and beyond the comprehension of human sight, their arms moving in blurs and blinding rotations as each man's brow drew the sweat of his efforts. Neither man rescinded his space but maintained his territory. And neither man by the plateau of his pride was willing to concede to defeat, as the fatigue began to weigh on both of them.

Breathless, both men reached into their inner selves and mustered whatever reserve power they had left, before being entirely sapped.

When Obadiah finally went in for a stabbing motion, Kimball came down and slashed his blade across Obadiah's forearm, a score that severed the muscle that incapacitated him.

With a savage cry, Obadiah dropped his knife and looked skyward, the veins in his neck sticking out in cords. When Kimball went for the kill, Obadiah rotated on his feet like a matador dodging the course of a charging bull and came around with a solid kick that sent Kimball across the floor and over the edge of the collapsed stairwell. Dropping his knives, Kimball reached for the exposed rebar and grabbed it, before plunging to the debris below. When he tried to pull himself up, Obadiah was standing at the edge of the concrete holding a hand over his wounded arm, the blood flowing freely between his fingers as he looked down on Kimball.

"You're indeed a truly magnificent warrior," he said. "But tell me, that crest and shield on your vest. Is it a symbol of your squad? Or is it the marking of something else?"

Kimball tried to pull himself up, but Obadiah placed a foot upon the rebar, his weight bending the bar downward.

"Your style is different," added Obadiah.

When Kimball's hands began to slide down along the bar, he reaffirmed his grip.

"Who are you?" asked Obadiah. "You're not with the FBI, that much is for certain. Your style is too unique. And I thought I had seen them all." Obadiah bent down as the blood of his forearm dripped on Kimball. In the background, opposing forces were moving in. But Obadiah didn't seem too concerned by their apparent encroachment, in Kimball's view. "You're not the Swiss Guard, either. As good as they are, you fight like no other. So again, who are—"

Obadiah turned to check the progress of the troops. Given this window of opportunity, Kimball lunged up and grabbed Obadiah by the front of his shirt and pulled him over the edge.

Too surprised to utter in protest, Obadiah traversed the open space to the debris below.

When the troops finally reached the precipice, a commando reached down and aided a tired Kimball Hayden to the landing.

"Are you all right?" asked the team leader.

"I'll live," said Kimball. He pointed to the rubble below. "You'll need to contact Special Agent Cohen of the FBI regarding that man down there," he said. "She's in the building somewhere."

The team leader looked over the debris. "What man?" Kimball immediately sat up and looked over the edge. Obadiah was gone.

CHAPTER FIFTY-FIVE

Washington, D.C.
September 30, Mid-Morning

The day had been a sweeping success for the FBI. And like a deprived addict, the media consumed the details. The pope was taken to Massachusetts General Hospital where he was recuperating from a bronchial infection. The overall prospect for complete recovery was rated excellent by all attending physicians. Once able to travel, Pope Pius would be checked into Gemelli Polyclinic in Rome, for a follow-up.

As an addendum to the lead story of the pope's health, there was a detailed account of the battle that procured the pontiff and the remaining members of the papal council, all unharmed.

The Soldiers of Islam weren't as lucky, as Shari Cohen of the FBI conducted a superior assault mission in which the Incident Command System was well established and performed with military precision. The Command's Ops Supervisor and Liaison Officer informed a special group of media members, who were discreetly predetermined by the president of the United States, that the Soldiers of Islam were eradicated. This, the media members were told, demonstrates to the world that terrorism will never gain a true foothold on American soil. The media went wild as they unknowingly served propaganda as the main course of public news sustenance. This in turn served the government's purpose of burying the real conspiracy involving the pope's kidnapping, and the true identities of the players involved.

On the surface, Shari had picked up various snippets regarding Misters Paxton, Murdock, and Pappandopolous—depending upon the source at the time. Mr. Paxton presumably took a post in the Oregon field office. But Shari knew the dark truth. This same dark truth also applied to the sudden retirement of George Pappandopolous, and the unreported imprisonment of solitary confinement for Punch Murdock. There was absolutely no doubt in her mind that all these players shared the same feared fate as Murdock, both ending up in a grave in potter's field.

The man known as Obadiah was never found. What was discovered, however, were several false walls and panels allowing for his escape, a contingency that was well planned by members of the Force Elite. Another panel located on the first floor by the rubble led to the network of sewer lines beneath Boston's numerous streets; a rabbit hole. And though Obadiah's name was never revealed to the media, it was, however, whispered within the smallest circles in D.C. But those who did so did it with caution since leaks sometimes proved fatal in high-profile situations. Coincidental to all the positive news washing across television and reported in the major papers, America suffered the pangs of losing Vice President Bohlmer to a brain aneurysm, an imperceptible bubble along the arterial wall that finally erupted, somehow missed by physicians normally stellar in their tending of White House dignitaries. After three days of closed casket viewing within the rotunda of the Capitol Building, he was buried alongside his wife in California. Shari did not attend.

As for President Burroughs, his policies continued in the war effort against ISIS. Only a few people on Capitol Hill contested him, however, while others remained silent.

Kimball Hayden and the Vatican Knights had simply disappeared. And Shari thought of him often during her trip back to D.C. When she returned to the archdiocese, the cardinal did not mention Kimball to her at all. Nor did she dare ask.

In her short time with Hayden, she had come to understand the man as someone dark and distant—a man not only in search of redemption but someone in search of himself. She admittedly found herself enchanted by the fact that even though Kimball was virtuous, there was something quite savage about him as well.

So, when she returned home and found Gary cleaning up the mess when he had taken on Dark Lord, they had laid eyes on each other as if to glean each other's thoughts.

Gary appeared solemn, his eyes carrying the sadness of

weighted sorrow. Yet she saw a man with integrity and kindness, a man who would never raise a hand to harm anyone but was willing to put his life in harm's way to protect the woman he loved unconditionally.

This was the Gary she saw, the Gary she had met years ago, the Gary she had always loved whether she realized it or not.

And then it came to them in a symbiotic rush, Shari realizing there was nobody else for her as they closed in and embraced each other. And for a long time, she maintained and hugged Gary very tightly, as if never wanting to let go, a reaffirmation of her love that somehow became lost to her over time, now newly discovered. And though Gary thought she might crush his ribs; he didn't care as his hug was just as affirming.

They had rediscovered each other while standing on the threshold of Death's doorstep.

#

After Shari was granted time at home to relax, FBI Director Larry Johnston called her to his downtown office to confront her on a few issues. Most notably he wanted to know who her CIRG Team was since all valid members had been accounted for at Quantico at the time of the assault.

When she arrived at the office, the director closed the door and gestured for her to take a seat in front of his desk.

"You look good," he told her, his tone congenial. "Thank you."

He examined a few documents before placing them on the desktop before him. "These are the documents by the Planning Ops Chief from the Incident Command Post."

Shari wanted to roll her eyes. *Here it comes.*

"None of your team checked out with the Incident Commander for accountability when they completed duty, which is against ICS protocol."

"I wasn't aware of that," she lied. She realized Johnston knew it as well.

"I'd also like to know who your squad was since everybody who made up the Strike Force was accounted for at Quantico, during the time your assault against the Force Elite commenced."

Shari remained composed and quiet. Johnston seemed almost paternal as he addressed her with a wry grin. "As a First-Team Assault Unit, they were fabulous in clearing the stage for the rest of the team's maneuvers, perhaps saving a lot of lives considering who they were up against." And then with a measure of gratitude, he said, "I'm proud of you, Shari. The Bureau, the president—you've made this agency shine. And for that, we are all proud."

"Why . . . I guess . . . thank you."

He picked up the papers. "The assault from beginning to end took less than eight minutes with no casualties or injuries to report on our side. A job well done."

"Eight minutes?"

"Eight minutes," he confirmed.

"It seemed much longer than that."

"Being on the front lines, I'm sure."

She diverted her attention to the papers he was holding. "What else does the report say?"

He placed them back on the desk. "Nothing damaging . . . That's for sure." He paused before posing the next question. "So, are you going to tell me who they were?"

Shari could only stare as her mind searched for an answer.

Then without so much as a quiver in her tone, she said, "I can't."

Johnston's face remained passive, despite her inability to confide in him.

"You know I should be admonishing the hell out of you for doing what you did," he told her. "But I can't argue the outcome of the situation. Despite the lack of protocol regarding the ICS, I'm going to send this report to the attorney general, who I'm sure will agree with the recommendation that your efforts be recognized. You and your team did a nice job, Shari. There are a whole lot of people who are proud of what you did."

Shari was beyond relieved. "May I ask you something?"

"Go ahead."

"Abraham Obadiah . . . Are we going after him?" Johnston's features became guarded. "No."

Shari couldn't believe what she just heard. "But this is the man who started all of this. He tried to start—"

He cut her off by raising his hand. "Abraham Obadiah does not exist, at least that's the viewpoint of the Mossad and the Israeli government. We've already checked. Even though we believe him to be a major player in Mossad's Lohamah Psichlogit Department, he might be something quite different."

"What's that?'

"He may be a part of the Kidon."

The Kidon was Israel's elite group of assassins, a legendary program kept very deep in the shadows. Little was known about them.

"So, we're just going to sweep this under the carpet?"

"And what do you suppose we do, Shari? Risk dredging up a conspiracy that could bury this country in the eyes of our allies—in the eyes of the world? I don't think so. If this man surfaces again, maybe we'll handle it. Until that time, we'll continue to work with our allies in a positive way. If they say this man does not exist, *then he does not exist*. Is that clear?"

She sighed. "Very."

"Then have a good day."

Shari got up from the chair and thanked the director.

"Oh, I almost forgot," he said. The smile returned to his face. "You have a special engagement to attend to this afternoon."

"Engagement?"

"The pope is being released from the hospital and has requested a personal meeting with you before his plane leaves. I believe he wants to thank you for what you've done, which is an engagement that most of us could only envy." He returned to the paperwork on his desk. "Your plane leaves for Boston in about an hour."

"But . . ."

"Don't worry," he said. "You'll be back in time to be with your family." For a moment, her heart hitched inside her chest. Would she get another chance to see Kimball and say goodbye? She at least wanted that privilege, to tell the man how much she deeply appreciated him, and that their courses were taking them in two separate directions. She just wanted to say goodbye to someone whom she would never see again.

"If I were you, Shari, I wouldn't miss the opportunity of a lifetime."

She thanked Johnston once again. And she certainly didn't have to be reminded that a plane awaited.

CHAPTER FIFTY-SIX

Boston, Massachusetts. Logan Airport
September 30, Late Afternoon

The crowd along the fenced-in tarmac at Boston's Logan Airport was far greater than when the pope arrived in Dulles several days before. The support was immense, but certainly far less than the Biblical proportions the pope joked about, as Cardinal Medeiros wheeled him toward Shepherd One.

Shari walked alongside them, the pope holding her hand lightly in his as they moved along the stretch of pavement. "I'm so glad you made it, my dear. But as much as I want to thank you, I need to speak to you regarding the Vatican Knights."

"I have already given my word, Your Holiness. I'll keep their secret safe."

"Of that, I have no doubt," he told her. "But you must understand that the Vatican Knights are not even a myth since their secret is *that* closely guarded."

"I understand."

"And for that, my dear, I truly thank you. And I certainly thank you for saving my life and the lives of my councilmen. If you should ever want to come to Vatican City, please let the good cardinal here know when you want to visit, and I shall roll out the red carpet for the one who saved my life."

"I deeply appreciate that, Your Holiness. But there's something I would like to ask of you."

"Of course, my dear."

"I would like to say goodbye to Kimball one last time."

The pope's face faltered a bit. "As much as I would like you to, I'm afraid I cannot let that happen. The Vatican Knights are mourning the losses of those whom I consider my children. Please understand that."

She looked up at the immense Boeing. "Is he in there?"

"Yes," he said. And then in a more sorrowful measure, he said, "He's in there with the others holding a ceremony. In a moment, I shall lead them in prayer."

"Then I'll respect that," she returned and continued to hold the pope's hand as they moved closer to the jet. "May I ask you something else?"

"Of course."

"The Vatican Knights," she began. "Why Kimball? Why the rest?"

The pope lowered his head as if the answer was on the surface of the tarmac before him. "The Vatican Knights, Ms. Cohen, are incredibly special people who come from squalor—mostly hard-luck cases who were either orphaned or abandoned and possess no future other than what the Vatican can give them. Serving me in the capacity that they do is ultimately their decision, in the end, knowing the full consequences of their choices by then and the dangers involved."

"And Kimball?"

The pope smiled as though he was reminiscing over a fond memory. "Kimball is an animal of a different color," he said. "He's unlike the rest because he stands within his personal torment and seeks redemption through his service to God. He believes his road is a difficult one in which salvation lies at its end, but impossible to achieve. What he fails to realize is that his journey is a lifelong endeavor paved with many mistakes."

"Kimball *is* a good man."

"Of course, he is. Although we see this he does not. It's up to Kimball to find his way. We can only give him direction. But it's Kimball who must have the faith to see it through."

"Is there anything you can do to help him?"

The pope smiled. "I can only provide the direction, my dear. Kimball has to do the rest. You see . . . Kimball *needs* evil in his life to recognize the good, which is something I learned from the man who held me captive. I saw the side of man that I've been sheltered from for so long. And because of it, I now understand Kimball more than ever."

"I don't understand."

The pope held a hand up to the cardinal who slowed the wheelchair as they neared the Boeing. "Kimball knows only one thing," he said. "He knows the dark side of man perhaps better than anybody else, and he knows what is needed to combat it. I, on the other hand, have lived in ignorance believing the Light inside of all men can be reached. Kimball knows different. He knows the Darkness, has lived in its depths and is working his way toward the Light. There has to be a balance in life, my dear. But right now, I believe Kimball does not feel that balance in his soul. When he finds the balance between the two, perhaps he will find the salvation that he has been so desperately looking for."

"I hope so."

"Kimball has to find his way."

The cardinal had moved the wheelchair to the center of an entourage who were dressed in priestly vestments. They were standing at the base of the stairs that led into Shepherd One.

"Well, my dear, my gratitude for your perseverance in this matter cannot even begin to be measured by my standards. I do wish you well. And I will tell the Vatican Knights that you wish them well."

"Thank you."

"And one last thing." The pope held his hand out to the cardinal, who opened a velour satchel and removed a thick volume with leather binding. He then handed it to Pope Pius XIII.

"This is a gift for you," said the pope, handing the book over to her. "Have you ever read *Paradise Lost* by John Milton?"

She shook her head. "I'm afraid not."

"There's several volumes total, but this will get you started," he told her. "And so that you know, there are four main characters: God, Satan, Adam . . ." He smiled and reached out for her free hand. "And, of course, there's Eve. Please accept this as a token of my appreciation. I even signed it for you."

"Why, thank you very much, Your Holiness."

"God bless you, Ms. Cohen. You truly are an asset to mankind, which makes me believe there's hope after all, even when I questioned myself that mankind was too far gone. It was a period in my life when I was at my lowest. Sometimes, my dear, it takes a tragedy to see the full picture. I now believe that tragedies are sometimes good for the soul that sometimes reminds us that we need misfortune in life to bring out the best in mankind. I have now seen that when things are at their worst . . . that is when *we* are at our best."

"I've always believed in that," she told him. "A perfect example was nine-eleven."

"Nine-eleven brought strangers together in a cause to heal not only a nation but one another. There was no prejudice, no animosity, all of which were forgotten due to a shared tragedy. From hatred came pure love. It was a balance that formed from the Darkness and Light of man. Let's just hope that Kimball finds his balance, too."

Shari leaned close and hugged the old man, as he got to his feet. She barely touched him, his bones as frail as a sparrow.

"Be good, my dear."

"And you take care of yourself."

"Don't worry," he told her. "Gemelli Hospital is one of the best in the world."

There was one last question she wished to pose to the pope.

"Your Holiness, if I should visit the Vatican someday, would it be possible to visit the Vatican Knights? Or Kimball?"

"If you should happen to see the Vatican Knights again," he informed her, "then it will be because something terrible has happened . . . So, let's hope not."

Aided by the archdiocese staff, Pope Pius XIII climbed the stairs and waved his hand in a loving gesture of saying goodbye. Once inside Shepherd One, the door closed behind him, and the mobile stairway was pulled back from the Boeing.

Along with Cardinal Medeiros, Shari walked away from the jet and made her way to the terminal.

#

Kimball Hayden had been sitting inside Shepherd One watching the pontiff being wheeled from the terminal and to the plane. Shari accompanied the pope and became his focal point, as the pontiff's party made their way toward the Boeing. Since Kimball knew the pope would never allow her passage onboard, he pressed his hand against the window. And with the tip of his forefinger, he traced the outline of her body against the pane, the closest thing to saying goodbye.

As the pontiff made his way up the stairway, Kimball thought Shari looked as pleasing as always—the way she smiled, the point of her widow's peak, the way her hair shined in the sun, all a mental picture he would carry with him for the rest of his life. *Perhaps,* he thought, *if I do right, then maybe He'll grant me the right to love someone openly.*

But if anything was taught and learned, it was the fact that Shari Cohen made him see that he was not the painted monster who held no feeling or remorse but as someone who was capable of loving.

Nevertheless, he knew he had a long way to go.

EPILOGUE

Somewhere off the shore of a Venezuelan beach, a luxury home lay surrounded by palm trees and tropical vegetation that bloomed in riots of bright colors. On the wraparound porch sat two men who spoke leisurely. Hector Guerra sat in a lounge chair with his brightly flower-patterned shirt unbuttoned, exposing a huge and hairy paunch. Although a breeze blew off the ocean, it barely moved his perfectly styled hair. Next to him sat a man who seemed comfortable in these surroundings. He wore a wide-brimmed hat and dark sunglasses. The most distinguishing feature was the pink scarring beneath his chin. On his arm, he wore a clean bandage from a recent battle. There was another tight wrapping around his chest.

from a fall that had broken three ribs.

"Unfortunately," said Guerra, "it was not meant to be. So, we pray that the Middle East will someday find its way back to stability. I would hate to see this progress into a war from which there may be no return."

The man who was Abraham Obadiah lifted his drink in the air, then sipped from it before he placed it back on the table beside his chair. "I will never give up the cause for the sake of my people. The shadows of war are coming too close to the homeland. One way or the other it must be stopped. It will be stopped."

"You know we could never risk another venture as we did with the pope."

"There will always be opportunities, my friend. We'll simply learn from our mistakes and make better judgments from them."

"But never at the risk of placing myself in jeopardy. Never

again."

"There will always be risks, Mr. Guerra. What you do is prognosticate the problems before they happen, and then you plan for them."

"Which is what you did with Kimball Hayden?"

"Kimball Hayden came out of nowhere."

"My point exactly. Sometimes you just can't prepare for everything."

"Next time we'll know better."

"And how does one prepare themselves against somebody who doesn't exist?"

"Kimball Hayden has a background," he said. "We all do. Someday I'll find him."

Both men remained quiet for the moment, each enjoying the light breeze coming off the surf, as well as the scenery of froth-laden waves lapping the shoreline.

Then Guerra queried him further. "And when you find this Kimball Hayden, what will you do with him?"

Obadiah paused to think this out before answering. "That's my business," he finally said. "Right now, I have far more pressing matters to deal with."

"If you meet up with this Hayden, make sure that you live to see another day."

"I would have to," he returned. "If I am to make a better life for my people, then I have to make progress. And the price for progress, my friend, is destruction. And the destruction of Kimball Hayden would surely remove any future nuisances from my life."

For a moment both men stared at each other, neither of their features betraying any thought or emotion, then turned to gaze at the incoming waves.

Printed in Great Britain
by Amazon

87425328R00172